THE RULE OF FEAR

Also by Luke Delaney

Cold Killing
The Keeper
The Toy Taker
The Jackdaw

LUKE DELANEY

THE RULE OF FEAR

HarperCollins*Publishers*

HarperCollins*Publishers*
1 London Bridge Street
London SE1 9GF

www.harpercollins.co.uk

Published by HarperCollins*Publishers* 2016
1

A catalogue record for this book
is available from the British Library

ISBN: 978-0-00-758572-4

Set in Meridien by Palimpsest Book Production Ltd,
Falkirk, Stirlingshire

Printed and bound in Great Britain by
Clays Ltd, St Ives plc

MIX
Paper from
responsible sources
FSC™ C007454

Dedication

I dedicate this book to all the police officers, the length and breadth of the country, regardless of rank, who work tirelessly under difficult and often dangerous circumstances so the rest of us can live our lives much as we please. Imagine a country without a strong and reliable police service and think how much that would damage the quality of all our lives – no matter how wealthy or powerful we may be.

Having done the job for many years, I know how testing – how physically and mentally hard – it can be, not just on the individual, but on their families and friends. It often demands complete commitment to the cause to the exclusion of everything else. It's simply what's required to get the job done, but it makes it a very demanding job indeed. We should all be very grateful there are still thousands of police officers serving their communities with such dedication and diligence, despite increasingly poor working conditions and pay. Without them there would be no society as we know it.

Some people will misunderstand this book and maybe even see it as an attack on the police, but I can assure you it is anything but. It is a warning – the character of Jack King representing an entire police service within one man. If we do not treasure and care for the things we value most, then it's only ever a matter of time before we lose them. Not everything can be pulled back from the brink. It is a very dangerous thing indeed to give people great power, as each officer has, yet through such poor pay place them perilously close to poverty. Desperate people will sooner or later take desperate actions.

Remember the old saying – *a society ultimately gets the police it deserves*.

So, to every cop out there looking after all of us, I say thank you and dedicate this book to you.

LD

1

Chief Superintendent Brian Gerrard looked down at the open file on his desk and nodded approvingly before looking up and smiling at the expressionless PC Jack King who sat in front of him.

'An excellent end of probation report,' Gerrard beamed, his shining blue eyes magnified by his spectacles as he sat straight-backed in his chair, trying to stretch his five-foot-eight body as far as he could. 'Wouldn't you agree, Inspector?' he asked Inspector Joanne Johnston who was prowling around the office like a caged leopard.

'Very impressive,' Johnston agreed.

King forced a smile onto his handsome face and continued to wish the meeting would be over and he could be free from the two senior officers he barely knew. He'd passed them in the corridor from time to time, respectfully said hello in deference to their rank, but this was the first time either had actually spoken properly to him. He didn't mind about that. He just wanted the meeting to be over so he could get back out on the streets. Like Johnston before him, he was on the Metropolitan Police's accelerated promotion scheme and knew his working life would soon be dominated by endless meetings and *coordinating*. Whatever time he had left on the front line was already precious to him. If it hadn't been for his parents, he may have even considered giving up his accelerated promotion to stay in the action indefinitely. Already he understood that the police was one organization that could only be truly understood by standing at the bottom looking up – not peering down at it from a glass tower.

His appearance was the opposite of Gerrard's, who looked grey and weak, albeit slim and tidy; whereas King was almost six foot tall and muscular, his short brown hair framing deep brown eyes, high cheekbones and a square jaw, and his skin a deep olive, the colour of someone who laboured hard outside. Johnston was undeniably attractive, but she looked like a lawyer in a police uniform. As he listened to their congratulations he imagined them avoiding as much real police work as they could – spending most of their time on courses and safe attachments, keeping themselves out of harm's way while also protecting their squeaky clean records, ensuring there would be no skeletons in their closets that could bar them from the dizzy heights of becoming Assistant Commissioners or perhaps even more. Whereas he had won the respect of his peers through hard work and a willingness to get his hands dirty – overcoming their natural mistrust of anyone on accelerated promotion.

'Thank you,' he answered through his forced smile. 'I really enjoyed the work.'

'Well that's all behind you now,' Gerrard spluttered a little. 'Onwards and upwards for you, Jack. First you'll need to complete your sergeants' course and then you'll have to go back to Bramshill for additional training. Then of course you'll serve the minimum amount of time possible as a sergeant before becoming an inspector and then, so long as you pass the exams and keep away from anything controversial . . . who knows what heights you could reach? The key is not having any skeletons in your cupboard, if you understand what I'm saying.'

'Doesn't sound like I'm going to get much of a chance to do any real police work,' he teased them.

'As you travel through the ranks,' Gerrard smiled, 'you'll realize that making policy and providing a general umbrella of supervision is the true backbone of the service. Anyone can charge around in a police car arresting people, but adhering to government targets of crime reduction and managing the borough budget is an entirely different matter. In many ways now is the time for you to put away such childish things and accept the responsibilities that come with having been selected for accelerated promotion.'

'Of course,' King smiled through gritted teeth. 'I understand.'

'Good,' Gerrard beamed.

'Excellent,' Johnston added through her assassin's smile.

'Well if that's everything, sir,' King stated more than asked, rising from his chair, 'I should be getting back to my duties.'

'Of course,' Gerrard agreed. 'Of course.'

'But I would like to say that I'm very much looking forward to returning to the borough as a sergeant,' King added, before immediately regretting it.

'Return?' Gerrard asked, the smile dead on his face.

'Here?' Johnston added. 'To Newham?'

'Yes, ma'am,' King confirmed.

'Well, that's your choice entirely,' Gerrard took over, 'but there are *easier* boroughs in which to complete the rank of sergeant. Ones in which you could say you're less likely to be . . . *tarnished* with anything unsavoury or unpleasant that for example the *media* could exploit later on in your career when you're of a suitably high rank. These are the sorts of things that a potential future Commissioner already has to start thinking about. You take my point?'

'Of course,' King nodded and tried to look serious, 'but I like it here. Newham will do me fine.'

'Well,' Gerrard recovered his smile, 'maybe after a few weeks at Bramshill you'll change your mind.'

'Maybe,' King lied and pointed at the door. 'Is it all right if I . . .?' he let his words trail away.

'Keen to make the most of your last few hours as a constable, eh?' Gerrard asked, pretending that he could understand what that might mean to someone like King.

'Yes, sir,' he answered, heading for the door as quickly as he could, turning the handle, only seconds from freedom before Gerrard stopped him.

'And remember, Jack,' he told him, 'the likes of you and I and Inspector Johnston here have been selected to rule over this organization of ours. We carry on our shoulders the heavy burden of responsibility.'

'I'll bear that in mind,' King answered before escaping through the door, blowing through puffed-out cheeks with relief as he closed it behind him. 'Thank fuck that's over,' he whispered under his breath and headed towards the station yard to hitch a lift back to his beat in an area of Newham he doubted either Gerrard or Johnston had ever seen.

Two hours later

King walked along Central Park Road in East Ham cursing the body armour and traditional-style helmet that made the intense heat of a London summer almost unbearable. He listened to every call that came out over his personal radio, determined to end his constable career with yet another decent arrest and maintain his reputation as a thief-taker, something that had surprised his peers and seniors alike, unaccustomed as they were to seeing anyone on accelerated promotion showing any street skills. But he felt born to be a street cop – his law degree nothing more than something he'd obtained to please his parents. Although they still expressed their deep displeasure at his chosen career, the accelerated promotion programme he'd been offered as a graduate had mollified them. He'd accepted the deal to keep the peace, but doubted he'd stick to it. Maybe he'd even join the CID proper – not just on an attachment as a future senior officer passing through, but as a trained and qualified detective. It would kill off his chances of ever being anything more than a detective inspector or at best a detective chief inspector, but at least he wouldn't be permanently trapped behind a desk.

Finally a call came out over his personal radio that interested him and that he could get to on foot within the acceptable response time: *suspected domestic disturbance at 15 Gillett Avenue – sounds of a disturbance in the background.*

'I'll take that, 914 over,' he said into his radio.

'*You sure, 914?*' the female voice from Control came back to him. '*It'll be your last shout as a constable. Sure you want to end on a domestic?*'

'Why not?' he answered, knowing that domestic disputes were always good for an arrest. 'I'm just round the corner. ETA two minutes.'

'*OK, 914,*' the female voice told him. '*I'll sort some back-up out and send them to your location.*'

'Fine,' he agreed and picked up his pace, determined not to let a mobile unit beat him to the shout and any possible arrests. But as he turned into Gillett Avenue and began to walk past the rows of neat terraced houses, a feeling quite unlike anything he had experienced before began to wrap itself around him – an unpleasant feeling of something terrible happening close by. The street was deathly quiet, only the sound of the leaves in the small trees moving in the faintest of breezes disturbing the stillness. The birds had stopped singing.

When he reached number 15 his sense of dread only increased as he found the house in complete silence with none of the usual reassuring sounds of screaming and shouting coming from inside – the small house looked somehow foreboding and threatening.

5

He slowly reached for his radio, pressing the transmit button a second before speaking. '914 to Control.'

'Go ahead, 914.'

'Any informant details for the domestic at 15 Gillett Avenue?'

'Negative. Caller was using a mobile number – declined to leave a name.'

'Can you call them back?' he asked. 'It's all quiet here.' But before Control answered, the front door began to slowly open, the darkness from inside seemingly spilling into the light outside as an unseen malevolence chased the warmth of the sun from the street. He slowly took two steps forward – unnerved enough to carefully draw his telescopic truncheon, extending it to its full length with a flick of his wrist as the door continued to open inch by inch, but still he could see no one.

'Police,' he called out to reassure himself as much as anything. 'Show yourself.' But his command was met only with a deathly silence, as if the street had been sucked into a vacuum in time and space. He took another step forward, squinting into the darkness of the house as a faint shape began to form – small and flowing white, moving towards the light like an ethereal being. His pounding heart sent torrents of blood rushing past his ears, creating an internal deafness as his vision tunnelled towards the shape that became increasingly human as it approached him. A young girl, no more than ten, slim and pale, dressed in what appeared to be a long white nightdress with long straight blonde, almost white, hair, staggered into the light – red blood spreading through her clothing as she walked towards him trembling, arms stiff by her side before falling forward into his arms. He caught her safely and lowered her to the ground, his mind still struggling to comprehend what he was seeing.

The girl's eyes blinked fast and hard as she used the last of her strength to whisper into his ear. 'They're inside.' Her eyes rolled back inside her head as she went limp in his embrace, dead or passed out, he couldn't tell.

'Jesus Christ,' he pleaded quietly as the adrenalin began to flow through his body, snapping him from the nightmare and allowing his training and experience to force his mind and body to act. But as he reached for his radio to call for an ambulance, a man came screaming from the house – his clothes and hands covered in blood, a kitchen knife held aloft above his head as he ran full pace straight towards King.

Without thinking, his instinct to save the girl made him turn his back on their screaming assailant – his own body becoming a human shield as he felt the first punch land on his shoulder. Only he knew it was more than just that – it was the knife being buried deep into his body. There was then a far more intense, violent pain as the knife was ripped from the muscle before he felt another punch, this time lower in his back, close to its centre, before once again the pain of the knife as it was torn from his body.

He screamed in pain and anger, the primeval response to fight for his life superseding all other emotions as he instinctively knew he had to react or die. He spun fast, brought the truncheon down hard on the madman's kneecap, but it had no effect. It was as if the man hadn't even felt it as again he plunged the knife towards him, only this time King was able to deflect it away as he pushed himself powerfully from the ground, launching his shoulder into the madman's midriff, driving him backwards until they both lost their balance and clattered to the ground. The man took the brunt of the fall as the knife fell from his grip and skidded away across the pathway.

King didn't hesitate in seizing the initiative, ignoring the pain and nausea sweeping through his body as he raised his metal truncheon and smashed it down over his attacker's head, splitting his skin to the bone as blood instantly poured from the wound, but in his wildness the man didn't even try to protect himself. Instead he clawed and grasped at King's face until his hands found his throat and wrapped around it, constricting his breathing. Over and over again King brought the truncheon down on the man's head and across his face until finally the man became human again and released his grip of King's throat to use his hands to protect himself. But still King rained down the blows, all thoughts of reasonable force banished to another time until the man underneath him was nothing more than a moaning bloody pulp.

Near exhaustion, he rolled his attacker onto his belly and stretched his arms out to the nearby metal railing and hand-cuffed him to it. The fight for survival over, he instantly felt close to passing out, drawing in long deep breaths to steady himself, but he knew he had only minutes, if that, before his injuries overcame him and when that time came he would welcome it – a blissful escape from the pain and sickness into darkness, but not yet. He had to check the girl. He had to check the house.

He staggered to his feet, but could only manage a crouching walk as he crossed the short distance to the motionless girl, although it seemed a mammoth trek to him. He kneeled next to her and first touched the base of his own back where all he could feel was a warm oily liquid. When he looked at his hand it was soaked in the darkest red blood he could ever remember seeing. He shook the image away and pushed the fingers of his other hand firmly into the side of the girl's neck, feeling for a pulse from her carotid artery. After a few seconds he found it – weak, but there – enough to spur him into tearing the bottom section of her dress clear and using it to press hard on the only wound he could find – a deep knife stab in her abdomen. He placed the little girl's own hands across the desperate bandage to provide some weight and breathed a sigh of relief as the bleeding seemed to slow, although he knew that her only chance of survival was to get her to an A&E unit as fast as possible. Suddenly he remembered his radio – pressing the transmit button, he steeled himself to speak.

'Officer needs urgent assistance and an ambulance on the hurry up at 15 Gillett Avenue.' He waited for the response from Control.

'All units, officer needs urgent assistance at 15 Gillett Avenue. Repeat, officer needs urgent assistance at 15 Gillett Avenue.' The female voice was then instantly followed by a cacophony of voices and call signs accepting the call to urgent assistance before Control spoke again. *'914, are you injured at all?'*

He managed the smallest of ironic laughs as he looked at his bloodstained hand before answering. 'Yes,' he spoke into the radio. 'Two, maybe more stab wounds.'

'Where have you been stabbed?' Control demanded.

'In the back,' he stuttered, his strength failing, giving him the urgency to press on. 'I have to check the house.'

'Wait till we get back-up to you, 914,' Control insisted. *'Stay out the house until we can get you some assistance.'*

'I can't,' he told them. 'She said "They're inside". I have to know.'

'Wait for back-up, 914. Stay clear of the house.' But King wasn't listening any more as he dragged himself to his feet and stumbled towards the doorway and the darkness beyond.

He steadied himself against the frame, allowing his eyes to adjust to the dimness, trying to blink the increasing amounts of sweat away before staggering inside, moving from room to room, quickly scanning each, but finding nothing. Somehow he knew the horror still waited for him – somewhere, until he finally, almost crawling now, made his way back to the front door and the foot of the staircase that looked like a mountain. As he reached out to grasp the bannisters he saw the bloody handprints for the first time. They reminded him of the sort of prints young children made with paint, but the marks on the wall opposite had no such childish innocence

9

as a long trail of smeared blood led his eyes back to the summit of the carpeted cliff.

The way ahead warped, constricting and elongating as his injuries threatened to overwhelm him, forcing him to his knees as his eyes tried desperately to close and surrender his body to blissful unconsciousness, but from some depths of humanity, a spirit to help his fellow man drove him on. It forced him to breathe in deeper than he'd ever done before and steady himself against all the pain, shock and blood loss as he literally began to crawl up the stairs one by one – each effort making him grimace and call out, begging for the strength to conquer the next step until somehow he found himself at the peak – on a hallway floor covered in thick, plush carpet where he collapsed, fighting to stay in the world.

If he stopped now he knew he'd at best pass out, so he pushed himself from the floor and sat with his back supported by the wall as he panted uncontrollably, fighting the nausea, his face ashen white, his lips turning grey as the blood flowed steadily from his body. He should have stopped and tried to shore up the wounds in his back, but he wasn't thinking straight any more, trapped as he was in a spiralling nightmare where nothing looked real or made any sense. Summoning his last remaining strength, he got to his feet, hunched and buckled, but at least he was walking.

The first door he came to was only slightly open, with the terrible telltale bloody fingerprints smeared on its panels and frame. He took one deep breath, sending searing, burning pain through his back, but with it came a moment of clarity as he carefully pushed the door open and stepped inside. The air rushed from his body when he looked at the bed and saw the body of a girl no more than twelve years old lying face up on the bed, her unseeing eyes staring at the ceiling, arms crossed across her chest as if someone had posed her – tried to make her violent death appear peaceful. Only a *parent* would take such care after death. He thought of the man

10

he'd beaten almost to the point of killing him. He was convinced that the life of the girl on the bed had been taken by her own father.

Although he already knew it was pointless, he staggered to the motionless figure and tried to find a pulse in her throat, but it was as still as a dead songbird. His eyes scanned her body, but could find no obvious sign of a wound other than reddening around her neck that would soon turn to widespread bruising. She'd been strangled. He swallowed deeply before stroking her brow and walking falteringly from the room, the blood from his hands mixing with the smears already on the walls as he tried to steady himself during the short walk to the next bedroom where the bloody handprints were heavier than anywhere else. He eased the door open and stepped inside. The approaching sirens wailed as if in mourning in the streets outside, but he couldn't hear them.

The woman who he assumed was the mother of the family lay on a double bed soaked in blood, as were the tangled sheets twisted around her tortured and mangled body. He stepped closer and could see she'd been stabbed more times than he could count – in her chest, neck and face, her hands and arms too covered in slashes and stabs as she'd tried to save herself. He remembered the bloodstains on the door of the other room and realized she must have been killed first – the father, the madman, killing her to stop her trying to save the children. King looked into her face – her eyes still wide open in horror, her mouth frozen in a twisted scream as she'd realized she could neither save herself or her children.

'Jesus Christ,' he managed to say before giving in to his swelling nausea and vomiting on the floor. His stomach continued to retch even after its contents had been violently expelled, the dizziness pulling him to the floor where he rested for a few seconds before he tried to flee the room, half walking, half crawling, when the sight of something froze him in his tracks: a foot on the floor protruding from the other side of the bed.

Again he used the wall for support, sliding along it until the boy's body came into view – lying on its side and, like his mother, heavily soiled by his own blood. Best he could tell the boy was fourteen or fifteen. King closed his eyes for a second and imagined the boy bursting into the room and seeing his own father slaying his mother – his bond with her so strong that he sacrificed his own young life to try and defend her from the wild animal his father had become, but it had all been in vain. The unarmed boy had had no chance. King opened his eyes, unable to comprehend what state of mind the man he'd beaten could have been in to butcher his own son and simply leave him dead on the floor of the bedroom as he went in search of his sisters. He fled from the room backwards – his eyes never leaving the boy on the floor by the side of his parents' bed.

Back in the hallway he struggled past the family bathroom – breathing heavily with relief as he realized it held no more horrors. But there was still one room he'd yet to visit and now it beckoned him, and although in his subconscious he was aware of approaching sirens and the sound of urgent radio chatter, the only thing that existed in his world was the door to the room. So he staggered forward, his youth and strength keeping him on his feet, though even they were rapidly failing now.

He knew he had only seconds before he surrendered to the blackness, falling more than walking to reach the door and push it open, the lack of any blood marks giving him hope that his living nightmare would end in an empty room of normality, but as he fell inside he realized the cruelty of life and death had saved the worst till last – the eerie peacefulness somehow making what he saw even more harrowing than what had gone before.

The pale young girl, no more than six, a perfect, younger

copy of the girl who'd fallen into his arms outside, lay still and staring on her bed, flanked by two empty, perfectly made beds either side. The beds of her sisters – one already dead and the other barely alive. The father's first victim. He'd taken the time to close her eyes and straighten her clothes before going in search of the rest of the family – no doubt planning equally clean and peaceful deaths for her siblings. But the mother was always going to feel his rage, and when the son fought back everything had changed.

Without warning King's legs buckled and he fell to his hands and knees, but even they could no longer take his weight as he collapsed onto his side, knocking the last of his breath from him as his eyes flickered and closed. At last the darkness came and took the nightmare away.

2

Nine months later

King sat in front of his computer inputting yet another crime report into the Met's CRIS system, feeling as bored and frustrated as he'd felt for the last few weeks. At first he'd been happy just to be back at work instead of climbing the walls in the hospital and then in the small flat he shared with his partner, Sara Taylor, a fellow police officer also based in Newham Borough. But now being stuck in an office was more than he could bear and he was longing for the streets. He was still treated as something of a hero after what had happened, but he knew that reputations didn't last long in the police and if he didn't make it back to the streets soon his peers would start to consider him as little more than a civvy – police slang for a civilian employee – who was no longer capable of the task of being an officer. He had to get back in the action, even if it meant lying about his true physical and mental state – even if it meant not telling anyone about the nightmares that plagued most of his sleeping hours.

The phone on the opposite desk rang loudly and made him jump. He hoped no one had noticed as he watched the civvy speak curtly into the phone before quickly hanging up and looking across the computer screens in his direction.

'Apparently the Chief Superintendent will see you now, Jack,' she told him, smiling. He smiled back and practically leapt from his chair. This could be the call he'd been waiting for – the green light to return to the streets.

As he hurried through the main CID office he almost bumped into Detective Sergeant Frank Marino coming from the other direction. Frank grabbed hold of his arm to steady them both.

'What's the big hurry?' Marino asked with a smile.

'Sorry, Frank,' King apologized. 'I just got a shout to go see Gerrard. I might be getting the OK to return to full duties.'

The smile slipped from Marino's face. 'Full duties? You sure you're ready for that? What happened to you was . . .' he struggled to find the words.

'I'm fine,' King tried to reassure him. 'Back and shoulder's still a little stiff and sore, but nothing I can't handle.'

'It's not the physical stuff I'm concerned about,' Marino told him. There was a silence for a few seconds. 'That was a tough situation you had to cope with. Fortunately the sort of thing not many of us will ever experience. It can leave scars no one else can see.'

'I'm fine,' King answered again and tried to smile, but couldn't.

They watched each other for what seemed a long time until Marino interrupted their silent conversation. 'Tough trial too. Wanker of a defence barrister grilling you for more than two days looking for holes.'

'Yeah, well, he was wasting his time,' King answered – the bitterness still thick in his voice.

'Yes he was,' Marino agreed. 'I've never seen a cop as young as you handle something like that as well as you did.'

King nodded, looking a little embarrassed before replying. 'Thanks. I just did what I had to do.'

Marino watched him for a few seconds. 'You're a good cop, Jack, you know. You had a lot of good results before . . . Real good arrests. Not easy to gain the respect and trust of other cops when you're on accelerated promotion – but you have. If you want to go the way of the CID I can make it happen. A couple more months flying the Crime Desk then we can get you on a plain-clothed squad and look to get you into a trainee detective slot as soon as we can. It's a good option, Jack.'

King took a deep breath before answering. 'I appreciate the offer, Frank – but I need the streets. Walking around out there in uniform makes me feel . . . makes me feel good. I missed it, you know. I need it.'

Marino gently let go of his arm. 'OK then. Good luck, but if you're not ready, or if you change your mind once you're back out there – you're welcome back here any time.'

'Thanks,' he replied. 'Anyway, mustn't keep Superintendent Gerrard waiting.'

'No. Of course not,' Marino agreed and watched King head off across the office.

King walked so fast through the station that several times he almost broke into a jog, nodding quick hellos to people he knew and some he didn't until he'd climbed to the top floor of the station and reached Gerrard's door. He took a deep breath and knocked, resting his hand on the handle in anticipation of a swift reply. He wasn't disappointed as almost immediately he heard Gerrard's voice calling him inside.

As soon as he entered he was greeted by the usual sight of Gerrard sitting straight-backed behind his desk as Inspector Joanne Johnston stood to the side. Jack knew it would be Gerrard doing the talking, but was in little doubt who was really in charge. Johnston had a fearsome reputation as being a ruthless self-promoter destined for the top – prepared to stab anyone in the back who got in her way, including Gerrard. Her appearance was, as ever, immaculate; her uniform tailored

16

at her own expense to best show off her athletic, thirty-three-year-old body, her brown hair cut into a short pixie style to best frame her pretty face. Looks that had already lulled more than a few male colleagues to drop their guard only to be crushed. A reputation that had already earned her the nickname of the 'Poisonous Pixie' at Bramshill Staff College.

'Ah, Jack,' Gerrard smiled. 'Please take a seat.'

'Thank you, sir,' King replied, sitting in one of the two chairs that faced Gerrard.

Gerrard looked down at the obligatory file that lay open on his desk and then back to King, looking as serious as King could remember seeing him. 'Inspector Johnston and I were just having a chat with HR about yourself – going over your latest medical reports, psychological reports, that sort of thing – something we need to do before considering anyone for full duties. Fortunately it's not like the old days when we'd have just patched you up and slung you back out on the streets. Times have changed. Things have moved on – for the better.'

King didn't agree. Being patched up and slung out sounded perfect to him. Talking to psychiatrists hadn't taken away his nightmares, but perhaps the streets could. 'I understand,' he managed to reply.

'However,' Gerrard smiled again, 'having taken everything into consideration, we have decided to allow you to return to full duties.'

King felt his heart soar with excited relief, but his stomach knotted with anxiety. He told himself it was nothing – that it was to be expected after everything that had happened. Gerrard must have seen something in his face.

'Are you all right, Jack?' he asked.

He recovered quickly. 'Sorry, yes, I'm fine. Just excited.'

'Good,' Gerrard beamed again. 'Now, having completed your sergeants' course while recovering on light duties, you'll no doubt be looking for more of a leadership role.'

It hadn't been something King had thought about – other people to look after as well as himself – but it wasn't enough of a fly in the ointment to put him off returning to the streets. 'Ideally,' he lied.

'Excellent,' Gerrard told him, 'because there's something that's come up that could be perfect.'

'I'm listening,' King encouraged him.

'We've been having a lot of trouble on the Grove Wood Estate this past year or so and, try as they like, the Safer Neighbourhoods Team down there can't seem to get to grips with it. So we,' Gerrard glanced at Johnston, 'have decided to try something new.'

'Such as?' King asked impatiently.

'We've decided to dedicate three constables to the estate on a permanent basis, or at least until they're no longer required. All have exceptional records and are known for their, shall we say, no-nonsense approach to policing. Your job, should you want it, would be to supervise the team and make sure they understand their parameters. We don't expect you to be walking the beat day after day yourself; after all, you should now be working towards achieving the next rank as you are still very much part of the accelerated promotion scheme.'

'I'd want to be out and about on the estate,' King blurted out.

'Then I take it you accept the position?' Gerrard asked.

'Of course,' King insisted. 'Sounds like fun.'

'I'm sure it will be,' Gerrard tried to play along, 'but don't lose sight of your ultimate career objectives. I see this as something to keep you out of harm's way – until you move forward to the next rank.'

'I don't need to be kept out of harm's way,' he argued, suspicious of Gerrard's intentions – fearful he and Johnston somehow doubted he was ready to return to the world outside.

'Of course you don't,' Gerrard quickly agreed. 'That's not what I meant. What I mean is we need to keep you away from anything that could hinder your future prospects, such as unfounded complaints from the public, for example. They can drag behind your career like an anchor on a speed boat.'

'I'll be careful,' he promised, 'but I've only been in the job a couple of years. I'm not quite ready for being stuck in an office behind a desk.'

Gerrard cleared his voice and managed to remain smiling. 'Well then, good. Good. Get out there and get it out of your system.'

'Thank you, sir. I will,' he assured them.

Gerrard grew serious again and appeared to look to Johnston for moral support before speaking, moving uncomfortably in his chair as Johnston looked on through her green eyes that shone with intelligence and ambition.

'Terrible thing that happened to you,' Gerrard finally spoke. 'Terrible thing that you had to see.' King just shrugged, dying inside at the thought of having to discuss it with two people he neither respected nor liked. 'The young girl – the girl you saved – eventually spoke to the Murder Investigation Team. She confirmed it was her father who'd tried to kill her – who'd killed the rest of his family. The investigating officers discovered he suspected the mother of having an affair and feared she was going to leave him and take the children with her, so he decided better to kill them all. Turns out she wasn't even seeing anyone else. He just imagined it.'

'I know,' King managed to say. 'The investigation team told me before the trial.'

'Yes,' Gerrard said, sounding more melancholy than King had ever heard him. 'I suppose they did. But after such a traumatic experience I was wondering how you felt – how you *really* felt? Never mind what you told the psychiatrist.'

'I'm fine, sir. I just need to get back to work. Proper work.'

19

'Very well,' Gerrard smiled, seemingly satisfied. 'As I've said, you'll be taking care of the day-to-day running of the Unit and will report to Inspector Johnston here who'll be overseeing things as a whole.'

'Fine,' King agreed, already rising from his chair, happy he'd heard everything he needed to before Johnston stopped him.

'You've been working on the Crime Desk, I understand?' Johnston finally spoke – her voice accentless and pleasantly toned. Designed to trap the unwary.

'Yes,' King confirmed, easing back into his chair.

'Then are you aware there appears to be a serial offender preying on young children on the estate and surrounding areas?' Johnston asked.

'I am,' King answered.

'Not as serious as it could be, thank God, although we take all offences against children, particularly sexual offences, very seriously indeed.'

'Yes, ma'am,' King went along with her, wondering where she was heading.

'It's time he was stopped,' she insisted, 'before he does something even worse.'

'I understand,' King assured.

'Good,' she smiled slightly – showing the tips of her straight white teeth as she turned to Gerrard to let him know she'd finished.

'You start tomorrow,' Gerrard told him. 'We've sorted out an office over at Canning Town for you. It's not much, but it'll do. Your new team will meet you there in the morning and you can all get acquainted. I'm sure you'll already know one or two of them.'

'Probably,' King shrugged and headed for the door.

'Inspector Johnston will email you a list of the team members before tomorrow,' he continued. 'Give you a chance to look them over.'

20

'Make sure you keep me fully informed,' Johnston told him, with a trace of a warning in her voice.

'Of course,' he assured him, guessing that Johnston wouldn't be slow in taking the credit for anything positive they achieved.

'And be careful,' Gerrard warned him as he headed through the door. 'I hear the locals occasionally take potshots from the tower blocks at passing police officers with unwanted television sets.'

'I'll bear that in mind,' King smiled as he pushed himself from his seat and headed for the door.

The next morning, shortly after ten, King entered the small office on the second floor of Canning Town Police Station that used to belong to the now reassigned Crime Prevention Officer. His three charges were already there noisily sorting out their new desks and trying to find places to stash the huge amount of kit that every uniformed officer now possessed: body armour, utility belts, riot helmets, normal helmets, flat caps, CS gas, extendable truncheons, fixed truncheons, light jackets, heavy jackets and a seemingly endless number of other items. He knew all three of them by name and sight, although they'd never worked closely. None of them were distracted from their mission to sort out the office when he entered, choosing to acknowledge his presence in a more casual manner.

'You must be mad to want to be in charge of this shit posting,' PC Davey Brown accused him in his strong Glaswegian accent – his hair still cropped exactly as it had been in his days as a Royal Marine before a shoulder injury had forced him to retire when he was only twenty-one. He had a tough, unpleasant-looking face, other than his striking green eyes, all enhanced by a muscular body that made him appear shorter than his five-foot-ten inches. Since joining the Met four years previously, he'd established a

21

reputation amongst his peers and the lowlife of Newham that was to be feared. 'I heard you actually volunteered for this shit,' he continued, stuffing his newly acquired drawers with kit.

'Maybe,' King played it cautiously, heading deeper into the office.

'Just like you did,' PC Renita Mahajan laughed at Brown who pulled a face of disgust.

'Did I fuck,' he insisted. 'First rule of being a police officer – never volunteer for fucking anything.'

'Well I volunteered,' she proudly admitted, her bright smile adding to her attractiveness before she pushed her shiny, short black hair out of her face and returned to emptying the previous incumbent's hordes of paperwork from her desk's drawers and throwing them into a confidential waste bag. At only five-foot-five and the tender age of twenty-three, she made up for her shortcomings by remaining strong and athletic, fearless and tenacious. She had only three years' service with the Met, but she was already confident and capable way beyond her years. 'Better than driving around in a patrol car all day with some old fart who doesn't want to get involved any more, delivering messages and taking crime reports.'

'You'll be wishing you were back in that patrol car soon enough when you're walking around the Grove Wood Estate in the middle of the night on your own, hen,' Brown smiled evilly.

'Ignore these two,' Danny Williams, the final member of the team, advised King. 'They think they're Laurel and Hardy.'

'Who?' Brown spat the question. Williams ignored him as he tried to close the tall metal locker he'd filled with equipment with no success, ramming it with his sizeable shoulder in frustration, before giving up and turning to King and straightening to his full six-foot-two, his lithe, athletic body augmented by his mahogany skin. He kept his Afro hair cropped so nothing would distract from his undeniably hand-some face, although at only twenty-four some boyish features still remained.

'We all volunteered,' Williams ended the argument, 'and so did a shitload more people, but we got picked because we're the best.'

'Aye,' Brown interrupted. 'Six months of this shit and I'll have earned enough brownie points to fuck off to the TSG. Borough policing's strictly for mugs. Territorial Support Group's the real show.'

'It's the CID next for me,' Williams explained.

'And you?' King asked Renita, who continued tidying her desk for a few seconds while she thought.

'I don't know,' she shrugged. 'Promotion maybe. What about you?'

'I haven't thought that far ahead,' he admitted before Brown answered for him.

'Have you not heard?' Brown grinned. 'Sergeant King here's on accelerated promotion. Oh, he's strictly just passing through on his way to the top.'

'You're on accelerated promotion?' Renita asked, suspicious.

'That's the rumour.' King knew he'd need to quickly earn their respect. 'If that's the way I want to go.'

'If?' Brown almost shouted. 'Listen, pal – take some advice. Never look a gift horse in the mouth. Fucking accelerated promotion – easy life, eh.'

'We're not pals yet,' King warned him. 'Let's start with Sarge and see how we get on, eh?'

Brown eyed him silently for a few seconds before answering. 'Aye. Fair enough.'

Williams calmed the tension. 'So what's the score – what's the brief with this estate policing unit?'

'What you been told?'

'Only what Inspector Johnston told me,' Williams explained.

'Police the Grove Wood Estate and sort it out. I was hoping you could be a little more specific.'

King moved deeper into the office and dumped his heavy kitbag onto the only desk that hadn't been taken. 'Fair enough,' he began. 'The estate's in a shit state. Local criminals and yobs seem to run the place. Reported crime's through the roof, so God only knows how much *unreported* crime's going on.'

'Powers-that-be won't like that,' Renita added.

'Safer Neighbourhoods Team tried to get on top of it, but failed,' King continued.

'SNT,' Brown scoffed. 'They couldn't get on top of a whore.'

King ignored him. 'Our job, to put it bluntly, is to kick some arse – within the confines of the law, naturally.'

'I like the sound of that,' Williams joined in.

'Can't make an omelette without breaking a few eggs.' Brown once more grinned his evil grin.

'I said within the confines of the law,' King reminded him.

'Aye,' Brown argued, 'but the local slags know the law better than most barristers. We want results, we're going to have to bend things a little. Know what I mean?'

'No one minds things getting a little *bent*,' King agreed. 'But it better be for the right reason and the right person. I don't want anyone overstepping the mark. Very low-grade stuff and only when there's no question of them being guilty. No stitch-ups – even on the local faces. We're better than that. Someone tosses a stolen phone when they see you coming and your evidence says you found it in their pocket when you searched them – hey, so be it. No one's going to get too worried about it, but no more than that. Everyone understand?' Everyone nodded in agreement, except for Brown who just shrugged. 'Good,' King left it.

'As I'm sure you all know by now, there are several fairly notorious drug dealers in the estate and at least one prolific handler,' he explained.

'I'll soon take care of them,' Brown crowed before King cut him down.

'No you won't,' he ordered. 'None of you will. Our job is to take out all the little shits who've been making life hell for everyone on the estate. Later on maybe we can move on to bigger fish, but right now we sort out these little bastards who are beginning to feel untouchable. The CID can deal with major crime. Our brief is to get the streets back.'

'The bloody CID?' Brown asked in his own unique way.

'Yes,' King answered – the fact he was losing patience plain to hear in his voice. Brown just shook his head. 'Now, I spent half of yesterday in with the Intelligence Unit getting the info on who's who on the Grove Wood and I've identified the people we should be looking at.' He pulled a folder and some Blu-tack from his kitbag and spilled the photographs from inside over his desk. As he spoke he stuck mugshots of the people he discussed to the closest whiteboard.

'Let's start with the local burglars, shall we?' he began. 'Tommy Morrison, seventeen-year-old residential burglar.' The mugshot showed a skinny youth with bad skin and unkempt brown hair. 'He specializes in daytime burglaries of homes on the estate.'

'So much for not shitting on your own doorstep,' Williams said.

'Morrison doesn't care about rules and sayings,' King told them. 'He only has one rule – steal it if you can. He doesn't care from who.'

'Why don't the locals just give him a good kicking and teach him a lesson?' Renita asked.

'Because they're all as bad as each other,' Brown explained. 'All fucking thieving from each other – all fucking each other over.'

'Probably,' King agreed, 'but the fact remains this kid is a one-man crime wave, so let's bring an end to it.' He stuck another photograph of a similarly unpleasant-looking youth to the board. 'Justin Harris. Another residential burglar and sometime partner-in-crime of the before-mentioned Morrison and just as prolific.' Yet another photograph was stuck to the board, this time of a black youth in his late teens. 'Everton Watson,' King explained. 'The last of our residential burglars, only he strictly works solo and is notoriously slippery.'

'I've dealt with that slag,' Renita told them. 'Nicked him for screwing a car. Looks like he's moved up to bigger and better things.'

'He has,' King agreed, 'and now he needs to be stopped. But speaking of screwing cars,' he continued, sticking two more photographs on the board, 'we shouldn't forget these two – Craig Rowsell and Harrison Clarke – a salt-and-pepper team specializing in theft from motor vehicles. Where you find one you'll usually find the other. Prolific isn't the word for these two. Next time you feel broken glass from a smashed car window under your feet, you can be sure it's probably down to these two clowns. They'll think nothing of breaking into a car just to see if there's anything worth nicking. They're looking for satnavs people have been stupid enough to leave inside or mobiles, but they'll take absolutely anything: loose change, adaptors, chargers, pens, CDs, even lighters in the past. If they had a motto it'd be "steal first – think later" and they are causing havoc to the borough motor vehicle crime figures.'

'Well now,' Brown added sarcastically, 'we can't have that, can we.'

'No we can't,' King reprimanded him. 'And then there's those who are slightly further up the food chain. As I've said, they're not our immediate problem, but you should be aware of who they are.'

The first mugshot was of an overweight man about thirty-four years old, with oily olive skin and hair pulled back in a ponytail. He was smiling in the photo, revealing his heavily stained teeth. 'This is Arman Baroyan,' King told them. 'By all accounts he's a proper Fagin – the main dealer in stolen goods on the estate, but judging by his lack of arrests he's no fool.'

Next he slapped a photo of a man in his mid-twenties to the rogues' gallery – tall and skinny with a poor pox-marked complexion, his head shaved, dead blue eyes staring from his skull-like face. 'Micky Astill's our main local heroin and crack dealer, selling out of his secured flat in The Meadows. He never seems to get turned over by any bigger or more violent dealers, so assume he's getting protection from somewhere.'

'Probably the Campbells,' Renita offered, referring to the area's most notorious crime family.

'Probably,' King agreed, 'but the Campbells neither live on the estate nor commit the sorts of crimes we're interested in.'

'More's the pity,' Brown snarled.

'And last but not least,' King ignored him, sticking his final photo to the board, 'Susie Ubana – our primary local cannabis dealer.' He tapped the photograph of the attractive black woman in her early thirties. 'If it's cannabis you want she's your girl. She deals from her heavily fortified maisonette in Millander Walk. Drug Squad have hit it before, but by the time they got through the metal grates any drugs had been long flushed or so well hidden they couldn't find them.'

'If we're not going to hit them, why we talking about them?' Brown demanded to know.

'Because they're a good source of arrests,' King told him. 'You see any local toe-rags coming from any of these addresses there's a strong chance they'll be carrying drugs or stolen goods. Never look a gift horse in the mouth – wasn't that what you said?'

'Aye, well,' Brown struggled for an answer.

King pressed on. 'And remember – in amongst the scum there'll be a lot of decent folk just trying to live their lives quietly. Treat them with respect when you're dealing with them and we might just win their support and confidence. We're there to police by consent – not just force. Everyone understand?'

Renita and Williams nodded, whereas Brown just shrugged.

'Now, most of the people we're interested in don't even get out of their beds till midday, lazy bastards, so there's no point us wandering around the estate at seven in the morning. We'll work two shifts between ten am and six pm and six pm till two in the morning – two of us per shift. You don't have to walk around holding hands, although sometimes we'll need to stick together. Any questions?'

'Aye,' Brown asked. 'When do we get started?'

'Right now,' King told him, clipping on his utility belt and pulling his body armour from his bag. 'The Grove Wood Estate's crawling with criminality. It's time to restore the rule of law.'

The small meeting began to break up before King stopped them. 'One more thing, before I forget.' The others stopped what they were doing and turned back to look at him. 'Apart from the before-mentioned rogues' gallery, the Grove Wood has an additional and very unwelcome problem.'

'Such as?' Renita asked.

'Some animal messing with the local kids,' King explained.

'The fucking kiddie fiddler?' Brown jumped in. 'CID still not caught the bastard?'

'Yes, the kiddie fiddler and, no, the CID still haven't caught him,' King answered. 'But this one's already up to half-a-dozen attacks to date and doesn't look like stopping until he's stopped. I spoke with DS Marino about it and he's convinced whoever's doing it is already escalating. Only a matter of time before he commits a serious sexual assault on a child. We have to stop him before that happens.'

'That's a lot of attacks in a relatively small area,' Renita questioned. 'How come he keeps getting away with it?'

'CID have had the Crime Squad down there a few times,'

King explained, 'but he never attacks out in the open, so observation posts haven't worked. They tried to put plain-clothed units on the ground, but you know what it's like on the Grove Wood – strangers stand out a mile and Old Bill even more so. As soon as the Crime Squad moved onto the estate the local slags put the alarm up – warning whoever we're looking for, even if they didn't mean to.'

'Forensics?' Williams asked.

'No forensics,' King answered. 'He's real careful. Uses his hands and hands only. Never leaves any body fluids behind for DNA.'

'And identification?' Williams tried again.

King just shook his head. 'We have little or no chance of that. He uses the oldest disguise in the book: a baseball cap, hoodie – hood up and sunglasses. Add to that the fact that the children are usually very young and traumatized – there's little chance of a positive identification. No. This one we're probably going to have to catch in the act.'

'Great,' Brown shrugged and pulled a face of disgust.

King ignored him. 'OK, people. That's the job, so let's get on with it. Starting right now.'

King walked through the estate feeling better than he had in a long time. He caught a reflection of himself in the stain-less steel doors of one of the many old lifts that ferried the inhabitants skywards to their homes. It had been a long time since he'd seen himself in full uniform. There'd been no need for body armour and a belt full of equipment answering a phone on the Crime Desk. He took a second to admire his appearance – a crisp white open-neck short-sleeved shirt under the armour. Black trousers and shiny shoes with rubber soles so he could move silently. He'd also chosen to wear his peaked cap instead of the traditional helmet and had told the others to do the same. He wanted them all to look the part – to look different from other cops on foot. He wanted the locals to know they were dealing with something unlike anything they'd dealt with before. He took a deep breath and straightened his cap to perfection and let the feeling of power surge through his body. Strange how powerful a uniform could make a person feel – like wearing an impregnable shield. A jolt of pain through his shoulder reminded him it was anything but.

His radio suddenly gave off two electronic-sounding peeps – letting him know someone was trying to contact him on one of its private channels. He checked and saw that it was Renita. He pressed the transmit button and spoke to her, knowing that only she would be able to hear him.

'Go ahead, Renita.'

'You still on the Grove Wood?' she asked.

'Yeah. In Manor Mead. Something going on?'

'I got Craig Rowsell under obs in Tabard Street checking out the parked cars,' she told him. 'I've already got enough to nick him for vehicle interference.'

'No,' King insisted. 'If he's that interested it's only a matter of time before he screws one. Give him a bit of rope. I'll make my way to you. Where are you now?'

'South end of Tabard Street,' she replied.

'I'll make my way to the north end,' he explained. 'You keep him under obs. If he screws one, show out and flush him towards me. I'll stay out of sight until you give me the nod.'

'Understood,' she confirmed as he made his way quickly through the estate's rat-runs to Tabard Street – staying out of view from anyone who might have shouted a warning to Rowsell of his impending approach. A few minutes later he'd hidden himself behind a recessed stairwell and let Renita know he was waiting to ambush their prey.

His radio hissed into life. 'Sarge,' Renita began. 'Rowsell's getting very interested in an old BMW 3 Series. He's been back for a couple of looks. Standby.' His radio went dead for a few seconds before coming alive again. 'He's picked up a small stone,' she continued. 'He's moving towards the BMW. Standby. He's done the window – repeat – he's done the window. Shall I move in?'

'No,' King insisted. 'Wait till he's stolen from the car.'

'OK,' she agreed, 'but whatever he's after he's taking his time. Standby – he's out the vehicle now – looks like he's had the stereo away.'

The stereo? King thought to himself. Any stereo old enough to be ripped in one unit from a car in this day and age could surely only be worth pennies. He wondered why the likes of Rowsell bothered. 'Show out now,' he commanded. 'Get him running towards me.'

'Already done it,' Renita told him over the radio, her voice making it clear she was running as she spoke. 'Stop there, Rowsell, you thieving little . . .' She released her transmit button before King could hear any more.

He peeked around the stairwell in time to see Rowsell haring towards him, stupid enough to be still clutching the old stereo, about fifty metres away, but closing fast. He waited, hidden, muttering barely audible encouragement to the advancing thief. 'Come on. Come on.' Only when he was sure Rowsell would neither be able to swerve past him nor turn and run in the opposite direction did he burst from his hiding place, making the thief's eyes widen with fear and nostrils flare as he realized he'd run straight into a trap.

King hit him hard with the palms of his outstretched arms, ploughing into Rowsell's chest and momentarily lifting him from the floor, knocking the wind from him and making him drop the stereo. Quickly King spun him around and pushed him up against the wall, pulling his arms behind his back and expertly wrapping his quick-cuffs around Rowsell's wrists, making him curse and complain.

'Get the fuck off me,' he demanded. 'Ah, fuck. The cuffs are too tight, you wanker.'

King pushed him harder into the wall to let Rowsell know who was in charge. 'Better watch your language, Craig, or I'll be adding violent disorder to theft from motor vehicle. Understand?'

'Who the fuck are you?' Rowsell asked. 'TSG?' Clearly he was experienced enough to know the difference between a relatively gentle arrest at the hands of the local police and the more *robust* treatment he could expect from the Territorial Support Group.

'Not TSG, my friend,' King smiled. 'Haven't you heard? You've got your very own police force now. The Grove Wood Estate Policing Unit. Remember the name, you little prick, because things around here are about to change.'

By the time King arrived home to his two-bedroom flat in Chadwell Heath, East London, his partner was already there, preparing dinner in their tiny kitchen. She kissed him on the lips and fussed around him, making him smile at the special treatment he was receiving.

'Sit down, sit down,' she insisted. 'I want to hear all about your first day back.'

He slumped in one of their only two kitchen chairs that lived under the small circular dining table, also used as a part-time desk, thankful to be sitting after spending the first day on his feet for more than nine months. 'Nothing to tell,' he lied. 'Just a normal day at the office.'

'I don't think so,' she reminded him. 'Your first day back on the streets. Your first day as a sergeant on full duties. Your first day in charge of the Estate Policing Unit.'

'OK,' he relented, nodding his head. 'It went well. Team seem solid, although Davey Brown wants to lock horns all the time.'

'Oh, I know Davey Brown,' she told him. 'The ex-Marine, right?' He just nodded. 'You know his type. They want to be sergeants, but they don't want to have to bother with the exams – think they've got a right to promotion just because they know what they're doing on the streets. But I know you. You'll soon have Davey Brown eating out of the palm of your hand.'

'Maybe what we do on the streets for real should dictate who gets promoted and not just who can pass exams?' he questioned.

'That's a little rich coming from someone on accelerated promotion,' she reminded him. 'Turkeys don't generally vote for Christmas.'

'Well, we had a decent arrest on our first day,' he explained, letting her comment slip away. 'Craig Rowsell for screwing a car on the estate. He nicked some ancient stereo from some clapped-out BMW. I mean, why would you bother nicking that? It wasn't worth shit.'

'Because he's a thief,' she reminded him. 'What does he care? He's not thinking about the logic of breaking a hundred-pound window to steal a ten-pound stereo. None of it's his loss. As far as he's concerned if he sees a ten-pence piece on the seat of a car why not smash the window to get it. At the end of the day he'll be 10p up.'

King unconsciously rubbed the back of his injured shoulder. 'I'll never understand these people,' he complained. 'If you're gonna be a thief, be a good one. Steal something that's worth something.'

'If you're getting it for nothing, then everything's worth something,' she tried to explain, before noticing he was rubbing his back and grimacing slightly. 'Giving you trouble?' she asked.

'Uh?' he replied, momentarily confused before he realized what he was doing and self-consciously pulled his hand away. 'I'm fine. Just a little sore, that's all.'

'Have you taken your pills?'

'I took some earlier,' he assured her. 'Probably due some more about now,' he added as he rose and headed to the cupboard where they kept all their medicines and first aid equipment and popped two four-hundred-milligram tablets of buprenorphine from their plastic and tinfoil homes and threw them into his mouth as he headed for the fridge and grabbed himself a beer. He used the bottle opener attached to the door to lift the lid and washed the pills down with a large swig.

'I thought you were supposed to let them dissolve on your tongue before swallowing,' Sara reminded him.

He swallowed hard to force the pills further into his stomach before answering. 'I know, but they taste shocking. What difference can it make anyway?'

'I don't know, but maybe you should stick to the instructions.'

'It'll be fine,' he tried to reassure her.

'And those ones are opioids,' she warned him. 'Perhaps you should try to come off them and use something else.'

'Fine,' he shrugged. 'I'll ask my GP next time I see her.'

'You mean the GP you never go and see?'

He looked her up and down with admiring eyes before taking another drink of beer and sitting on the chair in front of her. 'Maybe all it needs is a good massage?' he suggested.

'Oh,' she smiled, taking hold of his shoulder with both hands. 'You reckon that's *all* you need.'

He slipped his arms around her waist and pulled her a little closer, rolling his neck as her fingers dug deep and began to relax him. 'That feels nice,' he told her.

'Only nice?' she teased.

'It feels good,' he improved. 'Really good.' He felt tired parts of his body start to awaken as he pulled her a little closer and began to unbutton the white police blouse she still wore, pulling it open and kissing her soft, pale skin, making her gasp a little before she spread her legs and sat astride him, moving her mouth onto his as his hands moved upwards to cup her breasts through the lace of her white bra.

34

She whispered in his ear as she panted a little for breath. 'Not here. Let's go to the bedroom.'

'Here's fine,' he argued, kissing her neck and covering her body in goose bumps, but she pulled away, smiling seductively, taking his hand and encouraging him to his feet.

'The bedroom's more comfortable,' she told him, 'for what I have in mind.'

'And what would that be?' he asked, his voice hoarse with desire.

'Come with me and you'll find out,' she promised as she rose from his chair and he willingly followed her towards the bedroom.

3

King and Williams hid in a stairwell tower overlooking flats in Millander Walk – specifically the one belonging to the local handler, Arman Baroyan. Williams continued to explain the night's events as King listened intently, considering their options – his eyes never leaving the flat opposite.

'Two residential burglaries overnight – both on the estate, both very close together in time and location. They took so much stuff there's no way they could have shifted it yet. I figure sooner or later they'll bring it to Baroyan.'

'What did they take?' King asked.

'Like I said – shedloads. TVs, Blu-ray players, a laptop, a disc drive, jewellery, clothes, booze – you name it.'

'That's too much to shift in the open in broad daylight,' King argued.

'Unless they're stupid or desperate,' Williams grinned.

'I suppose we could get lucky,' King admitted.

'Or maybe they'll bring it here bit by bit – in which case what do we do?'

'If we catch them out in the open with any of the gear we'll nick them before they even reach Baroyan's. Remember what I told you all – we're not after the handlers and dealers yet. Instead let's use them as a source of arrests.'

Williams nodded in agreement. 'Fine by me.'

A few seconds later a clearly empty-handed youth casually approached Baroyan's flat, stopping and checking he wasn't being watched before he prepared to knock on the door. Once satisfied he was unobserved, he reached through the solid-looking metal grid covering the door and pounded on the reinforced wood.

'Allo,' King whispered. 'Who's this then? D'you recognize him?'

'I know this little slag,' Williams told him. 'That's Stuart Weller. He works as a runner for Baroyan – ferrying messages backwards and forwards for him, arranging where to drop nicked gear.'

'I guess Baroyan doesn't trust phones then,' King suggested.

'Would you?' Williams asked. King just nodded slowly as the door was answered by Baroyan, who briefly spoke to Weller before disappearing inside and closing the door. Weller quickly skulked away, still walking casually, as if it was just another normal day on the estate – and for him it was.

'Come on,' King told Williams, already running down the stairs two at a time. 'We need to follow him. He could lead us straight to whoever screwed the flats, and the stolen gear.'

Williams was after him now. 'How we gonna get close enough to follow him without showing out?'

'He'll take the rat-runs as much as he can,' he explained, 'and so will we.'

They tailed Weller for almost a quarter of a mile to the other side of the estate, always staying close to the building lines, looking for shadows to hide in, alcoves to conceal them, until finally they spied him climbing to the second floor of Abbey Mead – a long, low-rise block of flats with sweeping communal walkways made from dull grey bricks, where he stopped outside a flat. They hid behind a car in the building's car park and waited, although it was already clear from the state of the front door that the flat was semi-derelict and probably being used as a squat. After a few seconds the door was opened by a white man in his mid-twenties who looked gaunt and neglected – the yellowness of his skin clear even from a distance.

'D'you know him?' King whispered.

'Nah,' Williams admitted, 'but he looks like a scag or crack-head.'

The gaunt figure ushered the youth inside and closed the flimsy-looking door. 'I'm liking this more and more,' King told him, just as they saw an equally emaciated-looking white man appear from the stairwell carrying a thin plastic bag loaded with what looked like groceries and head towards the flat. He fumbled for a key in his trouser pocket before finally opening the door and disappearing inside.

'These are definitely our boys,' King insisted. 'Have to be.'

'I agree,' Williams whispered, 'but we haven't got a warrant and we haven't seen any stolen goods yet.'

'We don't need a warrant to search the flat if they're already under arrest,' King reminded him.

'That's all fine if the stolen stuff's inside,' Williams argued. 'If that's the case we can make up anything we like – make the facts fit the arrest – but if it's not, people might ask what power we had to search it in the first place. Maybe we should get a warrant.'

'It'd take too long,' King dismissed it, 'and there's no guarantee they'd give us one anyway. Trust me – the stuff's inside that flat and so are the burglars.'

'OK,' Williams reluctantly agreed. 'We'll do it your way.'

The single lock holding the door closed was wholly inadequate and unable to stand up to even one kick from Williams' boot as he and King seemed to charge through the small space simultaneously, screaming 'Police!' at the tops of their voices as they ran into the sitting room with truncheons drawn, catching the two men and the youth by complete surprise as they sat on the only sofa in the flat – a filthy remnant salvaged from a skip somewhere and dragged to the squat that stank of hard drug use, human desperation and impending death. It was also now filled with the stench of human excrement as the drug users struggled to control their bowels with muscles wasted by years of abuse with serious narcotics. On the battered table in front of them lay the remains of their latest attempt to escape the awful pointlessness of their lives – a homemade glass crack-pipe stained with over-use and numerous pieces of old tinfoil riddled with the track marks of burnt heroin. The drug users' eyes were wide open and vacant – as if they'd been hypnotized – whereas the local feral youth had the look of someone who realized they were just unlucky to have been caught in the wrong place at the wrong time.

'Nobody fucking move,' King screamed at them, making one of the men begin to shake uncontrollably and grimace as he tried not to foul himself. 'You're all under arrest for the two burglaries that happened on the estate last night. I'll assume you all know the caution off by heart so I won't waste my time explaining it.'

'I ain't done no fucking burglary, man,' Weller protested his innocence.

'Shut the fuck up, Stuart,' Williams told him, prompting him to exhale in exasperation and sink further into the reeking sofa.

'Get up and turn around,' King told the silent men who obeyed like lambs heading to the slaughterhouse as they secured them with quick-cuffs and sat them back down. 'You just stay there,' he told Weller, who knew there would be little point in running.

The suspects safely trussed, King and Williams began to look around the spartan flat, but it was immediately clear the drug-ravaged men hadn't even bothered to hide their stolen booty and had merely piled it in the corner of the front room – TVs, laptops, booze, everything. Even the jewellery lay on the floor.

'Fuck me,' Williams tormented them. 'You could have made an effort.' But still they said nothing, occasionally looking to one another as if they were communicating telepathically – their plight about to get significantly worse as King pulled open the only fitted cupboard in the room and stared inside almost disbelievingly.

'Danny,' he called over his shoulder without looking away from the contents of the cupboard. 'You'd better take a look at this.' Williams could tell by his tone that he'd found something even more serious than the stolen goods and approached almost in trepidation until he too stared into the cupboard and let out a long whistle before turning back to the men.

'You two are well and truly fucked,' he told them as King pulled the two black balaclavas, baseball bats, knives and – almost most damning of all – a roll of thick black gaffer tape from the cupboard and laid it all out neatly on the floor for the men to see.

'Things just got very serious, gentlemen,' King told them. 'This isn't just burglary any more – this is aggravated burglary. You could get *life* imprisonment for this.' Still they said nothing and King wondered whether they even cared. Their lives had been over the minute they started smoking crack and heroin. 'All right,' he told Danny, the excitement in his voice suddenly replaced with a resigned sadness. 'Call up some transport for the prisoners, will you? And you'd better let CID know what's coming their way. It's all over for these boys. By the look of them, has been for a while.'

King was in the custody suite back at Canning Town Police Station, having just finished booking in the last of the three prisoners from the estate, when Marino appeared quietly on his shoulder.

'That's a top job you've brought in there,' Marino told him

as he began to examine the paperwork on the prisoners. 'Two for aggravated burglary and one for handling. Very nice. But I don't see a search warrant anywhere here.'

'Didn't need one,' King answered with a stony face. 'We had reasonable grounds under Section 17 to enter and arrest, which then gave us power to search the flat under Section 18.'

'Reasonable grounds?' Marino looked him in the eyes.

'We followed Weller from a well-known handler's address to the squat and while we had it under obs we saw one of these slags approach and enter carrying a flat-screen TV I recognized from the crime report.'

'Uh huh,' Marino smiled. 'Good work. We'll take it from here.'

'I'd like to keep the job,' King asked, but Marino shook his head.

'Sorry, Jack,' he explained. 'Aggravated burglary is strictly a CID matter. They may be good for a few clear-ups elsewhere on the borough as well. Don't worry – I'll make sure you and your team get full credit for the arrests.' King shrugged disappointedly. 'You've done your job and you've done it well,' Marino tried to encourage him. 'You should be proud of it.' Still King said nothing. 'And I for one am certainly looking forward to seeing what else your team can bring in. Now finish up your arrest notes and drop them on my desk when they're done.'

King again remained silent as he watched Marino walk away with the paperwork for the job that he felt should have been his. He quelled his rising resentment by reminding himself that one day in the not too distant future the likes of Marino wouldn't be able to take anything off him unless he ordered them to. He decided to console himself by taking his team for a celebratory drink at the nearby pub favoured by the local police. He reckoned they deserved it.

*　　*　　*

King entered the Trafalgar pub. It was a stone's throw from the police station and therefore guaranteed to be popular with the local uniformed officers so long as the drinks were reasonably priced and place was kept clean; whereas the local CID preferred to hide themselves away in more far-flung watering holes, out of sight of indiscreet eyes. The pub was already busy and noisy with the late shift, but he found his small team easily enough, standing apart at the far end of the bar. He eased his way through the crowd and made his way over to them where he was greeted with smiles all round.

'I thought you'd bailed on us,' Brown accused him.

'Just had to finish up some paperwork,' he explained.

'Drink?' Renita asked.

'Of course,' he told her. 'Lager – a pint. Anything that's not Australian.'

'That'll be the Heineken then.' She pushed her way to the bar, getting served almost immediately despite the men who'd been waiting before her.

'Shame about having to hand over the burglary prisoners,' Brown reminded him.

King couldn't be sure if he was just making conversation or setting something up. 'Couldn't be helped,' he answered. 'Aggravated burglary's a CID matter.'

'Still,' Brown eyed him, 'would have been nice to keep hold of a job like that – take it all the way to court.'

'We could have dealt with it,' Williams joined in. 'The job was as good as done anyway. We had the prisoners, the property. What else was there left to do?'

'Interviews,' King pointed out, 'forensics, paperwork, pump them about other burglaries they may have committed. If we'd taken it on we'd be tied up in the station for the next two or three days. Better to let the CID have it so we can get on with patrolling the estate.'

'Or maybe the CID just didn't trust you to put the job

together properly.' Brown smiled unpleasantly just as Renita turned back towards them handing King his drink.

'Maybe,' he told Brown as he took the drink. 'Thanks.'

'You're welcome. Everything all right?' she asked.

'Everything's fine,' he assured her.

'Aye,' agreed the still smiling Brown. 'Everything's fine.'

'Drink up then, Sarge,' Williams encouraged him.

'On the streets it's Sarge,' King explained. 'In the pub it's Jack.'

'Fair enough,' Williams nodded, happy to oblige, as were the others. 'And here's to a solid start.' They all raised their glasses and took a drink before King spoke again.

'It's been OK,' he pulled them back, 'but it could have been better.'

'You think,' Renita asked. 'How exactly?'

'The burglars were good arrests – very good,' he admitted, 'but they weren't locals. They weren't *faces*. I doubt anyone on the estate even knew them. Probably glad to see the back of them. No one wants to see a couple of loose cannons running around with knives and baseball bats committing aggravated burglaries. Not even our delightful locals. As much as we can, we need to keep our efforts concentrated on the indigenous wildlife. Only that'll bring the estate to heel.'

'Aye, maybe,' Brown partly agreed, 'but it could have been even better if we took the gloves off a bit. It's all very well and good sticking to the rules, but I don't see the local slags playing by any rules. Maybe we should even the game up a little, know what I mean?'

'No,' King forbade it. 'I told you – neatening things up is one thing. Anything other than that is not acceptable. We're better than that. We keep our integrity.'

'Whatever you say,' Brown said in a sulk.

'You've got a lot to say for yourself,' Renita told Brown. 'For someone who hasn't had an arrest on the Unit yet.'

'Yeah, that's right,' Williams joined in. 'The only one who hasn't.' Everybody smiled but Brown.

'Yeah well,' he defended himself, 'enjoy it while you can. Won't be long before I'm top dog.'

'Come on,' King ended Brown's humiliation. 'Drink up. It's my round.'

4

King felt something rocking him and dreamt he was on a small boat lost in a large sea until Sara's voice broke through his tiredness and the remains of the alcohol and he realized he was in his own bed in his own flat with very much his own stinking hangover.

'Time to get up,' she told him unsympathetically loudly. 'You'll be late.'

He sat upright too quickly, the sudden movement of blood in his head making him feel like he was back on the boat. 'Shit,' he complained as he grabbed his head in both hands. 'What time is it?'

'Almost nine,' she said without looking at him. 'Good night, was it?'

He ignored her sarcasm, but could tell she was enjoying herself. 'Why didn't you wake me up?'

'I'm not your keeper,' she laughed.

'Ahh, Christ,' he complained as nausea crept up on him, making her laugh all the more.

'And it's a bit early to be celebrating your success, isn't it?' she warned him. 'A few days on that toilet of an estate – a few arrests and you think the job is done. I don't think so. You may be the talk of the borough right now, but you've

45

got a long way to go before I for one will be convinced. Now I'm off to do some *real* police work. I'm on one of the response cars again. Some of us have to cover the whole borough – not just one estate. Being the superstar that everyone thinks you are, I'm sure you're capable of getting your own breakfast.' She kissed him on the forehead and swaggered out the bedroom, while all he could do was flop back onto the bed and let out a groan of misery.

King entered the Unit's small office at Canning Town and found Renita and Brown already in full kit and ready to yet again take on the estate. Both somehow managed to look considerably better than he felt, despite having all left the Trafalgar at the same time. They passed knowing glances at each other and smiled at his misfortune, for the first time making him suspect they'd spiked at least one of his drinks. Still, he'd enjoyed the sensation of numbness and the sleep that was free of his usual nightmare.

'Morning, Sarge,' Renita grinned from ear to ear. 'You look well.'

'Very funny,' he told her, pulling a face.

'You wanna be more like me,' Brown unhelpfully advised him. 'Trained soldier, me. Take more than a few bevvies to bring me down.'

'I'm fine,' he lied. 'Nothing a decent brew won't sort out.'

'I'll get the kettle on,' Renita came to his rescue, heading for the old kettle in the corner of the office they'd commandeered from nobody quite knew where. She was in the process of filling it with water from a tiny, dilapidated sink when a gentle knock on the doorframe of the office halted her. They all looked in the direction of the disturbance to see Inspector Joanne Johnston standing in the entrance to the office – her green cat-eyes darting between King, Renita and Brown, as if she was deciding which mouse to pounce on first.

'Good morning, everybody,' she said cheerfully, if a little

drily. They murmured good mornings in return, but still Johnston didn't enter. 'Just thought I'd call by and congratulate everyone on the excellent start you've made. You're quite the talk of the Senior Management Team. It won't be long before everyone's beating a trail to your door wanting to know how you did it.'

The team looked at one another before King answered for them. 'Thank you, ma'am. But it's only a start.'

'Yes. Yes it is. I'm glad you understand that,' Johnston agreed with her famous pixie smile. 'But a good start all the same.'

'Thank you,' King said again, unable to think of anything else to say.

'Good,' Johnston replied, her clear, sparkling eyes boring deep into King's. 'I appreciate policing the Grove Wood can be very challenging and at times there may be a temptation to bend some of the rules to get the job done.' She waited for a reaction, only continuing when none was forthcoming. 'Just make sure bending doesn't mean breaking.' Again she waited for a reaction, but still the others just stared back at her until she gave up. 'Keep up the good work.'

'We'll do our best,' King told her with a look that let Johnston know he had nothing else to say.

'Very well then,' she smiled, looking satisfied with herself. 'Before I forget – any progress with this sexual assaults on children business? The SMT wants him stopped before things become even more serious. Sexual assaults of this nature are not a Service priority, even on children, but serious sexual assaults are. So far he's gone no further than exposing himself and touching them in *intimate* places. If he progresses to making them perform sexual acts on him, or worse, it'll make the whole borough look bad.'

'We're on it,' King assured her. 'But it's difficult.'

'Spare me the excuses,' she dismissed his plea. 'I've had enough of those from the CID.' She paused as she checked

47

their faces for a reaction. 'Just keep me informed.' King nodded once as Johnston spun on her slightly higher than regulation heels and disappeared from the doorway. They stood in silence, as if they had been temporarily frozen for almost thirty seconds, before simultaneously breaking into stifled laughter, more with relief that Johnston had left than anything.

'Some piece of work, that one,' Brown said what they were all thinking. 'Mind you I wouldn't mind giving her—'

'All right,' King stopped him. 'Just remember – you report to me. Not Johnston.'

'I'm beginning to understand why they call her the Poisonous Pixie,' Renita added, before looking more serious. 'She's sharp though. I wouldn't be trying to take the piss with the pixie around. Remember – the more beautiful the snake the more poisonous it is.'

'Enough fun and games,' said King. 'Let's get out there. Like I said last night, the aggravated burglary arrests were good, but they weren't locals, so let's get on with harassing those who need to be harassed. I want everyone on the estate to know who's running things now. Everyone.'

King walked along Millander Walk still nursing his hangover – trying to breathe in fresh air, but the air on the estate at the beginning of summer was anything but fresh. It was as if it had been permanently trapped by the surrounding buildings that never allowed a clean wind to blow away the stale smell of humanity piled too high on top of each other – the heat of the sun igniting the stench from the communal bins and rubbish chutes that were rarely cleaned. The odour of a thousand different meals escaped from seemingly every window and vented cooker hood, mixing with the smell of the dog excrement that sporadically littered the walkways and grassy play areas set aside for children, but which were only ever used by the local youth gangs and their cross-bull-terrier dogs who crapped where they pleased, undeterred by their owners who had no interest in cleaning the foul mess. King almost gagged on the stench until the sight of Susie Ubana standing outside her fortified maisonette distracted him from his sickness.

Her attractiveness and general appearance surprised him. He'd only ever seen her mugshot, which was from a few years ago and probably had been taken after she'd been in custody for hours, if not days. It was a stark contrast to the well-dressed, slim black woman in her early thirties he was looking at now. She stood casually smoking a cigarette, standing on the walkway looking over the wall at nothing in particular, staring in the direction of the grassed area and beyond, unbothered by his presence – whatever drugs she possessed being safely hidden away in her home. Her front door was open, but the metal grid across it remained securely locked. King knew Ubana wouldn't be stupid enough to have the keys on her, which meant there was someone in the maisonette holding the keys for her.

King decided it was time he introduced himself to one of the estate's better-known residents and walked the short distance to where she stood and leaned on the wall next to her, slipping off his flat cap and smoothing his hair.

'Good morning,' he told her with a smile. She neither looked at him nor said anything – smoking her cigarette as if he wasn't there. 'Thought it was about time I introduced myself,' he persisted. 'My name's Sergeant King. Sergeant Jack King.'

'I know who you are,' she finally acknowledged him, but still wouldn't look at him.

'You do?' King questioned.

'News spreads fast in a place like this,' she told him.

'Like a prison, eh?' he deliberately reminded her of her time behind bars.

'That's what this place is, isn't it?' she answered, surprising him a little. 'We're all trapped here.' She gave a short ironic laugh. 'That's what this place does to you. It traps you. Maybe one day you'll be trapped here too.'

'I don't see how,' he argued. 'Once my job's done I'll be moving on. Even now I arrive in the morning, do what I have to do then I go home to my nice flat and my nice girl-friend. All this,' he explained, waving his hand across the entire estate, 'means nothing to me. It's just a mean to an end.'

'Gets you up the next rung of the ladder?' she smiled.

'Exactly,' he smiled back.

'Well,' she continued, 'while you're here people will just enjoy having a bit of law and order about the place.'

'You telling me you're happy we're here?'

'Of course,' she answered, confused by his surprise. 'Too many little bastards on this estate running wild. It ain't good for living and it ain't good for business.'

'Even your *business*?'

'Especially my business,' she insisted. 'The shit they pull brings you lot sniffing around and that makes the punters nervous.'

'Is that how you see it,' he asked, 'as a business?'

'Of course it's a business,' she laughed. 'I just provide a quality product that people want. You don't see me selling crack and heroin to fucked-up losers, do you?'

'No I do not,' he admitted.

'I provide a leisure product that's less harmful than alcohol,' she explained. 'Not my fault a bunch of public schoolboy politicians decide to keep it illegal. Won't change nothing though. Where there's a demand there'll always be a supply.'

'Law's the law,' he reminded her. 'There are no good laws and bad laws as far as I'm concerned. Just laws and I'll enforce them all.'

'I know you will,' she told him. 'Your reputation precedes you.'

'Good,' King stiffened, pleased at what he was hearing.

'Yeah, well, don't get carried away with yourself,' she warned him. 'Coming down hard on the local tearaways and shit is fine, but some of the other people round here . . .' She gave a knowing shrug. 'I wouldn't ruffle too many feathers, if I was you. You never know who knows what – who's connected to who. You get my meaning?'

'So long as nobody draws unnecessary attention to themselves,' he smiled. She flicked her cigarette over the wall and onto the grass below and headed back to her maisonette. 'I don't suppose you're carrying the keys to that metal grid on you?' he asked still smiling.

'No,' she answered. 'Do yourself and everyone else a favour and catch this animal who's been messing with the kids round here. Feeling is, because it's *only* our kids, Old Bill don't care. You find him, you win everyone's respect – almost.' She turned away from him before shouting into the dimness of the concrete cave. 'Nakiya.' She saw the look of interest on his face. 'My daughter.'

'I see,' he nodded.

'And in case you're wondering,' she explained, 'which I know you are – the keys are never on the outside – always on the inside. Even if I'm just out here for a smoke or a friendly chat with a passing cop.'

'Of course,' he replied as her teenage daughter appeared on the other side of the grid holding a single key.

'Open it,' her mother demanded, causing Nakiya to eye King suspiciously. 'It's fine,' she told her. '*He's* fine.' Nakiya's expression changed from one of suspicion to disinterest as she quickly unlocked the grid and swung it open. Ubana stepped inside quickly, the grid being slammed behind her and immediately locked. She turned round and looked through the bars as King leaned back on the wall with the sun pleasantly on his face.

'Looks like you were right,' he smiled.

'Oh yeah,' she asked. 'About what?'

'About this place being a prison,' he told her.

Her eyes rolled as she unwittingly examined the bars in front of her. 'Maybe,' she replied, 'but if you ever want to stand on this side of the bars, you'd better have a warrant. Know what I mean?' She winked and closed the door before he could answer.

She was right about one thing, he thought to himself. *Word really did travel fast on the estate.*

A short time later King met up with Renita to patrol the estate together looking for trouble. As they headed down a huge vehicle ramp that led to dozens of underground garages, King spotted a large piece of plastic wall hanging a little looser than the other panels on the bottom section of a low-rise row of flats and maisonettes. He stepped towards it and pulled it even looser and peered inside the bowels of the building.

'Someone's pulled this loose deliberately,' he told Renita. 'Wonder where it leads to.'

'Probably the basement area of the building,' she guessed. 'It'll be where the water tanks and electrical stuff is all kept. Everything will be pumped into here before being fed out to the flats.'

'So why would somebody want to break inside?' he asked.

'I don't know,' she shrugged. 'Why don't we see if we can find out?'

He pulled the loose panel to one side so she could more easily enter. 'Ladies first,' he grinned.

'Well thank you,' she joked. 'You're such a gentleman.'

She clambered through the small gap into the semi-darkness and watched as King did the same. They both un-holstered their Maglite torches from their utility belts, instantly illuminating their surroundings, and realized they were in some sort of corridor with dozens of pipes running above their heads and along the walls next to them. Underneath their feet was nothing but cold concrete lit by the occasional safety light glowing red.

'Christ,' Renita complained. 'It's like being in a bloody submarine.'

'Not a side of the estate most people would ever see,' he replied, squinting as he followed the beam of light from his torch. 'Want to split up like they do in American horror movies?' he teased her.

'No I bloody don't,' she told him. 'Place gives me the creeps.'

'This way then,' he encouraged her and headed off along the corridor, following the long cones of light that stretched out ahead of them as they walked deeper and deeper into the strange underground world until the thin corridor suddenly and unexpectedly opened out into a cavernous room where there was a little more light from the weak overhead strips and seemingly grey metal box after grey metal box attached to the surrounding walls.

'Wow,' Renita declared. 'What d'you think's in the boxes? There's hundreds of them.'

'Not sure,' King answered, his torch sweeping every corner of the room. 'Probably the electrical circuit boards for the block.'

'Amazing,' she admitted. 'You wouldn't want to be the one to try and find the blown fuse if electrics failed.'

'No,' King agreed as he drifted to a corner where something had caught his eyes in the torchlight. 'I suppose not.'

'You found something?' Renita asked, slowly following him.

'Over here,' he told her as he passed his light over the arrangement of old sofa cushions, homemade stools and a crate that was clearly being used as a makeshift table, littered as it was with the remnants of drug use and alcohol consumption.

'Christ,' Renita surveyed the scene. 'Lovely place to talk the night away with friends.'

King bent closer to better examine the items strewn across the table. 'Don't be too harsh on them,' he told her. 'Looks like cannabis and alco-pops – nothing too heavy. Probably just kids looking for somewhere to hang out of the rain and away from their parents.'

'Speaking from experience?' she asked.

'I was a kid once,' he answered.

'Hard to believe,' she replied, trying to sound serious.

'Still,' he ignored her, 'can't have them hanging around off their faces down here. Only a matter of time before they start a fire and burn the whole bloody block down.'

'Idea?' she prompted him.

'Hope you brought a good book,' he told her.

'Ahh,' she complained. 'You're not serious, are you? You want to wait down here until someone shows up? Could be hours. Could be days.'

'We're not going to wait down here for days,' he began to explain.

'Good, because this place still gives me the creeps.'

'But let's give it a while.'

'Fine,' she reluctantly agreed and followed him to the darkest corner of the basement room where they prepared to lie in wait for whatever came their way.

Susie Ubana sat in her kitchen waiting for someone to answer the number she'd called on her untraceable pay-as-you-go mobile phone. Eventually a man's voice spoke cautiously.

'Hello.'

'It's me,' she replied.

There was slight pause before the man spoke again. 'What do you want?' he asked without any politeness or subtlety.

She drew deeply on her cigarette, exhaling as she spoke. 'We may have a problem.'

'Go on,' he told her.

'These new cops on the estate – the one in charge,' she

explained, 'I think he's planning on *upsetting* things around here.'

There was a long silence before the voice spoke again. 'Can he be *persuaded*?'

'Not like that,' she assured him. 'He's young. Clean. Untainted. He still has . . . *ideals*.'

'Do I need to do something right now?' he asked.

She sighed before answering. 'No. Let me keep an eye on him – for now.'

'OK,' the man agreed casually. 'But keep me informed.' The line went dead before she could answer.

'Shit,' she cursed under her breath before taking a long pull on her cigarette.

King and Renita waited silently in the dark shadows of the corner, their eyes well adjusted to the dim light. The sound of distant laughter made them look at each other as they visibly tensed, but as the noise grew louder and closer they realized it was more giggling than laughing – the sound of children. Soon they could hear their footsteps as well as their voices talking softly to one another as they filed into the opening and took what appeared to be their usual places on the stools and cushions; their conversation grew a little louder and coarser as they became increasingly confident they were alone.

'Now,' Renita whispered in his ear.

'Not yet,' he hissed back as he watched the five children aged between twelve and fourteen empty their pockets onto the table making a communal display of cigarette papers, lighters and broken cigarettes. The youngest-looking child pulled something too small to see from his trouser pocket and began to fiddle with it. King guessed what it was and what he was doing, but still he waited until he could be sure.

He didn't have to wait long before the boy began to heat whatever it was he was holding over the small flame of a lighter, immediately filling the basement with the smell of softening cannabis resin, but still they waited until he crumbled the resin into the waiting tobacco on a paper bed that another boy rolled and ignited with his own lighter. King tapped Renita on the shoulder and stepped out into the space, clicking his torch on and half blinding the youngsters. They looked to one another in terror before trying to scramble to their feet, but King and Renita were already on top of them.

'Police!' King half shouted, before lowering his tone. 'Everybody stay where you are.'

'Fuck,' one of the girls announced, dramatically clutching her chest. 'It's just the police. You nearly scared the hell out of us.'

'Nobody do anything stupid,' King warned them. 'You,' he spoke directly to the youth holding the joint. 'Put that out and drop it on the table. Everybody else – let's have any drugs, cigarettes or booze on the table too.' He gave them a couple of minutes to search themselves, but they produced little to add to the collection that they'd already made.

'Is that it?' he asked once they were no longer fidgeting in their pockets.

'That's it, man,' the one who'd brought the cannabis resin answered. 'What d'you expect – a whole *soap* or something?'

'Watch your mouth,' Renita scolded him, ensuring the silence of the others too.

'Right then,' King shone his torch in their faces one by one. 'Who do we have here?'

'I recognize *chatty boy* here,' Renita told him. 'Darren Stokes, right? Been causing trouble round here for years. And that one,' she pointed to a pretty girl with long, straight blonde hair, but the eyes of a battle-hardened street fighter, 'that's Crissy O'Sullivan. Don't be fooled by the angelic face.' Crissy gave them her best sarcastic smile before her face again turned to stone.

'Who else?' King asked, but no one answered. He tapped the nearest one on the shoulder with his torch. 'You. Name?'

The small, unhealthily slim boy sighed before answering, his translucent skin shining in the light. 'James.'

'James what?' King snapped at him.

'James Mulheron,' he admitted with another sigh as King moved to the next girl.

'And you?'

She brushed her short brown hair from her young face. He could see the fear in her eyes and guessed she was new to the group. *The weak link.* 'Kimberley Clarke,' she almost whispered.

'Your parents know you're hanging around with these clowns?' King asked. Kimberley just shrugged. 'Thought not,' he told her and turned his attention to the last of the group who, despite his boyish appearance and slight build, had a look of feral viciousness about him. King instinctively knew that if this was the boy's first contact with the police it certainly wouldn't be his last. He shone the torch directly into the boy's face, making his eyes appear black and red – like a trapped rat's. 'And you?'

'I don't have to tell you anything,' the boy snarled, summoning some fight from his urban, animal instinct.

'Have it your way then,' King warned him. 'If you won't tell me who you are we'll have to arrest you – for your own good, you understand.'

'Just fucking tell him,' Mulheron demanded, but the boy stood firm – his face a mixture of fear, defiance and hatred.

'And obviously if I have to arrest you then we'll have to arrest all of you,' King threatened, immediately turning the entire group on the isolated boy as they took turns to tell him to say his name – their fear of arrest making their young faces twisted and ugly until Mulheron could take no more.

'His name's Billy Easton,' Mulheron told them. 'It's fucking Billy Easton.'

King saw the fire burning in Easton's eyes. Betrayal on the estate to the police had clearly long been installed in the boy's fabric as the greatest of sins – even if it was just a name to save them from arrest.

'Billy Easton, eh?' King nodded, tapping the boy on his shoulder with his torch. 'I'll be sure to keep an eye on you.'

The boy never flinched – his eyes intense flames of intent that momentarily unnerved King.

'All right, you lot,' King suddenly barked. 'Leave all your shit here and fuck off.' The children looked to one another, unsure – suspicious of King's motives. 'I said fuck off,' he repeated, this time drawing a look of concern from Renita.

'Sarge?' she checked. 'You sure?'

'I'm sure,' he told her. 'Now go, all of you. Just go and tell all your friends this place is now out of bounds – understand?'

'Yeah, yeah,' Mulheron agreed. 'We'll tell 'em.'

They hurriedly scrambled to their feet and scampered off towards the corridor – all except Easton, who took his time getting to his feet, his eyes never leaving King's.

'Got something to say, Billy?' he asked, but the boy didn't answer as he turned towards the corridor and strolled after his fleeing friends. 'I'll see you around, Billy,' he tried to wrestle the initiative from the boy, but it was already too late.

Once the sound of their retreating feet had faded King examined the table, taking the remains of the resin and unsmoked joint before carefully placing them in a pouch on his utility belt.

'Better not leave this behind.' He spoke more to himself than anyone.

'No,' Renita agreed, sounding a little confused. 'I guess not.'

'Come on,' he told her. 'Let's get out of here.'

* * *

A few minutes later they were back in the bright sunshine that overheated the microclimate of the estate and made everything shimmer and dance – the warmth giving King's fading hangover new life.

'We should find a drain,' Renita told him.

'A drain?' he asked. 'What the hell d'you want to find a drain for?'

'You planning on booking that resin and joint in as property found when we get back to the station?'

'No,' he laughed. 'Got enough paperwork to get through without wasting my time booking this in.'

'Exactly,' she explained. 'So chuck it down the nearest drain.'

'Not this time,' he replied casually.

'Oh,' she said, sounding a little suspicious. 'You're not planning on getting stoned, are you?'

'No,' he laughed again. 'I don't even smoke cigarettes.'

'So why d'you want to keep it?'

'I'd just rather keep hold of it,' he smiled. 'You never know when it might come in handy – when we might need it to *encourage* someone to tell the truth.'

'That's a route fraught with danger,' she warned him. 'Every little toe-rag's got a mobile they can record shit on these days.'

'Don't worry about it,' he reassured her – a call coming through on his radio saving him from any further questioning.

'*PS 42.*' The voice on the radio used his shoulder number as his call sign. '*PS 42 receiving – Control over.*'

'Now what,' he complained, before answering professionally. 'Go ahead, Control.'

'*Can you take a domestic dispute,*' the male voice from Control Room back at Newham Police Station asked, '*at number 24 Millander Walk? That's your patch, I believe. Informant's a Debbie Royston – says her boyfriend is drunk and won't leave the house.*'

He froze for a second. It was his first domestic since the

incident. The familiar images from his nightmares rushed him – *the girl in the white dress staggering towards him, the maroon blood spreading through the pristine material. The mother and son lying together in a scene of carnage, but always worst of all – the tiny figure of the girl no more than six years old, lying still and peaceful, her eyes wide open in death with barely a mark on her body.* His radio blared again and brought him back to the present.

'*Can you deal, 42? Control over.*'

'Yes,' King answered, his voice almost too weak to hear. 'Yes,' he repeated more strongly. 'Show me as dealing. I'm with 274.'

'*Thanks,*' the voice acknowledged. '*I'll show yourself and 274 as assigned.*'

'You all right?' Renita asked.

'I'm fine,' he lied as they began to walk to the location of the domestic.

'Is this your first domestic since . . . you know?'

'Yeah,' he answered. 'Can't avoid domestics for the rest of my career. I'll be fine.'

'I can handle it on my own if you'd rather,' she offered. 'No one need know.'

'No,' he snapped at her slightly before gathering himself. 'No. I want to deal. I have to.'

As they approached the scene of the reported domestic, King was relieved to hear the normal sounds associated with such an occurrence – a man and woman screaming at each other – dispelling his fear that he was about to walk into another silent trap of horror.

'Sounds like things are in full swing,' Renita joked before they had to dive head first into other people's misery and anger.

'Great,' he replied through gritted teeth as they approached the front door and found it already open – the sounds of exchanged profanities spilling out onto the communal walkway. King knocked on the door once, called inside, 'Police', and then entered without waiting to be invited, quickly taking in his surroundings – looking for any immediate dangers, obvious or hidden. Other than the duelling couple he saw none, although he was surprised by the size and clever open-plan design of the kitchen and living area of the maisonette, noting that it was clean and ordered, with no shortage of decent mod-cons, least of all the oversized LED TV dominating the space. He was relieved the fight was taking place in the living area and not the kitchen where deadly weapons always lurked close to hand, denying the attacker time to think – time to take stock before they committed a serious armed assault or worse.

'Someone call the police?' he added to get everyone's attention.

The man looked in his direction and grimaced before continuing to shout at the woman standing only inches in front of him. 'Why did you have to go and call this fucking lot?'

'Because you're a drunken arsehole – that's why,' the woman King assumed to be Debbie Royston answered him.

'All right,' King said calmly as he moved towards them. 'That's enough. Who called us?'

'Me,' Royston answered, 'and I want this fucking drunk out of my house.'

'You Debbie Royston?' he asked.

'I ain't going fucking anywhere,' the man interrupted.

'You,' King pointed a finger into the man's chest, 'be quiet and don't interrupt me again.'

'Yeah, I'm Debbie Royston,' she now answered, 'and this is my house and I want him out of it.'

'I'll get to that,' King assured her, 'but right now we need to know if anyone else is in the house?'

'My kids,' she answered, still shouting everything she said.

'Hiding upstairs scared half to fucking death because of this bastard.'

'Shut up, you stupid slag,' the man began again.

'One more word,' King warned him. 'One more word.' He took a breath before continuing, but suddenly paused as he felt a strong presence for the first time since entering the home. It was strangely powerful and alluring, but dangerous too. He turned his head towards the source of whatever it was that had been strong enough to distract him from the couple who'd already started screaming at each other again and saw a teenage girl, no more than sixteen or seventeen. Intelligence and sexuality blazed from her almond-shaped eyes that were so brown they appeared quite black. Her strikingly angular face was covered with flawless olive skin and framed by long deep brown curls. Her tight jeans and top showed off her curved hips and full, shapely breasts. Despite the complete lack of style or subtlety in her appearance, she was undeniably beautiful.

'Who's this?' he asked the screaming woman, before realizing his virtual whisper was being drowned out. 'I said, who's this?' he shouted loud enough to match them as he continued to stare at the girl standing halfway up the stairs. She looked straight into his eyes, a slight smile of seduction on her lips as she seemed to ignore everything in the house but him.

The couple momentarily stopped shouting and looked in the direction he was facing. 'That's my eldest,' Royston told him. 'Kelly.' She looked to King and then back to Kelly before bellowing at the girl. 'I thought I told you to stay upstairs and watch your brother and sister.' Kelly casually shrugged and began to climb the stairs, looking back over her shoulder as she did so, her eyes never leaving his as she seemed to float from step to step with the grace of an old movie star.

'How old is she?' he asked Royston once the girl was out of sight.

'Why d'you want to know?' she asked, suspicious.

'For my report,' he told her, not even sure if he was lying or not.

'She's seventeen,' Royston finally answered. 'Be eighteen in a couple of months.'

'And the other children in the house?' he asked, recovering from the distraction of Kelly.

'Jason's thirteen and Sharmane's eleven,' she told him, before re-igniting the battle with her boyfriend. 'Not that it's got anything to do with the fact that I want him out of my house.' She stabbed an index finger at the man's chest.

'I ain't going nowhere,' he shouted back as King and Renita got in between them, easing them further apart. 'I paid for everything in here, so why the fuck should I go anywhere?'

''Cause it's a council house and it's registered in my name,' she screamed back with an ugly smile.

'All right,' King spoke loudly enough to be heard and silence the bickering couple. 'You,' he talked to the man. 'What's your name?'

'Chris O'Connell,' he answered truthfully. King could smell the alcohol on his breath.

'Is the house registered in your name?' King continued.

'No,' O'Connell admitted.

'No, it bloody isn't,' Royston refused to remain silent for long. 'I told you – it's in my name.'

'So fucking what?' O'Connell called to her over King's shoulder.

'Do you want this man to leave?' King went through the procedural questions he needed to ask.

'Course I want him to bloody leave,' she confirmed loudly.

'Then, Mr O'Connell,' he told him, 'you have to leave.'

'I ain't fucking going nowhere,' O'Connell hissed.

'I was hoping you were going to say that,' King replied before moving faster than O'Connell could anticipate, spinning him around and pushing him up against the nearest wall as he twisted an arm up behind his back, making

O'Connell call out in pain. 'Chris O'Connell,' King began, 'I'm arresting you for causing a breach of the peace. You have the right to remain silent, blah, blah, blah,' he continued as he pulled O'Connell's other arm behind his back and locked quick-cuffs around his wrists.

'Argh,' O'Connell complained. 'Get the fuck off me.'

'Be quiet,' Renita told him as she helped King restrain the struggling man.

'Oi, what you doing to him?' Royston tried to come to O'Connell's aid.

'What you wanted,' King told her, breathing a little heavily as he battled with O'Connell, who'd been made strong by anger and alcohol. 'We're removing him from your house.'

'Yeah, but,' she argued, moving towards them, 'there's no need for all this.'

'Back up,' Renita warned her, 'or you'll be getting nicked too.' Royston stopped in her tracks as Renita pinched her radio and called for a van to transport their prisoner. At the same time King looked over his shoulder to check any danger Royston could be to them, but he found himself looking past her to the figure that now stood in the shadows at the top of the stairs, looking down on him with the same smile of unknown intentions. For a moment it felt as if he and Kelly were the only people in the room before she gave a silent giggle and disappeared into the upstairs darkness.

'You all right?' Renita asked without being heard. 'Sarge. You all right?'

'Yeah,' he answered as her words cut through the intoxicating effects of Kelly. 'I'm fine.'

'Good,' she told him. 'Van's on the way.'

5

King had keys, but still he knocked on the front door then took a step back. He wrung the neck of a bottle of wine while he waited next to Sara, who was holding an elaborate bunch of flowers and a box of expensive chocolates.

They listened as heavy, military-sounding footsteps approached followed by the sound of at least two locks being freed. The door swung ceremonially open, revealing the tall, straight-backed figure of a man in his sixties standing unsmiling in the entrance, his hair cut short and neat, his clothes as clean and pressed as his uniform had been before he retired as a full colonel from the army.

'Made it here at last then,' he greeted them.

'Dad,' said King.

'And how are you, Sara?' his father asked, ignoring his son as he stepped aside to allow them to enter.

'I'm fine thank you, Mr King,' she answered through a nervous smile.

'No need to stand on ceremonies,' he told her. 'I keep reminding you to call me Graham. Everyone else does these days.'

'Sorry,' she apologized. 'I keep forgetting. I'm fine thank you, Graham.'

'You'd better come and say hello to your mother,' he told King. 'Let her know you're still alive. For some reason she still worries about you. Can't think why.'

'No,' King rolled his eyes at Sara when he was sure his father couldn't see. 'Nor can I.'

The two couples began to eat their way through the meal that King's mother, Emily, had taken hours preparing. King couldn't help but think what a pointless exercise it had been – taking so much time to make something that would disappear in minutes and probably not be appreciated by anyone. He became increasingly aware of the growing pain in his shoulder and back as he watched his mother picking at her food as she'd done all her life – ensuring she remained slim for *the Colonel*. Her ash-blonde hair was pulled back into a permanent ponytail and she spoke with a heavily clipped accent – on the rare occasions her husband allowed her to get a word in edgeways. Even now, King felt he hardly knew her. He had been sent to boarding school at seven years old and then on to university and finally the police. This was their home, not his. As far as he was concerned, they'd never shared a *home*.

'You still haven't asked about Scott,' Graham reprimanded him, with no attempt to conceal his annoyance at King's apparent lack of interest in his own brother.

'I was going to,' he replied, 'when Mum wasn't around.'

'What's your mother's presence got to do with anything?' Graham demanded.

'Well, I didn't know if she wanted to talk about it,' he explained. 'She gets upset.'

'Nonsense,' Graham insisted. 'Your mother's fine. It's not like he's not going to make a full recovery. It's not like he's lost any limbs or been disfigured. Many have, you know. If you ask me he's been bloody lucky.'

'Funny idea of luck,' King argued, 'being shot.'

'Could have stood on an IED,' Sara added awkwardly before realizing she wasn't helping – drawing stony looks from both King and his father.

'He's going to be fine,' Emily tried to end it. 'That's all that matters.'

'Quite,' Graham huffed as they settled into silent eating until Sara tried once more to break the tension.

'How long has Scott been back from Afghanistan now?' she asked.

'Six months or so,' Graham answered.

'Weren't we supposed to have left there more than a year ago?' she asked naïvely.

Graham cleared his throat to answer, but King spoke before he could. 'Not everyone,' he explained. 'The army left some military advisors behind.'

'Shot by the very people he was supposed to be helping train,' Graham spat the words out like bile. 'Let the whole lot of them go to hell in a handcart,' he added.

'Where is he now?' Sara asked, making King move uncomfortably in his chair.

'Still in hospital,' Emily quickly told her, as if only she had the right to answer the question.

'But he's getting out very soon,' Graham took over again, 'as Jack would have known if he ever bothered to visit him.'

'I did know he was being released soon,' King surprised them.

'You didn't tell me,' Sara smiled uncomfortably.

'That's because Scott doesn't like me talking about him to other people,' he explained.

'He didn't tell me you'd visited him,' Graham said, suspicion thick in his voice.

'What Scott and I do is no one else's business.'

'Christ,' Graham laughed. 'You're not schoolboys any more keeping silly secrets. For God's sake, it's not bad enough Scott got himself shot in Afghanistan – you manage to get yourself stabbed in the police. What sort of an idiot almost gets himself killed *walking the beat*?'

'It can be a difficult job, Mr King.' Sara had forgotten his father's instructions to call him by his Christian name. 'Policing London is dangerous. You can never be sure what you'll walk into round the next corner.'

'Nonsense,' Graham dismissed her. 'Joining the army in this day and age was always going to present certain risks. Scott knew that and so did your mother and I, but almost getting yourself killed walking around East bloody London. I mean . . .'

'Which is exactly why I *didn't* join the army,' King fought back. 'What's the point of doing a job where you've got a *good* chance of being blown up or shot? Sounds like a pretty stupid thing to want to do to me.'

'Which is probably why you got injured in the first place,' Graham accused him. 'A touch of karma, I think. You spent so much time avoiding joining the army because you were *afraid* of being injured, you got injured anyway.'

'I don't think so,' King replied, just about holding it together.

'The police,' Graham held his arms out dramatically. 'There's no future in it.'

'He's on accelerated promotion,' Sara reminded him.

'Accelerated promotion,' Graham scoffed. 'He's a sergeant. Now if he'd joined the army he would have started at lieu-tenant – the equivalent rank of inspector. None of this playing around in the other ranks nonsense. It's not too late, you know,' he continued down a familiar track. 'I could still pull some strings and get you into Sandhurst. You're still young enough, just.'

'It's not for me,' King insisted. 'I'm not like you or Scott.'

'And what exactly is wrong with being like me or Scott?' he demanded.

'Nothing,' King looked for a way to escape the conversation.

'Then at least think about it.'

'No,' he answered bluntly.

'Why not?' his father demanded.

'Because the army's for fools,' he couldn't stop himself from blurting out.

His father breathed in deeply, preparing to attack before his wife finally stepped in to bring matters to an end. 'That's enough, you two,' she insisted with a smile, as if the argument had been nothing more than friendly jousting. 'We're just glad that both you and Scott have fully recovered. You gave us quite a scare.'

'Indeed,' her husband forced himself to agree – the redness in his face and his slight trembling betraying the anger he still harboured.

'It wasn't intentional,' King told them, happy to continue with the fight until he felt Sara kick him under the table. 'But at the end of the day Scott's going to recover and that's all that matters.'

'Good,' his mother finished it for this occasion at least. 'Now eat your dinner. You're getting too skinny.'

Kelly Royston walked to Susie Ubana's maisonette and reached through the metal grid to knock on the front door. After a few seconds the door opened slightly and Ubana peered through the gap, relaxing when she saw it was only Kelly – someone she'd known for years, having watched her growing up on the estate. She opened the door fully, but kept the metal grid firmly closed. Their meeting looked like a prison visit in an American jail.

'You gonna open this . . . *barricade*?' Kelly asked.

'No,' Ubana answered bluntly. 'D'you want something?'

Kelly sighed and opened her clenched fist, revealing a crumpled five-pound note and a handful of loose change. 'I need an eighth of Lebanese red,' she told her. 'It's all there,' she assured Ubana as they both looked at the mess of cash in her palm. Kelly saw the look of distaste on Ubana's face at her offering. 'What d'you expect?' she asked. 'Brand new tenners out the cash machine?'

'Chance would be a fine thing,' Ubana answered, awkwardly holding out both her hands through the grid and cupping them as if she was holding water. Kelly tipped the banknote and coins into her hands and watched them retreat back beyond the grid. 'Wait there,' Ubana told her and disappeared inside.

Kelly leaned against the wall and looked out over the estate as the night grew ever darker, its silence punctuated by the occasional scream of a child, shout of a drunk or bark of a dog. Her mind wandered to the young cop who'd arrested her mother's boyfriend earlier in the day. She knew she'd affected him in a way she could affect pretty much any man she chose to, but he was different. Very different. He was a policeman. The men and boys on the estate were largely desperate fools she could manipulate like putty, taking whatever she liked from them with just the promise of intimacy with her at some distant, unspecified point in the future. At seventeen she already knew that to them she promised the chance of escape to a better world where they could have something wonderful and beautiful. Even if it only lasted for a few minutes, it would be the best thing that would ever happen to most of them. But would the young policeman be so easily enthralled by the drug of her beauty?

After a couple of minutes Ubana returned and ended her daydreaming.

'Here,' she told Kelly, easing her clenched fist through the grid. Kelly pushed herself off the wall and took hold of Ubana's fist as if they were shaking hands in a slightly strange way until she felt Ubana's well-practised fingers push the small parcel wrapped in clingfilm into the palm of her hand. Quickly she slipped it down the front of her skintight jeans and nestled it in her public hair, but she didn't then scamper away as Ubana had expected. 'Don't wait around here long,' Ubana warned her. 'Not with that on you. One of them new coppers might be hanging around.'

'Think they'll want to search me?' Kelly smiled mischievously, but her charms were wasted on Ubana.

'They'll want to arrest you,' Ubana told her grimly. 'And me.'

'I wouldn't mind being searched by *one* of them,' Kelly ignored her.

'Oh yeah,' Ubana looked her up and down. 'And which one would that be?'

'The one in charge,' Kelly answered, moving from hip to hip.

'That'll be the sergeant then,' Ubana said sarcastically.

'Yeah. Him,' Kelly agreed. 'The one with the stripes. The good-looking one – well, good-looking for a cop.'

'What you got in that young mind of yours?' Ubana asked suspiciously.

'Nothing,' Kelly lied, blinking her wide almond-shaped eyes and for once looking younger than she was. 'I was just saying . . .'

'I'd get those crazy notions out your head if I was you, girl,' Ubana cautioned her. 'I've spoken to the man. He ain't interested in the likes of *you*, unless he's arresting you. He's pure, you know. He's here to bring the bad times to us. Sure, he's starting with the local thugs and fools, but what d'you think he's gonna do after they're all gone? He's gonna come after people like me and that will not be good. Where would you get your puff from then, Kelly?' The girl just shrugged disinterestedly. 'Yeah, exactly,' Ubana told her. 'I've seen his type before. Best thing for us is he gets his promotion or joins the CID or whatever it is he's after and fucks off and leaves us alone, before he has a chance to do any real damage. He's already been here too long.'

'You shouldn't be so afraid,' Kelly dismissed her fears. 'You just need to know how to control him.'

'Really,' Ubana replied patronizingly.

'Really,' Kelly continued. 'There isn't a man on the planet I couldn't control.'

'What do you know about men?' Ubana asked. 'You're too young to know anything much. Too young to even know that.'

'We'll see,' Kelly answered, walking backwards and smiling before elegantly spinning on her heels, never looking back as she strolled away. 'We'll see.'

King nursed their car through the light evening traffic as Sara sat in the passenger seat still talking relentlessly about the evening they'd just spent with his parents – continually shaking her head and groaning with frustration. He listened to her many complaints as his head throbbed from the stress of being in the company of his parents, while his back and shoulder ached as if the knife was still buried deep in his body. But he said nothing to her as she continued to list the crimes against his parents and even managed to smile and appear amused by her ranting.

'Honestly,' she told him, 'I don't know how you got through the night without a drink. Jesus, your dad. How did you put up with that growing up?'

'I told you,' he explained. 'I was never at home or almost never. I went to boarding school.'

'Yeah. I remember,' she replied, rolling her eyes. 'Nice parents – sending you away for your entire childhood.'

'They're not that bad,' he half-heartedly tried to convince her. 'Just a bit *military*, I suppose.'

'Oh, God,' she reminded him, 'and all that crap about "it's still not too late to go to Sandhurst". Is he serious?'

'Yes,' he sighed. 'I think he probably is.'

'Christ,' she complained. 'You'd think he'd have had

72

enough of his sons being in the army after what happened to Scott.'

'Don't drag Scott into this,' he snapped at her.

'I'm not,' she said. 'It's just after what happened to him and everything, you would have thought the last thing your parents would want is for their other son to join the army too. It's not like you haven't already been through enough.'

'He just doesn't know what else to say,' he told her. 'Doesn't know what else to do.'

'Well, he could help Scott for one thing,' she argued, 'instead of having a go at you.'

'As far as he's concerned, Scott's all *fixed*,' he explained. 'Dad only sees the physical wounds.'

'He doesn't know Scott has post traumatic stress?'

'No,' he answered, 'and Scott doesn't want him to know.'

'Why?' she questioned.

'Do you really need to ask?' He looked at her quizzically.

'Fair point,' she conceded and allowed a silence to settle in the car for a while before breaking it. 'Do you ever think you might have it?' she asked a little nervously.

'Have what?' he smiled.

'PST,' she told him.

'No,' he managed to laugh it off, praying that the tightening in his stomach and the deafening sound of blood rushing around inside his head weren't somehow manifesting themselves in a form Sara could see. He'd convinced the psychiatrists he was fine, not that any of them had dug too deep, each seemingly in a rush to move on to the next patient – teenagers with eating disorders and suicidal housewives. Sometimes he even fooled himself he was fine, but never for long. 'There's nothing wrong with me other than a stiff back and a sore shoulder. I passed my psychs – remember?'

'It wasn't a test,' she corrected him. 'They were just trying to find out if you needed help.'

'And they found out I didn't,' he reminded her.

'So long as you were truthful with them.'

'Course I was,' he assured her.

'I doubt it,' she accused him. 'I know what you blokes are like – especially cops. You'd admit to anything before you admitted to struggling emotionally. You're such a bunch of macho losers.'

'If I was struggling I'd tell you,' he lied. 'But I'm not, so that's the end of it.' He dug his fingers deep into his aching shoulder, trying to ease the pain.

'I'm sorry,' she apologized. 'I wasn't trying to—'

'I know,' he cut her off, making her turn away. 'Look,' he softened. 'It's just my parents. They have a knack of pissing me off. But I'm fine,' he insisted. 'I'm absolutely fine.'

They shuffled through the front door of their small flat together feeling deflated and tired. They both kicked off their shoes and Sara threw herself into the inexpensive but comfortable sofa, before immediately jumping up again.

'I'm exhausted,' she told him. 'I need to go to bed. If I fall asleep on that sofa you'll never get me out of it. You coming?'

'In a minute,' he answered. 'I need some painkillers and a drink first.'

'I bet you do,' she said without smiling. 'Don't be too long.'

'I won't be,' he assured her, although in truth he had no idea how long he'd be.

'See you in a minute then.' She headed towards their bedroom while he went to the kitchen, turning on the under-cabinet lighting that only dimly illuminated the room. He pulled a beer from the fridge and popped the top off the bottle, placing it carefully on the small kitchen table before crossing the room and beginning to search for painkillers. Even in the poor light he found the buprenorphine easily enough. He pressed two tablets from the tinfoil and headed back to the table where he slumped in a chair, quickly throwing the pills in his mouth and washing them down with a long drink. The racing thoughts about his parents, his brother and Sara slowed to a flickering procession of still pictures in his mind, until finally they were pushed aside by the memories of the day he'd accepted a seemingly innocuous call to deal with a domestic dispute.

He shook his head, trying to expel the images from his mind, but they remained strong and vivid – the young girl walking like a ghost from the house, the crimson spreading slow and steady through her pristine white dress, collapsing into his arms as her father, her would-be killer, burst through the door. He winced as he once again felt the knife bury deep into his back and shoulder – his memory fast-forwarding to the point where he was beating the father unconscious and then he was inside the house and moving up the stairs to the room where he found the twelve-year-old girl lying face-down on her bed. He saw himself in the room standing over her, but not touching her as he had in reality – just standing there looking down at her dead body before walking back-wards out of the room.

And then he entered the other room – the scene of bloody slaughter – the mother lying stabbed over and over on the bed with her brave teenage son on the floor next to her, his failed attempts to save his mother costing him his own young life. Only now, in his conscious nightmare, there was even more blood than there had really been. So much more that it pooled around the soles of his shoes as he walked slowly into the room – his feet sinking into the blood-saturated carpet as thick maroon liquid still poured from every wound on the mother's body, yet more pouring from her son's mouth, ears, nose and eyes.

King fled from the room in a panic, stumbling into the hallway and somehow becoming lost and disorientated in the small house, leaving bloody fingerprints on the walls as he used them to try and steady himself before he finally fell through a door and into another bedroom – the bedroom

75

where he'd found the youngest girl lying peacefully on her back, pale and lifeless. Only in the terror of his waking dream she wasn't lying, but sitting on the bed, her dead eyes staring at him, now wide and crystal blue – not closed as her father – her killer had left them. He inched towards her, his hand rising slowly and reaching out to her as her pale lips parted, her tongue garishly red in contrast. Words formed in her mouth before finally escaping, although they took an age to reach him, as if he was watching a badly lip-synched film. But eventually he could hear what she was saying – her voice soft and broken, but more terrifying than the loudest screams. *Why didn't you save me? Why didn't you save me?*

'Fuck!' He jumped to his feet, grabbing his shoulder as he instantly became aware of the pain in his body. 'Jesus Christ,' he pleaded as he shook the last remnants of the day-terror away. He drained the rest of his beer in one and took several deep breaths to steady himself, his pulse rate slowing as he recognized his surroundings and realized the girl wasn't real – not any more.

He headed for the fridge, pulling the door open before immediately closing it and resting his head on the cold metal. 'There was nothing I could do,' he whispered to the ghost of the little girl. 'You were *gone* before I got there. There was nothing I could do. Fuck,' he said a little louder and yanked the fridge open, taking another beer from inside. 'You were *gone* before I got there.'

6

King and Brown were tucked away in a large shed-like building used to store some of the estate's many giant communal bins, keeping watch on the comings and goings from Micky Astill's flat in a particularly bleak part of the estate known as The Meadows, despite the fact it contained not a single blade of grass.

'Fucking stinks in here,' Brown complained in his sour Glaswegian accent, his face screwed up against the stench from the over-full bins. 'How much longer we gonna waste our time in this hole?'

'You wanna be a rat-catcher, you have to be prepared to go into the sewer,' King told him.

'What?' Brown pretended not to understand. 'Don't see why we don't just get a warrant and do the door.'

'Firstly,' King explained, 'by the time we got through the grids anything and everything would have been flushed. Secondly, what's the point? We take out Astill, it's only a matter of days before another dealer replaces him. Where there's a demand there'll always be someone to provide the supply and there's plenty of demand on this estate.'

'Fucking crack-heads and heroin addicts,' Brown grumbled.

'Let them kill themselves on it if that's what they want. Why should we care?'

'Because they steal to buy their shit with,' King reminded him, 'and that *is* our problem.'

'Well,' Brown still argued, 'at least if we put his fucking door in he'll get the message we're after him. Put the pressure on him, eh?'

'No,' King insisted. 'We leave him alone for now – pick off his customers on slow days to keep our arrest figures ticking over. If we can turn the odd informant, all the better.'

'Informants,' Brown scoffed at the idea. 'Nothing but trouble. Dangerous bastards. If they're happy to sell out their own friends and family then what d'you think they'd do to you given half a chance?'

'Quiet,' King suddenly told him, holding up his hand for emphasis. 'Looks like we've got a customer.'

Brown peeked through a spyhole in the rotting wood. 'Aye,' he admitted. 'We do indeed.'

'You know him?' King whispered.

'Aye,' Brown smiled as he looked at the tall, skinny figure loping towards the flat. Even from a distance his drug-induced acne and sickly, deathly pallor was clear to see, his hair badly shaven by his own hand to save money that could be better spent on hard drugs. 'That there's Dougie O'Neil. Well-known lowlife, thief and scaggy crack-head of this parish. Dougie doesn't care what drugs he's pumping into his system, just so long as they're class A.'

They watched O'Neil gently knock on the door before turning and checking the walkways below and above, as well as the forecourt littered with cars – always alive to danger, constantly alert, like an antelope on the Serengeti; prey to all and predator to none, except when he was engaged in acts of petty theft. O'Neil understood his lowly role in life to the point where he'd even had '*Born to lose*' tattooed on the side of his neck. After what seemed a long time, the door finally opened, although, as per the usual modus operandi for house-bound dealers, the metal grids riveted to the walls across the doors and windows remained secure and unopened. They could clearly make out Micky Astill standing in the doorframe looking like a clone of O'Neil – his body and skin ravaged by years of getting high on his own supply.

They watched as a short conversation took place before O'Neil handed something as surreptitiously as he could to Astill who disappeared back inside, closing the door behind him.

'Paranoid fucker,' Brown whispered.

'Yeah,' King agreed. 'Heroin and crack'll do that to you.'

'Aye,' Brown nodded as they continued to watch O'Neil waiting outside the flat, on edge the whole time – needing his fix – fearful he'd either be arrested or mugged before he got the chance to get as high as a kite and, for a time at least, escape the utter meaningless of his life.

Eventually the door opened, causing O'Neil to stand close to the grid, bobbing up and down like an excited puppy waiting to be thrown its favourite toy. Astill quickly put his hand through the grid and waited a split second for O'Neil to hold his own hand under it. Momentarily the two hands appeared to touch, causing Astill to immediately close his door and O'Neil to scamper away towards the stairwell.

'He can't see us once he's in the stairwell,' King said, watching O'Neil as he disappeared behind the brick wall. 'Now,' he told Brown and they both slipped silently from their hiding place and moved quickly across the car park to wait for *Born to lose* to appear from the bottom of the stairs. A few seconds later, O'Neil duly obliged, walking right into their arms as he stepped from the entrance.

Without warning Brown grabbed him one-handed around the throat and squeezed hard on his trachea to stop him from swallowing any drugs he had in his mouth, while King pulled his arms behind his back and forced him to bend slightly forward.

'Spit it out,' Brown demanded. 'Spit it out or I'll fucking choke you.' O'Neil spluttered and gagged as he tried to swallow, but Brown's grip made it impossible. After a few more seconds of struggling, O'Neil succumbed to the inevitable and allowed a small yellowish rock, no bigger than a child's fingernail, to fall from his mouth.

Brown snapped on a pair of latex gloves while King kept hold of the panting, gasping O'Neil and recovered the crack cocaine. Brown held it up to the light as if examining a diamond before dropping it into a small plastic evidence bag. 'That's you fucked then, Dougie,' he told the luckless prisoner and slid the bag into his trouser pocket.

'Leave it out.' O'Neil coughed as he tried to talk. 'It's just one rock. Just a bit of personal. Come on, man. Let me off.'

'We might think about it,' King told him, giving him renewed hope, even if the rock and therefore the chance of escaping to the paradise of oblivion was lost to him. 'But first I think we'd better search your flat. What d'you say, Dougie? Got anything to hide?'

His shoulders slumped at the prospect. 'Fuck,' he declared, closing his eyes and shaking his head in disbelief. 'I just wanted to get stoned for a while,' he told them.

'Never mind, Dougie,' Brown told him condescendingly, patting him on the shoulder. 'You know what they say – *Life's a bitch, then you marry one.*'

As soon as they entered O'Neil's squalid flat the smell of decaying humanity, burnt heroin, crack cocaine and hopelessness assaulted them. It was a devil's brew of a scent neither of them had ever experienced until they'd joined the police, but now they knew its signature all too well – a self-inflicted torture caused by the addict's fear of opening a window and risking attracting the attentions of a passing policeman. Better to live in a putrid, airless hovel, again and again breathing in recycled air that had passed through diseased lungs a thousand times before. They pushed O'Neil along the short hallway ahead of them and into the pit of a sitting room, sparsely furnished with items donated to charity and others pulled from the skips of the more fortunate. The battered coffee table was littered with burnt-out homemade crack-pipes and tinfoil that had been used over and over to chase the dragon. O'Neil had made no attempt to hide it away.

Filth was everywhere. King doubted they'd find a single cleaning product no matter how hard they searched the flat. The old, rancid carpet stuck to the soles of their shoes as they walked around, pushing the still handcuffed O'Neil onto the threadbare sofa riddled with burn holes and stains while the surviving flies repeatedly crashed into the opaque windows above the many bodies of their dead comrades who now lay unburied on the window sill.

'Jesus,' Brown gagged. 'I can't breathe in here. I need some air,' he told them and moved towards the window.

'Don't open the windows,' O'Neil said with urgency. 'You'll let the flies in.'

'Let the flies in,' Brown replied, pulling a window open. 'Poor bastards would rather commit suicide than stay in this shithole.'

'Got any drugs stashed away?' King broke them up.

'Do I look like someone who would have drugs stashed?' O'Neil asked. 'Anything I get, I smoke,' he assured them.

'Fair enough.' King saw his point. 'Something else then? Something you couldn't keep your thieving little fingers off?'

'I ain't got nothing,' O'Neil pleaded with them, his feet tapping away agitatedly.

'Best tell the truth,' King warned him, looking around the virtually unfurnished flat. 'Not like it'd take us long to spin this rat hole.'

'I swear,' O'Neil lied convincingly, but his startled eyes following Brown as he entered the bacterial bombsite of a kitchen betrayed him.

'Fuck me,' Brown declared. 'You need an NBC suit before coming in here. How can you fucking live like this?'

'A what?' O'Neil asked, confused.

'A nuclear, biological, chemical protection suit, you fucking moron,' Brown explained. O'Neil just shrugged, but his eyes grew ever wider as Brown went straight to the cooker that hid under a thick layer of ancient grease and kicked open the door. 'Well, well,' he called into the oven loud enough for the others to hear. 'And what do we have here?' He reached inside and pulled out a good-quality Blu-ray player before heading back into the sitting room and placing it on the coffee table in front of O'Neil. 'Why do you slags never think we'll look in the oven, eh?' he asked, smiling menacingly. 'First place we look, Dougie. Always the first place we look.'

'I didn't know that was there,' O'Neil tried in vain.

'Save your bollocks for the interview,' King told him, hoisting him off the sofa and pointing him towards the front door while Brown continued to open every cupboard and drawer he found – looking under everything and anything, anywhere illicit goods could be hidden, listening intently to every word being said as he did so.

'Oh come on, guv'nor,' O'Neil pleaded. 'Don't nick me.'

'We haven't really got a lot of choice, have we?' King told him. 'Possession of crack cocaine and a stolen Blu-ray. Serious offences, Dougie. Serious offences.'

'Come on,' O'Neil kept trying. 'I only got out a few months ago. I can't go back inside yet.'

'Might clean you up,' Brown offered as he tossed the foul cushions off the sofa to reveal even more foul things hiding under them – although nothing illegal. 'Do you a bit of good.'

'Listen,' O'Neil offered conspiratorially. 'Let me go and I can give you Astill. I can set him up for you. You can get him for *supply* – a proper result for you. Better than a fifteen-quid rock and a knocked-off Blu-ray.'

'So you admit it's nicked then?' Brown told him.

'Come on,' O'Neil looked from King to Brown and back, desperate to see some enthusiasm for his offer. 'I can help you make a name for yourselves.'

'We don't need your help for that,' Brown told him.

'What you thinking, Dougie?' King stepped in.

'You're joking, right?' Brown interrupted.

'Give him a minute,' King rebuked him. 'I'm listening.'

'I could guarantee you take him out with, what, an eighth of an ounce of crack on him,' O'Neil talked fast. 'That's too much for personal. You'd have him for possession with intent, easy.'

'And how would you do that?' King asked calmly.

'I could call him,' O'Neil explained. 'Tell him I want to score large. That I want an eighth.'

'Where would you get the money for an eighth from?' King pressed.

'I'll tell him I've had a top result,' O'Neil talked even faster. 'I'll tell him I screwed an office and found a petty cash tin stuffed with tenners and twenties. He'll believe me, I promise.'

'All a waste of time,' Brown intervened. 'Astill never comes out from behind his fortifications. Not while he's holding, anyway.'

'That's what you think,' O'Neil smiled.

'Fucking bullshit,' Brown insisted.

'To sell an eighth he'll come out,' O'Neil persisted. 'Astill won't be able to resist getting that much cash in his hands in one sale.'

'Won't he be afraid you could try and set yourself up as a dealer with that much crack?' King asked. 'Why would he risk having competition?'

'No,' O'Neil shook his head. 'I couldn't deal it because I couldn't buy from him and match or undercut his price. He'd be selling it to me at a punter's price – not as a dealer. I might get a bit of discount for buying in bulk, but not enough so I could sell it on and make money. And besides, he knows me, knows what sort of user I am. If I had an eighth I'd do it all myself. It wouldn't be around long enough for me to sell. It'll work,' he tried to convince them. 'Astill's dumb and greedy. It'll work.'

'But he's going to want to see the cash before he even shows you any drugs, right?' King asked. 'He's not that stupid?'

'Of course,' O'Neil shrugged, as if it was obvious.

'So where you going to get the cash from?' King questioned.

'You'll have to give it to me,' O'Neil answered casually, as if it was nothing.

King and Brown looked at each other, before Brown spoke. 'You fucking serious? Forget it, Dougie.'

'No,' King intervened. 'Let's hear him out.'

'Bad idea,' Brown insisted. 'Remember? You said it your-self – bending is one thing, but something like this . . .'

'Whatever happened to "you can't make an omelette without breaking a few eggs"? Your words, I seem to recall.'

'Saying it's one thing,' Brown argued. 'Giving cash to a fucking druggie to set up a dealer is another world altogether. Not somewhere we want to go. Trust me.'

'I just want to hear Dougie here out,' King smiled. 'That's all.'

They looked hard at each other for a few seconds before Brown relented. 'Fine,' he said, shaking his head. 'We hear him out. That's it.'

'So?' King turned back to O'Neil. 'How much cash would you need for an eighth of an ounce?' he asked.

'Two hundred and thirty-one or thirty-two pounds,' O'Neil told them.

'That's a very precise number,' Brown pointed out. 'What's with the pound difference?'

'Profit margins are tight on the street,' O'Neil explained. 'Nobody's getting rich selling this shit – except the big players.'

'Big players like who?' King pressed.

'The sort of people who supply people like Astill,' O'Neil answered vaguely.

'A name?' King tried.

'No names,' O'Neil told them. 'Even if I knew I wouldn't say. You don't fuck around with people like that. They're dangerous people. Very dangerous people.'

'But you still want us to hand over two hundred and thirty-odd notes for you to go play with?' Brown brought them back.

'If you want Astill, yes,' O'Neil insisted.

'You must be fucking joking,' Brown told him.

'But I thought we were making a deal,' O'Neil complained.

'I don't think so,' King explained. 'Nice try, Dougie. And by the way – you're under arrest for possession of a class A drug and suspected theft of a Blu-ray player. You know the caution.'

'Come on, guv'nor,' O'Neil pleaded. 'I'm more use to you out here than banged up. Let me go and I'll work for you, I swear on me mother's life.'

'Your mother's already dead,' Brown reminded him.

'Yeah well,' he replied weakly.

'Nice try,' King told him. 'Better luck next time, Dougie. Now move.'

King was standing next to the photocopier in the custody suite making clones of the paperwork he'd need to put together the file on O'Neil when Marino drifted alongside him.

'Another good arrest, I hear,' Marino told him. King briefly glanced sideways before returning to the copying.

'Thanks,' he replied.

'I see old Dougie had a rock on him,' Marino pried. 'Any idea who supplied it to him?'

'No,' King lied. 'We just saw him coming along the walkway

and took a chance he'd be holding. Davey Brown got him in a stranglehold and he coughed the rock.'

'Stroke of luck,' Marino said.

'I guess,' King answered without looking at him. There was a few seconds' silence before Marino spoke again.

'Any luck with the Blu-ray player?' he asked.

'It was stolen yesterday,' King explained, 'in a burglary on a flat on the estate. SOCO says they found plenty of finger-prints at the scene. Only a crack-head like O'Neil would be so careless. We'll charge him with the drugs and bail him on the burglary while fingerprints try and match his prints to the scene.'

'Sounds like a plan.' Marino suddenly sighed before speaking again. 'On the not-such-good-news side of things, while you've been tucked up in here dealing with O'Neil, there's been another child sexually assaulted on the estate.'

King stiffened. 'Serious?'

'It's always serious with kids, Jack,' Marino answered, 'but no – we're still at the lower end of the scale. For now.'

'Any leads? Forensics? ID?'

'No. Sticking to his MO this one. No fluids exchanged. Usual disguise. Girl's too young and too petrified to be able to ID him anyway. Sorry, Jack.' King just shook his head. 'You and your team are really ripping it up down there,' Marino continued after a couple of seconds, trying to lift the despondent mood. 'Keep going like this and you're going to run out of people to arrest.'

'I doubt that,' King forced a smile. 'There's plenty more where O'Neil came from.'

'Yeah,' Marino agreed. 'I suppose there is. Well, if you ever need any help just let me know and I'll do what I can do – lend you the Crime Squad for surveillance or something.'

'I will,' King assured him. 'I appreciate it. Anyway, much to do and all that.'

'Of course. See you around.'

King headed across the custody area and tapped the security code into the pad that unlocked the main door leading into the rest of the relatively small station. As he was making his way to the Unit's office, Renita intercepted him, her face a picture of seriousness.

'Sarge,' she began, steering him out of the way of the passing human traffic.

'Something up?' he asked.

'Just had a call from one of my friendlies on the estate,' she explained, impressing him with the fact she already had informants in place, even if they weren't official or registered. 'They're saying there's an older man hanging around with a group of young kids.'

'This happening right now?' he checked.

'Yeah,' she confirmed, 'a guy called Alan Swinton, male, IC1. I ran an intelligence check on him and he comes back no convictions for anything, but lots of suspicion around possible sexual involvement with minors.'

'Well if it's happening right now,' King nodded thoughtfully, 'then I guess we'd better check him out.'

Kelly Royston stood outside her maisonette on the walkway of Millander Walk enjoying the sun on her face, her eyes closed as she smoked a cigarette, her mind wandering wherever it wished – far from where she stood. Such moments of simple pleasure came rarely on the estate. Her finely tuned survival instincts alerted her to people approaching and her eyes fired open, but her manner remained relaxed as she scanned the two figures, a bounce in their step that told everyone they considered themselves players. Kelly groaned inside as she recognized Tommy Morrison and Justin Harris striding quickly towards her, as if they had a real purpose, although she knew they almost certainly didn't. Both had made it plainly clear to her in the past that they desired her, albeit only in the crudest of physical senses, and neither ever missed an opportunity to reinforce their intentions towards her. She always acted bored by their lewd, clumsy advances, but she enjoyed the attention.

Morrison, the more dominant of the two feral youths, sprang up to her, moving deep within her personal space. 'All right, Kel?' he asked, quickly glancing at Harris for moral support and grinning. 'Fancy sucking my cock yet?'

'Fuck off, Tommy,' she told him, pushing him away with a two-handed shove in his chest. 'I wouldn't suck it if it was the last cock on earth.'

'Yeah?' Morrison asked, half smiling, half snarling.

'Yeah,' she made it clear, leaning into his face for emphasis.

'Then what about sucking his cock,' he continued, motioning towards the grinning Harris, 'while I fuck you from behind.'

'Fuck off, Tommy,' she repeated. 'You wouldn't know how.'

'Oh yeah,' he smirked as he took a few steps backwards and began to unzip his dirty jeans.

'Jesus, Tommy,' she shook her head as if he was nothing more than a disappointing child. 'You're wasting your time. I wouldn't fuck you even if you were a millionaire and, anyway, how come you two haven't been nicked by these new cops yet?' Her words turned their faces to stony seriousness. 'You've heard about them, int'ya?'

'Yeah, we've heard about them,' Morrison told her.

'Got most of the villains on the estate scared of their own shadows, I heard,' Kelly baited them.

'Yeah well, not us,' Harris bluffed. 'Old Bill. Fuck the Old Bill.'

'Yeah,' Morrison pumped himself up. 'We're too fly and sly for any copper.'

'Is that right?' Kelly smiled in her special way – a mix of flirtation and condescension. 'Well I suppose we'll see,' she mocked them. 'Find out if you're as *fly and sly* as you think you are.'

'Fuck you, Kel,' Morrison snarled, aggrieved at her apparent admiration for the Unit. 'You need to remember where you're from.'

'What?' she asked indignant. 'I'm supposed to have some sense of loyalty to this . . .' she rolled her head and eyes at her surroundings, 'toilet – just because I'm unlucky enough to have to live here. You know what the difference between me and you is?' she continued. 'This is as good as it's ever going to get for you. But I'm getting out of here. One way or the other, sooner or later – I'm getting out of here. You won't see me pushing a screaming baby round before my eighteenth birthday. I know where I'm headed, but you're never gonna *escape*.'

'You ain't that special,' Morrison spat. 'See you round, Kel.' He motioned with his chin to Harris that it was time to leave, their legs springing to life as they scampered off along the walkway, moving at an almost frenzied pace like the habitual thieves they were – heads and eyes darting every which way, always on the look out for a window left open, a door left unlocked.

'See you round too,' Kelly whispered to herself. 'If you last that long.'

King and Renita walked through an ancient railway arch built by the Victorians in the early years of steam trains. Although a road still ran through it, it was rarely used by traffic and endless fly-tipping had all but blocked it. The graffiti daubed on the dirty bricks made it clear the favoured football team in the area was West Ham, while other tags, both new and old, some crossed out and replaced with others, enhanced with threats of death and acts of sexual violence, suggested the arch lay on the border territory between at least two street gangs.

'You sure about this?' King asked.

'Yeah,' Renita reassured him. 'I've been through here a

few times. The wasteground's on the other side and that's where my friendly says she saw Swinton and the kids heading.'

'OK,' King went along with her, casually reading the graffitied messages of impending doom from one gang to another. 'If you say so.'

As they exited the arch they immediately heard the sound of laughing children, but it still sounded distant. They skirted around the tall wild grass that hid their approach, heading towards the young voices that grew ever louder, until they heard the voice of a man mixing cheerfully with the others. King automatically held his hand up to stop Renita.

'Hear that?' he asked.

'Yeah,' she whispered. 'Looks like the friendly was right.'

'Come on.' He led them off, moving slowly until they reached the end of their cover, the wasteground stretching out beyond their hiding place. He slid his hand into the tall sheaves of grass and moved them aside just enough to enable him to spy on the children. They were all between ten and eleven years old, he guessed, sitting and lying on the floor, using whatever they could as makeshift chairs and sofas. In the middle he could see the figure of Alan Swinton, a un-attractive white man in his early thirties with unkempt greasy brown hair and thicker-than-normal spectacles. His thin arms and legs contrasted badly with his swollen pot belly and made him appear like some sort of hideous spider-type creature. It was if he was trying to make himself perfectly fit the public's stereotypical idea of what a paedophile would look like.

'Is that your man?' King whispered to Renita, leaning away so she could take a look, as if they were big game hunters spying their quarry through the long golden grass of the savannah. She looked through the parted stalks and began to nod slowly.

'Yeah,' she confirmed. 'That's him. He certainly looks the part. What do you want to do?'

'Give him enough rope,' he told her. 'You say he has no convictions, then let's wait until we have him bang to rights.'

'But they're kids,' she warned. 'If we wait until it's too late for him, it might be too late for them too.'

'We won't let it go too far,' he assured her, 'just enough so we can bury him.'

'How far is too far with children?' she asked, her voice thick with concern.

'So what do *you* want to do?'

'All we can do,' she explained in her hoarse whisper. 'Warn him off – let him know we're watching him. Maybe let the kids' parents know.'

'So he walks away again?' he complained. Renita just shrugged resignedly. 'Fine,' he gave in. 'Have it your way.'

Without warning they burst from their hiding place and strode into the open ground, not worrying about the two or three more experienced children who took advantage of the others' hesitation to jump to their feet and flee into the surrounding mess of rubble and trees. 'Everyone stay where you are,' he ordered, closing the distance quickly until he was in the middle of the group. 'What you doing here?' he asked the children, ignoring Swinton who sat wide-eyed and resigned on a stack of old cushions salvaged from God knows where, looking even more innocent and bewildered than the children around him.

The children shrugged, pulled faces and muttered a collective 'Nothing'.

'You know who these kids belong to?' he asked Renita.

'Yeah,' she confirmed, scanning the frightened faces. 'Most of them.'

'OK,' he nodded. 'All right, you lot – disappear.' The children looked at each other disbelievingly until King barked at them again, causing a small stampede of little feet. 'I said, disappear.'

Swinton tried to join the exodus until King's hand fell

heavily on his shoulder. 'Not you,' he whispered menacingly before turning and shouting after the fleeing juveniles, 'and stay away from this man,' he warned them. 'He shouldn't be around children.'

'Why, why, why did you say that,' Swinton stuttered. 'I, I haven't done anything wrong.'

'Haven't done anything wrong?' King mimicked him. 'How old are you?'

'Thirty-two,' Swinton replied, his eyes flicking from King to Renita.

'So what's a thirty-two-year-old man doing hanging around with a bunch of kids?' King asked calmly, leaning closer to the still sitting Swinton who just shrugged. King kicked him slightly in the foot to get his full attention. 'I asked you a question.'

'Take it easy, Sarge,' Renita intervened. 'He's not worth it.'

'No, he's not,' he agreed, 'but I still want him to answer the question.'

'I wasn't doing anything,' the scared-looking Swinton replied. 'We were just talking.'

'If you want to talk to someone, why don't you talk to someone your own age?' King questioned.

'I don't know,' Swinton shrugged again. 'I don't like listening to the things they talk about.'

'What things?' King pushed.

'You know,' he looked at the floor. '*Ugly* things.'

'You ever talk to any children about these *ugly* things?' King asked softly.

'No,' Swinton insisted, his face a picture of indignation and embarrassment. 'I'm not interested in that stuff. That's all other people talk about, but I don't care. The children don't talk about it.'

'So what do they talk about?' King demanded, his voice full of suspicion and distrust.

'Interesting things,' Swinton answered, sounding more

upbeat, as if the memory of childish conversations had lifted his spirits. 'You know, like school and toys and computer games.'

'And you like stuff like that, do you?'

'Yeah,' Swinton smiled nervously back.

'School?' King picked on one of the things Swinton had mentioned.

'Sometimes, I suppose,' he tried to backpedal somewhat, as if he sensed a trap.

'And why the fuck are you talking to children about their schools?' King turned on him.

'I, I just like to hear about the things they learn,' Swinton tried to explain.

'Fucking bullshit,' King almost shouted into his face, making Renita take a step closer.

'Sarge,' she tried to leash him.

'You're trying to find out about their friends, aren't you?' King accused him. 'So you can find out who the vulnerable ones are, right? So you can, what – follow them and pick them off? Just like you did the others?'

'No. No,' Swinton denied it all, twisting uncomfortably on his makeshift seat, his face contorted in confusion and fear. 'I, I don't do that. I wouldn't do that. The children are my friends.'

'This is getting us nowhere,' Renita intervened, trying to calm King, even resting a hand on his forearm.

'OK,' he nodded slowly, looking down on the fearful Swinton. 'Get the fuck out of here.' Swinton looked to Renita for confirmation he was free to go. She motioned with her chin and he scrambled to his feet. 'And if I ever see you hanging around children again, I'll kick your door in and take your computer – give it to our experts and see what they can find on it. Would you like that?'

'No,' Swinton argued naïvely. 'I need my computer – to play my games on. It's, it's all I have.'

'Get out of my sight,' King told him as if he was nothing. Swinton stood in front of him, straightening his spectacles and wiping his sweaty palms on the stomach of his shirt before tentatively walking away, only stopping once he was a safer distance away, turning back towards them to speak.

'I know what you think of me,' he called. 'But I didn't do anything wrong. You, you shouldn't talk to me like that.'

'Walk away,' Renita warned him before King could react. 'Just walk away.' He looked at them with a mix of disappointment and fear before disappearing into the long, straw-like grass, the reeds closing behind him in the breeze as if he'd never been there.

'Fucking paedophile,' King accused him once he was gone. 'We should have waited till he did something. Could have nicked him and turned his flat over. There's probably enough shit on his computer to send him down for years.'

'We couldn't wait until he *touched* one of them,' she reminded him. 'We would have been slaughtered once people found out.'

'Maybe we were a little too honest in our approach,' King tested her.

'Easy,' she warned him. 'You can't gild the lily when it comes to kids. They have a nasty habit of contradicting you.'

'I guess,' he nodded.

Renita looked for a long time in the direction Swinton had walked. 'If you're that sure we'll find evidence in his flat maybe we should nick him and search it. Or we could always try and get a search warrant.'

'No,' King shook his head slowly. 'Too risky. We'd never get a search warrant and if we do a Section 18 and find nothing we'll look like idiots. I'm not having someone like Swinton make a fool of me. No forensics, remember? And the victims can't identify him.'

'OK, Sarge,' Renita said. 'Then how do we stop him?'

'I don't know,' he admitted. 'Maybe for this once, we'll

have to bend a few rules. For the sake of the children, if nothing else. And stop calling me Sarge all the time. Driving me bloody mad.'

'I thought you wanted us to,' she reminded him.

'The others maybe,' he told her, 'but not you. Doesn't sound right coming from you for some reason. Just call me Jack, will you?'

'OK,' she nodded once, a little unsure, following his eyes as they continued to stare at the space where Swinton had disappeared into the long grass. 'Let it go,' she encouraged him. 'Swinton will come again.'

'Creepy little bastard, wasn't he,' King answered, his eyes still not moving.

'Maybe,' she only partly agreed. 'But looks can sometimes be deceiving. Maybe he's just a little simple or maybe he'd just rather hang out with the kids than the adults on the estate. At least they have some semblance of innocence. He probably couldn't handle the adults. They'd rip him up for arse paper.'

'So what you saying?' He finally looked at her. 'That he's just lonely or something?'

'We all need human contact,' she reminded him. 'Maybe talking to the kids is the only way he can get any?'

'Human contact?' King scoffed. 'I know what kind of contact he's after and when he gets it I'll be there to nail the little freak to the floor. Come on,' he told her, the bile still in the tone of his voice, the thought of Swinton like an oil slick in his mind. 'Let's get the fuck out of here.'

King and Renita stood with a small group of off-duty uniformed cops in the Trafalgar pub enjoying a drink at the end of another long day as they discussed the early success of the Unit while the others listened admiringly. Renita did most of the talking and teasing as King played along, increasingly distracted by the growing pain in his shoulder and back that spread and flourished in his head. He left his half-drunk pint on the bar, made his excuses and headed to the toilet where he found an empty cubicle and locked himself inside. He wasn't due to take any buprenorphine for a few more hours, but decided to tackle the pain before it got out of hand – exceeding his daily dose of the drug again. His GP had told him he should be thinking about coming off the opioid, reducing his dosage slowly, but things seemed to be going the other way. He popped two from the tinfoil and plastic capsules and hid them in the palm of his hand, assuring himself he'd come off the pills as soon as work became less hectic and he had time to try an alternative.

He left the sanctuary of the cubicle and headed back to the bar where it was apparent he'd hardly been missed as he recovered his drink and subtly transferred the drugs from his palm to his mouth, quickly washing them down with the warming, flattening beer, unaware he was being watched by intelligent, experienced eyes from the other side of the bar.

Frank Marino drained his drink and weaved his way through the revellers until he stood next to King – appearing almost surprised to see him. 'Jack,' he nodded.

'Frank,' King nodded back.

'I was just getting them in,' Marino told him. 'Can I get you one?'

'I'm good, thanks,' he replied. 'I'm in a round.'

Marino looked at Renita and the others. 'Of course,' he said, while checking they were too occupied with their own conversation to hear his. 'Same old faces, eh?' he suddenly asked, catching King unawares.

'Sorry?' he asked.

'This lot talking to Renita,' Marino smiled. 'I don't come here often, but whenever I do they seem to be in here.'

'Everyone has their way of winding down,' King defended them.

'Winding down or drinking to forget?' Marino questioned.

King just shrugged. 'You don't want to wind down too much,' Marino explained. 'Not if you want to go further than sergeant.'

'Maybe,' King half agreed.

'Hardly ever used to see you in here at all before you got hurt,' Marino reminded him. 'The occasional leaving-do maybe. What was it – rugby in the winter for the borough and cricket in the summer, keeping fit and studying when you weren't?'

'Something like that,' King answered, shifting a little uncomfortably.

'But not since you returned to duty?' Marino continued. 'I still pop along to watch the odd game when I can. Always a bit surprised to see you not playing.'

'My injuries,' King insisted. 'They need a little more recovery time.'

'Shame,' Marino told him. 'It sure is a better use of time than hanging around the pub.'

'Listen,' King snapped a little, the irritation coarse in his throat. 'Why you suddenly so worried about what I do in my own time?'

'You're very young,' Marino advised him, sounding almost paternal. 'I occasionally still get to hear what the senior management are saying.'

'And what are they saying?' King asked impatiently.

'What they're saying is you could go all the way,' Marino answered. 'Maybe even to the very top. And I agree. We could do with a few like you at the top, instead of the usual bean-counters who've never nicked anyone in their careers. But it won't happen if you get too used to . . .' Marino paused, looking around their surroundings to make his point more clear, 'this.'

King relaxed somewhat. 'It's just short term,' he tried to reassure him. 'Last chance to live like a real cop before they drag me off to Bramshill and tie me to a desk. Work hard, play hard – just for a while.'

'Of course,' Marino nodded. 'But I've been doing this job a very long time and I've seen many a promising career disappear in the bottom of a glass. This job'll chew you up and spit you out if you let it.' Once he was sure his comments had registered he placed his empty glass on the bar and made his excuses. 'Anyway, I'll let you get on with your fun. Take it easy, eh.'

King watched him wind through the drinkers and head to the exit, Marino's words of warning spinning around his head. He patted his trouser pocket and felt the pack of buprenorphine inside. So what if Marino had seen him take them – there was no way he could have known what they were. But why would Marino be watching him so closely? He shook the paranoia from his mind, reminding himself Marino had been looking out for him ever since he returned to light duties. Even before that – visiting him in hospital and calling at his flat. But all the same, the feeling of being watched made him uneasy.

7

King's eyes flickered open as the early summer light filtered through the thin curtains – the heavy blinds having already been hoisted to the ceiling. His hangover washed over him like an unwanted residue as he tried to focus on the figure moving around the bedroom, making no attempt to be stealthy. He squeezed his eyes tightly shut before slowly opening them and allowing Sara's form to take full shape. He tried to open his mouth, but found his lips had sealed themselves shut. He summoned what liquid he could from the back of his throat and rolled it around his mouth until there was enough to loosen the other moving parts.

'Christ,' he complained through the fog of the night before. 'What time is it?'

'About quarter past six,' Sara told him, speaking too loudly – he thought deliberately.

'What the hell you doing up so early?' he asked. 'And why have you pulled the bloody blinds? It's too bright in here.'

'I'm up because I'm on early shift,' she scolded him, 'and the blinds are open because I need to see what I'm doing.'

'Fuck's sake, Sara,' he grumbled, pushing himself up on one elbow, 'd'you need to open all the blinds?'

'Your *injuries* are all self-inflicted, Jack,' she reminded him.

'If you're looking for sympathy you'll find it in the dictionary between shit and syphilis.'

'Thanks,' he moaned sarcastically. 'I love you too.'

'You were bloody noisy when you finally came home last night and properly pissed too,' she ignored him. 'Woke me up crashing around the place and now I'm knackered for work. Keep this up and you'll flush your accelerated promotion down the toilet along with everything else,' she warned him.

'Christ,' he complained again. 'Not you as well.'

'Not me as well what?' she questioned.

'Nothing,' he lied.

'Oh and before I forget,' she told him, standing and straightening her clothes in the full-length mirror, 'I bumped into Chief Superintendent Gerrard yesterday.'

'And?' he asked tentatively.

'He asked me to tell you he wants to see you.'

'When?'

'Nine o'clock,' she casually answered. 'This morning.' She gave him a satisfied smile and headed for the door. 'See you later,' she called over her shoulder and was gone.

King slumped back onto the mattress, his eyes staring at the ceiling before he swore at the empty room. 'Fuck.'

King sat in the office of Chief Superintendent Gerrard at Newham Police Station – the Borough's headquarters – trying to swallow down the tides of nausea the remains of his hangover continued to bring as he watched Gerrard flicking through report after report, slowly nodding his head and mumbling his appreciation.

'Impressive. Very impressive,' he swooned. 'Still early days, I know, but still . . .'

King forced the acid back down his throat before answering. 'Thank you, sir.'

'Keep this up and we'll have the Grove Wood Estate cleaned up in no time,' Gerrard beamed.

'Could be a little while longer, sir,' King tried to temper his enthusiasm. 'There's still plenty of work to be done.'

'Of course,' Gerrard pretended he understood, 'but once you've broken the back of it you'd probably be better used elsewhere, or at least the Unit will – whereas I'm sure you'll be keen to press on with your promotion to the next rank. You've already been on the Grove Wood a fair time. You don't want to dwell in a place like that too long.'

'A fair time?' King asked, confused – convinced they'd only been on the estate a few weeks, whereas Gerrard was talking as if they'd been there for months.

Gerrard gave a little twitch before replying – as if he too now was confused. 'I just . . . I just mean you've been there a while now. Are you all right, Jack?'

'I'm fine,' King shook it away. 'And I'm fine where I am – for now. I feel I'm gaining a lot of leadership experience.'

Gerrard reacted as if he was being assessed by invisible judges. 'Of course. Of course. No need to rush these things.' They fell into an awkward silence before Gerrard spoke again. 'You look a little tired though, Jack. Not working you too hard, are we?'

The previous night's drinking flashed through his mind. 'No, sir. I'm fine. A few late nights processing prisoners – that's all.'

'You should hand them over to the CID more,' Gerrard smiled. 'That is what they're there for, after all.'

'I like to keep the jobs where I can,' King replied. 'Squeeze the prisoners for information.'

'Well, if you like the CID stuff that much we can always make you a DS and give you a team here at Newham to head up,' Gerrard offered. 'It's in my power to make it happen – given that you're on the accelerated promotion scheme. You wouldn't even have to go on a detective course. Such privileges aren't open to everyone, you know.'

'I know,' King assured him, 'but no thanks. I'm fine.'

101

'Of course you are,' Gerrard agreed, smiling inanely. 'Of course you are.' Another awkward silence fell between them until Gerrard summoned the courage to move forward. 'Listen, Jack,' he began, 'I don't like having to intrude like this, but it's very much the policy that I have to ask a few questions about yourself, because of, you know, what happened to you.'

King felt himself dying inside. 'Go on.'

'How's the body holding up with a return to full duties?' Gerrard asked, trying to sound casual, as if he already knew the answer.

'Good,' King lied. 'I'm fine. I've been working out again – running when I can.'

'Excellent,' Gerrard replied, looking down at his reports and tapping his fingers nervously on his desk. 'Excellent. And what about other things,' he continued. 'How you feeling in yourself?'

'You mean psychologically?' King asked, enjoying the look of discomfort on Gerrard's face.

'Exactly,' Gerrard said, the smile flickering on his face. 'Exactly.'

'I'm sure you've read my psych reports,' King bullied his senior officer.

'And they're accurate, are they?'

'Yes, sir.'

'And they say you're fine?'

'Yes, sir. They do.'

'Well then, all's good,' Gerrard suddenly beamed, his perceived duty done – the box ticked. 'And now all that's out of the way, I'd better let you get back to work – let you get this street-cop thing out of your system. Remember, good arrests and rolling around on the ground with the local villainy may win you a lot of friends with the rank and file, but being a senior officer isn't a popularity contest. Sometimes you have to be prepared to sit on your own in the corner of the canteen because you've had to make an unpopular decision

102

that nobody likes or understands. Such is the responsibility of being a senior officer.'

'That's good advice. Thank you. I'll remember that,' King replied, although his mind had already left the room. 'Is there anything else?'

'Just one thing,' Gerrard answered, trying to sound casual. 'These attacks on young children in and around the Grove Wood Estate – I hear they're still happening.'

King cleared his throat before answering through his rising anger. 'Yes, sir.'

Gerrard leaned back in his chair and sighed a little. 'Got to put a stop to it, Jack – before we end up dealing with something even more serious. Something that the media get a hold of. Could be very embarrassing. Understand?'

'Yes, sir,' he managed to reply despite the almost paralysing tension he felt in his jaw. 'Well, thanks for your time,' he added, rising from his chair.

'Don't mention it,' Gerrard assured him. 'Any time.'

Too late, King realized he was staring a little too intently at Gerrard.

'Something else I can do for you?' Gerrard asked, his smile only slightly wavering.

'No, sir,' King managed to say. 'There's nothing.'

King sat alone in the canteen back at Canning Town Police Station forcing down a late breakfast in an attempt to slay the last remnants of his hangover, glad to be away from the glare of the Borough headquarters and the senior officers who seemed to be everywhere. The atmosphere at Canning Town couldn't have felt more different. Here those above the rank of inspector were rarely seen and sergeants, constables and a small detachment of CID officers were largely left alone to get on with their jobs, bringing a kind of peaceful calm to the place, despite the relentless storm of crime just beyond the walls.

Danny Williams ghosted into the canteen, made his way over to King and took a seat. 'You look well,' he teased.

'I've been better,' King replied, moving unwanted food around his plate.

'Late night, Sarge?'

'D'you fucking want something, Danny?' King ended the joke. 'Because if not . . .'

'Just thought you should know there were a couple of residential burglaries on the estate last night,' Williams explained. 'Didn't get reported until late last night when the victims got home after a night on the piss at The Warrior.'

'Unfortunate,' King told him, 'but not unusual. Whoever did it was probably in The Warrior themselves and knew the victims. Saw they were there and knew they were out.'

'That's not all though,' Williams tried to intrigue him. 'Whoever did it left a calling card behind – at both venues.'

'Calling card?' King took the bait.

'Sprayed "Fuck the Old Bill" on the walls inside the flats,' Williams explained. 'Looks like someone's trying to send us a message.'

'Suspects?' King asked.

'Nothing solid,' Williams admitted. 'Just my opinion.'

'Which is?'

'Classic Morrison and Harris burglaries,' Williams answered. 'Although the graffiti's new, not that it'll do us any good. They rarely leave any usable forensics behind. They're no geniuses, but they're smart enough to glove-up.'

'And the stolen goods?' King tried another angle.

'They took a fair bit of stuff,' Williams explained, 'but nothing they couldn't carry in one trip. They're too experienced to risk return visits.'

'Any info on where they stash their nicked gear?'

'Not at home – if that's what you're hoping for.'

'Then we could start with Baroyan,' King suggested. 'Stake out his place and wait for Morrison or Harris to turn up.'

'If they even use Baroyan,' Williams questioned, 'which I admit is likely, would they be dumb enough or bold enough to take the stuff there themselves?'

'Uhhm,' King thought for a second, his eyes narrowing with the germ of an idea and a favour to be offered. 'I think I have an idea.'

Minutes later, King and Williams were pounding hard on the fragile door that covered the entrance to Dougie O'Neil's squalid little flat. They received no answer so pounded again without calling out who they were. After a while, a scared, angry male voice came from the other side, close to the door, no doubt trying to get a feel of who was waiting for him.

'Who is it?' he demanded. 'What d'you want?'

'Sergeant King,' he answered, 'and PC Williams. Open the door, Dougie.' His demand was met by silence.

'Probably shitting himself,' Williams offered. 'Stuffing a rock of crack up his arse as we speak.'

'Probably,' King agreed and sighed as he cupped a hand over his mouth and tried to ease his words through the door so no one else could hear. 'It's all right, Dougie. We're not interested in your *gear*. We just want to speak.'

Silence for a few seconds before O'Neil responded. 'What about?'

'Open the door and we'll tell you,' King promised, but still it remained closed. 'I can't talk to you through a door, Dougie, but I'm happy to kick it open if you like.'

'No,' came the panicked reply. 'No, wait.'

A few seconds later and the door swung slowly open, O'Neil's head jutting out and bobbing in all directions like an anxious deer. He checked the coast was clear before stepping aside and quickly ushering them inside then slamming the thin plywood barrier shut.

'That's better,' King told him. 'Don't want the entire estate knowing our business.'

'Which is?' O'Neil asked, walking away from them, heading to his desperate-looking living room where he flopped on the salvaged sofa and immediately lit the sad-looking remains of a homemade cigarette.

'I need information,' King explained. 'Information you might be able to help with.'

'I'm no grass,' O'Neil insisted. 'I ain't gonna grass on anyone.'

'No one's asking you to do that, Dougie,' King lied. 'Just a one-off piece of information is all we need. Besides – you were happy enough to try and serve up Micky Astill for us and save yourself.'

'That was different,' O'Neil tried to explain. 'Astill's a cunt. You're pissing up the wrong tree if you want information on anyone else,' he dug in, his expression blank and disinterested.

King circled around him as O'Neil remained seated – close enough to make his expression change to one of nervous anticipation. 'I should probably remind you you're still on bail, Dougie. The Blu-ray, remember? Nicked during a residential burglary. You could do some serious time for that.'

'Bullshit,' O'Neil squirmed. 'You can't do me for the burglary. Most you can do me for is handling.'

'With your form that's still enough to send you down, Dougie,' King said, standing directly behind him and resting a heavy hand on his shoulder.

'Or?' O'Neil asked.

'Or,' King followed his lead, 'you can help us out with a little bit of information and maybe, if things work out, I can make the trouble with the Blu-ray disappear.'

'How you gonna do that?' O'Neil questioned, his eyes narrow with suspicion. 'CID ain't never gonna drop it.'

'Job's not with CID,' King explained. 'I kept it and I can make it go away. No one will notice. No one will care.'

'And in exchange?' O'Neil warmed to the idea – his primeval, feral instinct to look after number one superseding all others.

'Like I said,' King repeated, 'information.'

'About what?'

'Tommy Morrison and Justin Harris,' Williams joined in. 'You know them?'

'Yeah,' O'Neil shrugged. 'I know them. Most people round here do.'

'Two burglaries last night,' Williams spoke matter-of-factly. 'Reckon Morrison and Harris are good for them.'

'So?'

'So where do they keep the gear until it's time to get it to Baroyan?' King bluffed, pretending he knew more than he really did.

'Slow down,' O'Neil insisted, sounding more confident than usual. 'Morrison and Harris may be young, but they can be vicious little bastards. You want info on them I'll need you to make the thing with the Blu-ray to disappear *and* I'll need a nice drink out of it.'

'You want cash as well?' Williams laughed. 'Fuck you, Dougie. Looks like we'll just have to charge you with the burglary after all. You want too much, my friend.'

'All right, all right,' O'Neil panicked. 'Fuck me. Morrison and Harris are too careful to keep their nicked gear in their homes—'

'We already know that,' King rushed him. 'Where?'

Dougie filled his damaged lungs and began to speak as he exhaled, as if he could rush the words out before he ran out of courage. 'They keep it in one of the small storage rooms in Millander Walk – the ones used by the caretaker. They slip him a few quid now and then to keep him sweet and he lets them have a key to the room. They can come and go as they please. It's a nice set-up.'

'I'm sure it is,' King spat his agreement. 'And how do they get the gear to Baroyan?'

'Well they don't take it themselves, if that's what you mean,' O'Neil grinned. 'Too slippery for that, those bastards.'

Williams leaned in close. 'So how?'

'Got a little runner, ain't they?' O'Neil tried to get him to back away. 'Little kid off the estate called Aaron Thompson. Good little thief in his own right, I hear. He meets Morrison and Harris at the storage cupboard and checks out the gear. He then goes to Baroyan who hears what's for sale and then sends the kid back with an offer. Eventually a price is agreed and the kid takes the stuff over to Baroyan and brings the cash back to the other two and they give him a small cut. It's a sweet set-up, but Morrison and Harris are vulnerable when they first show Thompson the gear and when he comes back to collect it. That's when you can catch them with the goods. If they're hanging around near the cupboard and Thompson appears, chances are the gear will still be inside.'

King and Williams looked at each other before both nodding in silent agreement. 'Very good, Dougie,' Williams told him. 'That's actually pretty decent information you've given us there.'

'So you'll make the Blu-ray go away?' he asked eagerly.

'Maybe,' King told him.

'Maybe?' O'Neil sat up stiffly. 'You promised.'

'I don't remember promising,' King argued. 'Do you remember me promising?' he asked Williams sarcastically.

'No, Sarge,' Williams shook his head. 'Don't remember that.'

'I said I'd see what I could do,' he told the hapless O'Neil who slumped back down into his chair. 'But I wouldn't get any ideas about telling Morrison and Harris that you've been talking about them,' he warned him. 'Wouldn't like to think what they'd do to you if they thought you were a grass.'

'Fucking Old Bill,' O'Neil complained. 'You can never trust the Old Bill.'

Tommy Morrison and Justin Harris loitered near one of the caretaker's storage rooms in Millander Walk smoking hard

108

and covering the floor with a constant barrage of frothy spit as they continually looked both ways along the walkway. Eventually they saw the person they'd been waiting for approaching. Aaron Thompson walked casually towards them – his carefree spirit instantly knocked out of him as Morrison clubbed him around the side of his head with an open-palm strike. Thompson winced and cowered before recovering his courage.

'What the fuck was that for?' he complained.

'You're late,' Morrison accused him. 'You were supposed to be here ten minutes ago.'

'My mum only told me a few minutes ago you wanted to see me,' Thompson complained, still rubbing the side of his head. 'What was I supposed to do?'

'Maybe he's too young to be reliable?' Harris teased him.

'Yeah,' Morrison snarled in agreement. 'Maybe you're too young.'

'I ain't too young,' Thompson protested, anxious at the thought of losing the much-needed income from his part-time job. 'I'll be thirteen next year.'

'So why don't you use some of the money you make from us to buy a decent mobile?' Morrison quizzed him. 'Then we wouldn't have to call at your old dear's and leave fucking messages for you.'

'I can't,' Thompson pleaded, looking a little sheepish. 'My mum won't let me.'

'You soft cunt,' Harris told him. 'Use your imagination. Get one without your bitch mum finding out.'

'All right,' he assured them, but their faces told him they weren't convinced. 'I said all right, didn't I?'

'Fine,' Morrison relented, his snarl turning to a grin as he pulled a key to the storage room from his pocket. 'Take a look at this tidy lot,' he told Thompson and moved to the door, sliding the large key into the hole and turning it smoothly and easily as Harris kept lookout. He pushed the door open and stepped aside, allowing Thompson to enter. Morrison slipped in behind him, closely followed by Harris, but as he began to close the door it exploded inwards as if a truck had just driven into it, sending Harris spiralling to the floor, his eyes wide with fear and shock as he prepared to assess the threat and make a snap decision whether to fight, attempt flight or beg. Thompson just froze where he was standing, struggling to control his bladder as Morrison darted from one side of the small room to the other, like a rat trapped in a corner, looking for an escape route that simply wasn't there.

King and Williams stood in the doorway watching the chaos their entrance had caused for a few seconds before King spoke.

'All right. Everybody stay where they are.' Harris ceased his scrambling on the floor, but Morrison continued to spiral around the room like a broken android until King stepped forward and grabbed him by the collar of his shirt and almost lifted him off the ground, pulling his face close. 'I said, stand still.' Morrison froze for a second before he began to convulse and struggle. King tightened his grip and shook him hard twice – Morrison's head snapping backwards and forwards until he managed to speak.

'All right. All right,' Morrison pleaded, holding his hands up in surrender. King pushed him to the side of the room and began to look around without speaking while Williams' sizeable frame guarded the door against any desperate escape attempts. It didn't take long to find the barely concealed stolen goods: two flat-screen TVs, a Blu-ray player, a large collection of DVDs and a small amount of gold jewellery.

King turned to Morrison, who was already gathering his thoughts and regaining some of his composure and swagger. 'Turn around,' King told him, 'and put your hands against the wall.'

'What?' Morrison argued.

'Just do it,' King demanded and gave him a helping hand as he twisted him around by the shoulder and pushed him forward.

'Easy,' Morrison complained.

'Shut the fuck up,' King told him as he began to search him, quickly finding what he was looking for and pulling a thin pair of polyester gloves from his pocket. 'You're so fucking predictable,' he told Morrison as he slapped him across the back of his head with them.

'My hands get cold,' Morrison sneered.

'In the middle of summer?' King raised his voice. 'Don't be a mug.'

'Yeah?' Morrison challenged him. 'Well, them gloves mean you won't find my prints on nothing.'

'That right?' King calmly asked before turning to Harris who was still on the floor. 'Get up,' he told him. With little urgency Harris pulled himself to his feet and began to dust himself down. 'Hand them over,' King insisted.

'Hand what over?' he asked, puzzled.

'Your gloves,' King explained. Harris just shrugged, pulled a pair of polyester gloves from his pocket and gave them to King.

'And that means his prints won't be on nothing neither,' Morrison smirked.

King seemed to ignore him as he turned to Thompson who'd barely blinked since they'd burst into the room. 'You,' King quietly barked at the boy, making him flinch. 'Fuck off.' But the boy didn't move – made rigid by his confusion. 'I said, fuck off,' King repeated. Thompson sprang to life and darted past the equally confused-looking Williams.

'You got nothing,' Morrison drew the attention back to himself. 'What you gonna do us for? Being in a fucking storage cupboard? All this shit could be the caretaker's.'

'It could,' King agreed, 'only *we* saw you carrying it in here – didn't we, Danny?' He looked at Williams in a defining

111

moment of truth. If Williams went with him now he'd probably have to go with him forever. But if he didn't, they were finished working together. Their eyes stayed locked together while Williams decided his future on the Unit.

'Fucking right we did,' he finally answered, but his face was blank and his tone neutral – hard to read how he really felt.

'See,' King told the feral youths. 'That's why we came in here in the first place – because we saw you two little fuckers sneaking in here with a couple of TVs under your arms. Lucky for us eh, Danny?'

'Very lucky,' Williams flatly agreed.

'This is a fucking stitch-up,' Morrison had the audacity to complain.

'And you were both wearing your gloves,' King continued, 'which is why your prints aren't on the gear.'

'You're out of order,' Morrison said indignant.

'Gloves in summer. Carrying gear that will be easy enough to trace back to last night's burglaries. Found in caretaker's storage room stashing the goods. You're fucked, boys,' King read them their futures.

'This is a fucking set-up,' Morrison bleated as he remained pushed up against the wall.

'You need to learn to play the game,' King snarled. 'Have to pay for your crimes eventually. Be a bit more professional and take this one on the chin – for all the ones you got away with. At the end of the day you brought this on yourself, boys – leaving a message for us at the burglary scenes. What was it again, Danny?'

'Fuck the Old Bill,' Williams answered.

'That's right,' King mocked them. 'Fuck the Old Bill. Trying to tell us something, were you?' he questioned Morrison, pushing him in the back. 'Trying to say this is your *territory* or something, were you?' Again he pushed Morrison in the back, but harder now and with the base of his palm only.

'Well you understand something,' he said through gritted teeth, 'this is *our* territory now,' and again he hit Morrison in the back, but now with a short punch into his spine that made his legs give way a little.

'Easy, Sarge,' Williams tried to warn him, but King didn't seem to hear or care.

'We own this estate now,' he explained. 'You and all the other scum like you are marked men. We're coming after you all. D'you understand?'

'Yeah?' Morrison remained defiant.

'Yeah,' King assured him.

'Yeah – well when you're long gone we'll still be here,' Morrison told him over his shoulder. 'This estate will *always* be ours.'

'We'll see,' King told him, pulling Morrison's hands behind his back and snapping on a set of quick-cuffs tight enough to restrict the blood flow into his hands and make him wince with the pain. 'But right now you're under arrest for burglary, so say goodbye to your beloved estate, Tommy. Could be a while before you see it again.'

He had to be more careful now than ever. The sporadic plain-clothed operation the police had tried had been easy enough to avoid – with everyone on the estate shouting and talking about it. All he'd had to do was lie low until they'd moved on to something else. But the new police that had turned up were clearly different and there to stay for some time. There were only four of them and they were young too, but they seemed to be on the estate all the time – watching everything – determined to make a difference. But still, the Grove Wood Estate was a very big place and their eyes couldn't be every-where. Initially he'd decided to put his special tastes to one side until they'd packed up and left, but they were still here and he couldn't simply wait until they weren't. His urges were too strong.

113

From the shadows of an abandoned garage he watched the group of children, at least a dozen strong, all aged between five and ten, as they strolled subterranean roads and walkways that crisscrossed the estate looking for new and exciting places to play – the official playgrounds and grassed areas long ago abandoned by the children to the local teenage gang and the pit-bull terriers that helped them keep hold of their turf while crapping everywhere.

The groups of children who wandered the estate made easy targets – their parents either not caring where they were or trusting in safety in numbers, even though they knew someone, probably one of their own, lurked on the estate preying on young victims. But such was life on the estate, where survival of the fittest and luckiest were the only true rules and parents pulled the safety net from under their children at a very young age so as to prepare them for lives of hardship and disappointment. Which was why he chose the Grove Park as his hunting ground.

He tracked the children at a safe distance, staying out of sight until he saw what he was waiting for – a small group of the younger children breaking off from the larger group to walk in a different direction. His breathing and heartbeat quickened as he began to close in on the small group, but still he couldn't strike until he had one alone. He couldn't risk moving on a group or even just two children – the chance of one raising the alarm would be just too great. No. He had to wait for the perfect moment. But the longer they stayed together the more frustrated he became, until finally a girl, no more than seven, slowed and stopped. For a moment he stopped breathing altogether as the others now also stopped to check on her. He was close enough to hear their shouted conversation.

'What you doing?' a boy called to her.

'I gotta go home,' she answered.

'Why?' the boy asked.

'I think it's almost time for me tea,' she told him. 'I promised my mum I'd get home on time.'

'You sure?' the boy checked.

'Yeah,' she assured him. 'I'd better go.'

'All right, Caz,' the boy gave up, turning and walking away with the others, leaving the small figure in her dirty white shirt and ill-fitting jeans standing alone, her straight blonde hair hanging limply around her face. 'See you later.'

'See you later,' she called after them before spinning and heading straight back towards him.

He stepped a little further back into the shadows until he could almost feel her – so close now – her tiny feet shuffling along the driveway until she was level with the garage he was hiding in. At the last second he pulled his baseball cap down, made sure the wide collar of his tracksuit top was pulled up high and slid his wrap-around sunglasses on as he stepped out in front of her, smiling. He could see the immediate tension in her body and fear in her bright blue eyes as her already developed survival senses readied her to run or scream or both. He needed to act quickly.

'Caz, right?' he quickly said. She eyed him suspiciously, but nodded a *yes*. 'I'm a friend of your mum's,' he lied. 'She told me you should have been back for your tea ages ago – asked me to come and find you.'

'I was on my way,' Caz explained – the thought of being in trouble with her mother overtaking her other concerns.

'That's OK,' he smiled, 'but we'd better get back.' Caz nodded enthusiastically and began to walk in the direction of her flat until he stopped her with a gentle hand on her shoulder. 'No, not that way,' he told her. 'It'll take too long. Don't want you to get in more trouble. Come on. Follow me. I know a short cut.'

King entered the Old Queen's Head pub in Islington – his brother's choice not his – and was slightly taken aback at the pleasantness of his surroundings. Red leather armchairs and sofas mixed with old wooden stools and tables spread across the wooden floor; a far cry from the Trafalgar back in Canning Town, or the pubs he and Sara very occasionally visited near their flat in Chadwell Heath. The trendy, well-heeled clientele were something he'd grown unused to as well. He was glad he'd bothered to go home and change before coming instead of just wandering along in half-blues. He spotted his brother, Scott, sitting at a small table next to one of the large windows, staring out at the passers-by, an untouched drink abandoned in front of him. He ordered himself a beer from the bar before heading over to Scott and sitting quietly opposite him, waiting to be noticed. When his brother still hadn't emerged from his trance after more than a minute, King decided he'd waited long enough.

'You all right there?' he asked loudly enough for Scott to stir, looking from the window to his brother, his face still blank for a few more seconds before he finally smiled and spoke, shaking his head at his own daydreaming as he did so.

'Christ. Sorry, Jack,' he apologized, offering a hand that King accepted. 'Didn't see you come in there.'

'Was it somewhere nice?' King asked, momentarily confusing his brother. 'When you were staring out the window,' he explained. 'Were you anywhere nice?'

'Oh,' Scott smiled. 'I see. No, not really.'

'Back in Afghanistan?'

'Maybe,' Scott shrugged. 'I'm not sure. I don't remember. Just thinking, I suppose.'

'I see,' King dropped it. 'How you doing anyway?'

'Good,' Scott answered unconvincingly. 'And you?'

'I'm good.' King was a much better liar than his brother. 'How're your wounds?'

'Pretty much sorted,' Scott told him. 'I should be able to get back to my regiment soon.'

'Good,' King nodded. 'That's good.'

'Seems a long time since I saw you last,' Scott suddenly said – surprising him a little. 'You must've been very busy.'

King's expression showed his confusion. 'Not that long. I don't know – maybe a couple of weeks. If that.'

'Oh,' was all Scott replied – looking concerned, before managing to smile a little. 'Whatever. Probably just me. My condition means I sometimes lose track of time. You should watch out for that yourself,' Scott warned him. 'After what happened to you.'

'I'm fine,' King dismissed it. 'And how is that stuff with you?' he asked, referring to Scott's post traumatic stress.

'The army shrinks tell me I should be fine,' he explained, 'in time and with some help. It's not like the old days. They're not going to execute me for cowardice or anything.' They both laughed lightly. 'But what about you? How are your injuries now?'

'Fine,' King shrugged. 'Bit stiff. Nothing a couple of pints can't sort out.'

'You always were a tough little bastard,' Scott told. 'You know, I can hardly ever remember you crying as a kid. No matter how hard the knock you took.'

'Didn't want to make myself a target,' King replied. 'Other kids saw you crying in boarding school and you became a target.'

'I suppose,' Scott agreed. They both took simultaneous sips from their drinks. 'I remember I was still lying in intensive care when they told me you'd been hurt. They didn't want to tell me how serious at first, but I made them. Even through the pain and the drugs I can remember what the first thing I thought was.'

'Which was?'

'What were the bloody chances of that?' Scott smiled. 'Two brothers almost getting themselves killed – a thousand miles apart and doing completely different jobs.'

117

'I tried to work it out once,' King joked, 'but I ran out of zeroes.'

'God knows what Mum and Dad must have thought.'

'God knows,' King shrugged.

'Speaking of which,' Scott asked, 'have you seen the Colonel lately?'

'Yeah,' King sighed. 'Sara and I went over a few days ago and had dinner with him and Mum.'

'Sounds like fun,' Scott smiled. King said nothing. 'He doesn't change, does he?' Again King didn't respond. 'He was all right when I got wounded though. Pulled some old army strings to make sure I got the best treatment.'

'He's all right,' King gave a little. 'He and I are just different people, that's all.'

'He was pretty damn worried when you got hurt,' Scott explained. 'He may not have wanted you to see it, but he was.'

'Well, if he didn't want me to see it then he did a pretty good job,' King complained. 'Seemed to think it was my own fault for joining the police and not the army – some kind of twisted karma.'

'Just his way of dealing with it,' Scott tried to make him less resentful.

'Whatever,' King told him. 'When you go back to your regiment will they put you back on full duties?' he asked out of the blue, keen to move the conversation on.

'I suppose so,' Scott answered without enthusiasm.

'Aren't you afraid they'll send you back to Afghanistan or somewhere *worse*?'

'We're not in Afghanistan any more,' Scott grinned.

'Yeah, right,' King told him.

'Anyway,' Scott said, glancing out of the window, 'if they do they do. I'll be fine.'

'Why don't you quit?' King asked. 'Join the Met instead.'

'I don't think so,' Scott answered, shaking his head. 'Christ, imagine what the Colonel would say. Anyway, looking at what happened to you, I'm probably safer in the army.'

'What happened to me was a freak incident,' King pointed out. 'Getting shot or blown up in some far and distant land seems a regular thing for you lot.'

'Maybe,' Scott answered, looking more serious, 'but I think I'll stick with the military. Why don't you quit the police and join up too – make the Colonel's day.'

'Fuck that,' King answered, horrified at even the suggestion. 'You sound like the old man. All that saluting and polishing your boots would drive me mad.'

'I can assure you it's not like that in Afghanistan and . . . *other* places. It'd be right up your street. You're still young enough.'

'No chance,' King finished it, taking a long sip of his drink to punctuate the end of the discussion.

'So what are you up to now?' Scott changed the subject. 'Made you superintendent yet?'

'Not exactly,' King explained. 'I'm still a sergeant – having a little fun before life gets serious . . . spreading my wings.'

'A sergeant doing what exactly?'

'Running a special unit,' King answered.

'What – anti-terrorist or something?'

'Hardly,' King told him. 'It's a uniform unit. One of our estates got out of hand and it's my job to bring it to heel.'

'Sounds fun,' Scott replied unconvincingly.

'It is,' King answered eagerly. 'Almost no supervision, just me and a few handpicked boys and girls miles away from the Borough HQ. It's proper police work.'

'Is that the normal sort of posting for someone on accelerated promotion?' Scott enquired suspiciously.

'Probably not,' King admitted, leaning back in his chair, 'but it'll do for me. It's like . . . it's like we're our own little police force. No one interferes with us, we do things our own way – make up our own rules and get things done – how policing should be everywhere. I tell you, we got the local slags well on the run.'

'Good for you,' Scott told him, before giving him a warning. 'But remember – *power corrupts and total power corrupts totally.*'

'No one's doing anything corrupt,' King reassured him, spreading his arms apart. 'We're just getting things done.'

'Just be careful,' Scott advised him. 'I'm guessing the police is probably a lot like the army. The senior brass like things nice and predictable. If the shit hits the fan, they'll throw you under a bus.'

'The senior management love us,' King insisted. 'We get them the figures they need.'

'All the same,' Scott cautioned him.

'Don't worry,' King assured him. 'Even if it came to that, they're not smart enough to trip me up.'

'Beware hubris, brother,' Scott reminded him.

'It's just *robust policing*,' King promised. 'No need to be so concerned. If the powers-that-be come looking for me, it'll be to pin a medal on me – not to fuck me over.'

'I hope so,' Scott replied. 'I hope so, although I don't understand this need to try and prove yourself. You've already done enough. You don't owe anybody anything.'

'I owe myself,' King answered quickly. 'I owe myself the chance not to become like them.'

'And who is *them*?'

'The stuffed-shirt brigade,' King told him. 'Senior officers – people like the old man. There has to be more to life than that.'

'It's not so bad,' Scott smiled. 'You've already earned it. Think of the nice life you and Sara could have together.'

'I'm twenty-four years old,' King reminded him. 'I need more.'

'More what?' Scott asked.

'I don't know,' King admitted before offering an answer. 'More *life*. More everything.'

Scott gave a small laugh before answering. 'A difficult thing to come by.'

'I know,' King agreed, his face as serious as Scott had ever seen. 'But I have to try.'

'Well then,' Scott said, still smiling as he raised his glass, 'a toast. To the condemned man.'

8

King sat at the small dining table in the kitchen of the tiny
flat he shared with Sara, grimacing and rolling his head in
discomfort as he rubbed and gripped at his shoulder and back
where the madman's knife had cut deep. His suffering was
enough to attract Sara's attention, even though she was in
the storm of getting ready for work.

'Bad?' was all she asked.

'Bad enough,' King replied, squeezing his eyes shut against
the pain.

'Take your pills then,' she told him.

'I already have,' he answered truthfully.

'Then do what I keep telling you to do and go and see the
GP to get different ones.'

'I will,' he promised. 'Next time I get a day off.'

'Pull a sickie,' she encouraged him, 'and see them today.
I'm sure your team can manage without you for one day. Or
is that what you're worried about?'

'I'll survive,' he told. 'Just go to work.'

'Just don't be a hero,' she answered, swinging her small
rucksack over her shoulder and heading for him. She held
his face in the palms of her hands and kissed him on the
forehead before heading out of the front door.

Don't be a hero, he thought to himself. As if he ever wanted to be a hero. The surging pain interrupted any thoughts other than finding a remedy. He pushed himself to his feet, headed for the cabinet where they kept medical supplies and surveyed the goods on offer, but none were as strong as what he'd already taken and most couldn't be mixed with an opioid. He slammed the cupboard door shut and spun back to the empty room looking for answers – his eyes falling on another cupboard where they kept their meagre supply of booze. Against his better judgement, he crossed the kitchen, opened the cabinet and peered inside at the small collection of bottles: drinks bought for special occasions but hardly touched, things bought for Christmas and quickly forgotten. His eyes passed over the slim pickings until they settled on a bottle of whisky – something he rarely touched and didn't particularly enjoy. His hand stretched out for the bottle before he pulled it away, shaking his head. If he turned up for work even slightly drunk people would notice it straight away. The smell alone of whisky on his breath would give him away. He sighed and closed the door, taking a seat back at the kitchen table, the frustration of not being able to dull the pain bringing him close to tears – until he remembered something.

He sprang to his feet and went to a kitchen drawer where he had casually dumped something a few days before. Unless Sara had found it and thrown it away it should still be there. To his relief the cigarettes, papers and the small piece of cannabis resin he and Renita had taken from the youths they'd caught in the basement on the estate were all in the drawer. Even the lighter he'd taken was still there. Everything he needed.

King grabbed the items and retreated to the table, spreading them out like they were a model or puzzle waiting to be assembled. He'd seen the odd joint being made before, but he'd never actually tried to construct one himself. He'd never even smoked a cigarette, except once in school, and it had made him feel sick enough not to try it again. A stab of pain in his back reminded him why the items were spread in front of him in the first place, encouraging him to pick up the cigarette papers.

After a few attempts, he'd constructed something that was reasonably oblong-shaped with all the adhesive side along one edge. The addition of the tobacco from a broken cigarette was easy enough, although he suspected he'd used too much, but now came the bit he was truly unsure of – adding the cannabis itself. He considered using the Internet, but paranoia of who may one day be checking on him stopped him. Instead he rolled the resin around in his fingertips and soon realized it was too hard to crumble into the joint. He deduced that must be why he'd seen people heating the resin first – to soften it – so carefully he took the lighter and waved the flame under the resin until he felt it become more pliable, at which point he began to crumble it into the waiting tobacco – the whole procedure going better than he could have expected, although the last, larger, piece of resin fell into the construction before he could break it up properly. *Never mind,* he told himself and carefully lifted the entire thing, dapping his tongue along the adhesive strip and attempting to roll it into a neat cigar shape. After a few frustrating aborted attempts he had something that looked like a lumpy, oversized roll-up, but it was good enough.

He put the flame to the end of the joint and tentatively drew the smoke into his mouth, blowing it out again without inhaling. The taste wasn't unpleasant, but neither did it appeal to him greatly. He waited for any feeling of nausea, but when none came he decided to risk smoking it properly. He took another cautious puff, only taking a small mouthful before partially breathing it into his lungs.

The first cough was more of a splutter before his virgin lungs started to object more violently, causing a choking fit that seemed to last for minutes until, red in the face, things calmed down. Having never used the drug before, the effects came quickly, accelerated by the coughing that speeded the cannabis through his bloodstream. He felt a little lightheaded and relaxed, although the pain was still strong. Once the stinging sensation in his throat faded he took another drag, a larger one this time, which, learning from previous experience, he took slowly and smoothly down into his lungs. As he exhaled he spluttered only slightly, the bigger hit soon having a more profound effect than the last as the pain faded considerably and his mind relaxed and calmed – a kind of peace he hadn't had since before the *incident*. For the first time in a long time he felt . . . *good*.

King rapped on the closed door in the corridor at Newham Borough headquarters where all the senior officers had their offices. As a mere inspector, Joanne Johnston should have had to share with two or three other inspectors, but somehow she'd not only managed to secure an office entirely for herself, but one of the larger ones as well. King waited for what seemed a long time before a voice finally came from the other side of the door.

'Come in,' Johnston called out in a voice that always seemed too strong and deep for its pixie-like owner. King did as he was told and entered the office that was at least three times bigger than the one he shared with the rest of the Unit.

'You wanted to see me?' he asked, making Johnston look up from the report open on her neat and tidy desk that mirrored everything else in the room. A far cry from what he was used to.

'Yes, Jack,' she told him. 'Take a seat.' Again he did as she asked. 'I'm afraid the CPS have a problem with one of your cases.'

'Oh?' he asked, shaking his head slightly.

'The aggravated burglary job. They're going to drop the prosecution.'

'What?' he almost shouted. 'Why?'

'They have concerns over your grounds to arrest them in the first place and therefore the legitimacy of your power to search the address, making the evidence found inside the address inadmissible. And as the evidence from the flat *is* the case, they don't believe they can prosecute without it.'

'What the hell are they talking about?' King demanded. 'The case is solid. We did everything right.'

Johnston leaned back in her chair and studied him for a while before leaning forward and looking at the report on her desk before looking back to King. 'You used Section 17 as your power to enter and arrest?'

'I saw a known runner coming from a known handler's address go straight to the squat where the suspects were later arrested. While I had the flat under observation one of the suspects returned carrying a TV I recognized from the crime report, giving me more than enough grounds to enter and arrest, which is what I did. After that I had powers under Section 18 to search.'

'And that's what the CPS have the problem with,' Johnston told him – her face expressionless. 'This rather convenient sighting of the stolen TV. I've been informed they feel it pushes the boundaries of what a judge or jury would believe a little too far and as a consequence would reflect badly on the borough as a whole.'

'This is all bullshit,' King complained. 'What the hell do the CPS want? I give them a gift-wrapped case of aggravated burglary and they want to flush it. I don't understand what's changed. They were OK with it before. Let us charge them.'

'It's now gone up to one of the senior solicitors and they feel it's too risky,' Johnston explained. 'You need to think of yourself here too, Jack. Remember you're on accelerated promotion. Destined for high places. You start getting black marks next to cases you're involved with and it could be very damaging. So what if a couple of crack-heads dodge a bullet?

Only a matter of time before they come around again. You need to think of yourself.'

'These guys were desperate and dangerous,' King argued. 'Next time they commit an aggravated burglary someone could easily get hurt. What's the point of us working our backsides off to get these people off the streets if the CPS are just going to let them back out?'

'A lesson to be learnt, Jack,' Johnston told him, looking deadly serious. 'This isn't the eighties or even the nineties. CPS, courts, even the good old public won't tolerate anything other than whiter-than-white policing. Understand?'

'Not really,' he answered truthfully.

Johnston leaned forward in her chair. 'Let's just say, if you want to make sure the evidence is . . . *sufficient* to justify arrests and searches, maybe something a little more subtle than seeing someone walking along the street with a wide-screen TV would be a good idea. Now do you understand what I'm telling you?'

'It was a clean arrest,' he answered.

Johnston relaxed back into her comfortable chair before answering. 'Not clean enough, Jack,' she told him. 'Not clean enough.'

'Jesus, Sarge,' Davey Brown complained as he and King kept watch from their hidden vantage point on Micky Astill's flat, 'you look completely knackered. Last time I saw eyes like that was when I watched *Night of the Living Dead*. What's the matter – that pretty little girlfriend of yours keeping you up all night, eh?'

'Hardly,' King replied, the pleasant effects of the joint having now been replaced by an increasingly intense headache, although the pain in his shoulder and back hadn't yet fully returned. 'Been spending too much time here, more like.'

'You wanna watch that,' Brown warned, 'before she runs off with someone else.'

'Thanks for the advice,' King lied.

'Aye. No problem,' Brown said in a tone that made it impossible whether to tell whether he really believed he'd been helpful or not. 'You sure you're all right? You sound as bad as you look.'

'Just a little pissed off, that's all,' he admitted.

'Oh aye. How come?' Brown asked.

'Had a meeting with Johnston today,' he explained. 'Before we came on patrol.'

'Meetings with the Poisonous Pixie are rarely good,' Brown joked.

'Yeah, well – this was no exception.'

'And?' Brown pushed.

'The aggravated burglary job,' King told him. 'The CPS are going to drop it.'

'Why?' Brown asked. 'Thought it was as solid as a rock?'

'It was,' King assured him. 'Apparently they think I made up the bit about one of them carrying a stolen TV into the flat to justify entry and arrest.'

'And did you?' Brown asked.

King glanced at him warily before answering. 'Well it doesn't really matter now, does it? Job's gone.'

'Aye,' Brown agreed with a shrug of his shoulders. 'I suppose not.' They were silent for a while before Brown changed the subject. 'What we doing here anyway? A few poxy arrests for possession hardly seems worth the effort.'

'It's a slow day,' King explained. 'Looks like the local slags are keeping their heads down. Might as well keep things ticking over until they resurface.'

'Aye,' Brown only partly agreed, 'but we could be doing better than this. Perhaps we should be trying to find this dirty bastard kiddie fiddler instead of picking off two-bob punters?'

'No need to try and find him,' King assured him. 'I know who he is.'

'Then what we waiting for?' Brown asked excitedly.

'The right opportunity,' King answered without looking at him. 'When we move on him, I don't want there to be any doubt. I want him bang to rights – so the children he's assaulted don't even have to give evidence.'

'Oh yeah,' Brown laughed softly. 'And how the fuck you going to—'

'Hold up,' King stopped him as he nodded towards Astill's flat. 'Looks like we have a punter.' They both watched as the small, slim woman in her early twenties with long, lank blonde hair warily approached the flat and knocked timidly at the door.

'It's just a wee bird,' Brown grumbled. 'Let her go.'

'Man, woman,' King argued. 'Makes no difference.'

'Aye it does,' Brown disagreed. 'We can't search a woman. We'll have to take her back to the nick and get a WPC to do it for us. Pain in the arse.'

'Maybe not,' King told him as they watched Astill open the door and study the woman, although, as always, the metal security grid remained firmly closed. 'We don't have to do everything by the book.'

'I'm not searching a female prisoner,' Brown insisted. 'Even if she is a scag head, she can still make allegations.'

'I mean maybe we won't have to search her,' King explained quietly as they watched her shake hands with Astill – clandestinely palming him a fistful of change. Astill disappeared inside and closed the door while the woman waited outside looking increasingly agitated – like a small deer drinking from the tiger's waterhole.

'How d'you plan on arresting her,' Brown asked, 'if you aren't going to search her? No drugs, no evidence, no grounds to arrest.'

'We'll see,' King answered as the door reopened and Astill reappeared. He said something to the woman who put her hand through the grill and made momentary contact with his – the door closing quickly as she scuttled off along the walkway to the stairwell. 'Come on,' King ordered. They immediately sprang from where they'd been watching and made their way around to the place the woman had approached from. As they waited hidden at the end of a small path that lay between two blocks, the woman appeared, jumping with fright as they stepped out, turning even paler as she realized there was no escape. King grabbed her by the arm and pulled her to one side.

'What you got?' he asked the now trembling woman who, despite the obvious effects of the use of hard drugs, remained reasonably attractive, with sharp blue eyes set in pretty face – her skin still porcelain-like and flawless. For a second he imagined what she would have looked like before she sacrificed everything to heavy-duty drug use.

'I haven't got anything,' she lied without any conviction.

'What's your name?' King asked quietly, but with authority – slightly intimidatingly.

'Vicky Richards,' she answered so quietly they could hardly hear her.

'Got any form?' he asked.

'Just some possession and some soliciting,' she confessed.

'A fucking Tom, eh?' Brown barrelled in. Vicky just looked embarrassed and shrugged – as if it was the inevitable, preordained path her life would follow.

'Give me what you've got,' King demanded, but she just looked from him to Brown and back again, as if hoping they would suddenly disappear. 'We've just witnessed you making a buy from a well-known drugs venue,' King tried to sound formal, 'so why don't you just hand it over?' Still nothing. 'If you don't,' he continued, 'we'll have to arrest you on suspicion of possession and take you to the station and have a female officer carry out an intimate search on you and then when we find the drugs we'll have no choice but to charge you – and you don't want that, do you, Vicky?'

'No,' she sighed.

'Then hand it over,' King repeated, 'and we may be able to sort something else out.'

'Like what?' she asked nervously.

'The drugs first,' King insisted, his clicking fingers hurrying her along. Finally she thrust her hand down the front of her jeans and seconds later produced a small fold of blue paper that she held out for him. King considered where the package had been pulled from and snapped on a single latex glove before taking the tiny envelope from the gutted-looking woman. Carefully he opened it enough to be able to peek inside, although he already knew it would contain heroin or cocaine – crack came wrapped in clingfilm. He looked up at Brown. 'Heroin,' he told him and placed it inside a small evidence bag before slipping it into his pocket.

'Serious offence,' Brown told her, 'possession of a class A drug – especially with your form.'

'You going to arrest me?' she asked, the tears of desperation welling in her eyes.

'Of course we are,' Brown gave her the bad news before King intervened.

'No,' he told her.

'What?' Brown almost shouted.

King ignored him. 'D'you live on the estate?' he asked her.

'Yes,' she replied.

'Where?'

'Moland Walk,' she answered.

'I do you a favour,' he explained, 'and one day perhaps you can do one for me?'

'Sure,' she shrugged.

'Now get lost,' he ordered and sent her scurrying away, continually checking over her shoulder that they weren't coming after her – that it wasn't some sort of sick police joke, until she turned a corner and was out of sight.

'D'you mind telling me what the fuck that was all about?'

131

Brown demanded. 'I thought the idea was to make a few easy arrests while things were slow – keep the figures ticking over.'

'Change of plan,' King told him coldly.

'To what?' Brown asked angrily.

'Suddenly occurred to me,' he explained, 'there's still a few main faces we haven't taken down yet. Still a few need a wake-up call.'

'Such as?'

'Everton Watson, for one,' he replied.

'Watson's a scumbag burglar,' Brown conceded, 'but he's no scag head. Don't see how taking a half-gram bag off some scaggy tart's gonna help us get Watson.'

'Where there's a will there's a way,' King told him and winked.

'Hold on,' Brown argued. 'I don't like the sound of this. Watson's not worth getting in the shit for. He'll come soon enough. No need to force the issue.'

'You're right,' King gave in. 'He can run, but he can't hide. All in good time.'

'Aye,' Brown relaxed. 'Only a matter of time.'

'Of course,' King agreed. 'Only a matter of time, but all the same,' he continued, patting the pocket containing the heroin, 'I think I'll hold on to this. Just in case.'

Brown entered the Unit's office back at Canning Town just as Renita was getting ready to go out on the late shift. Brown's mood was reflected on his face.

'You all right?' she asked as she loaded her utility belt with weapons and cuffs.

'Aye,' Brown answered sounding glum. 'Never better.'

'Could have fooled me,' she told him, smiling.

'Aye, well,' was all Brown could muster.

'Come on,' she laughed, to let him know he'd been holding out long enough. 'Why so serious?'

132

'Our beloved leader,' he said sarcastically. 'Notice anything different about him lately?'

'No,' she answered with a stunted laugh.

'Seems different to me,' Brown whispered. 'He's changed.'

'You mean he's enjoying himself?' she explained more than asked.

'I mean he's not himself,' Brown remained serious.

'Go on,' she encouraged him.

'He used to be so . . . *straight*,' Brown responded. 'To be honest I thought he was a bit too fucking straight – accelerated promotion and all that. Truth be told I was a little nervous about working with him – thought we may not see policing in the same way, if you know what I mean. But now . . .'

'What you talking about?' she asked, trying to sound dismissive but failing.

Brown looked around conspiratorially before answering. 'Like taking drugs off suspects and pocketing it instead of arresting them.' Renita said nothing, but her silence was her answer. 'Aye,' Brown said knowingly. 'What was it with you?'

'Cannabis,' she admitted before trying to make it sound like nothing. 'A tiny amount. No bigger than the nail on my little finger. You?'

'Heroin.' Brown said it like it was a venereal disease. 'About half a gram from what I could see. Put it in his pocket and fucked the scag head off. You ever see that puff again?'

'No,' she confirmed.

Brown shook his head with concern. 'He's a worry. He's a worry. Perhaps he's been on that cursed estate too long? Perhaps we all have? A few months in that place is enough for anyone.'

Just as Renita was about to continue the conversation King rounded the corner and entered the office. 'Who's been on the estate too long? We've only been at it a few weeks.' Renita and Brown looked at each other, confusion etched on their faces.

133

'A few weeks?' Brown spat the question. 'What you talking about – a few weeks?' but before King could answer, the unexpected appearance of Inspector Johnston in the office doorway silenced them all.

'Not disturbing anything, I hope,' she asked, smiling her warmest fake smile.

'No, ma'am,' King replied, trying to look as relaxed as he could. 'We were just having a bit of a team meeting – to discuss the way forward.'

'Good,' Johnston replied. 'Good. Just thought I'd drop by and once again say congratulations on results so far. Your figures are making the Safer Neighbourhood Teams very jealous.'

'Thank you,' King nodded, hoping Johnston would be satisfied and leave.

'You've really got them on the run down there,' Johnston told them. 'In fact things have been going so well that it might soon be time to move you from the Grove Wood Estate to some other troublesome housing area – see if you can't have the same effect there. God knows, there's plenty of them on the borough.'

King stiffened before answering. 'Really? I was under the impression we were to be given at least six months on the Grove Wood. There's still a lot of unfinished business – youth disorder, as well as a number of significant dealers still in place. We need more time.'

'Not sure the figures agree with you,' Johnston argued. 'From what I can see everything seems to be settling down very nicely.'

'Figures can be deceiving,' King insisted. 'We've had some early success, that's all. Local slags are just keeping their heads down. They're not stupid. They'll stay out of sight for a while and hope we go away and as soon as we do they'll take over again. Pulling the plug on the Unit's exactly what they're waiting for. Exactly what they want.'

'We're not talking about the end of the Unit,' Johnston explained, 'merely moving it. If things turn *bad* on the Grove Wood we can always move you back – make you more of a mobile unit – switching from trouble spot to trouble spot.'

'Our strength lies in our local knowledge,' King countered. 'If we're turned into some sort of borough-based TSG we lose our greatest weapon.'

'Well,' Johnston smiled, tired of arguing with a subordinate, 'we'll see. You've already had enough time to make an impact. In the meantime I also hear there's been another child attacked on the estate.'

'Yes ma'am,' Renita admitted. 'I took the report. Happened earlier today. Looks like the suspect followed the victim and—'

'I know the details,' Johnston interrupted her. 'And I know this was the most serious case to date. But what I really want to know is how are you going to stop him?' She paused as she took it in turns to look each of them in the eye before suddenly smiling again. 'Keep up the good work.' She spun on her heels and was gone.

'Fuck,' King cursed loudly once he was sure Johnston was out of range. Renita saw his anger, even if she didn't understand it.

'What's the problem?' she asked. 'New estates mean new faces to nick. Another few weeks of walking around the Grove Wood and I don't know about you two, but I'll be going out of my head.'

'Unfinished business,' King snarled. 'I don't like unfinished business and this prick who's attacking kids is really beginning to piss me off. We need to stop him – one way or the other. I'm going back on the estate,' he told them as he quickly checked his equipment. 'See if I can't find someone to nick. Earn a bit of overtime.'

'Your shift's almost finished,' Renita tried to persuade him. 'Why don't you just go home and see Sara?'

'No,' he answered bluntly, 'and if any of you see Everton

Watson out and about, give me a shout on the PR straight away. Understand?' They both just shrugged. 'Good,' he told them and strode from the office.

Renita exhaled deeply before speaking. 'What the hell was that all about?'

'I told you,' Brown replied, shaking his head. 'He's changed. Losing it.'

'He isn't losing it,' Renita defended him.

'Isn't he?' Brown snapped back. 'Well I guess we'll see, eh? We'll see.'

King moved silently around the estate unseen – keeping to the rarely used paths and hugging the lines of buildings, occasionally concealing himself in a stairwell and observing life below. All seemed quiet until the unfortunate Dougie O'Neil suddenly came into view – moving quickly past the cars parked at the roadside, his head bobbing and weaving as he looked into each and every one in search of an easy steal. He may have just been on his way to the rundown local shop for a loaf of cheap bread, but a lowlife thief like O'Neil was a constant thief – always on the lookout for something of value, any value, that had been left unattended and was within his oily grasp.

King circled ahead of him, hiding in a tight alleyway as he prepared to pounce. Once O'Neil was level, still bobbing along the pavement with the typical stride of a petty criminal, King sprang from the alley and gave a short, sharp whistle. O'Neil looked up, his eyes wild with alertness until he saw who it was – his whole body suddenly slumping as King summoned him with a flick of his fingers. O'Neil looked to the heavens and mouthed something King couldn't hear before walking towards him with head bowed.

'Weren't planning on screwing one of these motors, were you, Dougie?' King asked with a wry smile.

'No,' O'Neil pleaded his innocence, looking indignant.

'Really,' King sounded bored. 'First time for everything then.'

'Why you hassling me?' O'Neil argued, more spirited than usual.

'I'm not hassling you, Dougie,' King warned him. 'If I was hassling you, believe me, you'd know about it. For one thing, I'd have already arrested you by now for vehicle interference.'

'I didn't touch a single motor,' O'Neil pleaded. 'You can't nick me just for looking.'

'Shut up, Dougie,' King demanded. 'I can do whatever I like.'

'Whatever,' O'Neil surrendered. 'So why you pulling me in the street?'

'Couldn't come round your flat so soon after my last visit, could I?' King explained. 'That could get tongues wagging. Somebody might just be smart enough to put two and two together – drop you right in it.'

'So what you want?' O'Neil asked as King led him into the alley and out of sight of prying eyes.

'Information,' King answered. 'That's all.'

'More information,' O'Neil complained. 'You're getting obsessive. You should go home once in a while.'

'Why?' King asked. 'If I did that I'd miss out on all the fun I have chasing the likes of you around the estate. Why would I rather be at home relaxing, drinking a cold beer and watching TV than walking around this sewer?'

'Like I said,' O'Neil ignored the sarcasm, 'you're getting obsessed. You'll be fucking moving in next.'

'Information,' King ignored him. 'I need information.'

'No, no,' O'Neil found a backbone. 'You still owe me for last time. Heard you had a nice little result out of my last tip. Reckon that's more than covered the Blu-ray. Anything else'll cost you.'

'Fair enough,' King surprisingly agreed. 'You give me what I need and you'll be well rewarded. You have my word.'

'Your word don't seem to be worth much,' O'Neil pushed his luck.

'I had to make sure you were reliable,' King lied. 'Someone I could trust. Now I know you are we can move forward in a more businesslike manner. If your information's good, you'll be rewarded.'

'And the Blu-ray?' O'Neil checked.

'Gone,' King assured him. 'Disappeared, along with the paperwork.'

O'Neil eyed him with deep suspicion before finally agreeing. 'Fine. What you want to know?'

'Everton Watson,' King told him.

'Why so interested in Watson?'

'Let's just say there's nothing worse than an itch you can't scratch.'

'Fair enough,' O'Neil played along, 'but you'll only catch Everton if you get really lucky. You'll have to catch him while he's actually screwing someone's gaff or catch him out and about with stolen gear, but good luck with that one.'

'What d'you mean?' King questioned.

'Everton works alone,' O'Neil explained, 'so there's no one can grass him up, because no one knows what he's up to. Also he's completely random where and when he goes screwing – totally unpredictable, know what I mean.'

'Then we take him out the same way we took out Morrison and Harris,' King suggested. 'You tell me where he keeps his nicked gear and I'll plot him up.'

'Can't be done,' O'Neil shook his head, taking a second to look around the alley to make sure they weren't being seen together. 'Everton doesn't use a fixed place. Once he's screwed a gaff he hides the gear all over the estate – in bins, on roofs, in garages – all over the shop and rarely the same place twice.'

'Then his handler,' King proposed. 'We keeps obs on his handler and wait for him to come to us. I assume he uses Baroyan.'

'He does, but it's no good,' O'Neil dismissed it. 'Like Morrison and Harris he uses runners to get the gear to Baroyan, only he uses a whole bunch of different ones. Little kids mainly and he never meets them in a specific place. Everton's slippery – I tell you. Not an easy geezer to catch.'

'Errm,' King nodded his head in appreciation of Watson's tradecraft. 'I'll think about it,' he said before changing tack. 'What about drug dealers?' he asked. 'Are there any other dealers on the estate?'

'Astill's your main man for crack and brown,' O'Neil mused.

'I already know about him,' King reminded him.

'Yeah, yeah,' O'Neil grinned as he remembered. 'Then there's Susie Ubana if you're interested in puff.'

'Not interested,' King insisted. 'Class A only.'

'And if the info turns out good,' O'Neil checked, 'I get paid, right?'

'That's what I said, isn't it?' King snapped at him.

'Then there is one I know about,' O'Neil admitted.

'You mean one you've bought off,' said King.

'Yeah, well,' O'Neil shrugged before trying to move on. 'There's a black kid still lives on the estate with his mum, who knows nothing about what he's up to, hence he does his dealing on the street.'

'Got a name?' King pressed him.

'Tyrone Mooney,' O'Neil told him. 'He's only about eighteen and not too smart neither.'

'All very interesting,' King replied, sounding frustrated, 'but you haven't told me how I'm going to take him out.'

'He deals on the estate,' O'Neil explained. 'In the stairwell at Brody House. He usually holds about ten rocks, but he doesn't keep 'em in his mouth or shoved, he dots them around the stairwell – one under a Coke can, one in a crisp packet, that sort of thing. Then he phones his customers and lets them know he's open for business – then it's first come, first served. They give him the cash and he tells them where their rock is hidden. Once he's sold out he fucks off, till next time.'

'Sounds interesting,' King admitted. 'But how do I know when he'll be there selling?'

O'Neil spread his arms wide apart and grinned. 'Like I said, he phones his regular customers.'

'Fine,' King decided. 'When he calls you – you call me. Agreed?'

'Agreed,' O'Neil nodded once. 'Can I go now?'

'Soon,' King deflated him, 'but first I need another piece of information.'

'Ain't you had enough?' O'Neil appealed to him.

'Not that sort of info,' King told him, surprised by his own words – confused by his conscious being hijacked by his subconscious, thoughts and ideas that had been swirling in the darkness of his damaged mind fighting their way to the surface and finally finding a voice, even if that voice would only lead him down an ever darkening path – albeit one where his anguish and pain were dulled.

'Then what?'

'I need you to tell me how people take heroin,' King surprised him, 'and crack.'

'What?' O'Neil laughed. 'You mean you don't know?'

'I know the principles,' King explained, 'but I've never seen it done close up. I've seen plenty of pipes, syringes and foil lying around – seized a fair few too – but I've never had the interest to pay much attention to how they're actually used or the pipes made. I don't know exactly how they're put together. Not exactly something they're going to teach us in training school, is it, and I'm hardly undercover or working the drug squad, so,' he pointed a finger at O'Neil, 'you tell me.'

'Why don't you just look on the Internet?' O'Neil grinned. 'Plenty instructions on there.'

'Maybe I don't trust computers,' King explained.

140

'Man, you're paranoid,' O'Neil told him. 'Not thinking about trying forbidden fruits for yourself, are you, Sergeant?'

'And end up like you?' King looked at him with disdain. 'Don't be a cunt, Dougie.' The grin fell from O'Neil's face. 'Now you gonna tell me how it's done or not?'

O'Neil shrugged again. 'Sure. Why not?' He cleared his throat at if he was about to deliver a lecture. 'There's only one way to take crack – you gotta smoke it. You can hot-pipe or you can use a water-cooled bong. Most people start with a bong. It's safer – don't burn your lips and give yourself crack-lip – but once you're really into the stuff you just hot-pipe it.'

'Which is?' King sought to clarify.

'Just get yourself a little glass pipe, with a hole in both ends – the crack goes one end and the other you suck on. Put a lighter to the crack and smoke the fucker – only the pipe gets fucking hot, hence burnt lips.'

King couldn't help but study O'Neil's own lips and sure enough noticed the scarring and recent burn injuries from too many hot-pipes. 'I've seen plenty of pipes,' King told him, 'but not so many bongs.'

'People hold on to their bongs,' O'Neil explained. 'Even shitty homemade ones.'

'And how d'you make one?' King asked.

'Easy enough,' O'Neil answered. 'Get a small plastic water bottle. Cut a couple of holes in it – both pretty high in the bottle. Stick a hollow pen or something into one of the holes and seal it with chewing gum, whatever. Leave the other open – that's your blow-hole. Then you want to fill it with a couple of inches of water, but not enough to reach the holes or the pen sticking in it. Then you get a little bit of tinfoil and, like, poke it down inside the top of the bottle a bit and wrap the edges around the outside of the top and maybe use an elastic band to keep it in place, but you need to use a needle to put loads of little holes in the foil. Then put the crack on the top of the foil, light it and inhale the smoke through the hollow pen. The water cools it down so it don't burn. That's it.'

'And heroin?'

'Well,' O'Neil thought about it as if he was considering his preference between two fine wines, 'hardcore is to mainline it. Take you straight to fucking paradise, man, but it can be dangerous, especially if the gear's no good – been cut with too much shit, know what I mean?'

'Go on,' King encouraged him.

'Best to smoke horse too. You can use a bong, but best to just chase the dragon. Make a circle with the brown on some skinny tinfoil and heat it from below. When it smokes suck it up with a pipe, or straw, it don't matter, and inhale that bad fucker deep, man.'

'That it?' King checked.

'Yeah, that's it,' O'Neil confirmed.

'Why not just take cocaine?' King asked. 'Why bother with all the hassle when they could just do a line of cocaine?'

'Cocaine?' O'Neil asked, wide-eyed and smiling. 'That's a rare high around here,' he explained. 'This ain't a night out in a West End club. Cocaine's too expensive and the hit's nothing compared to crack or horse. Unless you're dealing big quantities of it it's fucking difficult to make any money dealing that shit – practically talking minimum wage. Nah, man. There was no money in cocaine until dealers started turning it into crack. Then they had the perfect drug. More than ten times as profitable as cocaine and a hundred times more addictive. What dealer wouldn't want to sell it?'

'I see,' King slowly nodded his understanding before changing the subject. 'D'you have a new mobile phone yet?'

'I ain't got no money for a mobile,' O'Neil tried to convince him.

'Don't fuck me around, Dougie,' King warned him. 'You're

a drug addict and a thief. You couldn't exist without a phone.' O'Neil shuffled around, looking anywhere but at King. 'I'm not interested in where you got it from,' King told him, 'if that's what you're worried about.'

'Fine,' O'Neil gave in and pulled a smartphone from his back pocket.

'Show me the number,' King demanded. O'Neil did as he was told and pulled up the phone's number – showing it to King who programmed it into his own device. 'Good,' he said, looking O'Neil up and down before speaking again, a troubling question forming in his mind. 'You know what, Dougie – drugs have destroyed your life. You live like an animal, like a pig, yet I don't hear any *regret* in your voice.'

'Regret?' Dougie looked confused. 'Why would I regret it? It's the best thing in the world. Better than anything. If I won the lottery tomorrow I'd buy a fucking huge pile of crack and brown and smoke that bastard until I was dead. Nothing can touch it.'

'You're a sad individual, Dougie,' King told him. 'Now get out of my sight.' O'Neil stood nodding – his eyes still wild with the fantasy of huge piles of drugs – just for him. Eventually he realized that was all it was – a fantasy – and started to walk away. 'When Mooney calls you,' King reminded him, 'you call me.' O'Neil mumbled something over his shoulder and disappeared around the corner.

King stood shaking his head – trying to forget the desperate sadness that was O'Neil, when he heard his call sign coming over his radio. Despite the distortion he recognized Renita's voice immediately.

'*PS 42 receiving?*' she asked. '*PS 42.*'

He grabbed the mouthpiece that was clipped high on his body armour and replied. 'PS 42 receiving. What is it, Renita?'

'*Just seen someone you're interested in,*' she told him, '*out and about on the Grove Wood.*'

'Who?' he asked bluntly.

'*Everton Watson,*' she replied. '*Gladstone Way, heading towards Millander Walk.*'

'Keep an eye on him,' he ordered. 'I'm on my way.'

As King strode along the passageway of Millander Walk he spotted Watson swaggering straight towards him looking cocky and self-assured, as if he couldn't be touched. He wore one of his collection of elaborate tracksuits, all affiliated to either an American NFL team or an American basketball team and always with a matching baseball cap. He approached King as if he hadn't seen him – not even glancing his way as they drew almost level. But he burst to life when King stretched a powerful, muscular arm across his chest and stopped him in his tracks, dancing up and down on his toes as if he was about to start a boxing match. King ignored his posturing – confident he could incapacitate the slim eighteen year old with one punch if he had to.

'Mr Watson,' he smiled unpleasantly. 'I've been looking for you.'

Watson maintained his aggressive approach, having seen it cause more than one lone policeman or woman to back down in the past, but already he was beginning to think this one was different.

'What you hassling me for, man?' he complained vociferously, hoping to attract the attention of anyone else on the estate who might rally to his cause. 'I ain't done nuffing.'

'Maybe not in the last five minutes,' King snarled at him. 'But you owe Her Majesty some time behind bars, Watson. Been having things too good for too long.'

'I ain't afraid of you,' Watson bluffed, moving close to King, spitting the words into his face before a hand landed on his chest and pushed him backwards, spinning him around and slamming him into the wall. 'You're out of order,' he managed to complain, but his veneer of courage was fading fast as King easily controlled him with only one arm.

144

'I thought this was going to be difficult,' King whispered into his ear, 'but you're making it easy for me.'

'What you talking about, man?' he asked, confused and increasingly concerned. 'Who the fuck are you, man? TSG?'

'Shut up,' King ordered as he began to pat Watson down, his hand dwelling on his rear trouser pocket. 'Got something for me?'

'I ain't got nothing for you,' Watson answered, his face twisted with doubt.

King held up two fingers next to Watson's face. Pinched in between them was the small paper fold he'd taken from Vicky Richards, the female heroin addict he and Brown had stopped outside Astill's block. Watson began to struggle to escape. 'That ain't mine, you cunt,' he screamed. 'You planted it, man. You fucking planted it.'

King leaned all his weight into Watson's back and pinned him to the wall, squeezing the air from his struggling lungs as he whispered in Watson's ear. 'Have that on me. For all the flats you screwed, but never got caught for. Time to pay your debts, Watson.'

'Wait,' Watson tried desperately. 'I don't do none of that shit, man. People will know you stitched me up.'

'Then if you weren't going to use it yourself,' King smiled, 'you must have been planning on selling it, eh?'

Watson attempted to break free, but it was useless. He scanned the walkways for someone who might help him escape, but they were deserted, although he could feel dozens of eyes peering from the surrounding windows – too scared to come to his rescue or even shout token obscenities at the hated Old Bill. It was an ominous sign – a sign that King had fear on his side. In a place ruled by fear, he who wielded it was king. 'That shit ain't mine,' he almost begged.

'Then have it your own way,' King told him, pulling his quick-cuffs from his belt and bending Watson's arms behind his back – fastening them tightly around his slim wrists. 'Possession with intent to supply it is.'

'Fuck you,' Watson expelled the last of his defiance.

'You need to learn to play the game, Everton,' King told him loudly, hoping that anyone listening would hear what he had to say. 'You owe, Watson. You've been screwing people's houses for years and getting away with it. Taking the few precious things people around here have so you can afford expensive clothes and have the latest phone and best drugs, while the people you've screwed are left afraid in their own homes. You're vermin, Watson, and you owe. You owe everyone you've ever stolen from. You've been getting away with it too long. Nobody round here escapes justice any more. Not even you.'

King arrived home later than he'd hoped, but was relieved to see he'd beaten Sara back. He dumped the two heavy bags of shopping on the small kitchen table and quickly tried to massage the pain from his shoulder away, promising himself some painkillers and alcohol once he'd got dinner underway. He'd barely seen Sara the last couple of weeks and had decided to try and make it up to her by preparing a decent meal for them both. They could sit and talk and he could try to anchor himself to her normality and softness – pull himself away from the seductive excitement of life on the estate. Cooking something for a partner was something normal people did and he hoped his mind would lose itself in the task in front of him and allow him to forget his pain, the estate and his increasing doubts about his own future. A normal night with Sara would surely slay his doubts and remind him of how much he had – how happy and content he was and that it was only a matter of time before the *incident* felt like nothing more than a distant memory – like something that had happened to someone else.

He tipped the items from their bags and selected what he

needed, moving between the cupboards and pans to the fridge. He washed and chopped and threw things into hot water and oil. As he wiped a mixture of sweat and steam from his brow, the door opened and Sara stepped inside, a look of shock spreading over her face as she slowly closed the door behind her, the beginnings of a smile forming on her mouth.

'Dinner,' he told her. 'On me.'

'Wow,' she replied, moving slightly nervously into the flat, as if she'd expected something even more unexpected than King cooking dinner. 'And to what do I owe this?'

'Just thought it'd be nice,' he answered. 'I haven't seen you much lately. Thought we could sit and have a proper dinner. There's a bottle of white in the fridge and red on the table. Why don't you get us both a glass?'

'Two bottles?' she questioned. 'Trying to get me drunk?'

'Probably,' he shrugged – the mischievous smile that she'd missed so much returning to his eyes and lips.

'So, Mr Master Chef, what you cooking?' she asked, kicking off her shoes and heading for the cupboard where their few glasses were kept and then the fridge.

'Some chicken thing with some sort of pasta,' he told her – stirring his pots and battling with the clouds of steam. 'It's a new recipe I made up while I was walking around the supermarket trying to work out what to buy.'

She pulled a face of concern. 'Sounds delicious,' she told him, pouring two large glasses.

'By the time we've finished the bottle I don't suppose we'll care too much what it tastes like.'

She handed him a glass and they toasted each other before kissing briefly and gently. Sara spun away and slumped onto one of their few kitchen stools, sipping her wine and rubbing her feet. 'Well,' she told him, 'it's just nice to have you at home, although I have to admit a decent meal's a bonus.'

'You look worn out,' he told her.

'Yeah,' she agreed. 'A bit knackered, I suppose. I've been given a couple of new probationers to puppy-walk. God, they're so keen they're wearing me out.'

'Listen to you,' he teased her, 'three years in the job and already an old sweat.'

'Yeah well,' she said, 'you grow up quickly working Newham.'

'Don't I know it,' he said casually, but Sara misunderstood.

'I'm sorry,' she apologized. 'I know you do.'

'That's not what I meant.' He tried to make light of it, but only made the atmosphere tenser. Quickly he moved them on. 'Someone senior must think you're doing something right to put you in charge of probationers.'

'More like I'm the only one prepared to do it,' she answered. 'No one else wants anything to do with them – poor bastards. How are they supposed to learn anything and stay safe if no one will show them?'

'They'll learn,' King told her as he stirred the pans, 'or they'll quit.'

'Or they'll get hurt,' she reminded him. He just shrugged. 'Still, the hours I've been putting in look almost civilized compared to you.'

'I know,' he agreed. 'Sorry. It's the Unit. We're so busy. You can hardly take a step on the estate without tripping over someone doing something they need to be nicked for. Once we get it sorted out things'll calm down – although the overtime's been nice. Not like we don't need the money.'

'Tell me about it,' she agreed. 'Our credit cards are looking bad, Jack. We're paying a small fortune in interest and the car's going to need insuring again in a couple of weeks. I don't know how we're going to pay it. Maybe we should sell the car – get some cash in?'

'I'll get the money,' he promised. 'Don't worry.'

'How you going to do that?' she asked, shrugging her shoulders. 'More overtime?'

'If I have to,' he told her. 'Never short of overtime opportunities working the Grove Wood.'

'You're on accelerated promotion,' she reminded him. 'You don't need this. We don't need this. We'll manage well enough when you get promoted again. I might even try for sergeant myself or better still quit and get a job that pays proper money. You just need to concentrate on getting the next rank and then we won't need the overtime. Until then we'll just have to do what we can. One of the reasons I thought we could work was because you're on accelerated promotion. No shifts. Normal hours. Enough money so we don't have to kill ourselves working extra hours. Two cops both working different shifts can be a bit of a nightmare. Hardly allows for a healthy relationship and you've already been on that bloody estate long enough.'

He narrowed his eyes and shook his head with confusion. 'Why does everybody keep saying that?'

'Saying what?' Sara asked disinterestedly.

'It doesn't matter,' he answered, shaking his doubts away. 'I wasn't planning on spending the rest of my career on that dump of an estate anyway,' he reassured her as he poured the boiling contents of a pan into a sieve over the sink. 'The SMT are talking about moving it to another estate anyway. If that happens I'll quit the Unit and look for something nine-to-five. Let me just see out the next couple of weeks until that happens.'

'Good,' she smiled. 'It makes sense, Jack, because this isn't good for either of us. I miss seeing you, you know. Feel like I'm either at work or sitting in this flat on my own worrying about you.'

'You don't need to worry about me,' he smiled. 'I can take care of myself.'

'I know,' she said before sipping her wine, as much to buy a few seconds as anything. 'But after what happened I do worry you jumped straight back into the deep end too soon.'

'Best way to learn to swim, isn't it?' he tried to be jovial. 'Jump in the deep end and swim or sink.' He immediately regretted his words. Sara stared at him in silence – her eyes wide open with concern. 'That's not what I meant,' he tried to recover.

'Isn't it?'

'No,' he told her, trying to salvage the mood and slay the fear he saw in her eyes. 'Bad comparison.' Suddenly it was his turn to feel fear as the shadows of his nightmares crept from the corners of the room and invaded his mind. He feared for the good and kindness that Sara represented – that somehow it would be destroyed if she stayed close to him for too long. The *incident* had changed him, whether he'd wanted it to or not – it had. He couldn't come back from that and be exactly the same person he'd been before. He wasn't growing back to the people who'd been most important to him before the madman pushed a knife into his back – he was growing further away from them, his life-changing experience cocooning him from their everyday lives. But he didn't want to hurt Sara or anyone else he cared about, although he now knew almost beyond any doubt that he was slipping away from them. He felt a lump in his throat as she suddenly felt quite unreal – as if she didn't really exist, like a fictional character he'd been watching on the TV for years, a distant thing of pretend. He was filled with a terrible sense of dread that he was going to hurt her – to fill her life with pain. Whereas all he wanted to do was make her happy, although he wasn't sure he knew how to any more. Preparing the meal instantly felt futile and pointless. He clenched his fists tight so she couldn't see the slight trembling of his hands.

'Just don't push yourself too hard,' she warmly warned him. 'OK?'

'I understand,' he managed to say, but his heart was filling with sadness as he looked at the pretty blonde-haired young woman sitting in front of him sipping golden liquid from a thin glass. He desperately wanted to want the life she had planned for them, but something inside of him screamed that it wasn't what he was looking for any more. Perhaps it never had been – a life of boring domesticity with a wife forever pressurizing him to *go further, be more successful*. No doubt soon she'd want children. And work – as little more than a bureaucrat – endless hours of pointless meetings and indecipherable management-speak, while all the time the streets would be tempting and tormenting him. Suddenly the estate seemed a bright place where people lived their lives on the edge. A place where a wrong look at the wrong person could get you stabbed or your head caved in with a baseball bat. A place where life was cheap, like a war zone, but because of it every moment of survival was to be celebrated and lived to the full – not wasted on future plans and aspirations. Just lived, there and then. A place where alcohol, drugs and sex were used extensively from a young age – not perhaps, as he'd first thought, to dull the miserableness of their existence, but to further heighten and intensify the adrenalin of living life so close to the edge so much of the time. At home with Sara, he'd started to feel like he was just acting out a role – playing the part of the person he used to be. The estate was where he became his true self. Sara, his parents and his friends were people he'd left behind in another world. He still felt strong residual feelings of love for Sara, yet they were intangible and ethereal – like feelings he had for the long-dead pets of his childhood.

The estate made him feel not just alive, but powerful, and it felt good. Sara was talking but he wasn't hearing a word she said. Instead his thoughts turned to one particular person on the estate, although he wasn't sure why. The brown curls of Kelly Royston's hair hanging perfectly over the curved bones and muscles of her shoulders. Her skin the colour of caramel, radiating warmth and softness. And her eyes, so dark they were almost black, shining out from her young, wise face. She was beautiful – her streetwise toughness and the danger she represented making her all the more desirable. He forced her from his mind as he realized Sara was talking directly to him – repeating the same question over and over. Kelly's image slipped into the darkness of his subconscious as if she was disappearing beneath a black pool of tar.

'You all right?' He finally heard Sara's question.

'Yeah,' he managed to answer. 'I'm fine.'

9

King sat alone in the canteen drinking a strong, foul-tasting coffee, trying to get the confusion of the previous night's thoughts out of his head – telling himself he'd just been tired and that Sara's nagging had made him suffer some sort of temporary delusion. Yet still he could barely wait to return to the estate and stalk the walkways and alleys. And if he saw Kelly, no doubt her reality would be a pale imitation of how he imagined her. He was just about to leave when Marino came up behind him carrying a polystyrene cup.

'Mind if I join you?' he asked.

A stab of resentment twisted in his belly, but he managed to hide it. 'Why not?' he answered.

Marino took a seat and began with a smile. 'I heard you nicked Everton Watson.'

'No big deal,' King answered, trying to kill the conversation before it started. 'Just a bit of possession.'

'Of heroin?' Marino checked.

'Yeah, so?'

'Just I've known Everton a long time,' Marino told him. 'He's a slag and a burglar, but I've never known him take smack. Always seemed too switched on for that – in a street-smart sort of way.'

'Something must have changed then,' King said, sounding disinterested.

'He says not,' Marino ambushed him.

'You've spoken to him?' King asked, still trying to feign casualness.

'Yeah,' Marino replied, giving his words a couple of seconds to affect King before continuing. 'When he was being bailed out last night. Said the drugs weren't his – that he still never touches anything more than a bit of puff.'

'Did he say anything else?' King pried, looking into his coffee and avoiding eye contact with Marino.

'No,' Marino answered, 'except something about he'd get even. I figured he was probably holding the smack for someone else when you pulled him. I guess he thinks he owes them one.'

'Or he had it to sell it,' King recovered his poise.

'Maybe,' Marino shrugged, 'but I doubt it. Everton knows he could do some serious time for residential burglary, but if you get caught dealing smack they throw away the key. He works alone for a reason – so no one can grass on him. But the world of dealers is a world of informants and treachery. Not Everton's style.'

'Things change,' King told him.

'That they do,' Marino seemed to agree. 'Speaking of change,' he suddenly continued, 'I was wondering if you might have had a change of heart.'

'About what?' King asked suspiciously.

'About accelerated promotion,' Marino explained. 'You're turning into one hell of a thief-taker. You always were pretty good at it. Maybe endless meetings and pushing a pen around's not for you after all?'

'Not sure about that,' King answered, relieved the subject had changed. 'Feel like . . . feel like a lot of people are depending on me following through with it. Other people have made plans – you know.'

'Take my advice, son,' Marino insisted. 'Don't worry about other people. Do what your heart tells you, or face the rest of your career being a boring disappointment. Maybe you should think about the CID. You're a good fit for it. I could have a word with the DCI if you like.'

'I'll think about it,' King told him and started to get up before Marino stopped him.

'But while you're still out there,' he warned him, 'just remember this isn't the eighties any more. It's not even the nineties. Every little slag out there's got a smartphone stuffed in their pocket just waiting for some unsuspecting copper to screw up and do or say something stupid. You don't want to end up on the *News at Ten*. Media likes nothing more than a dodgy cop story and don't expect the powers-that-be to come to your rescue – not in this day and age. Know what I'm saying, Jack?'

'I'll bear it in mind,' King replied, getting to his feet. 'Maybe if the CID had acted a little more like it was the eighties or nineties this child abuser wouldn't still be running around. Know what I mean? I'll see you round, Frank,' he told him and headed for the canteen exit – watched all the way by Marino.

'Be careful out there, son,' Marino whispered. 'Be very careful.'

King was back on the estate with Williams, hidden away at the top of the stairwell O'Neil had told him Tyrone Mooney used to deal crack cocaine from. They'd have a bird's eye view of Mooney's activities – if he turned up. While King was dressed in full uniform, Williams was dressed in civilian clothing – doing his best to look like he belonged on the estate – but still he needed to stay concealed until the last moment.

King felt good being back on the estate, free from offi-cialdom and the boring pressures of normal life. While he was on the estate anything was possible. He could end up arresting a dealer or a thief. He could end up being first on scene at a murder or serious assault. He could have a chance meeting with Kelly Royston. Again he shook her from his mind.

'Jesus,' Williams complained. 'We've been here for ages.'

'Patience,' King told him.

'Yeah but how do we even know this kid's going to turn up?'

'Because O'Neil said he would,' he reminded him.

'You trust O'Neil?'

'No, but I trust him to do as he's told,' King assured him. 'He doesn't really have a choice, does he?'

'Yeah but we've been here for ages,' Williams whinged again. 'Maybe O'Neil got it wrong?'

'What's to get wrong?' King asked, keeping his voice low. 'Mooney called him and said he'd be dealing within the next few hours so I reckon that'll be what he does.'

'Anything could have happened,' Williams tried to persuade him. 'He could have been nicked by someone else or mugged or maybe he just changed his mind – decided to stay indoors and watch *The Jeremy Kyle Show*.'

'Perhaps.' The sound of shuffling feet coming from the bottom of the staircase made King freeze. He sensed Williams was about to say something and quickly placed a finger across his own lips to let him know to keep quiet. They stared at each other for a while, not daring to move as they listened to the sounds from below, partly terrified that if it was Mooney he might climb higher and see them. He would run and, at eighteen and knowing the estate well, there was a decent chance he'd escape them or at least get a good enough head start to toss his crack. But to their relief the noises stayed below them.

King tiptoed to the bannister and carefully peered over, his flat cap held in his hand to prevent it falling. He watched as the slim black youth began to move around his immediate vicinity, repeating the same action over and over as he pulled something too small to see from his pocket and then bent down to place it beneath whatever he could find: a tossed drinks can, a crisp bag, a loose piece of paving – constantly looking around himself and pointing to where he'd just been, committing each spot to memory. *O'Neil was dead right*, King thought to himself. Mooney was hiding his rocks close by so he couldn't be caught in possession if the police stumbled across him. *Clever, but not clever enough.*

'Is it him?' Williams whispered in his ear.

'Has to be,' King told him.

'Shall I go now?'

'No,' King stopped him. 'Let's wait until he's served at least one punter. Just to be sure he's dealing.'

'OK,' Williams agreed as they both moved back from the edge – relying on their ears alone now to warn them of any approach. They didn't have to wait long as first the sound of footsteps and then voices drew them back to the railing overlooking the stairwell. They strained hard as Mooney spoke with a wreck of a white man who looked sixty, but who King guessed was really probably only in his twenties.

He couldn't make out what the crack addict had said, but Mooney was clear enough as he told him, 'There might be something under the crisp packet you can use. Just make sure you leave the cash there when you're done.' King watched as the punter retrieved something from under the packet, examining it closely, as if it was a jewel, before he eventually tipped a small pile of change from his hand and covered it with the packet, then headed off without another word being said.

'All right,' King whispered to Williams. 'You know what to do.' Williams just nodded and headed off down the stairwell like a man without a care in the world. When he heard someone coming, Mooney bent his head around the corner to see if it was danger approaching – relaxing when he saw a casually dressed young black guy skipping down the stairs not even making eye contact with him. But as soon as they were level Williams changed tack and without warning grabbed him by both arms.

'Police!' he shouted, despite their close proximity. 'Turn around and keep your hands up,' he demanded, spinning the stunned Mooney around and pushing him against the wall. 'Don't move.' A few seconds later they were joined by King.

'Nice one, Danny,' he congratulated his colleague before turning his attention to Mooney. 'You're in a whole heap of shit, Tyrone,' he told him. 'It is Tyrone, isn't it?'

The shaking dealer looked over his shoulder at King and seemed to shrink further at what he saw. 'Shit,' he cursed, closing his eyes and shaking his head. 'Not you.'

'You know me?' King asked – surprised, but delighted at his notoriety.

'I heard of you,' Mooney admitted. 'Sergeant 42, right?'

'Sergeant King to you. Now, I'll ask you again, you are Tyrone Mooney, right?'

'Yeah, that's me,' Mooney sighed.

'Well then,' King smiled, 'it appears we both already know each other. And by the way, you're in a lot of fucking trouble, my friend. A lot of trouble.'

'You got nothing on me, man,' Mooney insisted. 'I was just sitting here minding my own business, innit. I weren't doing nothing.'

'You know, Tyrone,' King mocked him, 'I've been hearing a lot of that lately. What you think this is?' he snarled into Mooney's face. 'Some reality cop show on the telly? D'you see any cameras? This is real life, son.'

'What you talking about?' Mooney asked – confused and concerned – looking over his shoulder as King moved from Coke can to crisp packet to loose plaster, collecting the rocks

158

he'd seen Mooney hide and holding them in his open palm so all could see.

'I'm talking about these,' King explained. 'You've been a very naughty boy, Tyrone. Dealing this shit gets you some serious prison time. *Serious* time.'

'I ain't dealing nothing,' Mooney lied. 'You didn't find nothing on me. I was just passing through, innit. So somebody left their gear here. Ain't me.'

'Wrong,' King told him, shaking his head in fake disappointment at Mooney's answer. 'You're getting . . . you're getting confused, Tyrone. You see, we did find these rocks in your possession,' he spelt it out, 'all . . .' he quickly counted the tiny waxy stones in his palm '. . . all twelve. Enough for possession with intent to supply. And then there was the one we saw you sell to the punter . . .'

'What you talking about?' Mooney began to panic.

'Which was right before you sold a rock to PC Williams here,' King continued, now drawing confused looks from them both, 'who was acting undercover.'

'I didn't sell nothing to nobody,' Mooney desperately complained. 'Come on, man. Don't stitch me up.'

'No one's stitching you up,' King insisted. 'You're a crack cocaine dealer. You peddle death and misery.'

'Please,' Mooney begged. 'Give me a break. I swear I'll never do it again.'

'Doubt you're going to last very long banged up in Feltham,' King ignored him. 'There's a lot of very violent young men inside there – most in gangs, which makes them untouchable, specially to an outsider like you.'

'Please,' Mooney pleaded again. 'I'll do anything.'

'Well,' King asked the increasingly worried-looking Williams, 'what d'you think we should do, PC Williams? Should we give this drug-dealing shit a break or not?'

'Sarge?' Williams questioned.

'Should we give him a break?'

Mooney's eyes stared wide and frightened at Williams who gave his answer. 'I think we should nick him and get back to the station where we can have a *chat* about our evidence – that's what I think.'

King pulled a face as if considering his options, but he'd already made his mind up. 'I don't think so,' he finally said. 'Everyone deserves a second chance, eh, Tyrone?'

'Oh God, thank you,' Mooney exclaimed, his legs almost giving out from under him with relief. 'Thank you. Thank you.'

'Sarge?' Williams tried to intervene. 'What we doing?'

'We're doing what has to be done,' King snapped at him a bit. 'Tyrone here's not my problem. He's just a fool – aren't you, Tyrone?' Mooney just nodded, prepared to do anything to avoid arrest. 'Where d'you get your drugs from anyway?' King asked.

'Some kid at college,' Mooney offered without resistance. 'He makes me do it. He gives me the gear and makes me sell it. The money goes back to him.'

'Does he live on the estate?' King asked, his interest piqued.

'No,' Mooney answered, instantly finishing King's enthusiasm. 'He lives over in Leyton somewhere.'

'What would he do to you if you refused?' King continued.

'Stab me,' Mooney told him, 'or worse. He's in one of them gangs you talked about.'

'Sarge,' Williams protested. 'This is bullshit. Let's nick him and get out of here.' King ignored him and started to search through Mooney's pockets, pulling a small wad of cash and some cannabis resin from one trouser pocket and a mobile phone from the other. He spun Mooney around so he was no longer facing the wall.

'This kid you're talking about,' King continued, 'he's going to want either his drugs or his money back, right?'

'Yeah, yeah,' Mooney hastily agreed.

'But you won't have either,' King smiled.

160

'Keep the drugs,' Mooney negotiated, 'and let me give him the money.'

'Can't do that,' King shook his head. 'I need both. Means to an end and all that. What you do is this: you tell this drug-dealing slag you were nicked, but not by just any copper – you make sure he knows you were nicked by me, and now I'm coming after him. He'll make some calls to scum he knows on the estate and they'll be sure to tell him all about me. After that he'll be too busy keeping his head down to bother you, but if he does – you come tell me and I'll pay him and his friends a little visit. Fair enough?'

'Fine,' Mooney hurriedly agreed. 'Can I have my phone back now?'

'Of course,' King agreed with a snake-like friendliness and handed it to Mooney as he pushed the wad of cash and cannabis into his own trouser pocket – catching the look of contempt that flashed on Mooney's face as he eyed the money. 'You think I'm going to keep this for myself?' King asked. 'You think I'm some sort of bent copper lining my own pockets?' Mooney just shrugged.

'Easy, Sarge,' Williams tried to warn him.

'This isn't for me, Tyrone,' King explained. 'I'm not scum like you. I'm going to use this to take down someone who's had it coming for a long time. Someone who thinks he can't be touched. Someone who needs to learn we own this estate now and we'll do what we have to do to clear it of all the filth. They can't hide behind rules and laws designed to protect the guilty. Only rules round here – only laws round here – are my rules and laws. Understand?' Mooney nodded, his eyes blazing with mistrust and fear. 'Now get the fuck out of my sight.' Mooney didn't wait to be told twice and sprang away, only to be grabbed around the arm by King. 'But remember – I did you a fucking huge favour here. One day I may need you to return that favour. Know what I'm saying?' Mooney just nodded once. 'Good,' King told him, releasing his grip and allowing the disorientated and fearful Mooney to jog away.

Williams waited until he was out of sight. 'What the fuck are you doing, Sarge? We had a quality arrest for supplying crack right in our hands. Why the hell did we let him go?'

'He's small fry,' King answered. 'Just a scared kid.'

'Yeah but it was a good arrest,' Williams persisted. 'We could have squeezed him back at the nick – turned him into our informant.'

'He's already told us everything he knows,' King dismissed it, 'and it had nothing to do with the Grove Wood, so it's got nothing to do with us.'

'All the same – it was a decent collar,' Williams complained. 'Only reason I go along with this shit is to get some quality crime arrests. I don't mind working on the edge so long as it gets me the arrests I need to get me into the CID. If we're going to start letting everyone go, what's the point?'

'Think about it,' King almost whispered. 'What evidence did we really have? We saw him moving a few bits and pieces around and later found drugs hidden there. So what? You'd be prepared to stand in the box at Crown Court and swear he sold you a rock, would you?'

'That was your idea – not mine.'

'There you go then,' King finished it. 'We had nothing. I just said all that bollocks to scare the shit out the little prick. Make him nice and compliant. Make sure he keeps his mouth shut.'

'And d'you think he will?' Williams asked.

'Well he won't be making a complaint, will he?' King assured him. 'If he tells anyone it'll just be the local slags, which will only help make them even more afraid of us and that's fine by me.'

'Fair enough,' Williams reluctantly agreed, despite fearing he was sinking deeper and deeper into King's potentially bottomless pit.

'Now forget him,' King insisted. 'We've got bigger fish to fry.'

As he headed for the main staircase inside Canning Town Police Station with Williams, King was concerned to see Johnston standing halfway up grilling another uniformed sergeant about something that had clearly displeased her – although he couldn't help but feel she was really just waiting for him. He let Williams go in front as he tried to skip past her without being noticed, only to be frozen by the sound of her voice.

'Sergeant King. A word if I may,' she told him, before turning to the berated sergeant. 'We'll finish this later.' She turned back to King and saw that Williams had also stopped. 'Alone.' Williams looked at King first who gave him a quick nod to let him know he should go. Williams just shrugged before walking away. 'I need to be back at Newham in a few minutes,' she told him, 'so you'll have to walk with me.' She immediately headed off back down the stairs with King trying to keep up.

'Is there something wrong?' King asked, not wanting to spend any more time with Johnston than necessary.

'More good arrests for the Unit, I hear.' She seemed to ignore his question.

'Then there's no problem?' he asked in hope more than belief.

'No problems,' she answered as they walked fast along the corridor. 'But as the Unit's overall supervising officer, it's necessary for me to check everything is as it should be. You understand?'

'Of course,' King told her – swallowing his irritation at being checked up on. 'And I can tell you everything is as it should be.'

'Good,' Johnston replied without looking at him as they burst through the door that led to the small car park just as

163

a patrol car screamed from it with its siren blaring and lights flashing, momentarily silencing even Johnston until its wail faded as it disappeared into the street outside. 'You're all young and keen, I realize that,' Johnston told him. 'All wanting to do the right thing and get the results that'll reflect well on the Unit.'

'Yes, ma'am,' he agreed, still unsure where she was going.

'And the results have been very good so far.'

'Thank you.'

'And as much as I would like to spend more time with you and the others,' she lied, 'my other responsibilities make that very difficult.'

'I understand,' he assured her.

'Which leaves you all, especially you, Jack, with a great amount of responsibility, hidden away over there on the estate. Out-of-sight, out-of-mind, eh?'

'Yes ma'am,' he answered for the lack of being able to think of anything else to say.

'Only you're not, Jack,' she told him as she reached her car and came to a stop. 'Or at least not out of mind. Not my mind anyway. That warrant card you probably keep in your back pocket gives you a lot of power, Jack. The power to use force to detain and imprison anyone you merely suspect has committed a crime. Not even the Prime Minister has that power. Being a truly *good* cop is knowing how to wield that power. In the wrong hands it could be a very dangerous thing.'

'Is this about the aggravated burglary job?' he asked. 'With respect, ma'am, I already told you that arrest was clean. CPS screwed up.'

'And yet the arrests keep coming, don't they, Jack?' she told him, searching in his eyes for any sign of weakness.

'The arrests keep coming because we're working our arses off to keep them coming,' he argued before Johnston raised her hand to stop him.

'I'm just telling you the way of the world,' she warned him. 'You're a big boy, Jack. A big boy on accelerated promotion – which means you need to get used to playing by big-boy rules.'

'Meaning?'

'Meaning so long as the *results* keep coming, everyone will be happy. They may not even look too closely at how they're being achieved. But know this, Jack – if you ever go too far, get a reputation for flying a little too close to the sun, even if it's just to take out the local thieves and thugs, you'll be on your own. No one's going to flush their careers down the drain to save yours. Including me. Understand?'

He nodded his head knowingly before speaking again. 'Success has many parents, but failure is always an orphan?'

'Exactly,' Johnston replied. 'I couldn't have put it better myself,' she told him, heaving the car door open and ducking inside before he could answer. She pulled the door shut and within seconds was driving away, leaving King standing in the yard alone with his thoughts.

'Christ,' he finally whispered. 'Where the hell did they find her?'

10

Renita patrolled the walkways of the estate alone – more nervous than she would have been during the daytime. It was approaching the end of her shift – almost one am now – but she still had another hour to go. She should have been with Brown, but he'd received a court warning for the morning and had headed off at midnight – encouraging her to spend the rest of her shift doing paperwork and stay off the estate. But she wasn't about to show any fear or weakness to her male colleagues and had stayed on patrol even after Brown had left. But still, the estate was a more intimidating and menacing place in the hours of darkness, the heavy silence punctuated by the occasional shout or scream, the barking of dogs or sound of breaking glass. She held her heavy Maglite torch in her hand, more for protection than illumination. It made for a very effective truncheon if it came to it. If someone leapt from the dark at her it would be easy to justify reactively striking them in the head with a torch. She could have drawn her extendable metal truncheon, known as an ASP, in readiness, but she preferred to keep her free hand close to her radio in case she needed to call for assistance and the big torch was arguably the better weapon too. Tricks of the trade passed from one generation of cops to the next and so forth, but all the same, there was something intangible in the atmosphere that made her even more nervous as she patrolled – something that was undeniably and increasingly spooking her. *Maybe Brown was right*, she decided. *Now would be a good time to catch up on some paperwork in the safety and comfort of the office.*

She was about to turn for home when the unfamiliar sound of soft laughter mixed with the scampering of soft-soled shoes drifted up along the walkway from somewhere ahead of her. She clicked on the torch and shone it in the direction of the disturbance, but saw nothing. *Investigate or head back to the nick?* She couldn't help herself, moving forwards with the dangerous curiosity of a cat. When she reached the place she was sure the sounds had come from she heard them again – only now they were coming from the rear of the block, close to the stairwell.

'Shit,' she cursed and took a deep breath to steady herself before heading to the back of the building – the beam of her torch assisting the weak overhead and wall lights as she hugged the edge of the building, trying not to expose herself to danger from all sides, moving closer to the source of the unusual disturbance. Again, as she thought she must be drawing close, she heard the sounds of mischievous, unpleasant laughter mixed with the sounds of light feet taking flight – like small mythical creatures come to torment and trick her.

Now the sounds drifted up from below. She shone her torch into the gloom, but saw nothing but shadows flickering on the walls as someone – something – moved quickly about the basement area where Renita knew the underground garages were. Few people used them any more, the darkness and the danger overriding their convenience. They'd long ago been taken over by the young criminals and drug users for their various vices, until the Unit had arrived and chased them away – at least, until now.

Renita decided it was time to call into Control using her PR. She pressed transmit and spoke, trying to sound as calm and precise as possible. Last thing she wanted was the reputation of being a flapper. 'Control, Control,' she called in before adding her shoulder number for identification, '274.' There was only a second's delay before she was answered.

'Control receiving – go ahead, 274.'

'I think some youths must have got into the underground garages underneath Tabard House,' she explained. 'I'm gonna go chuck 'em out before they start a fire and burn the whole block down.'

'All received, 274. Do you want some back-up before entering?'

She hesitated before answering. 'No,' she assured them. 'I'll be fine.'

'You sure?' Control asked.

'I'm sure,' she repeated, rolling her eyes at her own stubbornness.

'OK. We'll keep checking in with you. If you need assistance come straight back to us.'

'Thanks,' she replied and released the transmit button, returning the daunting, eerie silence. 'Some job this is,' she said out loud, trying to bolster her courage as she began to descend into the blue-black darkness below – the light from her torch a cone of comfort as she swept the stairs beneath her, heading lower and lower until she took the final step into the underground cavern.

She walked into the middle of what used to be the access road and turned a full circle as she took in her surroundings. Broken garage doors hanging on their hinges. A few burnt-out shells of long-ago abandoned stolen cars. Piles of rubbish in every unused slot and the remains of dozens of small fires quickly extinguished and left by the local fire brigade, bored of being dragged back and forth to the estate. The clawing stench of the rotting waste and old smoke mixed putridly with urine and human faeces left by bowels loosened by heroin and crack cocaine. She momentarily covered her mouth and nose against the stench before the familiar sound of a harpy's laugh snapped her head around to try and catch sight of whatever had led her into the bleak cave.

'Who's there?' she called out, trying to sound in control, but the tremble in her voice betrayed her and drew another laugh from the thing in the darkness. She shone her torch straight ahead and caught the flash of movement as something disappeared into one of the many garages. 'I'm a police officer,' she said loudly, managing to sound stronger as she headed towards the hiding figure. 'What you doing down here? Come on – come out.' But her commands were only met with more giggling. 'Kids,' she said to herself, feeling more relaxed now she suspected she knew what she was dealing with.

She moved quickly and confidently now, her footsteps making audible splashes in the water that seemed to cover the entire floor, until she reached the garage housing the bait that had drawn her in and shone her torch inside.

'I think we'd better have . . .' was all she managed to say before she saw who she was looking at. Lucas Dyson and Robbie Jones. Two of the estate's most loathsome and feared teenagers. Too late she realized it was a trap and tried to spin away, but Ronnie Butler was already on her from behind, covering her mouth with a strong hand as his other arm wrapped around her chest and pulled her close and tight. Dyson and Jones inched towards them like hyenas moving in on a lion's kill – their teeth glistening in the light of her dropped torch. Within seconds they all had hold of her – ripping away her radio and utility belt before Butler tore her blouse open, exposing her chest that heaved in and out as she failed to control her fear and her breathing – the distorted faces in the semi-darkness growing increasingly lascivious and wild-eyed at the prospect of what was to come. Butler began to yank at her bra as he spoke into her ear – his breath made foul by stale cigarettes and cheap booze.

'You think you run this estate,' he hissed at her as the others grinned and giggled insanely, their excitement almost out of control. 'I'll show you who runs this estate, you pig bitch. Time to have some fun. You ready to have some fun, pig? You want to have some fun, you slag bitch?' Butler paused for a second as he looked at his two demonic partners – their frenzy encouraging him to do whatever his evil, twisted imagination could think of. 'Yeah, course you do,' he whispered. 'I can see it in your eyes.'

The young girl stood alone in the middle of the completely white room as long bleached curtains blew wildly towards her – the only colour provided by the wooden floor and the crimson that spread across her white lace dress like ink on blotting paper – only faster. King stood rooted in the corner, unable to move forward or to flee as she stared at him with startling blue eyes – like crystals in the rain. They watched each other for what seemed like forever until finally she raised an arm and pointed towards him. Her mouth opened and closed, but no sound came out.

He found strength in places deep inside his soul and slowly, as if he was moving through drying cement, began to cross the room towards her, falling on his knees once he eventually reached her, trying to hear what she was saying, but it was no good. He pressed his hands onto her chest and belly to try and stop the flow of the crimson, but it just leaked between his fingers and ran down his forearms. He began to sob, pleading with her for forgiveness as he did so.

'I'm sorry,' he begged her. 'I'm so sorry.' She looked down on him and smiled a childish smile – warm, sympathetic and forgiving as she cradled his head in her arms and held him pressed against her abdomen, her blood smearing his face and mixing with his tears as the sound of the breeze from the windows was suddenly, startlingly, replaced by a scream that couldn't have been made by anything from this earth.

He looked up at the girl, expecting to see her mouth wide open as she emitted the terrible noise, but her lips were sealed, although her hand was now raised, pointing at a door behind them he'd not noticed before – the sound of heavy, fast footsteps approaching, bringing danger. He fumbled at his utility belt, but found all his equipment missing. He spun to face the door regardless, ready to defend the girl with his hands, feet – teeth if he had to – but as the door exploded and splintered into a million pieces he realized it was hopeless. A huge creature, part man, part serpent, part dragon, extended to its full height in front of him – baring its rows of long, razor-sharp teeth as it grinned and advanced towards them. King stood in front of the girl and spread his arms wide in a token offer of protection as he stared into the face of the advancing beast, his eyes squinting as slowly, surely, he began to recognize the distorted face of the monstrous being – the girl's father, come to tear them both apart.

As the beast was almost upon them King turned and snatched up the girl, holding her tight in his arms. 'Close your eyes,' he told her. 'Don't look and everything will be all right,' he lied.

He waited until he was sure her eyes were squeezed shut before looking once more into her father's demonic eyes as he opened his terrible jaws and lurched towards them. King now closed his own eyes, relieved it was almost over, and prepared to be ripped limb from limb . . . but the dreadful pain never came, instead just a far and distant sound – an electric sound imitating music. Slowly his eyes blinked open as he squinted, preparing to protect himself from the brightness of the room and the great man-serpent, but he found nothing but darkness and the distant noise growing ever closer and louder.

'Fuck,' he cursed as he tried to chase the last lingering traces of the nightmare away – patting his bedside cabinet in search of his mobile phone that chirped somewhere in the darkness. Finding it, he slid his finger across the screen to answer. 'Hello,' he said, sounding alert and awake – shocked into consciousness by the awfulness of the nightmare and the shrill of the mobile.

'Sergeant King?' the formal-sounding voice asked – the unmistakable noises of a police control room in the background.

King's mind raced as he tried to work out what the hell was going on. 'Yeah. This is Jack King.'

'It's Inspector Dhawan,' the voice told him. 'Night Duty Officer. I have some bad news about one of your team, I'm afraid.'

King still struggled to clear his mind. 'Go on.'

'PC Renita Mahajan was seriously injured on the Grove Park Estate tonight,' Dhawan told him.

King's heart momentarily stopped, bringing a deafening silence inside his head. 'How bad?' he managed to ask.

'She's been taken to the Royal London Hospital, Whitechapel,' Dhawan explained. 'She's still in critical care in A&E. Her injuries are very serious, but hopefully not life-threatening.'

'What happened?'

'Not completely sure yet,' Dhawan admitted. 'We know she was attacked in the garages under Tabard House. We already have two in custody.'

'Who?' King demanded, wide awake now.

'Probably best you liaise with CID for those sorts of details,' Dhawan advised. 'Why don't you catch up with them first thing in the morning?'

'No,' King insisted, already out of bed and searching for his clothes. 'I'm on my way to the hospital now.' He hung up before Dhawan could speak again. As he hurriedly pulled his jeans on he suddenly stopped and sat back on the bed taking a moment to think. 'Shit, Renita,' he whispered. 'What the fuck did you get yourself involved in? What the fuck?'

172

'What's going on?' he heard a voice on the other side of the bed ask. Sara was awake.

'Nothing,' he lied. 'I need to go into work. I'll explain tomorrow. Go back to sleep.'

King arrived at the Royal London Hospital's A&E just as the first sign of morning summer sun was rising over the city. He flashed his warrant card to anyone who looked like they were about to challenge him as he searched for Renita's cubicle without asking for help. He recognized two young uniformed constables from Newham Police Station and correctly assumed the curtained cubicle they were guarding contained Renita. He was sure they knew him, but they stepped in front of him to bar his entry anyway – although they looked sheepish in doing so.

'I'm PC Mahajan's supervising officer,' he told them. 'I need to see her.'

'She's with the CID at the moment,' the male officer tried to explain. 'Perhaps it's best you give it a few minutes.'

King was about to tear a strip off him when he heard a familiar voice from behind the curtain speak. 'It's all right,' Marino called out. 'Let him in.' They stepped aside and let him past – King's threatening eyes never leaving the young constables.

Once inside he looked straight past Marino to Renita lying unconscious on the bed, oxygen tubes snaking into her nose and an intravenous drip feeding fluids and drugs into her arm. Her facial injuries alone both shocked and repulsed him. Her lips were severely split in several places; her nose and at least one cheekbone broken and both eyes were already swollen shut and turning purple. The rest of her face was covered in small cuts and bruises and he could tell parts of her hair were still matted with blood.

'Fuck,' he cursed as he stepped closer, the anger and fury swelling with each second that passed. Once he was close enough to touch her he could see the beginnings of bruising around her neck where she'd been held in a stranglehold. He reached out to stroke her shoulder before Marino stopped him. 'Try not to touch her,' he told him. 'She's not been forensically examined yet.'

King nodded without looking away from her. 'How come you're here?' he asked.

'Night Duty CID called me,' he explained. 'I'm covering for the DI, so when this happened . . .' He stopped, as if he didn't need to spell it out. 'She's a good girl and a good cop,' he continued. 'Only seemed right to come and see her for myself.'

King just nodded. 'How's she doing?'

'They think she's going to be OK,' Marino assured him. 'They're still in and out of here every few minutes, but the major panic seems to be over. It's going to take her a while though,' he sighed. 'The cuts and broken bones will take a few months, but the other stuff . . .' King knew exactly what he meant.

'Was she . . .' He struggled to say the word.

'No,' Marino quickly answered. 'We don't think it went that far. But she was naked when they found her. Her torn-up uniform was found close by, along with the rest of her equipment.'

'Fuck,' King cursed again as he swallowed the rising nausea back down – the thought of some foul basement-dwelling sex offender touching her making him feel sick to his core. 'The Night Duty Inspector said you already had two in custody?'

'We do,' Marino answered. 'Renita was smart enough to call in where and what she was doing. When they couldn't get her on the PR they sent the troops to find her. Our suspects were still having their . . . *fun* when the first units on scene sneaked up on them and caught them in the act – although one still managed to get away in the confusion that followed. It's pretty dark down there.'

'Who?' King demanded.

'The two arrested?' Marino clarified. King just nodded. 'Lucas Dyson and Robbie Jones.'

King looked confused. 'Dyson and Jones?' he checked. 'This isn't their form. What the hell were they thinking? They're lazy, vicious parasites with their tin-pot protection racket, but this?'

'Probably not thinking at all,' Marino explained. 'They were pissed and stoned when the uniforms brought them in. Didn't even hide their faces or wear gloves . . . or condoms for that matter. If it had gone any further they would have left us a DNA goldmine. Probably already have.' He registered the look of distaste on King's face. 'Sorry,' he apologized.

'And if it was Dyson and Jones it doesn't take a genius to work out the one who got away was Ronnie Butler,' King told him. 'Where one goes they all go.'

'Probably,' Marino agreed, 'but the troops who were on scene can't . . . won't swear to it.'

'Pricks,' he complained. 'By-the-book pricks.'

'Like I said,' Marino reminded him, 'it's dark down there.'

'Yeah,' King said, without sounding like he accepted it. 'I suppose it must have been.'

Marino could hear the vengeance in his voice. 'Don't get any stupid ideas,' he warned King. 'We'll catch up with Butler and—'

'And what?' King cut him dead. 'You'll charge him with assault and maybe he'll get convicted and maybe he won't. You said it yourself – *it was dark down there.*'

'There'll be other evidence. Forensics for one.'

'So he gets convicted, so what?' King raised his voice. 'And gets two, maybe three years in a young offenders institution. Out in eighteen months – bragging to his lowlife friends about what he did to a cop.'

'Our job's to catch them,' Marino reminded him. 'Not to decide on their punishment.'

'But she's one of our own,' King snarled.

'You've got to put it out of your mind, son,' Marino warned him, getting to his feet. 'Right now, our job is to find him. Use your sources on the estate to find out what you can. I'll give you a minute alone,' he finished and walked quietly from the fabric cubicle.

Once King was as sure as he could be that they were alone he leaned in close to Renita – his lips so close to her ear that he could feel her hair touching his lips. 'Who did this to you?' he whispered, but she remained still, her peaceful breathing the only movement. 'Renita,' he tried again. As sure as he was that it was Butler, he needed to be certain before he unleashed his justice – his revenge. 'Tell me who did this to you. Tell me who did it and I'll make them pay. I'll make them suffer more than they could ever imagine.'

Her eyes fired open without warning and her body started to convulse as she remembered what had happened – unsure if she was still trapped in the underground garages with her rancid, verminous attackers, their fingers clawing at her clothes and skin as they fumbled at the strings of their own tracksuit trousers. She raised her hands to fend off the assailants only she could see, threatening to pull the drip from her arm and the tubes from her nose.

'Take it easy,' King whispered, putting his hands on her shoulders and easing her back onto the pillow. 'Take it easy. It's me – Jack.' She seemed to relax a little at the sound of his voice, but he could still see the panic in her face. 'You're all right now, Renita. You're in hospital. You're safe.' Still she looked terrified and confused, her entire body trembling as she tried to part her cracked and bloodied lips. 'Wait a second,' he told her as he picked up the beaker of water next to her and tipped some through the straw and onto her lips, breaking the glue of blood. After a few seconds she was able to open her mouth slightly and speak almost inaudibly. It was little more than a rasp, but with his ear so close to her lips he could just about hear what she was saying.

'I can't see,' she was barely able to say.

King swallowed hard before answering – her pain and suffering seeping deep inside him, stoking his fury for revenge. 'Your eyes are badly swollen,' he told her, looking away for a second to compose himself. 'When the swelling goes down you should be able to see again.' She managed the faintest of nods to let him know she understood. King looked around the cubicle to ensure they were still alone. 'Listen,' he hissed in her ear. 'We already got two of them. Dyson and Jones.' Her breathing instantly became more frantic and irregular at the sound of their names. He gave her a few seconds to calm down before continuing – once again quickly glancing over his shoulder at the empty room. 'But there was another, right? Who was the other?' he asked, but she couldn't seem to answer. 'Who was the other, Renita?' he asked more urgently – desperately. 'I have to hear you say it.'

Her lips parted just enough for the words to escape. 'Butler,' she told him in the weakest of voices. 'Ronnie Butler.'

'Good,' he told her, nodding his head as he watched her drift back into unconsciousness. 'Good.' He straightened and stood staring at her for a while before leaving the cubicle, only briefly stopping to tell her uniformed guards she was asleep now and not to be disturbed by anyone but the medical staff. Once he'd made his way outside to the ambulance bays he pulled out his mobile and speed-dialled O'Neil's number. Addicts like O'Neil didn't live by the time routines of normal people and King knew he was just as likely to be awake as in a crack- or heroin-fuelled stupor. After a long while his call was finally answered by an alert-sounding voice. King wondered what he'd disturbed.

'Hello.'

'It's me,' King told him. 'You recognize my voice?'

'Yeah,' O'Neil assured him. 'It's—'

'Don't say my name,' King silenced him. 'Just say if you recognize my voice.'

'Yeah,' O'Neil replied, 'I recognize your voice. What d'you want? What fucking time is it anyway?'

'Information,' King kept him on mission.

'About what?' O'Neil nervously asked.

'Ronnie Butler,' King said. 'Where is he?'

There was a pause before O'Neil answered. 'This something to do with what happened to that lady copper?'

'You know something?' King pressed.

'I heard something bad happened to her,' O'Neil admitted. 'Word spreads fast when bad shit like that happens.'

'Butler?' King reminded him. 'Where is he?'

'He'll be where he always goes when he's trying to keep his head down,' O'Neil explained. 'Flopped down at Tanya Murphy's – an old girlfriend of his.'

'Address?'

'17 Clifford House – on the Grove Wood.'

King hung up without another word. He needed to wake the Unit.

Ronnie Butler was in a deep, peaceful sleep – the consequences of his actions the night before not making even the slightest scratch on his conscience as he dreamed of money and power, twitching with pleasure as his dream became increasingly debauched – like a cat dreaming of hunting. A second later his fantasy was destroyed as the solid door of the fifth-floor flat exploded inwards and the heavy feet of men came running across towards him.

Instinctively he was wide awake and rolling out of the squalid bed he shared with Tanya Murphy and grabbing the baseball bat he always kept close to hand. He sprang to his feet just in time to see the three uniformed cops come running towards him across the bedroom. He pulled the bat back to take a swing at the first of them, but Williams was too

178

fast – catching him flush on the chin with the punch from a gloved fist, knocking Butler back onto the bed where he landed on top of Murphy, who was by now screaming, clutching the filthy sheet to hide her pale nakedness.

Before Butler could recover, King lifted him from the bed, slammed him into the nearest wall and punched him hard in the solar plexus – forcing every inch of air from his body with one strike before stepping back and watching him slide down the wall to the floor. King turned to Murphy who'd fallen silent as she watched the scene unfolding before her frightened and confused eyes.

'Get out,' he ordered. She looked to the others for support but they gave her none. 'Get out,' King repeated, louder this time, sending her fleeing from the room with the sheet she clung to trailing like a royal wedding dress.

'You don't scare me,' Butler panted. 'Arrest me. See if I give a fuck. I hear it was dark in the garages. Difficult to make a positive ID.'

'You're probably right,' King agreed, 'but there'll be more than that. Forensics. DNA. Fingerprints. You and your *boys* weren't exactly careful.'

'Yeah and?' Butler shrugged – smiling now despite the pain. 'So what? That pig bitch has been begging for it since she came here. What's the matter?' he asked. 'Didn't you know? Yeah, man, she's a proper dirty whore. Begged us to fuck her – all three of us together, dirty bitch.'

'Just keep talking, Butler,' King encouraged him. 'It'll just make it all the sweeter.'

'Make what all the sweeter?' Butler smiled. 'You think I'm worried about being arrested by you – just because you've got half the estate running scared? Fuck you. Go on – arrest me.'

'Arrest,' King replied, faking a confused look. 'Who said anything about arresting you? We're here to make you pay, Butler. *Really* pay.'

179

The smile slipped from Butler's face as he watched King and Williams adjusting their leather gloves. 'What you talking about? You gotta arrest me.'

'You thought what you did to her sent us a message?' King asked, moving ever closer to Butler as he picked himself off the floor. 'Well, this is how we deliver a message.'

Butler tried to duck the punch, but it was too fast and too accurate, catching him on the cheekbone and sending him spinning, although he kept his feet. 'Wait,' he managed to plead, a split second before King's other fist piled into his nose, fracturing the bone instantly and sending a thick spray of blood flying across the room.

Butler didn't speak again as King and Williams punched and kicked him to the ground and took it in turns to brutally beat him, hitting almost every inch on his body – the only sounds he made small, pathetic whimpering pleas until he could barely even manage that. Only when the fog of hate and revenge began to clear did King realize that Brown wasn't joining in and stop the savage assault. He took a few seconds to get his breath back before he could speak. 'Don't you want some of this?' he asked the pale-looking Brown.

'He's had enough,' Brown told him. 'Let's just arrest him and get him out of here – get our stories straight on how he got his injuries, although fuck knows how we're gonna do that.'

'Arrest him?' King almost laughed. 'Weren't you listening? I said we're not here to arrest him so some court can give him a slap on the wrist. We're here for *justice*. Justice for Renita.'

'Fuck's sake,' Brown said, looking sick. 'What is this?'

'You heard him,' King answered, moving close to Brown. 'Heard what this slag said about her. He needs to fucking pay.'

'He's paid,' Brown raised his voice. 'Enough's enough.'

'What?' King snapped back. 'You know what they did to her.'

'I know,' Brown reminded him.

'For all we know they could have raped her.'

'That's not what the CID are saying,' Brown argued.

'They know fuck all,' King insisted, 'and even if they did they wouldn't tell us. This is for Renita, Davey. This is for all of us. We don't do this and every slag out there will consider us fair game. The war will be lost.'

'Fuck's sake,' Brown said again, but King could sense a weakening.

'How you gonna feel when you have to look in Renita's eyes knowing you did nothing?' King kept at him. 'That you *bottled* it.'

'I'm not bottling anything,' Brown fought back.

'Then make him pay,' King demanded. 'Leave your mark.'

'Jesus,' Brown shook his head.

'You're either with us or against us,' King told him – his eyes wide with anticipation as Brown began to move to the still unmoving Butler. 'Do it, Davey. Do it.'

'Fuck,' Brown cursed as he half-heartedly kicked Butler in the ribs, making him whimper slightly.

'Again,' King encouraged. 'They were probably going to kill her. They didn't hide their faces, remember? Because they weren't going to leave a live witness to identify them. Now again.' Brown did as he was told and kicked out again – harder this time. 'Again,' King barked. 'Harder.' Brown did as he was told. 'Again,' King cheered as Brown increased the rate and intensity of his blows. 'Good,' King sneered and joined in the beating as Williams stepped back and left them to it – Butler's body rocking with every new kick to his body and head.

Finally, through tiredness as much as anything, King stopped his assault and pulled Brown away from the bleeding, swollen wreck that Butler now was. 'That's enough,' he panted. 'Don't want to kill the fucker.' Brown turned away from the body on the floor and looked as if he was going to be sick. 'Danny,' King said. 'Get me some water from the kitchen.'

'Excuse me?' Williams asked.

'Just do it,' King demanded. 'A bottle, a glass – it doesn't matter.' Williams pulled a face and headed off as King used his foot to roll Butler onto his side before squatting next to him to make sure he was still alive. Brown realized what he was doing.

'Jesus Christ,' he pleaded. 'Don't tell me the bastard's dead.'

'Course he's not,' King assured him. 'You know what these fuckers are like. Bastards are almost impossible to kill.'

Williams re-entered the room carrying an old pint glass filled with water. 'You really going to drink this?' he asked, pulling a face of disgust.

'It's not to drink, you muppet,' King explained. 'Give it here,' he told him and took the glass. He stood directly over Butler's head and tipped the contents on his face, bringing him back to life as if he'd been electrocuted – his eyes firing open back into his nightmare as his back arched impossibly – slumping still again once his brain told his body he was too badly hurt to move, though his swollen eyes somehow managed to stay open.

King leaned in as close to his face as he could bear before speaking. 'Sooner or later the CID are gonna catch up with you. They're gonna want to know what happened to you. You mention our names, it's going to be bad for you. You tell anyone it was us I'll put you in a shallow grave. Understand?' Butler somehow managed to nod that he understood before his eyes rolled back into his head and he passed out – blood still streaming from his mouth, nose and ears. King straightened and gave him one last stamp on the side of the head before spitting on him. 'Cunt,' was all he said as he headed for the door, the others following behind him, forever tied to him. Now they were inextricably in it together. They were truly King's men.

* * *

182

Only a few minutes later they'd made it safely across the estate to the basement area underneath Millander Walk where days before King and Renita had discovered the children preparing a joint. Now the three of them walked the main area of the underground room looking deflated and tired – the hate and anger all spent and left in a bloody mess on the floor of Butler's hideaway flat. Once they reached the open space King turned on a couple of electric lamps – the kind used for camping. In the eerie light they could see that King had already been busy preparing things.

'Get your shirts and gloves off,' he told them, already unbuttoning his own, 'and put them in the bin liner – epaulettes as well. Use these to wash the blood off yourselves,' he instructed them pointing to a tray of plastic water bottles, 'and then put the empty bottles in the bin liner as well.'

They all did as King had planned, pouring water over their hands and forearms until they were clean enough to use their hands to wash the blood sprays from their faces. Finally they all stood bare-chested in the semi-darkness.

'Jesus Christ,' Brown told them, shaking his head as he looked at himself and his co-conspirators shining with wetness in what light there was. 'What the fuck have we done?'

'What we had to,' King assured him.

'Had to?' Brown said. 'We didn't have to do this.'

'Yes we did,' King snapped at him a little. 'What they did to Renita was a challenge. It was them letting us know everything's changed. No one's playing by the rules any more. We had to hit back.'

'We went too far,' Brown fought back.

'Jesus,' King reprimanded him. 'Listen to yourself. Right from the beginning you've been saying we need to take the gloves off – fuck the rules. *The slags don't have rules*, remember? Well now we are. There was no guarantee Butler would have gone down for what he did to Renita. Now he's had justice. We didn't leave it to chance. Didn't leave it to some wanker in the CPS playing God.' None of them spoke for a long time as they looked everywhere but at each other.

'Now what?' Williams finally asked.

King took a few steps before returning with a sports bag. He unzipped it and tossed them each a white police shirt. 'Wear these for now,' he told them. 'Get back to the nick and grab whatever you need, then head straight home. Try not to stop to talk to anyone.'

'What you going to do with our shirts and gloves?' Brown asked.

'Burn them,' King answered abruptly, 'and any forensic evidence along with them.'

'What about our trousers?' Williams asked. 'What about our shoes?'

'They're passable for now,' King explained. 'Blood's hard to see on a black background. But take them home and wash the shit out of them and wash the shit out of these new shirts too and scrub your shoes. Then take a very long, very hot shower. Use all the soap you've got, then take all the clothing and shoes to a charity clothes bin far from your homes and dump everything in it.'

'That's why you told us not to wear our body armour and kitbelts,' Brown caught on. 'Because we couldn't just chuck 'em. Not to mention it'd be impossible to completely destroy any forensics.'

'Got to be one step ahead all the time,' King answered. 'If the shit ever hits the fan, first thing CID will do is seize and examine our kit and it'll come up clean and so will we. Now split up and get home. I'll wait here to give you a few minutes' head start.' Williams and Brown finished pulling on their clean shirts and started to make for the exit until King stopped them with his words. 'And remember,' he told them. 'We're all in this together now. There's no turning back. Together they can't touch us, but if one of us talks we'll all go down. Butler's not worth going to prison for. He got what he deserved. No one's going to cry for him. Butler won't talk to the CID, but he'll talk to people on the estate and once he does – no one will fuck with us.'

King stood for a long time in the shower, the steaming hot water almost more than he could bear as he scrubbed his skin and nails over and over again, washed his hair over and over again to remove any last, lingering traces of Butler. He'd already put his clothes through the most intensive cycle in the washing machine and had thoroughly cleaned his shoes too before placing them in separate bin liners and driving to a supermarket car park miles away where he dumped the lot in different clothes for charity containers. When he returned home he sprayed and wiped the driver's area of his car with disinfectant spray – burning the paper towels he used in his sink before heading to the shower to finish the process of destroying any forensic evidence that could link him to the crime. Even if they were able to find some minute traces of Butler's DNA or something belonging to Butler on him, it could easily be explained. He'd been in physical contact with Renita at the hospital and she would undoubtedly have traces of her attackers on her body – they must have been transferred from her to him. No forensic evidence against him would stand up under scrutiny.

After the shower he wrapped a towel around his waist and headed for the kitchen, hoping his mood would change, but the familiar sight of another pile of unpaid bills on the table only darkened his outlook.

'That's all I need,' he complained, pushing the unopened letters to one side, feeling disgusted by their mere presence. He had thought taking revenge on Butler would feel good – exhilarating – but he just felt numb and a little sick. He felt remorse and guilt, even fear, although he was confident he'd never be linked to the crime, but still he wanted the images of him and the others beating Butler out of his head, especially since they'd started mixing with older, more painful memories of the slaughtered family and the girl he'd managed to save from her own marauding father – all the beatings and the blood combining in one ugly kaleidoscope in his haunted mind.

'Christ,' he told himself before his head sank into his open hands. Instantly the memories of assaulting Butler intensified, making him sit bolt upright as he stared down at his reddened knuckles where the bruising was beginning to develop. 'Christ,' he pleaded again. 'What have I done? What the fuck have I done?' He leapt up from the table and began to pace around the room, unable to settle. 'Never again,' he promised himself. 'Never again. Jesus Christ, what's wrong with me? What's wrong with me?'

He waited for an answer, but when none came he took a beer from the fridge and drank it quickly. It had little to no effect, so he grabbed another, but while he was drinking it he remembered the cannabis resin he'd taken from Tyrone Mooney and hidden in one of the kitchen drawers with some of the tobacco and cigarette papers he and Renita had taken from the children in the basement. He was sure that Sara wasn't due home for a few hours yet so went to retrieve it – and found to his consternation it had all gone. He knew he'd used some of it before, but couldn't for the life of him remember using it all.

As the realization dawned on him that he wouldn't be able to use cannabis to numb his mind and body, the pain in his head and back seemed to intensify. He needed something. For a moment he considered using stronger drink before suddenly remembering something far more potentially powerful and effective. He headed for the cupboard under the sink, opened the door and dropped to his knees, fishing behind the outlet pipe until he touched what he was looking for. He carefully peeled away the Sellotape holding the plastic bag to the pipe. Back at the kitchen table, he examined the contents of the small clip-seal bag, touching them with his index finger as if they were alive. Eventually he took one of the rocks of crack from the bag, removed it from its tiny clingfilm jacket and held it up to the light between his fingers.

How could such a small, innocuous-looking thing cause so much misery, and yet also give much untamed joy to those who chose to use it? He remembered O'Neil's words – how he'd said it was *the best thing in the world. Better than anything.* 'Really?' he asked, as if O'Neil could answer. *Best thing in the world. Better than anything.* If he ever needed something like that it was now. He was no scumbag crack-head. He could handle it – just once. Just to find out for himself.

Getting to his feet, he began to search the kitchen as he tried to remember what O'Neil had told him about building a homemade crack bong. He found a small plastic water bottle easily enough in the shopping bag they used for recycling. He removed the innards from a cheap plastic pen, testing he could inhale through it well enough, which he could. *What else did he need?* He remembered and took some tinfoil from one cupboard, an elastic band and pin from another. He took a small sharp knife and cut two holes high in the bottle just as O'Neil had described, putting the pen through one and sealing it with Blu-tack, leaving the other unobstructed. He stared at the foil, pin and elastic band until O'Neil's words came back to him and he carefully poked a small piece of the foil into the top of the bottle, making a cradle for the crack, and secured it with the band before using the pin to punch a dozen tiny holes into it to allow the smoke to be drawn into the bottle. Too late he realized he should have put some water in the bottle before covering the top with foil, but he managed to carefully pour a couple of inches in through the blow-hole.

Once he was happy with his construction he almost ceremoniously placed the small crack rock into its tinfoil cradle and prepared to light it – stalling a few seconds to calm his breathing and to consider O'Neil's words one more time. *It's the best thing in the world. Better than anything.* Suddenly fear began to replace the excitement. *What if it really was the best thing in the world? Would his life become nothing more than the never-ending search for the next hit? Would he stop washing – eating? Would he start wearing the same filthy clothes day after day as his hair became a tangled mess and his fingernails filthy talons, his lips like cracked, bleeding reptilian scales, his teeth rotting black as they fell from pulped gums as he abandoned everything he once loved to worship at the altar of crack cocaine? Would he even become a common criminal, stealing from anybody and everybody in search of enough petty cash to buy a rock big enough to blow away reality and return him to crack-head paradise – even if it was only for a couple of hours?*

He looked at the lighter in his hand and the bong on the table and came close to dismantling it, before memories of Butler's beating again swarmed into his mind and mixed with the image of the girls in white. The pain returned to his back and shoulder mercilessly and without warning.

'Fuck it,' he told the world. He placed his lips around the hollow pen and carefully lit the crack. Almost instantly he saw thick grey-white smoke drifting from the melting rock – its sweet, acrid smell filling the air around him and making him feel immediately dizzy, reminding him to inhale through the pen-pipe.

As he took the cool smoke, the water having done its job, deeply and smoothly into his lungs, the effect was immediate. Firstly he felt more lightheaded than he'd ever done in his life, before the stronger feeling took over: a feeling of almost weightlessness and excruciating relief as all his mental anguish left him along with all physical pain and the warm blanket of nothingness washed over his mind and body. All he could hear was the peaceful, soft beat of his own heart as he was surrounded by a calmness and safety he'd not felt since he'd been a small child. He could never have imagined it was possible to feel this *good*. But it wasn't like drunkenness or dreaming; it was *real*. Everything he was feeling and seeing was *real*. He wasn't on some kind of hallucinating acid trip. He knew exactly who he was and where he was – even what he was – but suddenly everything was *perfect* beyond imagination.

Through the haze of paradise he remembered the still smoking bong and took another hit on the pen turned pipe, flooding his lungs with more ecstasy-bringing toxins that flew around his body and into his brain. He sighed with the absolute pleasure of the effects and closed his eyes so he could more quickly sink into this new painless, stress-free world of delights. For the first time since the *incident* he felt free from agony and anguish. He felt *good*. Without realizing it he began to hum O'Neil's words like a mantra. 'Best thing in the world. Best thing ever.'

11

Sara weaved her way through the corridors of Newham Police Station heading for the canteen, lost in her own world. She was wondering how she could teach shiny new probationary constables to survive the streets of the East End borough, when she was still learning to survive them herself, when a voice she barely recognized broke through to her.

'Sara,' Marino spoke as he drew level with her.

She looked at him a little suspiciously – it was unusual for a detective sergeant to seek out a relatively inexperienced constable. 'Sarge.'

'Just call me Frank. Where you heading?' Marino asked with a friendly smile.

'Canteen,' she told him as she kept walking. 'Can I help you with something?'

'Canteen?' He ignored her question.

'I need a coffee,' she told him. 'Before I take a new probationer out for the first time. Caffeine's the only way I can keep up with them.'

'That's a lot of responsibility,' he replied. 'I was heading that way myself. Do you mind if I buy?'

'No,' she answered a bit nervously. 'On my wage you never look a gift horse in the mouth.'

'It gets better,' Marino assured her.

'If you get promoted,' she smiled, 'or join the CID.'

'Well,' he told her, 'you're getting a decent reputation as a thief-taker. Why not put in for the Crime Squad? Guaranteed overtime and plenty of it.'

'Maybe,' she shrugged.

They walked in silence for a few seconds before Marino spoke again. 'You and Jack still together?'

She gave him a sideways glance. 'You're not hitting on me, are you?'

'What?' Marino answered, the surprise thick in his voice. 'No. No.'

'What then?' Sara asked. 'Why you talking to me? Why do you want to know if I'm still with Jack?'

Marino sighed a little before continuing. 'OK. Fair enough. Jack's a good man, we both know that, but I'm a little worried about him, you know.'

'In what way?' she asked without breaking stride or looking at him.

'Just a little concerned he went back to full duties too soon,' he told her. 'Was wondering what he's been like away from work.'

'I don't know,' she accidentally admitted. 'I mean he's been fine . . . sort of. To be honest, I haven't seen much of him. We've both been putting in a lot of hours, you know.'

They pushed through the double doors that led into the canteen and joined the small line for service. 'Christ,' Sara complained. 'Why's there always a bloody queue?'

'But you think he's OK?' Marino persisted.

'Look,' she told him. 'I love Jack, but I've got my own life. My own career and my own worries. It can't always just be about Jack. I'm trying to make it work – help him, but he's got to let me. He's got to help himself too. I can't do it all. I don't know. This Unit seems to be taking him over. That bloody estate's all that seems to matter to him. He's becoming obsessed.'

'And home? How's his behaviour at home?' Marino asked.

'He's fine,' Sara answered, unaware she was shaking her head at the same time.

'Really?' Marino continued. 'I'm surprised. So this . . . change in him is only at work then?'

Sara sighed before speaking, betraying herself. 'He's still Jack,' she insisted, 'but he's just not quite the same Jack. He's so anxious all the time. He never used to get anxious. Never.'

'He went through a lot,' Marino reminded her.

'I know,' she said sadly, 'but funnily enough I'm not sure it was what happened that changed him. When he came out of hospital he was OK. Quiet, but OK. But since he's been on this Unit he's been . . . different.'

'A delayed reaction perhaps,' Marino suggested. 'The pressure of being back on the streets might have triggered something.'

'Maybe,' Sara partly agreed. 'Or the drugs.'

'Drugs?' Marino seized on it.

'He's still on the same prescription drugs for the pain,' she explained. 'He should have come off them months ago, but he just keeps picking up repeat prescriptions from the chemist.'

'You talked to him about it?'

'Of course,' she assured him. 'He just says he'll make an appointment with the GP, but he never does. I've tried to get him to see someone, you know. Someone to talk to, but he insists he's fine.'

'Two pounds fifty,' the woman behind the counter interrupted them. Marino scrambled in his pocket and handed over the change before taking both cups and heading for an empty table where he set them down and waited for Sara to sit before he followed suit. He sipped his drink and grimaced.

'It's better than the instant rubbish,' he told her, 'but it still ain't good.'

'I won't live my life through Jack,' she told him, ignoring the small talk. 'I got a career of my own to think about. So long as he helps himself, I'll be there to help him. But not if he shuts me out. I can't help him from the outside.'

'I understand,' Marino assured her. 'Just do what you can and I'll keep an eye on him at work. He's a good man, Sara. Just maybe lost his way a little.'

'I know,' she answered. 'Why do you think I'm still there?'

King entered their office at Canning Town Police Station the next morning to find Brown and Williams sitting around looking subdued and thoughtful. He guessed they must have felt largely as he did. The beating of Butler hadn't made him feel as satisfied and justified as he'd hoped. It had just left a sick, empty feeling. Brown was the first to look up.

'You look like shit,' was all he said.

'Feel like it too,' he admitted before turning to Williams. 'Go get us some coffees, will you,' he told him, pulling five pounds from pocket. 'Here – get the decent stuff. Not that instant shit.'

'If you're paying, I'm going,' Williams attempted to be cheerful, but failed. He took the cash and headed out the office, leaving King and Brown alone.

'You all right?' King asked.

'Yeah,' Brown told him and looked away – getting back to cleaning his kit. 'Fine.'

'I mean about what happened,' King continued.

'I know what you mean,' Brown snapped at him.

'Because you know what happens to cops who grass on their own,' King reminded him. 'They don't stay long in this job. No one will work with a cop they can't *trust*.'

'Like I said,' Brown now looked deep into his eyes, 'I'm fine. I'm solid. You don't have to worry about me.'

Good,' King nodded with satisfaction before Brown added something.

'It's just . . . It's just . . .' he tried to explain.

'Just what?' King pressed.

'Just we went too far,' he answered, lowering his voice. 'What we did to Butler went too far.'

King slumped in his chair and let out a heavy sigh. 'You're right,' he admitted, unsure if he believed it or not. 'Butler got to me. He's such scum he just got to me. What he did to Renita it threw me, you know. He broke all the rules of the game. Trying to rape and probably murder an on-duty police officer . . . fuck . . . I just wanted to make him pay. But perhaps we went too far.'

'We should have just given him a few choice digs to let him know and handed him over to the CID,' Brown argued. 'We could have said he resisted arrest. No one would have questioned a black eye, bloody nose and split lip. But after what we did to him . . . Burning clothes, dumping stuff in charity bins – fuck. I felt like a *criminal*. What we did was *criminal*.'

'Butler fucking deserved it,' King fought back before softening, trying to keep Brown on side, 'but you're right – it wasn't for us to do.' Brown nodded in agreement. 'Look,' King assured him. 'It won't happen again. I promise. Good enough?'

Now it was Brown's turn to sigh in resignation. 'OK,' he replied. 'Good enough, but me and Danny were talking. Reckon we've been on the bloody Grove Wood long enough. Time to get the hell out of there.'

'What you talking about?' King asked through a confused smile. 'We've practically just got there.'

'What?' Brown snapped back, but the appearance of Inspector Johnston at the doorway ended any further discussion. As always she addressed them from where she stood instead of stepping inside the office – as if it was somehow beneath her to enter such a small, chaotic room.

'Morning, gentlemen,' she began without receiving any

reply. 'Just wanted to drop by and let you know how sorry I was to hear about what happened to PC Mahajan. A terrible thing. A truly awful thing.'

'Yes, ma'am,' King answered. 'We're sorry too.'

'I called by yesterday – as soon as I heard – but none of you were about,' Johnston explained. 'I even tried to get hold of you on your PRs but . . .'

'We were out and about,' King interrupted her. 'Turning over a few stones trying to find out who the third suspect is. It involved a lot of sneaking around. Our radios would have been off or turned down most of the time.'

'I see,' Johnston smiled and nodded, her bright green eyes gleaming with intelligence. 'Well at least you don't have to worry about finding out who he is any more. CID already have him in custody.'

'Excuse me?' King asked, trying to hide the anxiety in his voice.

'That's right,' Johnston told him. 'He's already been arrested. Bit of a strange one actually. CID were already looking for him – apparently he is an associate of the other two suspects – when they got a call from A&E saying they had a badly beaten and injured youth in for treatment, but refusing to say what had happened to him. When CID went to take a look for themselves they found the injured youth was none other than their prime suspect for the attack on PC Mahajan. They arrested him there and then, but he's still in hospital receiving treatment. Apparently someone has kicked the living shit out of him.'

'How bad?' Brown couldn't help but ask.

'Not life-threatening,' Johnston told him, 'but beaten to a pulp, so I'm told.'

'Who?' King asked. 'Who did they arrest?'

'Ronnie Butler,' Johnston told him without hesitation. 'A well-known local slag.'

'Ronnie Butler,' King shook his head.

'I take it you know him then?'

'I know him,' King replied. 'And I know he runs with the other two. There was always a good chance it was going to be Butler.'

'Well it appears someone else came to the same conclusion,' Johnston said, looking more serious. 'Vigilantes, I'm being told. Gave him a hell of a beating by the sound of it. No more than the little bastard deserved, but vigilantes are never good news. Sort of thing the media love to beat us with.'

'If there's vigilantes on the estate we'll deal with them,' King lied. 'Enforcing the law is our job.'

'Indeed,' she agreed – her eyes flicking over them like a lizard's tongue. 'Anyway, just wanted to make sure you knew about the latest arrest. I have to be at an SMT meeting in half an hour so I'll bid you farewell.' King and Brown said nothing as Johnston turned to walk away before spinning back towards them. 'Oh and Jack – just a gentle reminder that your monthly report is overdue. Your team's racked up a fair bit of overtime lately. We on the SMT all appreciate the excellent work you're doing, but such expenditure needs to be justified. If you could let me have it ASAP I would be grateful.'

'Of course,' King told her.

'Excellent,' Johnston smiled, happy she'd asserted her authority, before disappearing into the corridor.

After a few seconds Brown spoke first. 'She fucking worries me. Give me some by-the-numbers, accelerated-promotion robot any day of the week. At least they're easy to control.'

'I can control her,' King reassured him. 'She's not as smart as she thinks she is.'

'Aye,' Brown half-heartedly agreed just as Marino appeared at the door.

'Gentlemen,' he greeted them.

'Another visitor,' King mimicked surprise as he hid his bruised hands in his pockets. 'We seem to be very popular this morning.'

Marino ignored King's fake lightheartedness and walked into the office, slowly pacing around – lifting files from desks, casting his eyes over them before dropping them back where he found them, talking as he prowled.

'Interesting thing happened this morning,' he explained. 'We got a call from the hospital saying they had a badly beaten youth in receiving treatment. When we went to take a look guess who we found?'

'Ronnie Butler,' King answered calmly. 'Inspector Johnston just told us.'

'Taken a right kicking,' Marino told them.

'No more than he deserves,' King tested the water.

'Maybe,' Marino played along. 'I was wondering if you boys might know anything about it?'

'Not yet,' King stayed in control. 'Sounds like vigilantes to me.'

'Vigilantes?' Marino shook his head. 'On the Grove Wood Estate? I don't think so.'

'Maybe they came in from somewhere else?' King suggested.

'But how would they know about what happened to Renita?' Marino asked.

'Word gets around,' King tried to convince him. 'Maybe even the locals thought what happened to Renita went too far. Maybe someone higher up the criminal chain decided Butler's actions were bringing too much police attention to the estate – bad for business. Maybe they wanted to send a message to the lowlifes.'

'Could be,' Marino nodded in unenthusiastic agreement. 'But strange thing is, I've dealt with Butler plenty of times in the past and he's never talked to us. Strictly a "no comment" man. But when I saw him at the hospital he couldn't wait to confess everything. He's already admitted attacking Renita and that it was his idea. It's as if the devil himself was after him. Never seen Butler scared like that.'

'Did he say anything about who did him?' Brown couldn't help asking, drawing a damning look from King.

'He's giving us some bullshit about it's an unrelated attack,' Marino explained. 'Says he got jumped by some blokes wearing ski masks, although he can't remember where and he can't think why. Maybe once he's recovered enough to be interviewed properly he'll be able to give us a few more details, or you never know – he might decide to actually tell us the truth.'

'So you don't think he's telling the truth about attacking Renita?' King questioned, trying to manoeuvre Marino onto the back foot.

'No,' Marino admitted. 'I've no doubts it was Butler.'

'Then that's all that really matters,' King said bluntly. 'And once you have his confession you can put him and the others away for a very long time. That's our job, after all, isn't it? To uphold the law and punish the offenders. Before anyone cries too much for Butler they should remember what he did to Renita – what he *was* going to do to her.'

'I haven't forgotten,' Marino assured him.

'Good,' King remained strong – in control. 'Then when you charge him make sure you do him for serious sexual assault and attempted rape – so everyone in prison knows he's a sex-case. See how long he lasts inside once the other inmates find out what he's in for.'

'He'll be charged with whatever I can prove,' Marino replied.

'You'll have enough to prove it,' King smiled. 'I have every confidence in you.'

'Glad to hear it,' Marino said without feeling. 'You boys be careful out there,' he told them, heading for the door. 'Watch out for yourselves. I'll see you around.'

They watched him leave and waited a long time before they believed it was safe to talk. 'Fuck it,' Brown cursed, panic thick in his voice. 'I told you that bastard knows something.'

198

'Calm down,' King told him through gritted teeth. 'And what the fuck were you doing asking him if Butler had said anything about who gave him a kicking? Why don't you just tell everyone it was us?'

'Sorry,' Brown hung his head. 'It's just all this shit's beginning to make my head spin.'

'Stop panicking,' King demanded. 'Marino knows nothing – not for sure. All he's got is guesses, and even if he did know, how can we be sure he'd do anything about it? Marino's old school. You don't think he hasn't given the occasional toe-rag a spanking in the past? Course he has. He knows the score.'

'Then why's he sniffing around like a drugs dog in a cannabis factory?' Brown wanted to know.

'You said it yourself,' King explained. 'We went a little too far.'

'A little?'

'Whatever,' King silenced him. 'This is probably just Marino telling us to calm it down a bit before someone less sympathetic starts taking an interest.'

'I fucking hope so,' Brown told him.

'We'll be fine,' King assured him. 'Just need to take it easy for a bit. Let this all blow over and then get back to normal. For now we keep the policing whiter than white till the heat dies down.'

'Fine,' Brown grunted.

'Hey,' King snapped him to attention. 'Stick together and everything will be fine. If one of us starts to wobble we'll all end up in prison with Butler.' Brown just nodded that he understood. 'Good,' King ended it, pulling on his body armour. 'I'm gonna take a walk on the estate. I need the air.'

King walked through the estate trying to get everything straight in his head. After smoking the crack he'd slept a long, peaceful, painless sleep, but when he'd awoken the old ghosts of the past immediately seized him, making him long to return to that *other world*. Somehow he'd managed to sort himself out and get to work, only to be confronted by first Johnston and then Marino. He'd fed Brown a few lines to keep him calm, but he wasn't sure he believed any of it himself. How much did Marino really know? Suddenly the sound of boisterous young voices somewhere close cut through his thoughts and drew him towards them. As he turned the corner into Millander Walk he saw a gathering of half-a-dozen or so twelve to thirteen year olds – boys and girls. He recognized most of them – decent enough kids who'd never given him any trouble, but today their noise and lively behaviour bothered him more than it usually would.

He strolled towards the group who quietened down as he approached, but still talked enthusiastically amongst themselves – gently jostling each other and showing off, untroubled by his presence.

'What you lot up to?' he asked.

'Nothing,' several of them answered together.

'This is a residential area,' he told them, 'and you're making too much noise.'

'It's the middle of the day,' one of the boys complained.

'What's that got to do with anything?' King questioned. 'Aren't you all supposed to be at school?'

'Holidays, innit,' another boy answered.

'Whatever,' King grunted – not interested in anything they had to say. 'You're making too much noise.'

'We ain't disturbing no one,' one of the girls joined in.

'I don't want you hanging around here,' he ignored her. 'People don't want you hanging around here disturbing them.'

'Where we supposed to go?' another girl asked.

'I don't know,' he told them more forcefully, 'and I don't care. Just so long as you're not here.'

'But we live round here,' a different boy explained.

'Just fuck off, right,' he exploded, silencing the children

who looked shocked and afraid. 'Just do as you're damn well told.'

The children looked from one to another before shuffling away along the walkway, watched all the way by King. Once they disappeared into a stairwell one of them called out. 'Prick.'

'Fuck,' King chastised himself for losing his temper over nothing and leant over the wall that allowed him to look out over a large part of the sprawling estate, wringing his hands together as he tried to gather his thoughts – the fear in the eyes of the children burning into his already troubled mind. 'Fuck,' he swore quietly again before suddenly sensing a presence behind him that made him spin round, ready to defend himself if he had to – only to see Kelly Royston standing in the open doorway of her maisonette watching him intensely with eyes like black pearls. He looked her up and down once, causing stabs of anticipation and desire all over his body, but he managed to turn away and continue his vigil over the estate – even though he could *feel* her coming to him. After a few long seconds she was at his side looking over the wall at first, but then turning and, watching him as he wrung his hands together, his knuckles marked with bruising caused by the bones in Butler's skull. He glanced sideways at her once – his heart tightening and fluttering in his chest as he was reminded of her raw beauty. She casually combed her long dark brown curls back from her face with her fingers before speaking through a slight but enticing smile.

'You should wear gloves,' she nodded towards his hands.

For a second he thought about hiding them in his pockets again, before realizing it was pointless. Her street intelligence matched her beauty and she probably knew everything already.

'No one's crying about Ronnie,' she told him straight, 'or his idiot friends. Ronnie's a thick bully who's upset pretty much everyone on the estate at one time or another. Fool thought he was some sort of top dog round here. Truth is he's too stupid and lazy to go thieving himself. Easier to just run his little protection racket – taking his cut from other people's earnings.'

'I don't know what you're talking about,' King lied, as he breathed in the scent of her shampoo and skin cream which smelt better than even the most expensive perfumes.

'You should be proud of what you did,' she told him, making him glance at her in surprise. 'It's what a lot of people wanted to do to him anyway – if they only had the bottle. And what they did to that lady copper – that was well out of order,' she shook her head. 'That broke all the rules. All the rules.'

'What d'you know about what happened to her?' he asked quietly.

'Enough,' she answered through lips coloured naturally like roses. 'I talked to her a couple of times,' she told him. 'She seemed really nice – for a copper. Didn't deserve what happened to her.'

'No,' he agreed. 'No she didn't.'

They were silent for a while as she seemed to study him. 'You're a bit young to be a sergeant, ain't you? What are you – some kind of superstar cop?'

He laughed despite himself. 'Yeah,' he joked. 'I suppose so.'

'Gonna be the Commissioner one day, eh?'

'Maybe,' he smiled and turned to face her.

'But right now you're stuck here,' she told him, 'like the rest of us.'

'I'm not stuck here,' he answered. 'I want to be here.'

'And when you leave,' she ignored his answer, 'things here will go back to the way they've always been. Shame. People like the way it is at the moment. People are beginning to feel it's safe to leave their homes without worrying about it being screwed while they're away.'

'Glad to hear it,' he played along.

'People round here respect a strong man,' she explained. 'Someone who can keep little slags like Butler in their place.' He didn't answer. 'Next thing you need to do is take care of this nonce who's messing with the little kids. People think the only reason he's not been caught is because you lot can't be bothered. That kids round here don't matter.'

'That's not true,' he told her. 'They matter to me. Catching him matters to me.'

'I believe you,' she smiled. 'Catch him and you'll have the respect of everyone on the estate. No matter how you do it. Know what I mean?'

'I'm working on it,' he assured her as they stood in silence for a long time.

'Why don't you come inside?' she surprised him with an invitation. 'You look like you could do with a drink.'

He looked into her black eyes that seemed to reflect his entire world, trying to ignore her gently rising and falling breasts. 'Is anyone else home?' he found himself asking.

'No,' she answered and smiled. 'No one else.'

He couldn't speak for a few seconds as a battle raged inside him.

'Come on,' she encouraged him. 'You afraid of something?'

'Fine,' he eventually answered. He followed her across the walkway as if being led to a magical kingdom hidden behind a secret door on an East London housing estate. Once inside she closed it behind them. 'You should probably leave that open,' he told her.

'Why?' she smiled mischievously. 'Afraid people will talk?'

'Something like that,' he admitted.

'Let them,' she dismissed it with a wave of her hand. 'A bit of excitement in their otherwise dull lives. What would you like? Tea? Coffee? Or something stronger?'

'Coffee's fine,' he answered, looking around the maisonette for any signs of a trap. But he knew the only trap was Kelly.

'Black, no sugar,' he managed to tell her without sounding flustered.

'How did I know you were going to say that,' she grinned as she flicked the kettle on and searched the kitchen for the things she needed, talking as she did so. 'You do know you've made a big difference around here?'

'You said,' he reminded her.

'I mean it,' she told him, looking serious for the first time. 'Living here's not like normal living. It's a jungle. Imagine that – a jungle in the middle of East London. Survival of the meanest. The cruellest. No laws. Just a daily battle not to go under. Not to lose it. Trying to find a reason to go on. Until you came along, that is.'

'I'm part of a unit,' he said without believing it.

'You are the unit,' she argued. 'It's you everyone's scared of.'

'Even the children, it would seem,' he replied, remembering losing his temper outside.

'A bollocking now and then'll do them no harm,' she shrugged. 'Small price to pay for a bit of law and order round here.'

'I suppose,' he tentatively agreed as she handed him a mug of coffee – looking into his eyes as she did so, searching for something. 'Thanks,' he told her, not wanting to be the first to look away. Eventually she spun away from him, but stayed close.

'What's your name?' she pried.

'Sergeant King,' he answered coolly. 'Thought you'd already know that.'

'I mean your *real* name,' she insisted.

He took a few seconds before deciding to tell her. 'Jack. It's Jack.'

'Jack,' she repeated, considering it for a moment. 'Suits you. How old are you?' she dug further, cocking her head seductively to one side.

'Why d'you want to know?' he replied, removing his peaked cap and tossing it on the kitchen work surface, self-consciously smoothing his dark brown hair with his hands.

'Just curious,' she answered. 'You look quite young to be doing what you're doing.'

'I look young?' he questioned. 'Even to a . . . how old are you?'

'You first,' she smiled, showing perfect, straight white teeth.

'Fair enough,' he played her game. 'I'm twenty-four. Your turn.'

'Eighteen,' she said, as if she was teasing him somehow, 'or at least I will be in a couple of months.'

'Yeah,' he nodded. 'I remember your mum saying you were only seventeen.'

'Don't worry,' she reassured him. 'You grow up fast round here.'

'I'm sure you do,' he agreed, feeling increasingly nervous about being alone with her. Kelly seemed to sense she was somehow in control and bit her bottom lip as if deep in contemplation. Without warning she opened a kitchen drawer, pulled out a ready-made joint and placed it softly between her open lips. 'You must be joking,' he told her, but her eyes just shone all the more with mischievous intent.

'What?' she smiled and shrugged. 'It's just a *joint*. Isn't going to kill me. And besides,' she said as she lit it and inhaled deeply, blowing out a long stream of thick white smoke as she came closer, 'you look like someone who's got much bigger things on their mind than one joint.'

'All the same,' he told her, unsure what his next move needed to be. 'That stuff's not good for you.'

'Tried it, have you?' she asked, moving close enough for him to be able to reach out and touch her shining golden skin. 'Maybe you should. Help you chill out.'

'No thanks,' he told her as she held the joint out for him to take. 'I'm all good.'

She placed the joint carefully in an ashtray, her hands moving towards his. He knew he should pull away and head for the door, but somehow he just couldn't. He felt her soft, cool, but strong fingers take hold of his hands and turn them to better see his knuckles. A feeling of extreme pleasure shivered down his body – as if they were already making illicit love. He could neither move nor speak.

'You should know better,' she spoke softly. 'Leaving *evidence* like this where everyone can see.' He tried to answer but couldn't as her thumbs gently caressed his bruised hands. 'I wonder what your girlfriend said when she saw this. You do have a girlfriend, don't you – good-looking fella like you? I bet she's nice-looking. I bet she's really pretty.' He felt his body tremble a little, but still he couldn't take his hands from hers. Her touch felt like warm silk in a hot breeze. 'Is she a cop too? She is, isn't she? You and your pretty little cop girlfriend. What a lovely couple you must make. Let me guess,' she continued with unerring accuracy, 'I bet she's slim – slim and blonde – with crystal-blue eyes.' She opened her own as wide as she could as her face, her lips, came ever closer to his – as he willed them to press against his own, but somehow a strength inside him pulled his hands away from the almost overwhelming temptation that stood in front of him and he took half a step back.

'Wait,' he almost pleaded, swallowing his desires deep inside. 'I have to go.'

'No you don't,' she whispered sweetly. 'No one will ever know. It can be our little secret and then you can run home to your pretty blonde cop girlfriend.' She placed a hand gently on the side of his face. He covered it with his own, his stomach tight with fear and longing. 'I bet she won't do things for you that I would. She can't make you feel like I can.'

'I can't do this,' he told her and pulled her hand from his face – its warmth replaced by a cold reality. 'I have to go,' he repeated and grabbed his cap from the worktop and ceremonially fitted it so that the peak cast a long shadow over his face. 'See you round,' he declared and headed for the door, closing his eyes and blowing silently through pursed lips once he was sure she couldn't see him.

'You can be sure of that,' she assured him, still smiling – a mermaid drawing the ship to the rocks that will wreck it.

He managed to make it to the door and into the hot, still summer air outside, walking along the footway without looking back even though his eyes burnt to look at her again – even just for a second. He'd escaped his most dangerous temptation . . . for now at least.

King arrived home a few hours later. He felt a huge weight lift from his shoulders when he realized the front door was still deadlocked, which meant Sara wasn't at home. Once in the small kitchen he slumped in a chair by the table and realized he was still shaking from his close encounter with Kelly. He sprang back to his feet and headed for the fridge, eyeing the beers inside before deciding their alcohol content was too low to take away the growing pain in his back and the far more intense and worrying pain he felt spreading through his mind.

'Damn it, Jack,' he told himself. 'Just relax.'

He slumped onto a kitchen chair and took deep, painful breaths to try and calm the growing anxiety he felt crushing down on his chest – his head falling into his hands as he sat rocking in his chair. 'Jesus Christ,' he pleaded. 'Jesus Christ.' He leapt to his feet and stormed across the small kitchen to the cupboard under the sink where he kept his supply taped behind the pipework. He ripped it clear before emptying the contents onto the floor in front of him, searching through the spillage looking for any cannabis resin he could find – cursing himself when he realized he'd not yet replenished his stock. 'Fuck. Fuck.' He stared up at the ceiling, his eyes tightly closed against the kaleidoscope of haunting, menacing images whirling around inside his dark and damaged mind before slowly looking down at the drugs on the floor – like gleaming, precious stones.

'Fuck it,' he cursed before half burying himself under the sink again until he'd recovered the homemade crack bong. He dropped it next to the drugs as if it was a poisonous insect. He surveyed the things that could take him far away from the pain and memories before sighing long and deeply. 'Don't do this,' he told himself. 'Get back to who you were. Be the man you used to be.' But the images of the girl in white with the spreading crimson, mixed with those of Butler's broken face and Kelly's almost desperate, forbidden beauty, threatened to overwhelm him.

'No,' he almost shouted as he grabbed one of several plastic bags that habitually lived in the sink cupboard in one hand. With the other he scooped up the drugs and then the bong before throwing them into the bag which he tied almost ceremoniously with as tight a knot as he could pull. 'No,' he repeated more calmly, but with more resolve as he dragged himself to his feet, staggering slightly as he went to the front door and pulled it open – checking that no neighbours were milling about before stepping into the communal stairway and moving quickly down the stairs until he was at the front entrance. Again he checked there was no one about before moving fast across the ground to the shared bin area. One last glance around before he chose someone else's bin and tossed the bag of damning possessions inside. He walked back towards the block feeling like he'd won a huge victory. He'd tasted the sweet poison of crack – been temporarily seduced by its power and the magical escapism it offered – but he'd done what the likes of O'Neil could never do and pulled himself back from the brink.

He fled back up the stairs and into the sanctuary of his flat and closed the door behind him, standing with his eyes squeezed tightly shut and his back pressed flat against it, as if the bag and its contents would somehow try to force their way back into the flat.

'Jesus,' he said before exhaling deeply, his eyes opening again as he looked around the empty flat. 'Fuck. Too close, Jack. Too close.'

12

Marino was standing in the CID office in Newham Police Station handing out advice to a young detective constable when he spotted Inspector Johnston walking by. He made a hurried apology to the constable and headed off after Johnston – intercepting her in the corridor that led towards the back-yard of the station.

'Inspector.'

Johnston turned to see who was calling after her. She stopped walking when she saw it was Marino and waited for him to catch up.

'Frank,' Johnston greeted him. 'Something I can do for you?'

'I was just hoping we could have a chat about something,' Marino told her.

Johnston seemed to consider him for a few seconds before answering. 'Fine, but I don't have time to stand around. We'll have to talk as we walk.' She headed off at a fair pace as Marino walked fast to keep up alongside her. 'Well?' Johnston asked impatiently. 'What is it?'

'The Unit,' Marino began, 'on the Grove Wood Estate.'

'What about it?' Johnston tried to hurry him.

'I wondered if you had any *concerns*?'

'*Concerns*?' Johnston pulled a face of confusion. 'Such as?'

'About the Unit's leadership?'

'I am the Unit's leadership,' Johnston reminded him.

'I know that,' Marino tried not to upset her, aware of the Pixie's reputation. 'I was talking about the day-to-day, on-the-ground leadership. I was talking about Sergeant King.'

The mention of King was enough to bring Johnston to a halt.

'Sergeant King?' Johnston asked. 'I have no concerns about Sergeant King.' She started walking again. 'Why are you asking, anyway? The Unit's got nothing to do with the CID and as far as I know Sergeant King's got nothing to do with *you*.'

'Sergeants' Union,' Marino reminded her of the unwritten code of mutual support that existed between all sergeants in the Met. 'I'm just a little worried that giving him the Unit was a bit too much a bit too soon.'

'I don't think so,' Johnston dismissed it. 'Sergeant King's doing a tremendous job. The figures speak for themselves.'

'Figures can be misleading,' Marino tried to warn her.

'So the *CID* keep trying to tell me,' Johnston answered, squinting her eyes.

'What I mean is,' Marino tried again, 'I understand it looks like they're doing a good job, but are you sure this is the right position for Jack at this moment in time? He doesn't exactly have a lot of experience.'

'He's on accelerated promotion, remember,' Johnston reminded him, as if that gave King a shield of infallibility. 'Better people than us have decided he's a more than capable leader, destined for senior management. Who are we to disagree? If it's been decided one day he could be running an entire borough or possibly even the entire police service, then I'm sure he can handle three constables and a housing estate.'

'Two constables,' Marino corrected her.

'Uhh?' Johnston questioned.

'There's only two constables now. Since PC Mahajan was assaulted.'

'Yes. Of course,' Johnston replied, avoiding eye contact. 'A terrible thing.'

'And perhaps a sign things aren't as under control on the Grove Wood as they may first appear.'

'An attack like that could have happened anywhere,' Johnston argued.

'But it didn't,' Marino argued, lowering his voice as they passed a group of uniformed officers coming the other way. 'It happened on the Grove Wood and it happened on Jack's watch.'

'Frank,' Johnston advised him, 'let it go. The SMT have no concerns regarding either Sergeant King or the Grove Wood Estate and neither should you.'

'But I do,' Marino told her more forcefully. 'If you ask me—'

'Which I'm not,' Johnston interrupted him.

'If you ask me,' he continued unperturbed, 'he returned to full duty too soon. He suffered serious injuries saving that girl.'

'Injuries which healed,' Johnston waved it away.

'It was a horrific incident he walked into,' Marino reminded her. 'Even for a seasoned cop it was a real bad one.'

'Comes with the territory,' Johnston replied unhelpfully.

'I think it could have scarred him psychologically.' Marino put his cards on the table.

Johnston shook her head and even smiled her famous smile. 'Come on, Frank. You don't think we let him go back on full duties without having a psychological assessment? He passed with flying colours. He's fine.'

'If he has post traumatic stress disorder,' Marino wouldn't give up, 'he could be a danger to himself and others.'

'Post traumatic stress,' Johnston scoffed at the idea. 'This is East London – not Helmand Province.'

'I don't see how it matters where it happens,' Marino told her as they entered the station yard – the warmth of the bright sunshine unnoticed by both of them. 'It's *what* happens that matters.'

Johnston held her hand up and came to a standstill. 'This discussion is over,' she insisted. 'There's nothing wrong with Sergeant King and there's nothing wrong with the Unit. Everything is fine – better than fine. If only everyone else had such good results as they do. We'd all be much happier. And just in case you don't already know, the new policing model they're deploying is my idea. No one has more interest in its success than me. If I thought King was a risk to it I'd not hesitate to replace him.'

Marino knew he needed to try something else if he was to get through to Johnston. 'I take it you're aware we arrested Ronnie Butler,' he asked, 'for the assault on PC Mahajan?'

'Of course,' Johnston answered, sounding affronted.

'And you're aware of his injuries?'

'I know someone got to him before we did and gave him a bit of a going-over.'

'Not just "a bit of a going-over",' Marino told her. 'Beat him half to death.'

'If it bothers you that much,' Johnston replied, 'then I suggest you double your efforts to find the vigilantes who did it and bring them to book.'

'Vigilantes?' Marino asked quietly. 'That seems to be a very popular assumption round here.'

Johnston's eyes narrowed. 'What are you trying to say, Frank?'

'I'm saying I think we should keep an open mind on this one,' he explained. 'Don't close the book on it just yet.'

'Has this Butler character said anything?' Johnston asked with suspicion.

'Not as such,' Marino answered.

'Has he made any,' Johnston looked around to make sure she wouldn't be overheard, '*allegations*?'

'No,' Marino admitted. 'Says he got jumped by some men in ski masks – probably a rival gang.'

'There we are then,' Johnston nodded with satisfaction and started to walk to her car, but Marino followed her anyway.

'All the same – perhaps I should keep an eye on the Unit,' he offered. 'Make sure everything's OK.'

'That won't be necessary,' Johnston dismissed him. 'Everything is fine. Now if you'll excuse me.'

'Jack's a good man,' Marino almost pleaded with her, 'and a good cop. Before he was injured he was the steadiest, most decent young man you could ever wish to meet. He was doing OK when he was on the Crime Desk, but I could see the demons in his eyes. He's changed.'

Johnston looked hard into his eyes. 'If he fucks up, he'll be treated like anyone else. I don't make exceptions,' she warned him, climbing into the waiting patrol car and closing the door before being sped away while Marino looked on.

'Bitch,' he said loud enough for anyone who cared to hear. No matter what Johnston and her SMT cronies said, he'd be keeping an eye on King and the Unit – if for no other reason than to save them from themselves . . . if it wasn't already too late.

King and Williams knocked on Dougie O'Neil's battered front door as loudly as they dared without attracting too much attention. After the fourth time of asking, O'Neil's voice finally came from the other side.

'Who is it?' he asked, sounding pissed off as usual.

'Sergeant King, Dougie,' he answered. 'Open the fucking door.'

A second later the door opened to reveal the typically ravaged figure of O'Neil. 'Why didn't you just say so?'

'Christ's sake,' King shook his head and pushed past him into the hovel of a flat, with Williams close behind. Once they were all inside O'Neil closed the door and followed them into his rancid-smelling front room.

'I assume you brought something for me,' O'Neil said.

'And why would I do that?' King asked as he checked they were alone in the small abode.

'The information on Butler,' he reminded them. 'It was good, wasn't it?'

'Yeah, it was good,' King agreed, still searching the flat.

'Then I get a reward, right?'

'You'll get your reward,' King assured him, 'but first there's something else I need you to do.'

'Hey,' O'Neil complained. 'I'm well overdue a payment here.'

'Oh I got something nice for you,' King teased him, 'but I need this one thing.'

'Go on,' O'Neil sighed, slumping on the sofa neither King nor Williams dared sit on. 'I'm listening.'

'Micky Astill,' King told him.

'What about him?' O'Neil shrugged and leaned forward as he prepared to roll a cigarette.

'Once upon a time you had an idea to take him down,' King reminded him.

O'Neil squinted his eyes with the effort of trying to remember. 'Oh yeah,' he eventually recalled. 'When you first nicked me.'

'Right,' King told him as Williams continued to circle the room like a shark smelling blood in the water. 'You said you could get him out of that bunker he calls home while he was carrying enough to have him for possession with intent.'

'Well,' O'Neil tried to back away, 'that was then and this is now.'

'What the fuck's that supposed to mean?' Williams asked.

'Means I'm not sure it can be done,' O'Neil answered as if it was obvious.

'You said you could call him,' King reminded him, 'tell him you wanted to make a larger than normal buy, but that you were nervous about going to his flat with so much cash. You said it could draw him out.'

'It might do,' O'Neil agreed, 'but you still haven't said what's in it for me. Why would I want to help you again? I ain't earning out of it. The debt with the Blu-ray's well paid off.'

'Fair enough,' King nodded his head slowly, slipping his hands into his pockets. From one he produced the crack cocaine they'd taken from Tyrone Mooney and from the other the cash taken from the same. He held it out for O'Neil who eyed it disbelievingly.

'What's this?' he asked, his eyes glued to the items seemingly on offer.

'It's yours,' King told him smiling. 'Take it. There's about ten rocks there and close to a hundred and fifty quid. Payment for what you've done in the past and what you're going to do in the future. Fair enough?'

O'Neil leaned forward before suddenly snatching the drugs and cash from King's hands, like a starving man grabbing at bread. He stuffed it into his pockets before it could be taken away. 'All right,' he agreed. 'What you want me to do?'

'You phone Astill,' King explained. 'Tell him you had a nice result dipping a tourist in the West End – a couple of hundred quid cash that you're looking to blow partying the weekend away and you want to buy ten rocks.'

'He'll want to see the cash before agreeing to anything,' O'Neil pointed out. 'Ten rocks'll cost a hundred and sixty.'

'You got the cash,' King reminded him, looking at O'Neil's pocket.'

'So I got to give Astill the cash?' O'Neil moaned. 'I ain't never gonna get paid, am I?'

'Don't fret,' King told him. 'You'll get it all back and more. So long as you help us out – and you don't have much choice, do you, Dougie? Unless you want people on the estate to find out you've been *helping* us.'

'Fine,' O'Neil reluctantly agreed, fully aware that if people found out a severe beating would be the least he could expect.

'So you tell him you want the ten rocks,' King picked up the thread, 'but that you don't want to risk coming to his flat with that amount of cash – in case you get robbed or nicked. Same after the buy – tell him you don't want to be out in the open with ten rocks on you. OK?'

'Sounds reasonable enough,' O'Neil nodded slightly.

'But as you said – he's gonna want to see the cash,' King continued. 'No problem. You get him to come here for the cash. He won't mind being out of his bunker with cash – it's drugs he doesn't want to be caught with.'

'Yeah but how's he gonna get the drugs to Dougie here?' Williams asked. 'Astill ain't gonna bring them round here himself.'

'He'll use a runner,' King answered disinterestedly. 'Send someone else round with the goods – for what it's worth.'

'I don't understand,' O'Neil admitted. 'How you gonna nick him if you can't catch him with the rocks? You can't nick him just for carrying a bit of dough.'

'Let me worry about that,' King smiled. 'You just make the call and don't fuck it up. Fuck it up and we might not be so understanding. Clear?'

'Yeah,' O'Neil answered, swallowing his fear and trying to control his loosening bowels. 'I understand.'

Micky Astill sat in silence on the faux-leather sofa with his drug-ravaged girlfriend smoking endless cigarettes while they watched *The Jerry Springer Show* together and waited for the next customer to rap on their front door. Just as the guests on the show were reaching a climax of insults and accusations,

Astill was disturbed by the sound of his mobile chirping and vibrating on the coffee table. He picked it up without much interest and checked the caller ID. The number wasn't blocked, but it wasn't one he recognized or had in his contacts, which usually meant a new customer – someone given his number by one of his existing clients. He stared at the phone hard, wondering whether to answer it or not. New customers were always potentially dangerous. They could be a police informant or even an undercover cop or they might just be a rival dealer setting him up to rob. There were no friends and no code of conduct in Astill's world. He decided it was worth the risk answering. His existing customers were imprisoned or died on a regular basis. He had to continually expand his client base or risk running out of addicts to sell to.

'Hello,' he answered cautiously.

'Micky,' O'Neil replied. 'It's me – Dougie.'

Astill immediately relaxed. O'Neil was one of his oldest associates. 'Got a new phone?' he asked.

'Yeah, yeah,' O'Neil confirmed. 'Lost my other one somewhere,' he lied, knowing that the mere mention of the police and certainly the fact he'd been arrested would put Astill on high alert. Drug addicts on bail always had the potential to be an informant – something Astill would know as well as anyone.

'I'll change your number in my contacts,' Astill told him.

'Can you speak?' O'Neil got down to business.

Astill glanced at his girlfriend. He trusted no one, but considered her harmless. 'Yeah, sure.'

'I've had a nice touch and looking to score large,' O'Neil spoke in virtual code.

'How large?' Astill asked.

'Ten rocks,' O'Neil told him bluntly, 'if you've got it.'

Astill was silent for a few seconds before he replied. 'That's a lot for you, Dougie. What you planning on doing with a score that size?'

218

'Party,' O'Neil lied, trying to sound cheerful and excited at the prospect of getting his hands on more crack than he'd ever had before.

'Party, eh?' Astill checked. 'Gonna be a one-man party, is it?'

'I ain't planning on sharing,' O'Neil confirmed.

'It'll cost one sixty,' Astill warned him. 'You sure you got it?'

'I got it,' O'Neil stuck to the plan. 'Had a nice result dipping a tourist in the West End.'

Again Astill was silent while he considered O'Neil's request – trying to recall if he'd ever heard of him dipping before. He thought O'Neil was strictly a theft-from-motor-vehicle man with the occasional burglary thrown in. After a few seconds he shrugged, deciding a thief was a thief. Maybe O'Neil was expanding his repertoire, and the money was hard to turn down. Ten rocks in one hit would give him enough cash to go straight back to his suppliers and re-stock. By the end of the week he could be as much as fifty pounds up on his normal profit margin. At Astill's level of the trade that was a significant gain. His was not the world of the TV drug dealer – smart suits, flash cars and briefcases full of pristine fifty-pound notes. His was a world of scratching out a living, risking everything just to make ends meet, where each deal only brought a small profit; maybe a couple of pounds a rock if he could get a decent price when buying in bulk – bulk on the street meaning twenty to thirty rocks at a time. He was in the business of surviving and little else. Even the money he dealt with was small time: filthy, crumpled five-pound notes, pound coins, fifty-pence coins – even one-pence coins. His customers scraped together what they could, stole what they could and used it to pay him for the drugs. It was the nature of the business and a pain in the arse. Laws introduced to force the banks and other financial institutions to inform the police of any suspicious deposits or transactions meant the likes of Astill found it almost impossible to change their coins and fivers for anything more user-friendly. They were stuck with it. Even if he wanted to buy something like a new TV, he'd have to buy it with small change, which meant he couldn't risk using a reputable supplier – in case they tipped off the police. His chosen trade had ensured he was trapped in a neverworld of illicit trades where even the smallest purchase could be fraught with danger.

'All right,' he finally answered, the thought of getting his hands on some clean cash in decent-sized notes proving too tempting. 'Bring the cash round here and I'll serve you up.'

'Er, not sure about that,' O'Neil answered. 'Don't fancy being close to your gaff with a hundred and sixty notes on me and I don't fancy being on the street with ten rocks under my tongue.'

'So you want me to take all the risks?' Astill laughed. 'I don't think so.'

'No one's gonna rob you,' O'Neil tried to persuade him. 'People know you must be connected.'

'Don't bet on it,' Astill told him. 'And what about the Old Bill. They'd like nothing more than to catch me out in the open while I'm holding. It's too risky, Dougie.'

'Why don't you use a runner?' O'Neil encouraged him. 'You got people you can use, don't you?'

'Yeah,' Astill admitted, 'but no one I'd trust with a hundred and sixty notes.'

'You don't have to,' O'Neil explained. 'Come round here and get the money yourself. Better that way anyway. Then you can send the runner with the gear later.'

'And if the runner takes off with the rocks?'

'My problem, I guess,' O'Neil told him. 'You'll have already been paid so what the fuck do you care?'

Astill once more considered the details of the potential transaction before replying. 'All right,' he agreed, 'but just because I like you so much I'll send the runner back and forth. They can bring you the rocks a couple at a time – just in case they get tempted.'

'Fine,' O'Neil agreed. 'When can you come round for the paper?'

'No time like the present,' Astill answered.

'Suits me,' O'Neil agreed before hanging up.

Astill dragged himself to his feet, surprising his girlfriend who'd never seen him miss any of *The Jerry Springer Show* before for anything other than a customer at the door. 'Where you going?' she asked, sounding a little concerned.

'Take care of some business,' he told her. 'I'll be back soon. I'll lock the security grid behind me. You ain't planning on going nowhere, are you?'

'No,' she replied, satisfied with his explanation. 'You can lock it behind you.'

Astill moved quickly up the stairwell towards the walkway that would take him to O'Neil's flat. The thought of crisp, clean tens and twenties – the sort of cash tourists carried, newly obtained from airport bureaux de changes – put an extra spring in his step. But his happy thoughts came to an abrupt end when he reached the walkway only to have King step out in front of him and push a strong hand into his chest. 'Shit,' he cursed before remembering he was neither in possession of any drugs or even cash. He instantly relaxed to the point of cockiness. 'Can I help you, officer?' he grinned.

'Help me?' King repeated as Williams and now also Brown stepped from the doorways that concealed them. 'Yeah, you can help me.'

'Go ahead and search me,' Astill told him as he looked at the others – some instinct for survival telling him that bumping into them was no accident and that this was no routine check. 'You won't find nothing.'

'Depends on what I'm looking for, doesn't it?' King replied

and spun Astill round, pushing him against the wall before he began to rifle through his pockets.

'I told you,' Astill insisted, 'I ain't got nothing.'

'I'd have to disagree,' King replied, pulling his hand from Astill's pocket and waving the set of house keys in front of his face. 'I'd say you've got exactly what we're looking for.'

'You can't take them,' Astill argued – confusion and panic setting in. 'I ain't done nothing.'

'Time we took a look around that bunker you call a home,' King told him. 'See what you've been up to.'

'You can't do that,' Astill continued to protest. 'You can't search my house if I'm not under arrest and I don't see no search warrant.'

'Well,' King said, 'if it makes you feel any better – Micky Astill, I'm arresting you for conspiracy to supply a class A controlled drug. You know the caution.'

'Fuck's sake,' he complained as King cuffed his hands behind his back. 'I might expect this sort of shit from the area drug squad, but the local beat cops . . . What you want – a pay-off?'

'Don't insult us,' King warned him. 'You think we're on the take? You got us confused with someone else, Micky.'

'Then what the fuck *do* you want?' Astill demanded.

'Your head,' King snarled at him, 'to go with all the others on our office wall. But don't worry – I'll be sure to mount yours pride of place. You're my lion's head, Micky. You should be proud of yourself.'

'Fuck you,' Astill spat at them. 'Fuck you all.'

Brown kept trying the keys on the small bunch they'd taken from Astill – working silently despite the frustration of another failure, his stealth training from his army days serving him well. He could hear the television blaring on the other side of the door and guessed at least one person was inside. If he made a sound any drugs that might be waiting for them could be flushed down the toilet in seconds. King and Williams waited in the close-by stairwell where the latter held a large gloved hand over the still-cuffed Astill's mouth to stop him calling out any warning to the occupants. They'd asked Astill to show them which key was for the grid, but he'd refused to help them, even after they'd threatened him. Either he didn't take them seriously or whatever he had in the flat was worth trying to protect – was something that could send him down for a very long time.

Finally a key turned the lock and the metal cage door swung an inch or two open under its own weight, but the movement made a noise loud enough to be heard inside the flat.

'Shit,' Brown cursed as he tried the front door handle and found it locked. 'Shit,' he cursed again and began to fumble through the keys trying to find one for the lock, but it was too late – he could already hear footsteps coming towards him from inside. He froze, desperately turning back to the stairwell where the others looked on with increasing confusion.

Suddenly the front door swung open and inwards as Astill's skeletal girlfriend stood in front of him, her mouth open and ready to greet her returning boyfriend and supplier. Too slowly her crack-ravaged mind registered the grid was open as Brown came back to life and seized on her mistake – almost running towards her and driving her backwards into the flat with his shoulder. The others saw him disappear inside and ran to the open door, pulling Astill along with them until they were all inside. King slammed the door shut and barked his orders.

'Make sure no one else is here,' he told his subordinates. 'Take her with you,' he ordered Williams. 'You stay with me,' he said to Astill, before leading him to the front room where the trappings of a low-level dealer were on show: a decent TV and sound system and a larger than average DVD collection to keep him entertained during the long boring hours of waiting for customers to come calling. The place was a tip: overflowing ashtrays, empty beer and cider bottles mixing with unwashed plates, cups and glasses. 'Nice place you got here,' King insulted him.

'Fuck you,' Astill bit back. 'Just do what you gotta do and fuck off.'

'Temper, temper,' King told him as the others joined them.

'It's clear,' Brown said. 'No one home but these two.'

'Good,' King nodded and pushed Astill onto the sofa. Williams did the same with the girlfriend. 'Give me the keys,' he told Brown, holding his hand out. Brown did as he was told. King dangled the keys in front of Astill before pinching a small but heavy looking one. 'I recognize this sort of key,' he explained. 'You got a floor safe somewhere in here, Micky? That where you keep your gear?'

'I don't know what you're talking about,' Astill tried to bluff it out.

'That's the trouble with people like you,' King ignored him. 'You don't trust anyone. If you did you could have left the key here and I'd never have known, but you had to take it with you, didn't you? You,' he turned on the desperate-looking woman. 'What's your name?'

'Tracy,' she answered in a faltering voice. 'Tracy Stevenson.'

'You his girlfriend?' King asked. 'His partner?' She shrugged and nodded at the same time – unsure of what she really was to Astill. 'See,' King said triumphantly. 'He doesn't even trust his own girlfriend. Probably thinks you'd empty the safe and do a runner first chance you got.'

'Probably right too,' Brown added.

'Probably,' King agreed. 'So where's the safe, Micky?'

'Fuck you,' Astill replied, but he sounded worried.

'You?' King asked Stevenson. She shook her head and shrugged unconvincingly again. 'If we have to rip this place apart we will,' he warned them. Still nothing. 'D'you hear what happened to Ronnie Butler?' he asked without warning.

Astill and Stevenson looked at each other and then back to King. 'I heard he took a serious kicking. D'you hear that?'

'I heard,' Astill answered.

'What else did you hear?' King continued.

'Heard it was a rival gang or something,' Astill told him truthfully.

'Rival gang,' King smiled to let him know he was wrong. 'I heard it was vigilantes. Maybe you're next on *their* list – if you know what I mean – unless you *cooperate*.'

Astill said nothing, but the reality of his situation was beginning to dawn on him, like a patient realizing the doctor had just told them they had cancer.

'No?' King nodded his head slowly, speaking to Brown over his shoulder. 'Davey – put the kettle on. Make sure it's nice and full. Just in case you're wondering,' he addressed Astill and Stevenson, 'it's not for tea or coffee. Apparently there's nothing more painful than being burnt with boiling water. Shall we find out?'

'You're fucking mad,' Astill told him and tried to stand, but King moved too quickly, stamping on his genitals and collapsing him back onto the sofa. He lay writhing and moaning – unable to reach his injured body parts because his hands were still handcuffed behind his back.

King pulled his black leather gloves from his pocket and made a deliberate show of slipping them over his hands. He leaned forwards and slapped Astill hard across the face, making Stevenson flinch and curl into an ever tighter protective ball. 'All you have to do is tell me where the safe is,' he insisted. 'Don't make *me* do something *you'll* regret.' He went to slap Astill again, but he spoke before he could.

'Wait,' Astill pleaded. 'How much d'you want? I can pay you.'

'I've told you,' King reminded him as he brought the first slap down on his face, 'we're not here for a pay-off. We're here for everything. You're finished, Astill. At least make the end easy on yourself and this wretch you call your girlfriend.'

'I can't,' Astill appealed to him. 'This is not how it fucking works.' King grabbed him by the collar and gave him a short, hard punch in the eye, making him call out in pain, but King showed no mercy as he hit him again square in the nose, causing it to immediately start bleeding.

'Sarge,' Brown tried to warn him. 'Let's not let things get out of hand.'

'Out of hand?' King turned on him. 'Too late for that. We're all in this together now. There's no going back after Butler.' He looked again at the terrified couple and realized what he had to do. He pushed Astill onto the sofa and grabbed Stevenson by the hair on the back of her head, pulling her straight and almost lifting her from her seat.

'No,' she begged him, but his open palm was already heading towards her face – King holding her still as he hit her hard on the cheek. Her crying intensified as he pulled his hand back again.

'The safe?' he demanded.

'I don't know,' she lied as a second later his palm struck her again. 'Please,' she grovelled.

'Leave her alone,' Astill tried to defend her.

'Well, well, well, Micky,' he tormented them. 'I never knew you were a man of honour. Are you a man of honour, Micky? You want to stop this – tell me where the safe is.' But Astill said nothing, his lips trembling with the effort of remaining shut. 'No?' King asked. 'Very well.' He tightened his grip on Stevenson's hair and turned his open palm into a clenched fist.

'Maybe there isn't a safe,' Williams tried to stop him – growing as concerned as Brown.

'There's a safe,' King insisted and jabbed his fist into Stevenson's cheekbone. 'Where is it?' he called through her hysterical crying, but she couldn't or wouldn't answer. 'Where

226

is it?' he repeated and smashed his fist into her mouth, splitting her upper and lower lips simultaneously. 'Where is it?' he demanded again, showing her his fist that was drawn back as far as he could.

'Fuck's sake,' Brown interrupted and stepped forward, to do what he didn't know – just something. Anything. But Stevenson broke first.

'In the bedroom,' she spluttered through the pain and blood.

'Shut up, you stupid fucking bitch,' Astill screamed at her, but he was quickly silenced by another kick in the groin from King who lifted Stevenson off the sofa by her hair and pushed her towards the hallway.

'Show me,' he told her and allowed her to lead him to the bedroom that mirrored the front room – some decent belongings, but otherwise squalid, dirty clothes strewn on the floor and yet more overflowing ashtrays along with the usual paraphernalia associated with smoking crack. 'Where is it?' he barked at her, throwing her onto the bed.

She pointed a crooked finger at the built-in wardrobe. 'In there,' she told him. 'Under the carpet in the floor.'

King smiled and nodded before walking to the wardrobe and pulling the doors open, digging his way through the clothes and shoes until he uncovered the carpet – like a treasure seeker hitting something solid underground. He ripped the carpet back and saw the heavy metal safe, about twenty inches by ten, cemented into the floor. Without ceremony he pushed the key into the keyhole and turned it. It twisted smoothly – the sign of frequent use. The handle turned just as easily. He pulled the heavy lid up and open, letting it fall to the floor as he stared into the box. His first impression was that he was looking at far more than he'd ever expected to find at someone like Astill's – much more.

'Fuck me,' he swore as he began to pull the contents of the safe out – spreading them across the floor next to him.

There were ten- and five-pound notes mainly, with the occasional twenty, and heaps of coins all neatly placed in small plastic bank bags, as well as pound coins, fifty-pence pieces and every other type of coin too. But there was something else – another plastic bag containing, he estimated, at least fifty to sixty rocks, and yet another with about an eighth of an ounce of brown powder he assumed was heroin, as well as a smaller clip-seal bag containing a small amount of a pure white substance he guessed was cocaine – a relatively rare find in such a deprived area. Clearly he'd underestimated Astill. Evidently he was a much bigger player than they'd thought.

He counted out the cash as quickly as he could, stopping when he got to a thousand pounds. He rolled the money as tightly as he could before pushing it into his shirt chest pocket under his body armour. He also separated out about half the rocks and stuffed them in one of the coin bags he'd emptied of small change. These he placed in his other chest pocket. He eyed the bags of heroin and cocaine before he snatched them up and stuffed them both into his trouser pocket. Finally he separated off two wads of five hundred pounds each before placing all the remaining drugs and cash into an evidence bag he'd pulled from a pouch on his utility belt. He felt eyes burning into the back of his head and turned to see Stevenson staring at him – her eyes wild with hate and disgust.

'It's not what you think,' he told her, although he didn't really believe it himself any more as he spiralled ever further from the man he had once been. He got to his feet clutching the evidence bag and walked towards Stevenson who flinched as he reached out for her. Grabbing her by the bicep, he pulled her from the bed and dragged her back to the front room where he unceremoniously threw her on the sofa next to the now recovered Astill, whose eyes locked onto the evidence bag – experience of a hundred drug deals telling him the bag was light. King dropped the bag on the coffee table and re-sorted the two wads of five hundred pounds.

'Here,' he told Brown and Williams, holding out the money in separate hands for them to accept. 'Take it,' he told them, but they just looked at each other and then back to King. 'You've earned it,' he encouraged them before pointing with his chin to the evidence bag. 'There's enough cash in there with the crack to send him down,' he tried to persuade them. 'This is your reward. Think of it as a bonus for all your hard work.' But still they didn't move. 'Come on,' he practically chastised them. 'Don't be so fucking naïve. You don't think this is normal practice? The money we're supposed to survive on – when you get the chance to make a little on the side, why the fuck not? If we don't have it it'll only go back to the government to waste. No one's going to increase our wages any time soon.'

'Doesn't seem right,' Williams argued.

'Fucking take it,' King insisted. 'Of course it's right. We all got mortgages to pay – debts. Nobody's going to help us, so best we help ourselves. Don't tell me you don't need it.'

'What about them?' Williams asked, jutting his chin towards Astill and Stevenson who were watching in silence. 'They'll know.'

'So?' King shrugged. 'What they going to do – tell someone we took their *drug money*? That's as good as admitting they've been supplying class A drugs. They'll get fifteen years each. No. They'll say what they always say – no comment. Right, Micky? They won't admit to any of the money or the drugs being theirs. They can't.'

Astill's eyes burnt with hatred as he listened to the truth of what King was saying.

'And even if they did tell someone,' King elaborated, 'who's going to believe a couple of drug-dealing crack-heads? They'd hardly be the first to make malicious allegations to try and get the cops who nicked them in the shit.' He checked the faces of Brown and Williams and saw they were still unconvinced. 'It's drug money,' he reassured them.

'Untraceable cash. No one will ever be able to prove anything. No one will ever try to.'

Brown was the first to step forward and snatch the cash from his hand. 'Why the fuck not? Haven't been able to afford a holiday since I joined this shit job.'

'In for a penny,' Williams gave in and took his cut. 'Motor needs a new clutch anyway.'

'Good,' King nodded. 'Now we're all singing off the same page. Time we got what we deserve.'

'You don't know what you're doing,' Astill suddenly piped up. 'Only a small bit of this is mine.'

'Aye,' Brown smiled as he slipped the cash into his pocket. 'Tell it to the judge, see if he believes you.'

'No,' Astill pleaded. 'Look – I'm just a salesman. I buy what I can and sell it on. I make what I can on each deal, but this, and the cash, it's not mine. It belongs to *other* people.'

'Like who?' King asked, deadly serious. 'Maybe if you can give us a way to take them down we can overlook this. So long as you can be sure it'd be worth our while.'

'I can't,' Astill shook his head, 'but you don't want to fuck with them. You steal from them, you pay the price.'

'You think they'd mess with the police?' King asked. 'You think *anyone's* going to mess with the police?'

'Straight ones, no,' Astill answered, 'but bent ones is different.'

'We ain't bent,' Brown snapped at him. 'You think we do this all the time?'

'Doesn't matter,' Astill warned them. 'If you hadn't taken any for yourselves they'd let it slide. Not much you can do about honest Old Bill. Losing the occasional bit of merchandise to the Old Bill is all part of the business. But if they think you're screwing them over for profit – they won't let it go.'

'Bullshit,' Williams said slightly nervously, knowing Astill was probably telling the truth.

'Who gives a fuck who they are?' King interrupted. 'They can't touch us anyway. I'll lock them up the same way I'm gonna lock you up. Round here we *are* the law. No lowlife drug dealer can touch us. Just let them try.'

'You're all fucking dead men,' Astill threatened them. 'When they find out who you are they'll come looking for you.'

'And who's gonna tell them who we are?' King demanded. 'You open your mouth to anyone and I'll hound you to your dying days.'

'If you live that long,' Astill warned him.

'You've been watching too many gangster films, Astill,' King told him. 'I don't care if this shit belongs to the Godfather. You all run scared of the police.'

'Sure of that, are you?' Astill asked.

'What?' King spat the word at him. 'You trying to scare me? You think I could ever be scared of any criminal? As far as I'm concerned you're all just weak-minded cowards.'

'We'll see about that,' Astill grinned a little for the first time. 'We'll see.'

Marino entered the canteen at Canning Town and easily found King and his two cohorts silently eating dinner together, looking subdued. Marino strode over to them and took a seat before asking, 'Mind if I pull up a chair?'

'Looks like you already have,' King answered, trying to sound relaxed, but Brown and Williams couldn't help but tense – the money from Astill's safe burning guiltily in their pockets. King warned them to calm down with a quick glance.

'I saw you brought in Micky Astill,' Marino began.

'Correct,' King continued, trying to sound almost flippant. 'Possession of crack cocaine with intent to supply.'

'Strictly speaking a CID matter,' Marino reminded them. 'He should have been handed over to us for further investigation.'

'No need to bother the CID with this one,' King told him. 'All very straightforward.'

'Custody record says he had almost thirty rocks in his possession and close to three thousand quid,' Marino explained.

'So?' Brown couldn't help himself.

'Thirty rocks is a little top-heavy for someone like Astill, although possible,' Marino explained, 'but almost three thousand in cash? That's a hell of a lot for someone at his level. Makes you wonder what he was saving up for. Did he have a big score lined up or . . . was he holding it for someone else? Someone bigger and badder?'

'There you go, you see,' King tried to end Marino's hypothesizing. 'Like I said, a straightforward case. He had the money and the drugs in decent enough quantities to sink himself. No need for the CID.'

'What d'you mean?' Brown ignored King – Astill's warning ringing around his head. 'Why the fuck would a major player give someone like Astill that much in drugs and cash to hold for them?'

'It happens,' Marino shrugged. 'Custody record says you found the cash and gear in a floor safe?'

'Aye,' Brown answered. 'So what?'

'Maybe Astill's supplier gave it to him, so he could use him for safe storage. If they were Astill's regular supplier he'd have no choice but to do as he was told.'

'Yeah, but why would they do that?' Brown continued. 'Why trust a scumbag like Astill with that much cash?'

'Sometimes they don't have a lot of choice,' Marino explained. 'A reasonably major dealer's gonna be cash-rich, but it'll all be in small notes and coins. They can't bank it because the banks have to tell us and it'd put us on to them. So they use the likes of Astill to stash cash for when they need it or can get it out to the British Virgin Isles or Switzerland and get it into the banking system there. They can't risk keeping it in their own homes or in one place in case they get hit in a raid and lose the lot or get turned over by a rival firm. Difficult business being a drug dealer.'

'So the drugs and cash we took could belong to a proper firm?' Brown asked, the concern tangible in his voice as he remembered Astill's words of warning – a warning he hadn't really believed until now.

'That amount?' Marino pulled a thoughtful face. 'Probably.'

'That's interesting,' King interrupted, managing to sound genuine, 'but Astill's already been interviewed and charged. He's in court in the morning, when he'll be remanded. If he ends up in the shit with a serious firm who cares? Just life catching up with him.'

'As it does with all of us,' Marino warned them, giving them a few seconds to consider his words. 'By the way – any particular reason why you processed him so quickly? Looks like he was interviewed and charged before the ink on his custody record was even dry.'

'No need to drag it out,' King answered. 'We've got plenty of other stuff to get on with.'

'Sure it wasn't to stop CID getting our hands on him?' Marino asked bluntly – increasing the tension between them.

'Why would we want to do that?' King managed to reply.

'Not sure,' Marino played along. 'Maybe he had some information you didn't want him sharing with us?'

'Information?' Brown jumped in. 'About what?'

'Oh, I don't know,' Marino told him. 'About his supplier perhaps?'

'You think we're using Astill as an informant?' King smiled. 'Trying to keep him for ourselves?'

'Wouldn't be the first time someone didn't want to share a decent snout with the CID,' Marino reminded him.

'Very unprofessional,' King shook his head. 'Look – we pumped him for information but he wasn't having it. We told him if he didn't want to speak to us we could have a suit come see him, but he told us to get fucked. Astill doesn't want to play the game, so we interviewed and charged him. Job done. No need to waste any more time on him.'

'Fair enough,' Marino shrugged once and stood to leave before halting. 'I almost forgot – how did you manage to get past Astill's security grid? Custody record didn't say anything about any damage being caused?'

'We took him out on the street,' King explained. 'He had a few rocks on him so we nicked him and did a Section 18 search of his flat. He had the keys to the grid on him when we stopped him. Made it nice and easy for us.'

'Micky Astill on the street while he was holding?' Marino questioned. 'Never thought he'd make a stupid mistake like that.'

'First time for everything,' King told him, trying to stay calm.

'Guess you just got lucky then.' Marino seemed to let it go.

'Guess so,' King answered.

Suddenly Marino began to look all about the canteen, as if he didn't want to be overheard. 'Jack. I need a word with you in private. Something I need to tell you.'

'I have no secrets,' King told him. 'You can speak in front of these two.'

'No,' Marino insisted. 'This is for your ears only.' With that he got up and walked across to the far corner of the canteen where a small area for watching an old TV was set aside, with a random arrangement of scruffy but comfortable seats. King rolled his eyes and shrugged his shoulders before standing and heading off after him.

Marino slumped in one of the chairs and used the remote to turn the TV volume up loud enough to camouflage his words while he waited for King to catch him up – who chose a chair close but not next to Marino.

'So?' King asked, sounding disinterested.

'Jack,' Marino began, his voice full of concern. 'There's something I need to tell you.'

'You said.'

'It's about Peter Edwards,' Marino told him.

King's blood stopped flowing at the mere mention of the man who'd lost his mind and slaughtered almost his entire family as well as nearly killing him. The frail little girl in the white dress with the spreading crimson falling into his arms crashed into his mind and robbed him of the ability to speak.

'Jack,' Marino tried to break through to him. 'Jack.'

'Yeah,' King managed to reply, shaking the images from his head. 'What about Edwards? Someone get to him inside? Please tell me they did.'

'No,' Marino answered, shaking his head and looking as serious as he ever had. 'Listen, Jack – he's appealed against his sentence.'

'*What?*' King asked, his face pale and his hands trembling. 'We buried him. There's no grounds for appeal.'

'His defence team did some digging into the psychiatrists that examined him. Turns out one of them may have not been qualified enough to declare him sane enough to stand trial.'

'He's sane,' King snapped. 'He knew exactly what he was doing. He meant to do it. He meant to kill them.'

'We all know that,' Marino agreed, 'and no doubt whoever hears his appeal will too. It's the last throw of the dice for him – that's all.'

'But if he wins his appeal?' King asked. 'What then? He's released? He gets away with murder?'

'No,' Marino explained. 'He'll be sectioned under the Mental Health Act. Sent to Broadmoor and detained indefinitely.'

'Unless some time in the future he's declared sane,' King pressed. 'Then what? Then he does walk?'

'It's complicated,' Marino told him. 'It's possible, but

unlikely. More likely he'll be returned to prison to serve out the rest of his sentence.'

'So he serves out his sentence in a hospital instead of a prison and then drops the mask of insanity and gets himself released. Jesus Christ.'

'Maybe,' Marino admitted.

'Great,' King complained.

Marino took a deep breath before continuing. 'Jack. You need to know there's a good chance you'll have to give evidence at the appeal.'

'What?' he snapped. 'Why? What's the psychiatrist got to do with me?'

'Nothing,' Marino answered, 'but CPS tell me you'll be considered the key witness as to Edwards' state of mind at the time of the murders. Look, Jack, I'm not saying it will happen – just that it could. I really didn't want you to hear about it from some CPS clerk sending you an email.' King sat motionless staring at the wall. 'You going to be OK?' Marino asked. King didn't answer. 'Any time you want to talk about it I'm here to listen.' But still King remained in his trance. 'Jack?' Marino raised his voice.

'I'll be fine,' King lied.

'I'm sorry, Jack,' Marino told him as he got to his feet. 'Come see me – whenever you feel the need.'

'Yeah sure,' King replied without conviction.

'You know where to find me,' Marino reminded him, before patting him on the shoulder as he walked past him and headed for the exit, leaving King with his own dark thoughts.

He had no idea how long he'd been sitting staring at nothing before his eyes blinked him back into the real world. He pulled himself to his feet and trudged across the canteen, returning to Brown and Williams who watched him in silence for almost a minute before anyone spoke.

'Jesus,' Williams broke the silence. 'You look like you've just seen a ghost.'

'I have,' King told him, his eyes dead to the world.

'What?' Williams asked, confusion etched into his face.

'Nothing,' King recovered. 'Forget it.'

'Then what was your private little chat about?' Williams pushed.

'None of your business,' King warned him. 'Something else.'

'I'm telling you that fucker knows something,' Brown brought things back to the present.

'Stop panicking,' King shut him up, recovering with each passing second. 'He knows nothing.'

'Then why did he come looking for us?' Brown asked. 'Why mention the cash if he wasn't trying to rattle us?'

'Because it *is* an unusual amount for someone like Astill to have,' King reminded him. 'You know that. Marino's probably just pissed off because he's missed the chance to turn Astill into his grass.'

'I'm not so sure,' Brown shook his head.

'I told you,' King tried to calm him, 'don't worry about him. He's old school. He's not out to cause us trouble. Besides, I know how to deal with Marino.'

'Oh yeah,' Brown said. 'And how's that?'

'What d'you do to keep a dog off your back?' King asked.

'I don't know,' Brown replied. 'What do you do?'

'Throw him a bone,' King smiled. 'Give him something to chase.'

'Like what?' Brown demanded.

'Don't worry about it,' King told him. 'I'll think of something. Just finish up your paperwork and get yourselves home – and make sure you put your *bonuses* somewhere safe.'

'Fuck home,' Williams said. 'I need a drink. Anyone coming?'

'Aye,' Brown agreed, getting to his feet. 'Sounds like a good idea to me.'

'Sarge?' Williams asked.

237

'No,' King shook his head. 'I'm knackered. You go ahead. I'll catch you tomorrow.'

As soon as he arrived home he checked every room to make sure he was alone. He couldn't remember what shift Sara was on and the truth was he didn't care – so long as he was alone. Once he was happy the small flat was deserted he emptied the crack, heroin and cash onto the kitchen table from his jacket pockets and stared at it, wondering where it was all leading to. As his fear faded he was better able to focus and realized his latest illicit haul was lying on a bed of unpaid bills Sara had obviously left out for him to see, most likely in the hope that he'd pay them. It momentarily flashed in his mind that at least he could now afford to pay off some of his credit cards, before the enormity of what he'd done swept the flicker of hope away.

'Fuck,' he swore before slumping into a chair. 'Fuck.'

The drive home had been a nervous and paranoid one as he continually checked his rearview mirror, made sure he stopped at every amber light and kept his speed at exactly twenty-nine mph – always terrified he'd be crashed into by an uninsured minicab driver and have to wait around while the police attended. In truth, bringing the drugs home was the real reason he hadn't gone to the pub with the others. If he got pulled for drink driving and searched they'd have found quite a stash and it would have been all over for him, but sober he could simply flash his warrant card and be sent on his way with the crack and heroin never being discovered.

He massaged his aching forehead, the stress of the day finally hitting him, despite his best efforts to push his worries away. Away from the excitement and thrill of being in the moment with the others alongside him – now the desire to show off his power to Astill and his rancid girlfriend had been spent – the seriousness of what they'd done suddenly seemed as if it was going to overpower him. Now he had to face the fact he could once more be standing in the dock reliving the moment of horror that changed him forever. He closed his eyes to try and chase away his own troubling thoughts, but all he could see were the faces of Astill and Stevenson and their looks of fear and disgust.

'Jesus Christ,' he moaned out loud as he squeezed his temples hard looking for a solution – a way out. Perhaps if he destroyed the drugs and dumped the cash in some charity collection box somewhere he could forgive himself – make promises to himself it wouldn't happen again. But what about the others? For all he knew they might have spent their cut by now – new TVs all round. 'Fuck,' he chastised himself again. The genie was out the bottle now. Even if they never did anything like it again, what happened today would follow them around forever – the feeling of not being *clean* – of not being *real* cops any more.

'Somebody help me,' he suddenly found himself whispering as his eyes filled with tears, releasing thin streams of salty water that flowed down the contours of his face. 'Somebody please help me.'

Without warning the ghosts of the past began to mingle in his mind with the demons of the present until only they remained. The girl in the white dress with the spreading crimson pattern staggering towards him as the monster that was her own father closed quickly on her from behind – only he wasn't carrying a knife, he was wielding a giant curved sword above his head. He plunged the blade towards the girl as if to cut her in two just as King threw himself between them – sacrificing himself to the razor-sharp metal.

'No,' he called out loud and jolted from the darkness – unsure if he'd fallen asleep and dreamt the images or whether something else was happening to him. Either way, he needed to go to a place where neither the past nor present could touch him.

He began to handle the bag containing the heroin – an

innocuous-looking brown powder like the sort of thing found in glass jars in the kitchens of everyday folk all over the country. But this powder had the power to destroy lives and build criminal empires. He considered laying a small amount on some tinfoil and chasing the dragon as O'Neil had described, but he was too afraid. Not many people survived the seduction of the powder they also called horse and he wasn't arrogant enough to believe he could be one of the rare few who would. And besides, he'd already tried crack and still been himself in the morning. He hadn't felt the immediate need to take more and had even disposed of his stash. Clearly he could control crack, so why risk the heroin?

Decision made, he leapt to his feet and fled from the flat and back down the stairs to the outside bins. After a quick look to ensure he wasn't being watched he began to search the bin, tolerating the foul stench and slimy, unmentionable things until he found the knotted bag he'd dumped in there. He pulled the bag clear and skulked back to the entrance, constantly checking for watching eyes until he reached the safety of his flat. Once inside, he opened some windows before retrieving his homemade bong. He quickly made a new tinfoil lid for the rock to rest on – this time remembering to part-fill the plastic bottle with water before securing the foil with the elastic band. He used a needle to punch holes through the top, returned to the table with a lighter, took one of the rocks that looked a little larger than the others from the bag and placed it on the base. He lit the rock with his lips already around the hollow pen tube and sucked gently and steadily, drawing the thick smoke from the melting rock into the bottle and then into his mouth. He inhaled without coughing or spluttering, exhaling once he felt the smoke was spent before quickly inhaling again – repeating the process over and over until the rock was dead.

The increased quantity and intensity of his smoking hugely amplified the effects from the first time he'd taken a hit. He felt so light he could have sworn he was about to start floating around the room as the pain, guilt, sense of responsibility and demonic nightmares left him and he entered a world of peace and pleasure so intense his eyes rolled into the back of his head. A small waxy rock the size of a baby's fingernail had taken him to a paradise no other experience or amount of money ever could. Sixteen pounds to leave the world and all its troubles behind. No more working all the hours God sent trying to find a better life. No more striving for materialistic things in the hope they could bring true happiness. No more slaving to get the admiration of his colleagues to make him feel wanted or important. Just smoke an innocuous waxy-looking little rock and achieve heaven on earth.

His head slumped forward onto the table and crashed on the surface, but he felt no pain – just the exquisite descent into oblivion.

13

Next morning King walked the estate on his own, which was how he wanted it. After the night before he still felt jaded, his mind foggy and unfocused. He'd made sure he'd eaten well and taken on plenty of fluids – avoiding a common trap most crack-heads fell into, so determined to hunt down their next fix that they forgot to eat or drink – but still he felt strange and disassociated from himself. Like being hungover without the headache and nausea. The high he'd felt after smoking the crack was now being matched by a long-lasting low. He caught a glimpse of himself in the window of a flat and was surprised at just how tired and pale he looked.

He ducked out of sight under a stairwell, pulled out the small clip-seal bag of cocaine he'd taken from Astill's floor safe and examined the contents. He'd heard that crack-heads and smack-heads often used a hit of cocaine to sober up – to bring themselves back from the lows that could ensue after using the far more potent crack or heroin. That was if they were lucky enough to find what was becoming a rare and expensive drug in areas like Newham – the vast majority of it being turned into the hugely more profitable crack. He didn't have the time or equipment to take it like he'd seen them do in films so he tipped a small amount into the valley between his thumb and hand, as if taking snuff, and inhaled it in one go through a single nostril. Immediately his nose began to burn, but in a strangely pleasant way, while at the same time the back of his throat and tongue were covered with a stinging, bitter taste – giving him the almost irresistible urge to spit. He waited for a while. It was a far cry from the instant effects of the crack, but slowly he began to feel his heart rate quicken and his mind sharpen – even his body returned to him as the tiredness retreated and he felt strong and capable again. His radio blaring in his ear snapped him further back into life.

'*Any Grove Wood Estate Unit out and about can deal with a call in Millander Walk, please? Control over,*' the female voice asked.

He tried to speak into his handset, but his voice was scratchy and inaudible. He cleared his voice and tried again. 'Yeah,' he managed to say. 'PS 42 will take a look. What you got?'

'*Not sure,*' Control admitted. '*We've had a call from a hysterical female saying something's happened to her young daughter, but we're not getting a lot of sense from her – lots of screaming and shouting and not much else. Call was made from a landline number that comes back to a Carroll Bickley at 214 Millander Walk.*'

'OK,' he told them. 'Show me assigned.'

'*Will do,*' the cheerful voice told him. '*Keep us informed.*'

'Yeah, yeah,' King said after releasing the transmit button. He began to stroll towards Millander Walk, in contrast to a few weeks ago when he would have virtually jogged to get there. Suddenly the misery and fears of others didn't seem important to him any more. These people lived like animals anyway – why should he break his back trying to help them? Kelly was right: the entire place was just a jungle and he was the tiger. He rushed for no one.

Eventually he reached the address of the distressed woman who'd called the police and hadn't even been able to articulate her complaint. Wearily he knocked on the door and half-heartedly called to whoever was inside. 'Police.'

243

Within seconds the door was flung open by a hard-faced woman in her thirties although she looked like she was in her late fifties. Her greying hair was pulled back tight over her scalp to reveal all of her flabby-looking red face, which matched her huge sagging breasts and tyre of fat perfectly. Cheap tattoos covered her Popeye-like forearms and neck. King was repulsed at the sight of her, not helped by the stink of stale sweat and food that emitted from both her and the maisonette.

'Oh, thank God it's you,' she greeted him. 'Come in. Come in.' Her voice was thick with a desperation that he found even more repulsive than her appearance and smell.

'What's the problem?' he asked without moving, hoping it would be something he could resolve without entering the house.

'We can't speak here,' she whispered conspiratorially. 'Inside.'

'Look,' he told her impatiently. 'You called the police. Why did you call the police?'

She looked him up and down before sticking her head out the door and looking both ways along the walkway to ensure no one could hear. 'My daughter,' she managed to say, fighting back the tears and the anger. 'Someone touched my daughter.'

'Touched?' he asked, his eyes narrowing with sudden concern.

'You fucking know,' she told him – her frustration growing by the second. '*Touched* her.'

'OK,' he relented. 'Let's talk inside.' He stepped past her and heard the door close behind him as he scanned the room for signs of danger or squalor. Last thing he wanted was to step in dog or human excrement – but he found neither. The maisonette was relatively clean and orderly, but the furniture, carpets and curtains were cheap and old and trapped the smell of thousands of meals and unclean bodies. He swallowed his nausea and controlled his breathing while he talked, taking short breaths so the sickly sweet smell of the place didn't penetrate too deeply into his lungs.

'Where's your daughter now?' he asked, still hoping the matter could be quickly resolved.

'She's here,' Bickley answered frantically.

'Is she hurt?' he enquired immediately, praying the answer would be no.

'I don't know,' she told him. 'I don't know what he could have done to her.'

'Didn't you check?' he chastised her.

'No,' she said, puzzled. 'I ain't a doctor.'

King sighed at her stupidity.

'You said she's your daughter?' he checked.

'Yeah,' she nodded repeatedly.

'What's her name?'

'Rosie.'

'And how old is Rosie?'

'Ten,' she answered, dabbing away her tears with the sleeve of her top.

'Was she with anyone when this happened?' he tried to find out.

'No,' she told him before looking confused, 'but why you asking all these questions? Just sort it out.'

'That's what I'm trying to do,' he assured her.

'No,' she told him. 'I mean properly sort it out.'

'I don't understand,' he told her truthfully.

'Yeah,' she nodded rapidly. '*Properly* sort it out. And if you don't, I know someone who will. Paedophiles don't deserve prison. That's too good for the likes of them.'

'I think you should calm down,' he insisted, beginning to understand what she wanted him to do, 'and tell me what happened. What did Rosie say?'

'She told me enough,' Bickley answered, less frantic now.

'Which was?'

'She was playing with some of her friends over on the

wasteground by the old railway arches, but got bored and wanted to come home,' she explained. 'She said she was walking back on her own when a man came up to her and started talking. She don't remember what happened next, just that he took her behind some bushes and . . .' She started hyperventilating – patting her own chest with a fluttering hand as if fending off an impending heart attack.

'Just take your time,' King encouraged her.

She calmed down enough to continue. 'He . . .' she struggled to say the words. 'He made her take off her trousers and . . . and he . . . he pulled down her knickers and . . . he touched her . . . with his fingers.' She covered her mouth with her hand, unable to describe any more.

'Did he . . .' King pushed '. . . did he do anything else? Did he make her do anything to him?'

'Isn't touching her enough?' Bickley almost shouted. 'So what you going to do about it?'

'You say this happened over by the wasteground near the arches?' he ignored her.

'Yeah,' she answered, unsure of its relevance. 'Why does it matter?'

'Did Rosie say who did this to her?' he asked. His mind was already turning to the last time he'd been on the wasteground and his encounter with Alan Swinton.

'No,' Bickley answered, hate and vengeance suddenly filling her eyes and chasing the sadness away. 'She's gone into some sort of lock-down. Won't talk to me. Won't say nothing. But we all know who done it. There's only one pervert who'd do this to a kid on this estate.'

'Really?' King checked they had the same suspicions. 'And who would that be?'

'You fucking know,' she accused him. 'That sick bastard Swinton. Only you ain't never done anything about it, have ya?'

'I need evidence,' he reminded her.

246

'Evidence?' she questioned. 'You mean the same sort of evidence you had against Ronnie Butler?'

King froze for a second before being able to answer. 'I don't know what you're talking about.'

'Not what I heard,' she almost threatened him. 'Not what *everyone* on the estate's saying.'

'Look,' he tried to move on, 'I need to get Rosie interviewed by a specially trained SOIT officer who'll know how to find out exactly what happened to her.'

'A what?' she asked through her anger.

'A SOIT officer,' he repeated. 'It stands for Sexual Offences Interview Technique. It's especially important in the case of a child victim.'

'I ain't having Rosie interviewed by no . . . whatever you said,' Bickley told him. 'I ain't having her messed with by shrinks and doctors – cross-examined in court by some pervert or his smart-arsed barrister. I want this piece of scum punished properly. I want him taught a lesson – like Butler was. I want justice.'

'I don't know anything about Butler,' he bluffed, 'except he got turned over by a rival gang.'

'Say what you like,' she told him, 'but what you did to that slag Butler was the right thing to do. If you want the people round here to keep on respecting you – if you don't want people *talking* to your bosses – you have to do the right thing here. Swinton has to be punished according to *our* laws.'

'Your *laws*,' he looked at her with disgust. 'What do you know about the law?'

'I know enough to know something has to be done about Swinton,' she demanded.

His radio breaking into life interrupted him before he could argue with her any more.

'*PS 42 from Control,*' the same female voice as before asked. '*You receiving, Sarge?*'

247

'Yeah, go ahead,' he acknowledged.

'Have you got an update for the distressed female calling from 214 Millander Walk? I need to update the CAD.'

He stared at Bickley in silence for a long time – knowing which way he had to go, but not wanting to hurry the moment when he finally jumped.

'PS 42 – you still there, over?'

'Yes,' he answered, knowing the time had come.

'Any update?' the voice asked, sounding quizzical. *'Millander Walk?'*

'Yes,' he finally told her. 'The occupant's ten-year-old daughter was missing for a while, but she's home safe and sound now. Mother just got a little over-anxious. No allegations made. No offences disclosed. Words of advice given to the mother about calling 999 so fast.'

'Thanks, 42,' the voice accepted his account. *'I'll update the CAD.'*

'Well?' Bickley demanded. 'What you gonna do about it?'

'Just leave it with me,' he assured her as he stared out of the window across the sprawling Grove Wood Estate stretching out in front of him – ugly with a rotting heart, like a cancer that devoured and transformed everything good around it, ultimately destroying itself. He and the estate deserved each other – increasingly belonged to each other and neither could ever go back now. 'I'll take care of it.'

Brown and Williams walked together in a different part of the estate – as far away from Millander Walk as they could get, knowing King was there dealing with the call. The unnatural quietness of the estate was not lost on either of them – the occasional person they did see scurried past them avoiding eye contact.

'Don't feel like a cop when I'm here any more,' Williams complained. 'People are scared of us. I feel more like some sort of gangster than Old Bill.'

'Aye,' Brown sadly agreed. 'Not much we can do about it now except be careful. While King's around we're all in this together.'

'I don't like it,' Williams told him, his nervousness tangible. 'What if he does something else that involves us?'

'Try and talk him out of it,' Brown answered. 'If we can't . . .' He gave an unconvincing shrug.

'He's got us by the bollocks, hasn't he?'

'We've all got each other by the bollocks,' Brown reminded him. 'King's right about one thing – we all stand or fall together.'

'Should have never taken that money,' Williams lamented his decision. 'As soon as we did that we were fucked.'

'Nah,' Brown disagreed. 'We tied ourselves to King before that. The thing with Butler made sure of that. We should have just nicked him. Handed him over to CID and taken the pats on the back. Jesus, what were we thinking?'

'I reckon Butler had it coming,' Williams argued. 'What he did to Renita. What he *would* have done to her. I'm not about to lose too much sleep over a piece of shit like him, but taking the money felt . . . felt dirty.'

'Aye,' Brown agreed. 'You spent any of it yet?'

Williams smiled. 'I bought a bottle of very expensive scotch and gave the rest to a beggar.'

'You what?' Brown laughed.

'Seriously. I gave it to some beggar outside the shop I bought the scotch in. Should have seen his fucking face. Figured I didn't want it so might as well try and do something good with it.'

'Fuck,' Brown laughed. 'I didn't think of doing something like that.'

'So what did you do?'

'Burnt the fucking lot,' he admitted. 'Made me feel like shit just knowing it was there.'

'Burnt it though?' Williams shook his head.

'Aye,' Brown smiled. 'So paranoid about forensics I thought burning it would be best.'

'Forensics?' Williams laughed at him. 'Now that is paranoid.'

'Aye, well,' Brown agreed. 'Wish I'd done what you did though or just stuffed it in some charity box somewhere. Oh well, fuck it. Too late now.'

They walked in silence for a few steps until Williams spoke again. 'So what do we do now?'

'Way I see it is we just play it out until the Unit's disbanded or King's moved on somewhere else,' Brown explained. 'Then we can get back to normal policing and try and forget about what happened here. The more time we put between ourselves and this place the better it'll be.'

'And the more distance we put between us and King,' Williams added.

'Aye,' Brown nodded. 'I'll fucking buy you a drink when that happens.'

'If we survive that long,' Williams added gloomily. 'If we're not already banged up.'

'Jesus,' Brown warned him. 'Don't even say things like that. You know what happens to Old Bill in prison.'

'But King bothers me, man,' said Williams. 'He's not the same person. He's got that fucked-up look in his eyes. Like he's enjoying this shit. Like he's capable of anything. I don't know what happened, but he's changed, man. He could drag us all down.'

'I hear you,' Brown agreed, 'but you better not let him hear you saying that. Fuck knows what he might do.'

'I don't know,' Williams shook his head. 'Don't know how much more of this shit I can take. Turning me into a nervous wreck. I feel sick all day and that Marino bothers me. And what's with King and how long we've been on the estate for? Every time I mention we've been here too long he looks at me as if I've gone mad. Like he's losing track of time or something – I don't know. Freaks me out.'

'I know,' Brown shook his head. 'He's fucking losing it, I tell you.'

'Listen,' Williams almost whispered. 'I got to tell you, I'm thinking about just bailing.'

'You can't,' Brown warned him. 'We can't do anything that could draw attention to the Unit. We can't afford to have people asking questions about why people are bailing from it. Also you'll probably be replaced. Then what happens if King tries to turn them too – tells them a little about what we've been doing – tries to give them a taste for it? Only maybe they're not interested and go running to Johnston blabbing their mouth off about what they've found out. That'd be you and me fucked along with King. No. We don't have a choice here. We have to keep our heads down, our mouths shut and see it out to the end. No matter how bitter. We got no choice, Danny. We just got no choice.'

King sat on a couple of crates he'd put on top of each other, creating a makeshift seat in the middle of the wasteground where he'd first encountered Alan Swinton, although there was no sign of him now. Being back on the patch of desolate land, littered with bricks, rubbish and thrown-out furniture, reminded him of Renita. He hadn't thought of her as much as he should have lately or even been to see her in hospital. He wondered whether she'd heard about what happened to Butler and if she'd worked out who did it. He figured she probably had, but couldn't even guess how she felt about it. He had a terrible feeling she wouldn't approve, although he was sure she wouldn't say anything to anyone. She'd want to speak to him face to face, though. Perhaps that was why he'd avoided going to see her – because he couldn't bear the look of disappointment and disgust he imagined she'd wear. Sounds of someone approaching snapped him from his self-grappling and made him stand to see who was fighting their way through the coarse grass and debris towards him. Finally Dougie O'Neil stumbled into view.

'Fuck,' O'Neil immediately exclaimed. 'Why the fuck we gotta meet here?'

'Didn't think it would be wise coming to your flat again,' King explained. 'Not so soon after Astill's arrest.'

'Why couldn't we just talk about whatever it is you want to talk about over the phone?' O'Neil questioned.

'No,' King insisted. 'This is not something I want to discuss over a mobile phone and from now on you remember that. You can use the phone to arrange meetings, but never use it to discuss business and never say my name. Understand?'

'Business?' O'Neil picked up on King's own word. 'What business?'

'Our business,' King told him. He pulled the crack he'd kept from the raid on Astill's flat from his pocket and tossed it to O'Neil who caught it in one hand and stood staring at the windfall. 'Thirty-one rocks there – I've counted them, so don't try and fuck me over,' King made it clear. From a shirt pocket hidden under his body armour he pulled a wad of notes adding up to several hundred pounds and held them out for O'Neil to see. 'Take it,' he encouraged, as if trying to hand-feed a sparrow. Finally O'Neil stepped forward and plucked the cash from his hand – looking down at it as if it was the greatest fortune ever discovered before confusion spread across his face.

'What d'you want me to do with this?' he asked.

'Not smoke it for one thing,' King warned him. 'You want the occasional rock, that's fine, but you pay, just like everyone else's going to pay.'

'You want me to sell it?' O'Neil checked, barely able to believe what he was hearing.

'What the fuck else would you do with it?' King mocked him. 'With Astill out the way you're the only crack dealer on the estate and as he was so kind as to give us our first supply free, you can sell this batch cheap. Get the customers lined up and maybe bring in a few more from further afield and then put the price back up to normal. We split the profits forty–sixty in my favour. For that you get my personal protection and the Unit's. No one will fuck with you. Anyone else is stupid enough to set themselves up in the same business, you let me know and I'll take care of it. I'm the police around here. Can't get a reputation for tolerating drug dealers. Once I've moved on they can all come creeping back in for all I care. Everything clear?'

'Yeah,' O'Neil answered with a shrug, 'but . . .'

'But what?'

'You sure you want to do this?' O'Neil asked.

King hadn't expected to be questioned – hadn't expected O'Neil to open the doubts in his mind.

'If people want to kill themselves on crack that's their problem,' he justified himself – the image of himself drawing long and hard on his own homemade bong invading his mind. 'As far as I'm concerned all drugs should be legal. With me controlling the local crack trade I'm removing the criminal element. Way I see it, I'm just doing on a local scale what the government should be doing nationally and taking the likes of Astill out the equation. Keeping drugs illegal is like handing organized crime billions of pounds every year. They're the last people who want to see drugs legalized. And unlike you, Dougie, I have bills to pay. Mortgage, credit cards, insurance – stuff you know nothing about. I'm sick of working my arse off and still only living hand-to-mouth, day-to-day. I deserve a little more and this is the best way to get it quickly. Once I've paid off a few bills we'll quit, but still keep the other dealers away.'

O'Neil didn't believe a word King said. 'Fair enough,' he answered anyway. 'When d'you want me to start?'

'Now,' King ordered, 'and by the way – do you know anyone who can keep us supplied? But not someone from round here. I don't want people round here knowing my business. Think of me as the silent partner.'

'Yeah, no problem,' O'Neil answered casually. 'I know a crew in North London can do the business for us.'

'Good,' King replied. 'Use them.'

'How much?' O'Neil asked.

'How much what?' King checked.

'How much d'you want me to buy? How much d'you want me to sell?'

'As much as you can buy – as much as you can sell,' King told him. 'I'll tell you when to slow down if I think things are getting too big.'

'That's all fine,' O'Neil cautioned him, 'only you should know I heard a lot of rumours that Astill was getting his gear from the Campbell family. They ain't gonna be too happy when they find out you've replaced one of their best earners with someone else and you're not even using them to get your gear.'

'Fuck the Campbells,' King swore. 'I've heard all about them. Bunch of wannabe gangsters. They won't bother us.'

'I ain't so sure,' O'Neil argued. 'They can be dangerous.'

'What they gonna do to me?' King asked. 'What they gonna do to the Unit? We're the police. They can't touch us. Just let me worry about the Campbells and you worry about shifting those rocks.'

'Fine,' O'Neil agreed. 'We'll do it your way.'

'Yes,' King snapped at him. 'We'll do it my way. Now I need to take care of something. I'll check with you in a couple of days. Have my cut ready.' O'Neil just nodded meekly as King turned to leave before stopping. 'One more thing – before I forget. Couple of guys will be coming round to your flat later today to fix a grid over the front door and windows. There's no need for you to speak to them. They know what to do and have already been paid. You just make sure you're there to take the new keys when they're done. And try and stay off the gear,' he warned him as he started to walk away. 'At least during the day. Remember – you work for me now, but if I have to replace you I will. You're no good to me stoned.'

By the time King reached their usual meeting place in the basement underneath the estate, Brown and Williams were already there just as he'd told them to be.

'Where the fuck have you been?' Brown snarled.

'Easy, Dave,' King told him and dropped a sports bag at their feet. 'I had some business to take care of.'

'We've been hanging around down here for ages,' Brown continued to argue before Williams changed the subject.

'What's in the bag?' he asked cautiously.

King grinned and bent to unzip it, silently pulling a sinister-looking mixture of items from inside and laying them on the floor in front of them: miniature baseball bats, ski masks, gloves and boiler suits.

'What the fuck is all this for?' Brown demanded, looking on in horror.

'Get dressed,' King explained. 'We got a job to do.'

'I'm not up for ripping off any more dealers,' Williams insisted, shaking his head. 'Especially not like this.'

'Same here,' Brown backed him up. 'I'm out.'

'We didn't *rip* Astill *off*,' King snapped at them, 'or Mooney. It was a means to an end to bring drug dealing on this estate under control. Anyway – this isn't for any dealer.'

'Then what the hell is it for?' Williams asked.

'Another young girl on the estate's been attacked,' he told them matter-of-factly. 'Sexually assaulted – just like the others.'

'Jesus,' Brown shook his head. 'Then let's hand it over to CID and let them deal with it.'

'That's not what the mother of the girl wants,' King explained. 'She doesn't want SOITs and psychiatrists. She

255

doesn't want to fuck around with courts. Even if we could get a conviction he'd only appeal – put all the kids he's abused through giving evidence all over again. She wants *justice* and she wants it now.'

'Fuck what she wants,' Brown argued. 'The people on this estate live like animals. They don't care about the law or justice – just revenge and brutality. Butler was bad enough, but at least I can convince myself he had it coming to him for what he did to Ren. But this . . . I want no part of it.'

'And a paedophile who attacks a young girl doesn't?' King demanded.

'Wait,' Williams jumped in. 'We don't even know who attacked her.'

'Yeah we do,' King corrected him. 'Alan Swinton.'

'She told you that?' Williams checked.

'No,' he admitted, 'but the mother did.'

'The mother?' Brown asked. 'And the girl told the mother, right?'

'Not exactly,' King answered without looking at them as he began to pull on one of the boiler suits.

'Then how d'you know it's Swinton?' Williams said what Brown was thinking.

'Because the mother just knows it was,' King replied impatiently, 'and so do I. Who the fuck else could it be? Swinton's a paedophile and deserves to be punished. I even caught him myself hanging out with a bunch of kids when I was with Renita. He's a filthy child molester and needs to be taught a lesson.'

'No,' Brown wouldn't give in. 'I'm not doing this. I know what people think about Swinton, but nothing's ever been proved.'

'Me too,' Williams supported him. 'This is too much for me.'

'Get dressed,' King ordered, throwing the boiler suit into Brown's chest who caught it but then let it fall to the floor.

'No,' Brown repeated.

'You think this is some sort of game?' King asked calmly. 'We're in this now. This is how things get done now. We don't do this we'll lose the respect of everyone on the estate. They're all watching us – waiting to see if we've got the balls to *deal* with Swinton. Do this or everything we have done will all be for nothing.'

'To tell you the truth,' Williams explained, 'I don't really give a shit and I sure as hell don't give a damn about what anyone in this shithole thinks about me. Butler. Astill. It's all gone too far.'

'Still don't get it, do you?' King shook his head. 'People on this estate *know* what's been happening – understand? If we don't do this, the girl's mother is gonna march down to the nick and start telling anyone who'll listen about what's been going on. Do you really want that? You think we'd survive that?'

'You're forgetting one thing,' Brown reminded him. 'There's no evidence. Astill won't talk to Old Bill and *you* made sure we got rid of anything that could link us to Butler.'

'Yeah,' Williams joined in, sounding slightly panicked. 'You took our shirts. You burnt them.'

'Did I?' King silenced them. 'Sure about that, are you?'

'You fucking bastard,' Brown cursed and jumped forward, fist clenched and arm pulled back, but Williams stepped across him and intercepted him before he could land a blow. 'You set us up. You were never gonna burn the shirts.'

'Just thought it would be wise to keep a little insurance, to ensure everyone's loyalty to the Unit. Nothing personal. Now let's all agree to do as I say.'

'Fuck you,' Brown cursed him.

'Let's just get on with it,' Williams implored him. 'But this is the last time. After this I want off the Unit.'

'Aye,' Brown agreed. 'Me too.'

'Fine,' King told them without emotion. 'As soon as I can find suitable replacements you can leave. But not until then.'

'How long will that be?' Williams asked. 'Weeks? Months?'

'As long as it takes,' King tormented them before softening. 'Maybe a couple of weeks. But once you're gone you keep your mouths shut.'

'Whatever,' Williams went along with it.

'So be it,' Brown did the same.

'Good,' King nodded his head and retrieved another boiler suit from the bag.

'Where the hell d'you get all this stuff from anyway?' Williams asked.

'Property store,' King smiled.

'Fucking property store?' Brown threatened to explode again. 'Are you insane?'

'Relax,' King waved his concerns away. 'It's all old evidence from dead cases – all marked for destruction. Once we've finished with it I'll put it back where I found it and wait for the Commissioner to do the rest and incinerate it. It couldn't be sweeter.'

'You really are insane,' Brown shook his head, but began to dress in the things King had brought all the same, as did Williams – both resigned to the inevitable – inextricably tied to King since the moment they transcended the law and tried to become it.

'Nothing insane about planning ahead,' King argued.

'Speaking of which,' Williams questioned, 'what is the plan?'

'We get kitted up and go to Swinton's house,' King explained. 'This time in the evening he'll be home alone watching the telly or surfing the net for child porn. We grab him from his flat and bring him back here.'

'We drag him kicking and screaming across the estate?' Williams queried.

'Not screaming,' King told him and tossed him a roll of insulating tape from the bag.

Williams stared at the roll in his hands. 'Jesus Christ.'

258

'And the kicking part?' Brown asked, unable to even look at the tape.

'Swinton's a loser and coward,' King dismissed it. 'He won't give us any trouble.'

'And if someone tries to interfere, or worse, calls the police?' Williams kept attacking the plan.

'They won't,' King insisted.

'How can you be sure?' Brown questioned.

'Because by now I reckon most of the estate know what's gonna happen,' he told them. 'Except for Swinton, of course. They want this to happen. They're waiting for this to happen. Nobody's gonna get in our way.'

'This is a fucking nightmare,' Williams complained.

'Aye,' Brown agreed. 'A living nightmare.'

'One there's no escape from,' King reminded them, 'unless we do this thing. Here,' he continued, pulling the small clip-seal bag of cocaine he'd taken from Astill's shirt pocket. 'Have a hit of this – it'll make it easier.' He tapped a thin line of the crystalline white powder onto the back of his hand and snorted it in one go up his nose – squeezing his eyes together against the rush of the hit. 'Fuck,' he cursed in approval and handed the bag to Williams who looked at it quizzically.

'I thought you were supposed to chop it up with a playing card or something and snort it through a rolled-up banknote?' he asked.

'I think that's for the TV,' King told him. 'Works just as well this way.'

'Already tried it, have you?' Brown accused him.

King ignored him as he watched Williams tap a small amount onto the back of his hand and eye it cautiously. 'It's only coke,' King assured him. 'It'll just give you a little pick-up is all. Like being drunk without making a fool of yourself or losing control. One hit's not gonna kill you.'

'Bollocks to it,' Williams relented. 'If it helps get this over with,' he declared before inhaling the minute white crystals, wincing against the stinging effects, shaking his head against the sensation, like hundreds of fire-ants in his nasal passage and throat, until the burning eased and the effects began to kick in. 'Shit,' he said and offered the bag back to King who jutted his chin in the direction of Brown. Williams understood and turned and offered it to his partner.

'You must be joking,' Brown refused it as he continued to get dressed.

'Feels good,' Williams encouraged him. 'Better than doing this sober.'

'Fuck's sake,' Brown moaned as he snatched the bag from him and tipped more than the others had onto the back of his hand.

'Take it easy,' King warned him. 'Don't want you thinking you can fly.'

'Fuck you,' Brown replied and sniffed hard at the powder, wincing and shaking his head violently to chase away the burning. 'Jesus,' he complained. 'Can't believe people take this shit for fun.'

'Give it a minute,' King told. 'You'll see. Now remember, we don't want to kill this fucker, just fuck him up badly enough so everyone knows we've done our job. Hit him in the face if you must, but no kicking to the head or stamping. I don't think he could take it. Remember your self-defence training – try not to use your fists or you'll end up with broken fingers and bruised knuckles. Let's not give the likes of Marino cause for suspicion. Use your forearms, elbows, knees and boots. Once we're done we'll dump him some-where on the estate and hope someone calls him an ambulance.'

'And when he starts shooting his mouth off in hospital?' Brown questioned.

'What's he gonna say?' King asked. '"I'm a child molester and the locals gave me a kicking to teach me a lesson?" I don't think so. He'll tell them he fell down the stairs and crawl off to hide under a stone somewhere. He's no threat to us.'

'Fucking madness,' Brown complained, but King just smiled, pulled a ski mask over his head and spread his arms wide as he turned towards them.

'Well?' he asked. 'How do I look?'

Susie Ubana stood outside her flat, with the metal grid securely locked behind her as usual, smoking a cigarette, enjoying the warm night air and listening to the sounds of the estate at night – so familiar to her they now sounded strangely peaceful. But tonight the estate had that special atmosphere of fearful anticipation. The sort of atmosphere that spread like a forest fire when word got out that something *serious* was going to happen. It usually meant one criminal planned to kill or seriously injure another or one street gang planned to attack another while the rest of the estate collectively held its breath and waited. She sensed Kelly approaching before she heard or saw her, but still it made her jump slightly.

'You're out late,' Ubana almost warned her.

'So,' Kelly shrugged. 'No law against it.'

Ubana continued to smoke in silence, wishing she were still alone to stare at the stars in the clear sky above.

'Quiet tonight, innit?' Kelly continued.

'I suppose so,' Ubana agreed, slightly irritated.

'Like . . .' she pried, 'like everyone's waiting for something to happen.'

'Yeah,' Ubana softened a little. 'Something bad in the air tonight, that's for sure.'

'Something's got people scared enough to stay indoors,' Kelly told her.

Ubana looked hard and deep into her eyes before speaking. 'The devil's out tonight,' she warned her.

Kelly just smiled, unafraid. 'I heard a whisper it's that nonce Swinton they're coming for.'

'They?' Ubana asked.

'You know,' Kelly shrugged. 'The same ones who did—'

'You shouldn't talk about them,' Ubana cut her off to save her from herself. 'They hear you been spreading rumours they might come looking for you next.'

'They don't scare me,' Kelly told her – her black eyes shining with confidence and fearlessness.

'Oh?' Ubana questioned. 'And why's that?'

'They're only men,' Kelly explained. 'I know how to handle men.'

'Yeah,' Ubana agreed, flicking her cigarette over the edge of the walkway and heading for her flat. 'I suppose you do.'

'I heard they might even kill him,' Kelly added casually, stopping Ubana in her tracks.

'This whole thing's out of control,' Ubana decreed. 'It's going too far.'

'Reckon he deserves it,' Kelly disagreed as she watched Ubana fumbling with the keys to the grid. 'Nonce practically raped that little Bickley girl. Teach him and his kind a lesson. Nice to see someone around here who's finally got the balls to do something.'

'Stay away from him, Kelly,' Ubana snapped her advice. 'I know what you're thinking, but I'm telling you he's bad news that one. Bad seed. Jesus, we don't even know it was Swinton who attacked her. I heard the little girl isn't speaking.'

'Course it's him,' Kelly casually damned him. 'Who else could it be?'

'I don't know,' she admitted as she slipped past the grid and into her secured maisonette. 'Best to stay out the way and not get involved. Is your mum at home?'

'No,' Kelly replied. 'She's round at Chris's.'

'Then get home now,' she told her. 'Lock your doors and stay inside. Don't come out for nothing. No matter what you hear. That's what I'll be doing. That's what everyone'll be doing. By morning – hopefully it'll be all over and may God forgive us all.'

Marino sat in the small CID office in Canning Town Police Station reading through the paperwork on two street robbers uniformed officers had arrested earlier and handed over to him for investigation and processing. He drank strong coffee in anticipation of a long night ahead – his concentration broken by the sudden ringing on his mobile phone. The caller ID had been withheld, which either meant it was a call from a police line or someone was being very cautious. He sighed heavily at the unwelcome distraction but answered it anyway.

'Frank Marino speaking.'

'It's me,' the woman's voice told him.

'It's late.' He passed on the pleasantries. 'Something wrong?' There was a long silence, as if the person on the other end was already regretting calling him. 'You called me,' he reminded her, 'so I'm assuming you've got something you want to tell me.' He waited for her to regain her nerve.

'I . . . I think something really bad is going to happen,' she warned him.

'Oh?' he asked, his eyes narrowing with concern. 'Like what?'

'Someone's about to get seriously hurt,' she explained. 'Maybe even killed.'

'Who?' he asked with urgency. 'Where?'

'On the Grove Wood,' she explained. 'Alan Swinton.'

Marino searched his mind, trying to remember why he knew the name, until finally it popped into his head. 'I've heard of him,' he said. 'Some people think maybe he's a danger to children.'

'That's your business,' the voice answered. 'All I know is he's getting *hit* – tonight.'

'Why?' Marino quickly moved on. He needed fast answers. 'Why's he getting hit? Is it something to do with . . . kids?'

'Yeah,' the voice told him quietly. 'Rumour is he touched up some young girl on the estate. That he's the one attacked the other children. Her mum's going mad about it. She wants payback.'

'That's weird,' Marino replied. 'I haven't seen any reports of another child being attacked on the Grove Wood. If something like that happened I should have been told.'

'No one informed the police,' the woman explained. 'The girl's mother didn't want them involved. She wants it taken care of another way.'

'D'you know the girl's name?' he asked – his question met by more silence, as if by telling him the caller would be getting too close.

'Bickley,' she finally gave in. 'I think it's Rosie Bickley.'

'Shit,' Marino cursed. 'I know the family. Old man's inside for burglary. Not exactly pro-police. Can't see her talking to us. You said this was going to go down on the Grove Wood,' Marino changed tack. 'Any idea who she's got to do her dirty work for her?'

There was another long silence – more pronounced than previously. Marino could feel the caller's fear even down the phone. 'Hello,' he encouraged her, but still nothing, although he could feel she was still there. 'I know the uniformed cops who cover the estate,' he told her, referring to the Unit. 'Maybe I could get them to show a presence? Might put our would-be attackers off.'

The silence seemed to intensify before she spoke again, but only to end the conversation.

'I've said all I can say,' she told him. 'Rest's up to you.'

He heard the line go dead before he could argue – his mind suddenly racing with possibilities and fears. He snapped himself out of it, grabbed his desk phone and pressed the extension for the Unit's office, but after more than a minute of listening to the ringing tone there was still no reply. After hanging up he scrambled around in his desk drawer until he found his rarely used personal radio, but having switched it on and prepared himself to speak he suddenly paused – some instinct telling him it would be a bad idea for him to make the call himself.

'You got your PR there?' he asked the DC sitting opposite.

'Yeah,' the DC replied a little suspiciously.

'I need you to make a call for me,' he explained.

'Your . . .' the DC enquired ' . . . your radio not working then?'

'Just do me a favour,' Marino ordered him with some irritation, 'and make the call.'

'OK,' the DC shrugged, turning his radio on. 'Who d'you want me to call?'

'The Grove Wood Estate's Policing Unit,' Marino told him.

'Any one of them in particular?' the DC asked.

'Just try them all,' Marino hurriedly demanded. 'Quickly.'

The DC pulled a face to show he didn't understand, but made the call anyway. 'Any Grove Wood unit receiving, DC Hutton, over?' The reply should have been almost instant, but there was none.

'Try again,' Marino insisted, but the result was the same, spurring Marino to his feet. He grabbed his jacket and started filling his pockets with the detritus from his desktop – his face serious and urgent. 'Do me a favour, will you?' he asked the young DC.

'Sure,' he replied without much interest.

'Babysit the two robbers banged up downstairs until I get back. I won't be long.'

'Going somewhere?' the DC asked sarcastically.

'The Grove Wood Estate,' Marino answered.

'Trouble?' the DC asked, more intrigued now.

'Could be,' he answered noncommittally.

'Want some company?'

'No,' Marino answered firmly – thinking of what he might find and what he may want to keep quiet. 'It's better I go alone.'

'Suit yourself,' the young DC told him and returned to the pile of reports on his desk as Marino headed for the yard and the unmarked car that would take him to the Grove Wood Estate.

Alan Swinton sat alone in his small, unpleasant flat watching children's TV while he ate a simple sandwich and drank a glass of milk. It was his usual evening diet and one of the few things he was capable of preparing for himself. Abandoned to the state by his parents who couldn't cope when he was just a young teenager, he'd spent most of his adult life in and out of mental health institutions until finally someone in a suit with a name badge that said Doctor decided that he had some learning difficulties, but was capable of looking after himself and should no longer be under care or super-vision. At which point the health system had spat him out into the care of social services who'd found him an unwanted flat on the Grove Wood Estate, showed him how to sign on at the job centre and cash his unemployment benefit cheque and bid him farewell. Having been in the system once and thrown out the other end he was now all but barred from it – abandoned to solitude and a daily battle to survive he was barely equipped to win.

His only pleasure was the simple company of children and enjoying the same uncomplicated things as they did. Most adults, especially the ones he'd encountered on the estate, were scary and intimidating and they talked about things he neither understood nor wanted to discuss – crude and ugly things that had no place in his life.

Suddenly a gentle knocking at his door made him tense and cock his head. Had he imagined the sound? He had very few callers at all, let alone late evening ones. Occasionally one of his young friends would call at the flat, seeking refuge while the latest domestic disturbance in their own homes subsided. He'd feed them snacks and let them watch TV with him until they thought it would be safe to go home. But this knock at the door didn't sound childlike. Children tended to almost slap his door, but this was a subtle rap of someone's knuckles, although the sound was somehow muffled, as if the caller was wearing gloves, despite the warm summer evening.

He muted the sound on the TV and listened hard, jumping with fright as he heard another knock on the door. He decided it must be one of the children from the estate needing his help and so lifted himself from his chair and headed to the front door – forgetting to look through the spyhole like the lady from social services had shown him – forgetting to use the door chain like the man from the housing association had shown him. Swinton was ill-equipped to survive on the estate. He had no instincts for danger. Already the local teenagers had identified him as a target and a victim – occasionally hammering on his door and screaming obscenities through his letter box, something he dealt with by hiding in his flat and holding his breath until they grew bored and went away. But tonight the men on the other side of the door were no troublesome teenagers.

He swung the door wide open to find three figures in dark boiler suits and ski masks standing in front of him. All he could see were their eyes, burning with malignant intent. He froze where he stood, unable to even try and close the door – resigned to whatever fate they'd decided for him. The man in the middle stepped forward and punched him hard in the stomach, making him collapse to his knees. He held a forlorn hand out in self-defence, but it was easily pushed away as another punch crashed into the bridge of his nose – blood spraying onto the hallway wall before it began to run in thick streams from both nostrils. He collapsed onto his side and grabbed his own nose in both hands, feeling the warm flow of thick blood, the sight of his hands being quickly covered in crimson panicking him into action as he grovelled and tried to crawl away from his attackers, making terrible, pathetic sounds like a wounded pig.

Soon the men were on him, hauling him to his feet, pulling his arms behind his back and clamping his wrists together with something that felt like cold metal before pulling a cloth hood over his head at which point he lost control of his bladder, urine flowing down his legs – his trousers becoming stained dark where the warm liquid ran. If they hadn't been holding him he would surely have collapsed.

'Fucker's pissed himself,' one of cruel voices accused him.

'You should have listened to me when I warned you,' another told him – the man's mouth close enough so he could feel the warmth of his breath through the material of the hood. 'Now it's time to pay.'

'I . . . I didn't do anything,' he pleaded through the blood that clogged his nose and mouth.

'Fucking sex-case,' another voice with a strange accent damned him.

'Get him out of here,' the most dominating voice ordered before stopping them. 'Wait,' the man seemed to change his mind. A second later Swinton felt the bottom of the hood being lifted above his mouth and a strong hand gripping him around the jaw and forcing his mouth open, then pushing a large ball fashioned from some fabric into it – filling nearly all the space. He heard something being ripped before his lips were taped shut. The only sound he could now make was a desperate, sad mumbling noise. 'Let's go,' the leader demanded and Swinton was pushed and pulled from his inadequate sanctuary into the warmth and dread of the estate beyond his door.

Marino climbed the stairwell with an increasing sense of urgency as he headed for the address he'd been given for

Alan Swinton – the words of the informant he'd spoken to on the phone becoming more concerning each time he replayed them in his mind. At best it sounded as if Swinton was going to receive a serious beating at the hands of some local avenging angels. Maybe they even intended to kill him. But even worse than that possibility, increasingly he had to consider the unthinkable – that the very people who were supposed to be protecting Swinton were the ones who'd taken it upon themselves to administer a brutal, maybe even fatal punishment. He'd seen with his own eyes what they were capable of, even if he couldn't prove Butler's injuries had been caused by them. Any hope he'd had that that was an isolated incident fuelled by what had happened to Renita was fading by the minute. He was beginning to regret not at least speaking to Professional Ethics and Standards confidentially and having the Unit looked into. If something happened to Swinton he would have his blood on his hands too. But like it or not he was old school. Turning on other cops just wasn't in his DNA. He needed to sort it out in-house.

As he reached the top of the stairs and turned onto the walkway, some movement about forty metres ahead in the gloom of the next stairwell along alerted his senses to impending danger – the figures of men in dark clothing disappearing into the darkness like bats into a cave. He hadn't run in a long time, but he ran now as silently as he could, only stopping when he reached the open door of Swinton's flat. He quickly peered inside, but saw no signs of life, although the TV was still showing children's cartoons.

'Shit,' he cursed quietly before running the rest of the distance to the stairwell and looking over the metal bannister. He squinted into the darkness, and could just about make out four figures moving slowly but silently – the figure in the middle of the group seemingly struggling as the others dragged it along. 'Damn it,' he told himself. Moving at that speed he knew he could easily catch up with them, but then what? The way he figured it he'd be outnumbered at least three-to-one.

He patted the mobile in his trouser pocket and for a second considered calling the CID office and getting some help sent, but by the time they arrived it would be too late, and if he was right about the Unit he would have opened up a horrible can of worms that he'd never be able to get the lid back on. No, he decided. He had to do this alone. If they saw him perhaps he could persuade them to stop – to hand Swinton over to him and the CID for investigation. He'd assure them no one else need ever know – so long as they swore never to try and pull anything like this again. At the end of the day they were still relatively young and dumb. He was sure he could pull them back from the precipice. Save them from themselves.

He ran down the stairwell, moving at speed, but being careful not to trip and fall, until he reached the bottom and jogged quickly towards the corner of the block they must have disappeared behind. But as soon as he rounded it he was struck in the solar plexus by a hard and accurate punch that doubled him over in pain and panic at not being able to breathe. Before he could think about straightening, his legs were kicked from under him and he fell hard onto the concrete ground. He managed to outstretch a hand towards his attacker – looking through his spread fingers at the lithe figure in dark clothing and a ski mask.

'Wait,' he managed to say. 'Just wait. You don't want to do this.'

'I'm not going to hurt you,' the figure told him in an obviously faked voice. 'Just stay out of our business.'

'It's not too late,' he pleaded. 'Just let Swinton go and I swear that'll be the end of it. It goes no further than here tonight.'

The figure stood over him, threatening and imposing. His eyes were hidden by the darkness so Marino couldn't be sure it was who he thought it was. If he could see the eyes he'd know.

'It's already too late,' the figure told him with more than a trace of sadness in his voice. 'Don't try and follow us. If you do I'll have to hurt you. I don't want to do that. Understand?' he demanded, suddenly more urgent. 'Just don't try to follow us.'

Before Marino could answer the figure sprinted off into the darkness, leaving him feeling more alone than he could ever remember – lying abandoned and vulnerable on the ground in the middle of one of the most brutal housing estates in London. Gingerly he got to his feet, using the wall to steady himself – looking in the direction Swinton had been dragged off in, but knowing he had no intention of trying to pursue them. The stark decision he now faced made him feel sick to his stomach. If he went back to the station and said nothing, then he could be signing Swinton's death warrant. But if he raised the alarm questions would be asked as to why he hadn't already informed Professional Ethics and Standards of his suspicions. He was already guilty of complicity, which for a cop meant loss of his job, his pension and even probable prison time. Somehow he'd unwittingly allowed himself to be drawn into the Unit's darkness. He knew what they were doing and had done nothing and that would be enough to damn him in the eyes of the police service and the law. He'd have to find another way to stop King and his band of brothers.

'If you kill him I can't help you,' he shouted as loudly as he could into the darkness, his voice echoing off the hard surfaces that surrounded him, not caring who heard him calling out. 'If you kill him I can't help you any more.' He slumped against the wall and clutched at his painful chest – his voice dropping to a whisper. 'Don't kill him. For God's sake, just don't kill him.'

* * *

271

Brown ripped his ski mask off and threw it on the floor of the basement. His hair was matted to his face with sweat and his eyes burnt red with the fading effects of the cocaine and exhaustion. Swinton knelt in front of him still hooded and bound – like a prisoner waiting to be executed.

'Jesus Christ,' Brown shouted. 'What the fuck was he doing here?'

'Don't worry about it,' King reassured him as he too removed his mask and tossed it casually aside. 'I took care of it.'

'What do you mean, "you took care of it"?' Brown demanded.

'I mean I warned him off our business,' King tried to explain.

'You told him it was us?' Brown panicked.

'No,' King laughed at him. 'Course I fucking didn't.'

'But he knows it's us, right?' Williams asked once he too had removed his mask.

'Maybe,' King shrugged, seemingly unconcerned. 'Can't be sure.'

'Jesus,' Williams shook his head. 'Then we need to dump this bag of shit somewhere back on the estate and get the fuck out of here.'

'And why would we do that?' King smiled. 'Do you hear any sirens screaming around the estate? Do you see any helicopter circling above? No,' he answered for them. 'No you don't, because Marino hasn't told anyone. Because Marino's not going to tell anyone. If he was, he already would have.'

'Why?' Brown demanded. 'Why's he not going to tell anyone?'

'I'm not sure,' King admitted. 'Maybe he's stupid enough or arrogant enough to think he can bring us down on his own.'

'Or save us,' Williams offered.

King ignored him. 'Maybe it's too late now for him to blow

272

the whistle without dropping himself in it for not blowing it when he first suspected something.'

'Yeah,' Brown clutched at this like a drowning man reaching for an overhanging branch. 'That's it. He left it too late.'

'But he'll still come for us, right?' Williams pointed out. 'He's not going to just quit.'

'Maybe he will now,' Brown argued, buoyed by a new belief that Marino couldn't touch them. 'Maybe he'll be scared off.'

'I don't think so,' King calmly warned them. 'But if he's working alone we can handle him.'

'Aye,' Brown agreed in desperation. 'We can handle him on his own.'

'I still think we should get rid of this nonce and disappear,' Williams insisted, 'or get back on patrol and make like nothing happened.'

'Watch what you're saying,' King reminded him, pointing with his chin towards the kneeling, shivering Swinton who made the occasional mumbling sound from behind his hood. 'And we can't just let him go. That wasn't part of the deal. People expect.'

He stepped forward and rolled the hood above Swinton's mouth then ripped the tape off and allowed him to spit the ball of material out – coughing and gagging as he did so. Once his convulsions were over King rolled the hood back down, causing Swinton to panic until he realized he could still easily draw air through the thin material.

'Who are you?' he spluttered a question. 'Why am I here?'

'Questions,' King told him coldly. 'Questions that need answers.'

'I . . . I don't understand,' he answered truthfully.

King slapped his hooded face hard enough to knock him off-balance and fall over sideways from his kneeling position, the sound of the blow reverberating around the walls of their underground interrogation centre.

'Don't lie to me,' King hissed into his face – the material of the hood curving in and out of Swinton's mouth as he threatened to hyperventilate. 'You know exactly why you're here.'

'I . . . I'll tell the police,' Swinton tried to threaten them. 'I swear I'll tell the police.'

'Tell them what?' King laughed at him. 'That you tried to rape a young girl and got found out? That the people on the estate made you pay for it?'

'What?' Swinton asked, his voice faltering with confusion.

King lifted him to his knees, only to knock him back down with a punch to the side of the head, before grabbing him by the scruff of his neck and pulling him back again. 'The girl,' he venomously accused him. 'Her name is Rosie and now she's too frightened to even speak.'

'I don't know . . .' Swinton shook his head behind the hood, 'I don't know what you're talking about.'

'Liar,' King screamed at him and punched him where he guessed his nose would be, sending him tumbling backwards over his own bent legs.

'Jesus,' Brown stepped closer. 'What's the point in questioning him? We know what we have to do. We don't need a confession. Let's just get on with it.'

'I want to hear him say it,' King snarled. 'I want to hear him admit it.'

'Why?' Brown continued. 'Don't you think it was him?'

'No,' King answered before correcting himself. 'I mean yes. I know it was him, but I still want to hear him say it.'

'Fuck this,' Williams joined in. 'Let's just do it and get the fuck out of here.'

'No,' King insisted before turning his anger back on Swinton. 'I want to hear him say it. I want him to admit he did it.'

'Who cares,' Williams complained.

'I care,' King told him through gritted teeth, momentarily confusing the here and now with the past – the girl who'd been attacked becoming the girl in the white dress and Swinton her father. 'He was going to kill her – like he killed the others.'

'What?' Brown frowned 'What are you talking about, "like he killed the others"? No one's been killed.'

King turned on him, his eyes blazing with hatred and retribution as he tried to work out where he was and why Brown and Williams were there with him. Eventually he shook his head to chase away the demons and bring himself back to the present.

'You all right?' Brown asked.

'I'm fine,' he answered unconvincingly. 'I'm fine.'

'What others?' Brown repeated. 'You said he would have killed her like the others.'

'It's nothing,' he lied. 'I meant there will be others, if we don't teach him a lesson.'

'There's already been others,' Williams reminded them, trying to convince himself that what they were about to do was justified. 'And there'll be more, right? He won't be able to stop himself. That's what they're like, yeah?'

'Right,' King confirmed and swung a kick into Swinton's rib cage that made him fold in two on the floor. King leaned over him, grabbed his collar and lifted his head off the stone floor. 'That's right, isn't it, you nonce? There's already been others, hasn't there?'

'I . . . I don't know what you're talking about,' Swinton pleaded before King again punched him in the bridge of the nose and sent a spray of blood flashing to the ground. He gargled and spat blood before being able to speak again. 'Why are you doing this? I haven't done anything.'

'Liar,' King spat into his face before taking a deep breath. 'If you admit what you've done it'll go easier on you. Your punishment won't be so bad.'

'Admit what?' Swinton panted, unwittingly fuelling King's rage. Without warning King punched him hard in the mouth – the sound of teeth falling on the hard floor and scattering away like fleeing beetles seemed to fill the large room. King sprang to his feet and kicked Swinton hard in the stomach and again quickly in his exposed ribs as he writhed to escape the beating.

King turned to the two passive onlookers. 'Well?' he questioned them. They looked at each other before reluctantly stepping forward and each tentatively kicking Swinton in his torso – the lightness of their blows making him flinch, but little more.

'What you doing?' King moaned. 'Like this,' he ordered and aimed a full-force kick into Swinton's unprotected kidney that made him straighten in pain before recoiling back into as tight a defensive ball as he could make with his hands still tied behind his back.

Brown and Williams understood it was impossible to avoid the inevitable and began to stab kicks into the prone body – without conviction at first, but with increasing ferocity as King looked on, nodding his head and voicing his encouragement. Swinton's beaten body was the vessel he could pour months of fear and frustration into as he drifted ever further from the person he used to be. His new-found acceptance of the brutality and ruthlessness of existence was shaping him into a new and stronger man who could not only survive its harshness, but thrive in it.

Their dark demons spent, Brown and Williams' kicks lost their vigour and slowed to nothing more than prods. 'What you doing?' King asked them – confused by their mercy.

'He's had enough,' Brown told him, stepping back from the body on the floor that could do little other than rock slightly from side to side.

'Enough?' King questioned. 'I'll tell you when he's had enough,' he told them and spun towards Swinton, kicking him hard in the side of the head.

'Jesus,' Williams complained, turning away, unable to look.

'Don't go too far,' Brown tried to warn him, but King fired

another kick into Swinton's head. Brown quickly stepped forward and grabbed hold of him and pulled him away. 'For Christ's sake, you'll kill him. You kill him and we're as good as dead ourselves. We can't hide a murder.'

'Can't we?' King rounded on him.

'Jesus,' Brown asked. 'What's happening to you?'

'Nothing I can't handle,' King snarled and pushed him away, bending down and punching the unmoving Swinton in the face. But Swinton didn't respond – not even with a quiet moan.

'You're wasting your time,' Brown tried. 'He's passed out.'

'He's not . . .?' Williams asked, unable to bring himself to finish his question.

Brown kneeled close to the tortured wreck and listened carefully. 'No,' he declared with a sigh. 'He's still breathing.'

'Thank fuck,' Williams said, shaking his head in disbelief at what he was involved in – the last remains of the cocaine having long since faded.

'Fair enough,' King relented. 'He's had his punishment. Take him out and dump him somewhere on the estate.'

'Aye,' Brown agreed. 'Funny though.'

'What?' King asked.

'He never did confess,' Brown reminded them. 'He never admitted it was him who touched the girl, even when you said it would go easier for him if he did. He never said it was him.'

King sniffed to let them know he didn't think it was import-ant. 'His type don't,' he tried to explain. 'They don't even know what they're doing is wrong. They think we're the sick ones because we see children as children – not things to be abused and preyed on. Fucking nonce.'

'Aye,' Brown said, although he didn't agree. 'Maybe. Come on. Let's get this piece of shit out of here then get the fuck out ourselves. I need a drink and I mean I *really* need a drink.'

'Fucking right,' Williams agreed.

'Just don't go round here,' King warned them. 'Don't use the Trafalgar. You don't want to run into Marino. Best stay out of his way for a while – at least tonight anyway. Go home. Use a pub local to where you live.'

'Fine,' Brown reluctantly agreed, stepping over the stricken Swinton, unlocking the cuffs from his wrists and taking hold of an arm. 'Give us a hand,' he told Williams who duly obliged. They draped the hooded figure between them and started to drag him away before Brown stopped and turned to King. 'You coming or what?'

'No,' King replied. 'I need to be somewhere else.'

'Oh aye,' Brown looked him up and down suspiciously. 'And where would that be?'

King's red eyes narrowed with anger. He didn't like being questioned. 'None of your business,' he warned Brown. 'Just get rid of him and then drop your gear back here. I'll take care of it in the morning. Anyone asks where you've been, tell them we were doing close obs on Ubana's flat and had to keep our PRs off. Understand?'

'Aye,' Brown didn't argue. 'Whatever you say, King. Whatever you say.'

King knocked on the door of the maisonette in Millander Walk and stepped back to wait for an answer, straightening his uniform and flat cap, having left the boiler suit and mask behind in the basement. The curtains were drawn, but light and sounds from the TV leaked through the gaps and spilled out across him. His stomach was tight with anticipation, but it felt good – he felt good – alive and wanting to live – really live – in the extreme zone of pleasure, pain, intensity and recklessness that few would ever experience. And he knew now without doubt that the girl inside the maisonette would help take him the rest of the way to where he now wanted to be. He felt a presence on the other side of the door – someone looking through the spyhole, checking him out for what seemed forever – before finally he heard the locks being clunked open and the door pushed slowly ajar. Kelly looked through the gap smiling, confident – as if she'd known he was coming, sure she had the same power over him as she did all the men in her life.

They looked at each other for a long while without speaking, neither wanting to be the first to blink in the game of dare they both knew they were playing. To her own surprise it was Kelly who cracked first. Normally if the man in front of her couldn't find his tongue she would have simply closed the door on him, but there was something different about this one. She'd had her share of wannabe gangsters before, but King's blend of menace and intelligence was something new and she found it intoxicating.

'Haven't seen you in a while,' she said, opening the door a little wider so he could better see her.

'I've been around,' he answered, trying to remember how long ago it had been since he'd seen her, sure it had only been days at most as his eyes lingered on her body for a long while – every inch of her perfection. Her small red silk shorts and matching cropped top left little to his imagination, but enough. 'Is your mum in?' he continued.

'No,' she answered casually, swaying the door back and forth slightly. 'She's round at Chris's.'

'Oh,' King nodded.

'Was it her you wanted to see?' Kelly asked, 'or . . .?' King just shrugged his shoulders, but his eyes never left hers. 'You wanna come in?' she offered.

He gave it a few seconds before answering. 'Sure.'

Kelly opened the door to allow him to enter and leaned on the doorframe – the harsh fabric of his body armour brushing against her as he entered – the smell of fresh sweat and deodorant further piquing her desire. Once he was inside she closed the door and secured the locks before trailing close behind him like a falcon stalking a dove.

'You want something to drink?' she asked, keen to rush through any pre-functionary niceties he may expect. 'Tea or something?'

'I was hoping that offer of something a little stronger might still be on the table,' he replied.

She smiled and led him into the kitchen, opening the cupboard where her mum stored their booze supply. 'Whisky? Vodka? My mum's got all sorts in here.'

'Whisky's good,' he told her, still deadpan and expressionless.

'D'you have anything with it?'

'No,' he answered flatly.

'Don't say much, do you?' she teased him.

'I say enough,' he finally smiled. 'Where's your brother and sister?'

'Mum took 'em with her,' Kelly explained. 'Chris likes having them around anyway for some reason. Spoils them rotten. Mum don't care.'

'But not you?'

'I like the time on my own.'

'And you can be trusted?' he asked, taking the glass of whisky she was offering from her hand and momentarily allowing his fingers to entwine with hers, the sensation from the touch of her skin firing a bolt of pleasure straight to his groin.

'With some things,' she answered before taking a sip from her own glass. 'Sometimes.' She moved a little closer and reached out with her spare hand, running her index finger over the back of his knuckles that gripped his glass – some fresh signs of bruising already possible to see. 'You been enforcing the law again?'

'Something like that,' he answered as he watched her finger draw increasing circles on the back of his hand. 'You got something to smoke?'

'Sure,' she told him, gently releasing his hand and taking

the things she needed from a kitchen drawer – her well-practised fingers quickly going about preparing a joint. 'How long you been smoking this shit for? Isn't it supposed to be illegal?'

'Round here,' he told her, 'it's only illegal if I say it's illegal.'

'So that's what you are now?' she told him more than asked, between dabbing her pink tongue tip along the edge of the cigarette paper and rolling it neatly. 'The law?'

'I've always been the law.'

'Judge, jury and . . . executioner?' She lit the joint and took a deep hit before passing it over to King who accepted it, his hands shaking slightly. Kelly noticed it. 'You all right?'

He sighed before speaking. 'Just . . . just maybe things have gone too far, you know. I let things go too far. Fuck.'

'So,' she asked, stroking the side of his face with her fingers, 'what you gonna do about it?'

'I don't know,' he admitted. 'Just make things how they used to be. *Normal* policing again. Play it completely straight again. You break the law, you get nicked. Simple. Some of the things that have happened have . . . have been bad. Really bad. I need to turn it around before it's too late.'

'You can do that?' she asked, sounding unconvinced.

'I have to try,' he told her. 'I have to try and find me again. People don't look at me the same any more. I'm not sure I know what I am now. Nothing's straightforward any more.'

'Why you telling me all of this?' she questioned, looking confused, but unconcerned.

'I'm not sure,' he answered, smiling a little. 'I'm not sure.'

'Smoke some,' she told him, glancing at the joint in his hand. 'A last taste of badness before you go back to your safe little world.'

He did as he was told. 'Strong,' he told her as he exhaled the thick smoke.

'I don't buy crap,' she smiled. 'Dealers round here always looking to palm you off with crap if you don't know what you're doing.'

'But not you?'

'I just know what I want,' she told him.

'And you always get what you want?'

'Always,' she warned him, picking the joint from his fingers, holding it softly in her naturally red lips and inhaling deeply. 'Take this,' she told him – talking while holding her breath, dropping the joint in an ashtray and snaking a hand behind his neck, pulling his mouth towards her – her lips shaping to kiss him, but instead gently blowing the smoke from her lungs past his lips. He inhaled it as if he was drawing the soul from her body. He held it in his lungs until there was nothing to exhale.

'That felt good,' he admitted as he looked at his own reflection in her black eyes.

'Not as good as this'll feel,' she assured him and gently pressed her lips into his, the tip of her tongue exploring the opening of his mouth, brushing his teeth and the underside of his lips. The pleasure in her mouth was like nothing he'd ever felt before – as if she was a different species from another world. His arms coiled around her back and pulled her close and tight – a sound of thrill and surprise escaping from her. He could feel her lips tighten into a smile as his hands stroked and explored her back then he moved one hand between their clasped abdomens and slid it into her shorts and under her tiny pair of knickers. As his fingers slipped between her legs and gently moved back and forth she broke away from their kiss and rested her head on his chest and body armour – gasping and moaning softly as she began to tremble more and more until she finally reached climax for the first time in her young life. She'd been with other men and boys, but none had ever taken her here. They'd always been rough and rushed, only interested in themselves or had been inexperienced fumbling fools. King's touch was altogether different.

'Fuck,' she told him as her fingers worked fast to remove

his utility belt. Next she quickly and expertly opened his more conventional trouser belt and fly – her fingers eagerly searching him out and pulling him free. She stroked his penis a few times before realizing he was already fully erect, at which she slid like a dancer to her knees and took him into her mouth. The pleasure he felt bordered on painful, and all the while she looked up at him with eyes like ink wells filled with black oil.

'Jesus,' he complained against the almost unbearable pleasure before he gently took hold of the sides of her face and pulled her carefully off him. He lifted her from the floor, bending to meet her lips with his own as she rose – the sensation in his groin now turning to a desperate need to release.

As she reached her full height he quickly spun her around and held her tight, kissing the back of her neck and biting the perfect skin of her shoulders, one arm wrapped around her breasts as the other hurriedly and roughly pulled at her shorts and knickers until they were around her knees. Her back arched as she reached over her shoulders and cupped her hands behind his neck – feeling for his erection with the gap between her buttocks, trying to guide him into her. 'Yes,' she almost pleaded. 'I want you to do it to me. I can't wait any longer.'

He lifted her from the floor and carried her the few feet to the kitchen table then bent her over it, watching her spread herself over it – arms out to her side, her face largely obscured by the long waves of her dark hair.

'Fuck me,' she whispered. He leaned forward and allowed his weight to push him into her as deeply as he could sink, making her moan out loud and partially push herself from the table before crashing back onto its surface. 'Oh fuck, yes,' she encouraged him. 'Don't stop. Don't stop.'

He moved rhythmically now – sliding deep inside her before pulling almost all the way out, before again pushing as deeply as he could into her body. He couldn't help but think of all the other women in his life he'd slept with, including Sara, who all seemed so lifeless in comparison. With Kelly it was different – how it should be: an uncontrollable urge to physically devour each other and form a bond between two people that could never be broken. Even if they never saw each other again, neither would ever forget these few minutes spent together for as long as they lived. Too soon he felt the irresistible urge to ejaculate and she felt it too.

'Come in me,' she pleaded, looking over her shoulder at him as they moved together. 'I want to feel you come inside me.'

'But . . .' he hesitated. 'But what about . . .?'

She guessed his chief concern. 'It's OK,' she panted. 'I'm on the pill.'

It was all he needed to hear and he quickly increased the rate of his thrusting, making Kelly call out in approaching ecstasy each time he pushed deep until he could delay no more. Even once the burningly wonderful moment had passed he held himself deep within her. For Kelly, it was the first time in her life a guy she'd just had sex with hadn't immediately wanted to abandon her to return to the pub, or his friends or just the TV. They always came back begging for more once their balls were full again, but she'd never been held like this before. It was the best feeling she'd ever had in her short life.

'Jesus, Kelly,' King was eventually able to speak.

'What?' she asked, concerned, as she eased his shrinking penis from inside her and twisted around to face him. 'You don't regret it, do you?'

'Fuck, no,' he admitted. 'I don't regret any of it.'

'Good,' she smiled a little, leaning forward, wrapping her arms around the back of his neck and gently pulling him forward to kiss her. 'Now take me to bed.'

'What?' King asked with a slight laugh. 'What about your mum?'

'She won't be back till late tomorrow,' she reassured him.

'You do want to be with me all night, don't you? I got other things I need to show you.'

He knew he should leave, but her magic was already too deeply embedded in his soul. 'Sure,' he told her. 'Lead the way.'

She smiled brightly and stood, allowing her shorts and knickers to fall to the floor instead of trying to pull them up – her confidence supreme. She wrestled her crop-top over her head and revealed small, perfect breasts for the first time as she let it slip to the floor. She gave him a few seconds to feast upon her beauty and headed off across the room towards the stairs, stopping to look back over her shoulder, waiting for him. He took the hint and quickly zipped himself back up, grabbing his utility belt and heading towards the creature of hypnotizing perfection who waited for him at the foot of a council house staircase.

The sound of someone knocking hard on the front door cut through his hangover and exhaustion and dragged him slowly back into the waking world. But as his eyes opened for a moment he had no idea where he was and felt instantly disorientated. After a few seconds he realized he was naked and in a bed, but where and why still eluded him until he turned his head and saw Kelly stretched out next to him. He couldn't help but reach out and brush perfect ringlets from her perfect face – the sight of her naked breasts stirring his groin despite himself. But more pounding on the front door quickly chased the desire away and brought Kelly closer to consciousness.

He jumped out of bed with paranoia quickly replacing lust and tiptoed through the debris of clothing strewn across the floor to the window. Flattening his back against the wall he moved the curtain just enough so he could see – his heart almost stopping at the sight of Marino waiting impatiently for an answer.

285

'Shit,' he cursed as he pressed himself even further into the wall just as Kelly sat up, stretching and yawning.

'What's going on?' she asked in a quiet, sleepy voice.

'Sssh,' he told her, placing a finger across his own lips. There was another knock at the door.

'Who is it?' she asked, ignoring him.

He crossed the room quickly and knelt on the bed next to her. 'Keep it down,' he ordered. 'It's the police.'

'Police?' she asked in an urgent whisper. 'What do they want?'

'I don't know,' he admitted, weighing up the possibilities. 'They can't know I'm here,' he told himself more than her. 'Must be something else,' he explained, the image of a hooded and handcuffed Swinton flashing in his mind. 'They can't know I'm here,' he repeated as he began to gather strewn items of clothing and uniform.

'I'm over sixteen,' she reminded him. 'I can sleep with who I like.'

'Yeah,' he laughed. 'I don't think the Met will quite see it like that.'

'Fuck them,' she smiled and leaned back into her pillows looking around for something to smoke.

'No,' he tried to bring her up to speed on the urgency of the situation. 'I need you to go and find out what they want – why they're sniffing round here.'

'What you so worried about?' she asked. 'You're one of their own.'

'Kelly,' he appealed to her. 'I really need you to do this.'

'OK,' she said with a heavy sigh and slipped from the bed, taking a thin t-shirt from a coat hanger and pulling it over her head – straightening it out as if it was a Chanel dress.

'That all you wearing?' he questioned as she headed for the door. She just fluttered her eyelids and pouted her lips as she slipped from the room.

A few seconds later she was opening the door to Frank Marino who eyed her suspiciously. He had no intention of falling prey to a teenage honey-trap.

'Hello,' she told him almost sweetly.

'Police,' Marino informed her, holding up his warrant card.

'I know who you are,' she smiled.

'Yeah,' Marino nodded. 'I suppose you do. Your mum or dad in?'

'I don't have a dad,' she answered matter-of-factly. 'Mum's round at her boyfriend's.'

'I see,' Marino nodded. 'Mind if I come in and speak with you?'

'Can't let anyone in the house when Mum's not here,' Kelly lied.

'Fair enough,' Marino let it go, trying to see inside the maisonette over her shoulder. 'Maybe you can help me anyway?'

'With what?'

'We're just doing some door-to-door,' he explained, 'trying to find anyone who may have seen or heard anything last night.'

'Why?' she jumped in too eagerly. 'What happened?'

'About ten-ish,' he told her, 'a local man was abducted from his flat and dragged off somewhere. A while later he was found dumped on the estate barely alive.'

'What local man?' she asked.

'Alan Swinton,' Marino answered. 'Know him?'

'No,' she shook her head trying to look concerned, before suddenly brightening. 'No, wait a minute. Alan Swinton? Isn't he that nonce always hanging around with kids?'

'Nothing's ever been proved against him,' Marino argued.

'Just telling you what I heard,' Kelly smiled cruelly.

'Really,' Marino replied. 'And what else have you heard?'

'Well,' Kelly told him, stretching and hooking her arm over the top of the door, threatening to raise her t-shirt above her crotch, 'maybe I heard he got caught touching up some young girl on the estate.'

'You heard that?'

'I said *maybe* I heard.'

'I see,' Marino nodded. 'And you believe the fact that some people think he may have assaulted a young girl had something to do with the attack on him?'

'I never said anything,' Kelly smiled, 'but it sounds like he got what he deserved. Nobody round here'll be crying for him.'

'And if he didn't touch the girl?' asked Marino. 'What then?'

'If he didn't touch her then he's touched someone else,' Kelly shrugged. 'That's what them paedophiles do – innit? They can't help themselves.'

'So I'm guessing you heard nothing?' he asked anyway.

'That's right,' she told him. 'Nothing.'

'And you saw nothing either?'

'Right again,' she smiled infuriatingly. 'We done now?' she asked, as if he'd been interrogating her.

'Sure,' he agreed. 'Thanks for your time,' he added sarcastically as the door closed softly in his face.

Kelly quickly climbed the stairs back to the bedroom as nimbly as a cat – entering the room to find King already pulling on his body armour and utility belt. 'You leaving?'

'Yeah,' he told her. 'I have to.'

'Don't you want to know why CID are all over the estate?'

'I heard what he was saying,' he replied. 'I need to get back and keep a lid on things.'

'What if they see you?'

'They won't,' he reassured her. 'I'll use the rat-runs. I know this estate like the back of my hand. Besides – I need to take care of a few things before someone thinks to let a dog unit loose.'

'So it was you?'

'You're surprised?' he asked, holding her with his eyes.

'No,' she finally admitted, moving forward and sitting on the bed. 'What did you do to him?'

'I did what everyone wanted me to do,' he answered.

'What everyone wanted you to do or what *you* wanted to do?'

'He had it coming,' he told her as he placed his flat cap on his head and straightened it in the mirror. 'I have to go.'

'When will I see you again?' she asked.

He looked into her eyes – black, swirling vortexes of life that could make any man a fool. 'Tonight,' he told her. 'I'll see you tonight.'

King entered the Unit's office and found Brown and Williams already at work – although they both looked as if their night had been a long one.

'About time,' Brown started them off.

'You think I just got here?' King asked with bitterness in his voice. 'I've already been out and about on the estate cleaning up after last night.'

'Jesus,' said Williams. 'You spend the night there or something?'

King realized his slip. 'Don't be a clown. I got myself home and grabbed a few hours' sleep while things calmed down – then I headed back there early.'

'You got rid of the clothing?' Brown whispered as loudly as he could.

'Back in the property store,' King allowed himself a small smile. 'No one will ever be the wiser.'

'Thank fuck for that,' Williams exhaled as the relief washed over him.

'So we're in the clear?' Brown asked, his voice urgent and afraid.

'More or less,' King deliberately tormented him.

'More or less?' Brown took the bait.

King waited until they were both staring at him in silent

anticipation. 'I saw Marino and some of his CID cronies sniffing around the estate this morning doing door-to-door.'

'Oh,' Brown threw his hands aloft, 'that's just fucking great. Door-to-door trying to find out what happened to Swinton – right?'

'Of course,' King told him calmly. 'What else would they be there for? You haven't forgotten our little run-in with Marino last night, have you?'

'Not fucking likely to, am I?' Brown argued.

'Yet I don't hear anyone talking about it – do you?' King asked. 'In the canteen this morning – the front office – the CID office – d'you hear anyone saying "Did you hear what happened to Marino last night?" No you don't.'

'So?' Williams tried to follow him.

'So he hasn't said anything, has he?' King explained. 'Which means he's not going to say anything – or at least not to anyone who could cause us a problem.'

'I don't like it,' Williams exclaimed. 'What's his angle?'

'Maybe he doesn't have one,' King suggested. 'Maybe he just doesn't want to get involved in our business or maybe it's too late for him to tell anyone without hanging himself in it too – I don't really care. What matters is that he hasn't made anything, which means he probably won't, and that means there's nothing he can try to do to us that we can't handle, so relax. I'll deal with Marino if it comes to that.'

'You said he was sniffing around on the estate?' Brown suddenly changed the subject. 'Where on the estate?'

'Millander Walk,' King told him.

'And you just happened to see him while you were cleaning things up?'

'Yeah,' King answered cautiously. 'Something like that.'

'You sure you weren't getting your head down somewhere on the estate?' Brown pressed.

'Why don't you just say what you really want to say?' King pushed back.

'OK,' Brown steadied himself. 'Are you fucking someone on the estate? Have you crossed that line as well?'

'What?' King tried to sound incredulous.

'You heard him,' Williams backed Brown up.

'Don't be ridiculous,' he bluffed. 'I wouldn't fuck anyone on that estate with yours. God knows what you'd catch.'

'No bullshit?' Brown stared at him hard.

'No bullshit,' King lied. 'Everything on that estate is toxic – including the women. I wouldn't touch any of them.' He tried to block the image and taste of Kelly from his mind as he spoke – the merest thought of her stirring his groin and twisting his stomach in a longing to be with her again.

'Fair enough,' Brown relented with a nod.

Before King could speak again Marino appeared at their door looking confident and unafraid, despite the previous night. 'Not interrupting anything, am I?'

'No,' said King, making a show of sorting out his body armour. 'We were just heading out on patrol, as it happens.'

'You heard what happened last night then?' Marino played the game.

'Swinton?' King asked without looking at him. 'We heard.'

'Maybe you can use your local knowledge to help us find whoever it was beat the crap out of him?' Marino tried to toy with them – test their nerve now they weren't hiding behind masks.

'Yeah, sure,' King casually agreed. 'Got any idea who you're looking for?'

'Not much,' Marino shrugged. 'Best we know, it was two white men and a black guy, all in their twenties. Ring any bells?'

'Not really,' King pretended to dismiss it. 'Could be anyone. But word on the estate is he's the one who's been attacking young girls. No one's going to put up with that shit. I'm hearing a few of the local dads got together as vigilantes and took the law into their own hands. No names yet, but as

291

soon as we get them I'll be sure to pass them on to the CID.'

'You do that,' Marino replied, 'because this is the second person found beaten nearly to death that's turned up on *your* estate. Powers-that-be will soon start asking questions – questions that could be difficult to answer.'

'The powers-that-be'll leave us alone,' King dismissed it. 'All they're interested in are crime figures and ours are the best on the borough. Reported crime is down to almost zero.'

'Except violent crime,' Marino pointed out. '*Serious* violent crime. Incidents like the one with Butler and now Swinton are making your unit look bad. Haven't you seen the new government directives? Violent crime is top of the politicians' wish lists. You need to find a way to make sure no more of this shit happens on your patch, before the senior management decide to close you down.'

'We're working on it,' King insisted, no longer attempting to hide his irritation at being challenged.

'I hope so,' Marino replied. 'I really hope so, because even now I reckon everyone can walk away from this intact.' He spoke cryptically but clearly. 'But it's important there are no more unfortunate, high-profile incidents. You want my advice – disband this unit. Tell the SMT you've done all you can to improve the estate.' He nodded at Brown and Williams. 'You two go back to your uniform teams and you,' he looked directly at King, 'you should probably move to another borough to best facilitate your accelerated promotion. In a few weeks everything will be back to normal and Swinton will have been forgotten. At least think about it,' he told them as he headed for the door. 'It's not just your best option – it's your only option.' He disappeared through the doorway, leaving his words hanging heavy in the air. They all waited in silence for an age before Brown broke the vigil.

'Fuck,' he swore. 'That bastard knows everything.'

'Davey could be right,' Williams added his concerns. 'He sounds like he knows our every move.'

'Course he does,' King dismissed its importance. 'But he's not gonna do anything about it – otherwise he already would have.'

'That's a big fucking risk to take,' Brown argued. 'He's got nothing to lose by dropping us in it. Maybe a slap on the wrist for not saying something sooner, but that's all.'

'He's no grass,' King insisted, 'and he'd get a lot more than a slap on the wrist.'

'But after you gave him a smack last night maybe he figures he owes us one,' Williams suggested. 'Owes you one. All his talk could be bullshit – biding his time while he figures out how to fuck us properly.'

'I don't think so,' King shook his head, but he could feel he was losing them.

'What he said about disbanding sounded like an offer to me,' Brown reminded them. 'We should take him up on it, right now. Get back to our teams and let this shit blow itself out.'

'No,' King raised his voice. 'I got too much time and energy invested in the estate to just walk away from it because of Marino.'

'What you talking about?' Brown demanded. 'We're just here to police that shithole – not to invest anything in it. It's not a fucking business – unless . . . unless you mean it *is* a business.' The reality of what he was saying suddenly hit him. 'Oh Jesus. What else have you been doing down there?'

'Calm down,' King warned him. 'Everything's under control. No one's going to say nothing to no one. You two just do as you're told.'

A sudden knock on the doorframe ended the conversation and they all turned to see a handsome young constable of Asian appearance looking tentatively into the office.

'Who the fuck are you?' King barked.

'PC Rana Knight,' he told them without smiling. 'The replacement.'

293

'Replacement for what?' King asked.

'For PC Mahajan,' he explained.

The mention of Renita's name momentarily stunned him. Would he have fallen as far as he had if she'd still been around? He doubted it.

'No one told me anything about a replacement,' King said with suspicion.

'Inspector Johnston told me she'd informed you I was coming, Sarge,' Knight assured him. 'She sent you an email.'

King hadn't read his emails for days. 'Oh yeah,' he lied. 'Now you mention it. Welcome to the Unit. Grab yourself a chair and some desk space and make yourself at home. You need to know we only have one rule here – we all watch each other's backs and we stick together, no matter what. Understand?'

'Sure,' Knight replied sheepishly, having been expecting the usual talk about honesty and integrity.

'Davey here will show you around,' King told him as he prepared to leave. 'I need to be somewhere.'

King made his way through the ward in the Royal London Hospital in Whitechapel towards one of the isolation rooms where he knew he'd find Renita still recovering. A uniformed guard sat outside her room, looking up and acknowledging King with a nod of his head as he passed him and entered the room where he found Renita sitting propped up in her bed reading a glossy magazine. Her wounds had improved dramatically since the last time he'd seen her, but she was still heavily bruised with butterfly tapes holding her deeper cuts together.

'Hard life, eh?' he told her.

'Jesus.' She looked up and smiled, taking care not to split open a painful-looking gash on her bottom lip. 'Wondered when I was going to see you again.'

'Sorry,' he apologized. 'Work's been a nightmare.'

'Ah,' she suddenly looked serious. 'Work.'

'Yeah,' he confirmed, pulling up a chair next to her. 'Speaking of which – any idea when you'll be back?'

'I . . .' she stuttered a little ' . . . I'm not sure.'

'Doctors give you any idea?'

'Another few weeks and I should be fine, apparently,' she answered unconvincingly, 'but . . .'

'But what?' he pressed.

'I'm not sure I'll be coming back,' she finally admitted.

'No one would expect you to come back to the Unit,' he smiled understandingly. 'You could go back to your team or even another borough.'

'I don't know,' she told him with her eyes closed. 'It wouldn't be the same.'

'You just need to take your time,' he insisted. 'That's what I did. There were times when I thought I'd never walk the streets again, but now it's fine. Time's a great healer.'

'I know,' she answered sadly, 'but what they did to me . . . what they were going to do to me. I can still see their faces . . . whether I'm awake or asleep, I can still see their faces.'

'The chances of something like that ever happening again are millions to one,' he tried to explain. 'It was a one-off freak occurrence. You're a good cop.'

'A good cop wouldn't have walked into that trap,' she argued. 'I should have seen it coming.'

'You did what any good cop would do. You wanted to find out what was going on so you checked it out. Butler and the others got the drop on you this time. It won't happen again.'

'No it won't,' she agreed, 'because there won't be a next time. Let somebody else do this shit. I'm going to work for my uncle's business. Twice as much money and no more sneaking around in the dark.'

'You like sneaking around in the dark,' he tried to cajole. 'You're good at it.'

'Not any more,' she cut him cold.

He could see she'd all but made her mind up. He had only

one more thing to try. 'If you're worried about Butler, you needn't be.'

'I heard,' she answered, looking hard into his eyes. 'They say it was vigilantes,' she said disbelievingly, 'upset by a woman cop being attacked.'

'That's what we think,' he lied.

'Bollocks,' she told him. 'No one on the Grove Wood's going to get pissed off about a cop being done – male or female. Someone else took care of Butler.'

He wanted to tell her the truth, but he knew her integrity was unbending. He wouldn't burden her with what really happened. Even though he knew she suspected as much, *knowing* would put her under a different pressure altogether. 'All that matters is Butler got what he had coming to him.'

'Not in my name. I want to see him arrested and prosecuted. I want to see his face when he goes down for ten years. I don't want to see him beaten by the mob for what he did. I don't believe in summary justice. That makes us no better than them. I believe in the system, despite all its faults.'

'Sometimes the law's not enough,' he found himself arguing. 'Sometimes people like Butler need something they can . . . feel.'

'He'll get ten years locked in a cell the size of a shoebox,' she reminded him. 'Imagine what that must be like. The only thing that can help him now is the fact someone beat the crap out of him. *Whoever* thought they were helping me have done the exact opposite.'

King felt an anger and resentment rising towards her he hadn't expected. The risks he'd taken to punish Butler had all been for her. It had even put Marino on his tail. And now he realized it wasn't even appreciated.

'Butler was laughing at you,' he tried to convince her. 'He was laughing at all of us. He's not laughing any more.'

'He'll be laughing if the CPS drop the case to save too many awkward questions being asked in open court about who it really was attacked him,' she warned him. 'He may not have thought of it yet, but as his trial gets closer and no one's been arrested for nearly killing him, sooner or later his barrister's going to start having their suspicions. If Butler thinks it'll save him ten years in prison he'll start making allegations. Just you wait and see.'

'Butler won't say anything,' he told her without conviction.

'We'll see,' she said before reaching out and resting her hand on his. 'Even lying here I hear things,' she explained. 'Break up the Unit. Move somewhere else and concentrate on your promotion. Get off that estate. Place like that's poisonous. You stay there too long it'll destroy you, like it destroys everything. Go back to being the person you used to be.'

King felt his chest constricting uncomfortably as her words sunk in, making him suddenly and unexpectedly long for the simple person he'd once been, living in a black and white world of good and bad, unlike the universe of grey he now inhabited. He felt tears welling in his eyes and he found it difficult to speak. 'I don't think I can ever be that person again,' he admitted. 'I'm not sure I even want to be. Too much has happened.'

'Of course you do,' she whispered intently. 'Just get off the Grove Wood.'

'And do what? Get a desk job? Go home to Sara at six o'clock every night? Have kids we can't afford?'

'Is that so bad?' Renita asked.

'But it's not living,' he insisted, his doubts falling away as quickly as they'd come. 'I'm doing things I could never have dreamed of and it feels good. It feels right.'

'Jesus, Jack,' she asked. 'What *things* are you doing?'

'Things that make it all worthwhile,' he smiled almost manically. 'Things that mean no one even takes a piss on the estate without me knowing about it.'

'On second thoughts,' she shook her head, 'I don't want

to know what you've been doing – just so long as none of it's being done in my name.'

'It isn't,' he assured her, rising to leave, knowing they had nothing more to say. Neither of them recognized the people they used to be. 'Nothing will come back to you. No need to worry about anything. You just rest and get yourself back to duty.'

'Yeah, sure,' she answered, although they both knew it would never happen and that the chances were they'd never see each other again. Just as he reached the door she couldn't help call out to him one last time. 'Take care, Jack,' was all she wanted to say.

He turned back and looked at her, the sorrow returning to his young face. 'I always do,' he lied to her. 'I always do.'

A short time later King walked through the estate – the memory of the conversation with Renita and the oppressive heat of the late afternoon intensifying his headache. He needed to take something and take something soon before his head burst open. The sound of his own mobile ringing on the shoulder of his body armour momentarily distracted him. He already had an ear and mouth piece attached to the device so he could speak without talking into his shoulder. He slid his finger across the screen to answer.

'Hello.'

'Jack, it's your mother,' she announced, making him regret not checking the caller ID before answering.

'Now's not a great time,' he told her. 'I'm at work – out and about.'

'There's never a good time to call you, Jack,' she complained. 'Anyway, it's just a quick call to remind you we're expecting you and Sara for dinner tonight.'

'Tonight?' he questioned before he could stop himself.

'Yes,' his mother told him with some irritation. 'Tonight. You haven't forgotten, have you?'

'No,' he lied, his heart sinking as he recalled some distant memory of agreeing to meet up. Unable to think of a good excuse not to go, he found himself agreeing in the hope he could think of something later. 'We'll be there.'

'Good,' she said with some relief. 'About seven then.'

'Fine,' he agreed before the line went dead. He tried to remember when he'd ever had a long and meaningful conversation with his mother over the phone, but couldn't, which reminded him he hadn't had a proper conversation with Sara for weeks and hadn't seen her in days. Even if he had forgotten about dinner, he was sure she wouldn't have and imagined her waiting for him in their small flat, dressed attractively, but conservatively – her soft blonde hair framing her pretty face. Yet the thought of her stirred no feelings in him – no life. Quickly her image faded to be replaced by Kelly, almost naked, lying on her front across the kitchen table offering herself to him – wanting him as much as he wanted her – an almost animalistic passion enveloping them as they came together. She was so alive, making all that had gone before her seem lifeless – including Sara. He vowed to take a hit of something to get him through the night of small talk and veiled criticisms – while all the time he'd be thinking of Kelly.

He tried to shake the picture from his mind and calm his rising excitement as he realized he'd almost reached Dougie O'Neil's front door. Once his mind was clear he knocked and waited a long time for an answer – O'Neil eventually opening the door and standing behind his new metal security grid.

'Oh,' O'Neil said with barely disguised disappointment. 'It's you.'

'You were expecting someone else?' King asked, stepping closer to the grid in anticipation.

'Another punter maybe,' O'Neil answered.

'I take it business is up and running then?'

'No problems,' O'Neil smiled before King barked at him.

'You going to open this fucking door then?'

'Yeah.' O'Neil jumped to action. 'Sorry,' he apologized as he fumbled in his trouser pocket for the key. King waited impatiently – looking back and forth along the walkway until the grid finally swung open and he was able to step inside.

'Well?' he asked. 'Aren't you going to lock it?'

'Yeah, yeah,' O'Neil realized his mistake and pulled the grid over and secured it.

'You need to switch on a bit more,' King told him as they moved deeper into the filthy flat. 'You leave the door open like that when the wrong people are watching you're going to get robbed – robbed of things that belong to me.'

'No one's going to rob me now they know you're my protection,' O'Neil argued.

'Assume nothing,' said King. 'There's always the chance of a bunch of cowboys coming in from outside and trying a hit and run. The grid stays shut all the time. Understand?'

'But what if I need to go out?' O'Neil asked.

'Lock the grid behind you,' King answered as if it was obvious.

'But I'll have the key on me,' O'Neil explained. 'What's to stop someone robbing me in the street and taking the key?'

'Fair enough,' King saw his point. 'If you need to go out you call me first and I'll babysit the flat and key while you're gone, or I'll send Brown or Williams if I'm not around. But I don't want to see you out and about partying with my cash or getting stoned on my drugs. Understand? You can have a rock a day, that's it.'

'One a day,' O'Neil enthusiastically agreed. 'Got it.'

'Now how's business going?'

'Good,' O'Neil assured him. 'I've almost sold the gear you gave me.' He pulled a mixture of small notes and coins from his pocket and offered it to King. 'You want to take your cut now?'

'No,' King told him, eyeing the dirty-looking cash. 'I need you to take it to your contacts in North London and buy some more gear.' He shook his head at the sight of the cash all dealers had to trade in. 'Look at this shit,' he complained. 'Fivers and loose change. Once the cash comes rolling in we're gonna have to clean it up. I can't be walking around with pockets full of coins.'

'How you gonna do that?' O'Neil asked. 'You try and change it in any bank and they'll tell the Old Bill – guaranteed.'

'You're forgetting one thing,' King reminded him. 'I am the Old Bill. I'll tell them I run the station social fund and tea club. They won't question it. I'll even be able to open a bank account so we can get the cash into the banking system. All things our competitors can't do. Which means we can offer clean cash in large denominations or even bank transfers and therefore demand a lower retail price – which means more profit for us.'

'Sounds like you got it all worked out,' O'Neil replied.

'I'm not here to make pennies,' King told him. 'I'm here to make as much as I can as quickly as I can before they shut the Unit down and move us all somewhere else. When that happens I'll never get my hands dirty again. Once I've cleared a few debts I'll be OK and can move on. I'll be finished with this shit.'

'Move on?' O'Neil asked, concerned. 'But if you go what am I supposed to do? Without protection I'm a dead man.'

'You stop dealing,' King explained without sympathy. 'You be glad of the cash you made and go back to being a small-time thief.'

'Shit,' O'Neil complained. 'I thought we were in this for the long run. I thought we were partners.'

'Don't be so fucking naïve,' King chastised him. 'They're not going to leave me down here forever, you moron. But while I'm here this estate belongs to me, and everything on it. Speaking of which, tell me what you know about Susie Ubana.'

'What you want to know?'

'Everything,' he insisted. 'Anything.'

'She's a dealer,' O'Neil shrugged. 'Has been for years. Cannabis only – she never touches anything class A. Guess she thinks the Old Bill will leave her alone if she keeps to puff. At the end of the day, who cares about puff, right?'

'What about other dealers?' King pressed. 'How come she's never been turned over by a crew looking to take her business?'

'Because she's got protection,' O'Neil answered as if it were obvious.

'Who from?' King demanded.

'I hear the Campbells,' O'Neil warned him. 'They may have moved off the estate years ago, once they started earning large, but they still run things around here, or least they did, till you turned up. But chances are she's got police protection too.'

'Oh?' King was interested. 'How so?'

'Never met a puff dealer who wasn't a grass,' O'Neil grinned. 'They throw their police handlers a bone now and then – usually a crack or heroin dealer – and in exchange they get left alone. Susie's been in the game so long she must have some tame Old Bill looking out for her. Must have.'

Marino immediately jumped into King's mind. He'd be just the sort to have someone like Ubana keeping an eye on things on the estate for him. Could that be how he seemed to know so much already?

'You're not thinking of messing with Susie, are you?' O'Neil asked worriedly. 'Better to let that sleeping dog lie, if you ask me.'

'I'm not asking you,' King told him. 'Why shouldn't she pay? You want to deal on this estate you pay me my cut. Ubana's been having it her own way too long. Time she fell into line with everyone else.'

'You sure that's wise?' O'Neil warned him. 'If she's got protection from Old Bill and the Campbells – especially the

302

Campbells? For all we know you may have already pissed on their chips when you cleaned out Astill. They're not just gonna sit around and let you mess with their business.'

'What they going to do?' King asked, spreading his arms for emphasis. 'I'm a cop. They can't touch me . . . and they know it.'

14

Inspector Johnston sat at the desk in her office reading through the borough's latest expenditure on diesel fuel and dreaming of the day she'd have an even bigger office, hopefully at the Yard if everything worked out well. Her work and dreams were interrupted by an unexpected knock at the door. She cleared her throat before calling out, 'Come in.' The door opened and Marino entered, making Johnston lean forward in surprise.

'Guv'nor,' Marino greeted her.

'Frank,' Johnston replied, hiding her concern. Visits from the CID were rarely good news. 'To what do I owe the pleasure? Please. Come in. Take a seat.'

'Thanks,' Marino replied, taking up the offer before getting straight to the point. 'I was wondering if you'd heard about the incident involving a man called Alan Swinton on the Grove Wood Estate last night?'

'I heard about it,' Johnston replied. 'An unfortunate incident. Sounds like the same vigilante gang who attacked that nasty little Butler character. Still, vigilantes cannot be tolerated on the streets of Newham. I'm sure it's only a matter of time before Sergeant King and his unit bring them to heel.'

'Maybe that's the problem,' Marino told her.

'What are you saying, Frank?' Johnston calmly asked.

'I mean I find it difficult to believe there could be a vigilante gang on the Grove Wood without the Unit knowing about it.'

Johnston eyed him with suspicion before speaking. 'Are you suggesting someone is turning a blind eye to a group of vigilante thugs? Or worse still – that there is some degree of cooperation or complicity involved?'

'No,' Marino answered deadpan. 'Not *cooperating* with them.'

'Then we have nothing to worry about,' Johnston smiled.

'I'm saying it's more than cooperation,' Marino quickly added. 'More than complicity.' For a second he thought he saw a moment of fear and panic in the previously unshakeable Johnston, but she recovered quickly.

'Do you know what you're saying?' she questioned him.

'Yes.' Marino answered.

Johnston leaned back in her chair and locked eyes with Marino. 'As far as I'm concerned no one has made any allegations *yet*. Including you, Frank. If you were to get up and leave my office now then that's how things would remain. Do we understand each other?'

Marino sighed deeply before answering – fully aware of the offer she was making. 'I can't do that.'

Johnston drummed her painted fingernails on her desk before speaking. 'I want to be absolutely accurate here,' she warned him. 'You're saying they could actually somehow be *involved* in these attacks?'

'Yes,' Marino admitted. 'That's what I'm saying.'

Johnston leaned forward in her chair. 'These are very serious accusations.'

'I understand,' Marino agreed.

'And not the first time you've inferred something untoward may be going on in the Unit.'

'I appreciate that, but this is different.'

305

'Different how?'

'Different in that I know it was them who attacked Swinton.'

'And how d'you know that, Frank?'

'I can't say.'

'Can't say or won't say?' Marino didn't answer. 'Are you sure there isn't a *personal* problem between you and Sergeant King?'

'That's not the issue here,' Marino insisted.

'It's just on the face of it these look like more unfounded allegations. King and his team have been on the estate for months and apart from your . . . *suggestions* there've been no allegations or complaints. Just first-class arrests and falling crime figures.'

'If you want to protect King and the others that's fine,' Marino assured her. 'They're young and maybe they've been dumb. No one's going to cry for Butler. Swinton's unfortunate, but the fact is no one's looking out for him. King and his people can still walk away from this.'

'Ah, Swinton,' Johnston changed tack. 'The sex offender.'

'Right now I don't see how that's relevant,' Marino argued. 'Even if it was him, there's not a single piece of evidence against him.'

'Well I suppose that's the CID's job, isn't it?' Johnston told him. 'To find the evidence – instead of making unfounded allegations against other officers.'

'I'm not making any allegations,' Marino replied. 'I just want this to stop, before it gets even worse.'

'You do your job, Frank, and let me do mine.'

'Meaning?' Marino pushed.

Johnston sat back in her chair and sighed. 'Meaning you find evidence against Swinton and leave the Unit to me.'

'So you'll do something?'

Johnston sighed again as if she was being forced to reveal a great secret. 'If you must know, in the light of our previous conversation I decided it might be prudent to have someone I can trust implicitly *inside* the Unit. I'm not the sort of person who leaves things to chance, Frank.'

'Oh?' Marino questioned.

'PC Mahajan's replacement, PC Rana Knight, joined the Unit as of today. He's a very competent and *ambitious* young officer. If there's any sign of . . . inappropriate behaviour, he'll report it to me immediately and if necessary the Unit will be disbanded. If I find something more serious then they'll have to be reported to Professional Ethics and Standards, although I'm sure it won't come to that.'

'And this PC Knight's up to the job?' Marino asked.

'Absolutely,' Johnston assured him. 'Handpicked by myself.'

'That's reassuring,' Marino replied. 'But you could just play safe and disband the Unit almost immediately. That way everyone walks away with their careers and reputations intact – no need for Knight to go sniffing around looking for evidence of misconduct or worse.'

'That won't be necessary,' Johnston dismissed the idea. 'To date you're the only person who's expressed any concerns about the Unit. I can't just disband them on the basis of one man's unsupported allegations. Officers do have rights, you know. And besides, their crime figures are the envy of the borough, probably of the whole Met. They can be held up as a model of what modern policing should be – community officers accepting long-term responsibility for policing specific areas of a borough, instead of anonymously speeding from one 999 call to another, never stopping to actually get to know the people they police or finding out what they want from the service. You need to understand the powers-that-be *like* what the Unit is doing and they like the results they're getting. Don't rock the boat too much, Frank.'

'A model of modern policing?' he questioned. 'A model designed by you?' Johnston just gave a little shrug of her slim shoulders. 'And the serious assaults?' Marino reminded her. 'How do the powers-that-be like the fact there've been two serious and unsolved attacks on the Grove Wood? Can't exactly be good for the crime figures.'

'Then you'd better solve them,' Johnston snapped back. 'Last time I checked, serious assaults fall within the CID's remit.'

'And you want us to investigate them fully?' Marino checked. 'Regardless of where that may take us?'

'Of course,' Johnston replied. 'Although I expect you to use your *full* discretion and judgement in this matter. And I wouldn't be telling too many people about your . . . suspicions. We don't want any negative publicity. God knows we've had enough of that lately. By all means investigate these assaults, Frank, but tread carefully. Tread very carefully indeed.'

'Of course,' Marino assured her, but remained seated to let her know he hadn't finished.

'Something else?' Johnston asked, leaning back in her chair.

'You heard about Peter Edwards appealing his conviction?' Marino asked.

'Of course,' Johnston answered. 'It was discussed at senior management level. An unfortunate occurrence.'

'Tough on Jack,' Marino suggested. 'Can't be helping his state of mind – his belief in the rule of law. In justice.'

'I'm sure Sergeant King will handle it and if he can't we'll soon know, won't we,' Johnston reminded him before moving forward in her chair. 'The rule of law is all very good, Frank, but every now and then, what a place like the Grove Wood Estate needs is the rule of fear. It's what people like that understand best.'

'That's not what Jack needs to believe right now,' Marino argued. 'He needs to have faith in the justice system.'

'Don't we all, Frank.' Johnston smiled. 'Don't we all.'

* * *

King watched from his vantage point as Susie Ubana finally appeared from her fortified flat, her daughter locking the grid behind her as she lit a cigarette and leaned over the walkway wall to look out over the estate. King moved quickly and quietly down the stairwell and was next to Ubana before she could react. He noticed she looked afraid, but stood her ground anyway – as if she'd been expecting a visit from him.

'Nice evening,' he told her, joining her in leaning over the wall.

'If there can be such a thing around here,' she answered.

'Oh, I don't know,' King argued. 'It's not so bad – now things have calmed down.'

'"Calmed down"?' she repeated. 'Is that what's happened?'

King said nothing for a while – examining her. 'I take it you heard what happened to Micky Astill?'

'I heard you paid him a visit.'

'It was more than a visit,' King reminded her. 'Arrested. Charged. Remanded. All his gear and cash seized. He's finished. He'll be going away for a long time.'

'Why you telling me this?' she turned on him.

'I hear your business is doing very well,' he told her coldly.

'You got something to say, just say it,' she insisted.

'All right,' he said, straightening to his full height. 'Nobody deals on the estate without my permission and everybody pays a commission.'

'Don't go too far,' she warned him. 'I have protection.'

'Fuck your protection,' he snarled at her. 'The only protection round here worth shit is mine. You pay or you get shut down. Consider yourself lucky. I'm doing you a favour. I could replace you tomorrow as easy as that.' He clicked his fingers for effect. 'But I'm going to give you a chance to stay in business.'

'You're getting out of your depth,' she tried to reason with him.

'Why?' he smiled. 'Because you have *police protection*. I

know you're an informant. I even know who your handler is. But here's the deal: you tell him anything about me and I'll let the entire estate know you're a grass. Wonder how long you'll last once that gets out? Wonder how long your *daughter* will last?'

'You're a fucking lowlife,' she told him through clenched teeth.

'I'm the fucking law,' he reminded her, 'and I can do whatever I like.'

'Yeah?' she challenged him. 'What if I don't pay?'

'Then I'll have one of my boys standing outside your front door twenty-four-seven. Won't get many punters knocking with Old Bill hanging around. You'll be out of business within a week and replaced by someone else. Someone who's glad of my protection.'

She considered her options for a few seconds before realizing it was useless. 'And if I pay?' she asked. 'How much?'

'Fifty percent of your profits,' he told her. 'Not your gross, just your profits. I can't say fairer than that.'

'Why?' she suddenly asked him. 'Why d'you need the money?'

'Money gives you options,' he told her. 'I like to keep my options open and I got bills to pay.'

'And drugs to buy,' she accused him. 'Doesn't matter how much money you have, those types of poison will take everything you've got.'

'I don't know what you're talking about,' he lied.

'I've been living here too long not to recognize the signs,' she reminded him. King said nothing. 'What you really doing this for?' she pressed. 'So you got a few debts – so what? You'll survive. What d'you really want the money for? Planning on running off into the sunset with someone? You're dreaming, King. Dreaming. Or maybe you don't even know why you're doing it.' She paused for a moment as he stood quietly watching her. 'Get out,' she warned him. 'Get out and take what you've made. Pay your bills or whatever, but forget the rest. If you don't this can only end one way for you – badly. Save yourself while you still can.'

After a few seconds King seemed to blink and shiver his way from his trance. 'Fifty percent,' he told her coldly. 'Starting now.'

'Fine,' she reluctantly agreed, flicking her cigarette away and heading for her front door. 'Have it your own way.'

'One more thing,' he stopped her. 'For now you can keep using whoever it is supplies you, but soon you'll be supplied by me and only me. More profit for both of us.'

'You're going to piss off some serious people,' she warned him.

'Let me worry about that,' he told. 'First payment's due at the end of the week. Don't disappoint me. I don't like it when people disappoint me. You understand what I mean, don't you, Susie?'

'Yeah,' she answered, what happened to Butler and Swinton foremost in her mind. 'I understand.'

'Good,' he told her. 'The end of the week then. Don't be late.'

Inspector Johnston entered Superintendent Gerrard's office when beckoned and stood in front of his desk. Gerrard sensed Johnston's tension and instinctively knew something must be wrong.

'Something you want to tell me, Joanne?' he asked.

'Something I thought I should bring to your attention, sir.'

'Well, go on.'

'I've been talking with DS Marino from our CID,' Johnston explained.

'And?'

'He's voiced some serious concerns about the Grove Wood Estate Policing Unit.'

'Such as?'

'Such as they could be behind the vigilante attacks on

311

the estate,' Johnston told him without a hint of concern herself.

'What?' Gerrard scoffed. 'Ridiculous. Bloody CID. Probably just jealous of the success a uniform unit is having. You know what a bunch of glory hunters they can be.' But the blank expression on Johnston's face told him there was more to it than he'd hoped. 'Or are you going to tell me I should be worried?'

'No,' Johnston answered unflinchingly, 'but just in case I've placed someone I can trust in the Unit.'

'And they know what they're looking for?'

'Yes, sir.'

'And their . . . *discretion* can be trusted?' Gerrard checked. 'Nothing like a bit of police malpractice to bring everything crashing down around our ears.'

'He can be trusted,' Johnston assured him.

'Good,' Gerrard relaxed. 'If any evidence arises that could damage the reputation of the borough I want to be told immediately. Although I'm sure it's all nonsense – uniformed officers acting as vigilantes, for crying out loud. This isn't the seventies or even the eighties. Things like that simply don't happen any more.'

'I'm sure you're right, sir,' Johnston agreed. 'Although there is another way – a way to be completely sure nothing can damage the reputation of the borough or the Met.'

Gerrard looked over the top of his spectacles at her. 'Which is?'

Johnston moved a little closer. 'Disband the Unit,' she said quietly.

'And raise everybody's suspicions?' Gerrard pointed out. 'As good as confirm to the CID something's wrong? I'm not sure that's the best idea.'

'Not immediately,' Johnston explained. 'We do it quietly, over the next two or three weeks. Let it all fizzle out and any . . . *malpractices* along with it. It's probably the best way to be sure.'

'I see,' said Gerrard as he looked at Johnston. 'And this is your idea?'

'Largely,' Johnston lied. 'We phase it out over the next few weeks, keeping control of the situation – doing it our way, instead of anyone else's.'

Gerrard considered the situation for a few seconds. 'Well,' he finally said, 'best to be sure I suppose. Leave your man in place on the Unit, just in case we have to expedite our intervention.'

'Of course, sir,' Johnston nodded. 'You can leave the matter in my hands. I'll take care of everything and if it comes to the worst and my man finds evidence of serious wrongdoing, then it would be best for us to be seen to be taking the lead on the matter. Make it clear we share a zero tolerance on corruption and malpractices of any kind. At the very least it'll ensure that our reputations are not damaged in any way.'

'Good,' Gerrard nodded slowly. 'Very good, Joanne.'

'No problem, sir,' she told him with one of her infamous pixie smiles. 'No problem at all.'

PC Rana Knight reached the open door of the Unit's office and warily looked inside, breathing a sigh of relief when he saw it was empty before entering and heading for his own desk. He shed his body armour and utility belt, dumping them on his chair before he checked the door to make sure no one had magically entered without him noticing.

'Fuck,' he cursed his own nerves, aware that if anyone ever found out he'd been snooping on other rank and file cops he'd never be able to work with them again. Worse – he'd forever have to watch his back and could never be sure again whether other cops would rush to his side if he ever needed assistance. But Johnston had made it clear that any information he provided would be treated as confidential and that if he was to accept the job she could pull strings and make sure he would soon be driving around in an Armed Response Vehicle with a Glock on his hip and a Heckler & Koch on his lap. It's what he'd joined the police to do and he wasn't about to pass up the chance to be fast-tracked to his dream job.

He moved tentatively across the room, eyes always fixed on the door until he practically bumped into the pushed-together desks shared by Brown and Williams.

'Shit,' he cursed under his breath and rubbed his thigh. Without much enthusiasm he began to check the tops of the desks, but found nothing other than stationery and bits of kit. Stirred by his failing he started going through their stacked in and out trays, but again found nothing of interest, just CPS memos and half-completed paperwork.

After checking the door again he pulled at the drawers under Brown's desk. The top two were open, but after a quick search he realized they were full of nothing but Brown's day-to-day debris. When he pulled at the bottom drawer, though, he found it was locked – piquing his interest as he slipped the long, thin skeleton key Johnston had told him would open any locked desk in the Met from his pocket. He shook his head disbelievingly, but to his surprise when he slid it into the tiny keyhole and turned it he was able to smoothly slide it open.

He wasted no time in diving into the contents of the drawer, but was soon disappointed to find nothing other than neatly organized files and folders containing case papers and an application to join the TSG. 'Fuck it,' he spat as he closed the drawer and re-locked it, just as a voice behind him almost made his heart stop.

'Looking for something?' King asked.

'Jesus,' Knight betrayed himself. 'No. No. I was just . . .'

'Just what?' King asked, smiling – happy to play with his catch.

314

'I needed . . . I needed an FPN,' Knight managed to think and say.

'Yeah?' King toyed with him. 'What for?'

'Running a red light,' Knight began to recover.

'Running a red light?' King laughed a little. 'No traffic lights on the Grove Wood.'

'On the way to it,' Knight made it up as he went along. 'The junction of Canning Town Road and Long Street. Saw some drivers really taking the piss today. Thought it couldn't hurt to stick a few on. It's all good figures for the Unit.'

'You think?' King told him, stripping himself of his body armour and other equipment. 'This is the Grove Wood Estate Unit. We're not really about sticking on hapless motorists. We exist to keep a foot firmly pressed on the throat of the local criminals. I would have thought Inspector Johnston would have made that clear to you?'

'She did,' Knight struggled, 'but I just thought—'

'In the trays,' King interrupted him.

'Excuse me?' Knight asked.

'The FPNs for running a red light,' he explained. 'In the trays over by the far wall. No need to look on anyone else's desk. People might get the wrong idea. Know what I'm saying?'

'I was just looking for an FPN,' Knight tried to convince him.

'We're a tight team here,' King warned him. 'You want to be part of that team, we have to know we can trust you. Trust you completely.'

'You can trust me,' Knight lied.

King watched him for a long time before replying. 'Why you here, Rana? What are you doing here?'

Knight felt his mouth go dry. 'I don't understand,' was all he could say.

'Here,' King said. 'On the Unit. Ordered or volunteered?'

'Volunteered,' Knight replied – the relief washing over him.

315

'Why?' King continued his interrogation.

'I want to try for the TSG,' Knight lied again. 'I need to up my crime arrests and here seemed like a good place to do it.'

'We'll get you your arrests. So long as we can be sure you're one of us.'

'Don't worry about me,' Knight assured him. 'Whatever it takes. Know what I mean?'

'Good,' King nodded. 'That's all I needed to hear.'

Susie Ubana paced around her kitchen waiting for the person she'd called to answer her untraceable pay-as-you-go mobile phone while her head spun with the implications of what King's ambitions meant for her and everyone else on the estate – their status quo of drug dealing and petty crime shattered by the intervention of the Unit. She shook her head in disbelief that a small number of uniformed cops could turn the lives of people on the Grove Wood upside down. She had to do something. Finally the man answered the phone.

'Hello,' was all he said.

'It's me,' she told him, but it was enough for him to recognize her.

'Trouble?' he immediately asked.

'King,' she simply answered. 'He's going too far – getting out of control. He's taking over all the dealing on the estate – even moving in on me.'

'What you talking about?' the voice asked.

'I mean it,' she warned him. 'Word is he's got that loser Dougie O'Neil dealing crack for him and now he wants me to pay him fifty percent of my profits every week.'

'I'm taking care of it,' he tried to reassure her, 'but I need something solid. They're cops. I can't do anything without proof.'

'What about when I pay him at the end of the week?' she asked. 'That could be enough.'

316

'And implicate yourself as a drug dealer?' he reminded her. 'Is that really what you want to do? There's no immunity in British law. You could testify against them, but you'd have to do time yourself.'

'I can't,' she told him, shaking her head. 'My daughter – they'd take my daughter away.'

'Then you'd better leave it with me,' he replied. 'I'll think of something. We don't necessarily need enough to send them down, just enough to get rid of them. Save them from themselves as much as anything.'

'I don't care what you do,' she admitted, 'so long as they're gone. But remember – if you can't solve this problem, then I know people who can. King's crossed the line now. He's in play. The people I know won't see him as a cop any more. They'll see him as a villain dressed as a cop trying to muscle in on their territory and they know how to deal with people who try to move on their business.'

'It doesn't need to come to that,' he appealed to her. 'I'll handle it.'

'You'd better,' she warned him, 'because time's running out. Can't keep the wolves at bay forever.' She hung up and lit another cigarette, unsure of what to do. The people she was thinking of had probably already heard rumours about King and the Unit. She knew that King and the others had taken down Astill, but had they done more than that? Had they been stupid enough to take his supply and cash for their own purposes? The people Astill worked for could tolerate losing the odd batch of drugs during a legitimate drugs raid, but local cops taking it for their own profit was not something they'd stand for and if she didn't tell them about King demanding protection money they might get the impression she'd willingly crossed to his side. And that would be bad for her. Bad for her daughter. 'Christ,' she complained. King could fuck everything up, but she didn't want blood on her hands. Especially not a cop's – even one who barely acted

317

like it any more. She decided to give her contact a few more days – then she'd have no choice but to tell them King was trying to move in on her. After that – God help him.

Marino stayed out of sight in the small cark park at Canning Road Police Station, keeping an eye on the door he knew King would use to exit the building before heading to his car and home – if indeed home was where he was spending his nights. Marino was in luck as King appeared through the door and headed across the asphalt towards his car looking like a man in a hurry with a lot on his mind. Marino caught up with him quickly enough – King turning on him and looking to the heavens once he knew who it was.

'What the fuck do you want now?' he snapped aggressively.

'Just a chat,' Marino answered calmly, noting how exhausted and strung-out King looked.

'I've got nothing to say to you, so why don't you just stay out of my business and stop bothering me.'

'What are you taking?' Marino cut to the chase. 'Amphetamines? Cocaine? Crack?'

'You know fuck all,' King snarled at him.

'I know someone on drugs when I see them,' Marino reminded him. 'And I know the prospect of Edwards' appeal is causing you more problems than you'll admit. No one would want to have to relive something like that more than once.'

'More than once,' King almost laughed – remembering the hundreds of times he'd already relived the nightmare incident in his mind. 'Just leave me alone, Frank,' he warned him. 'If I have to bury Edwards again I will. I'm not afraid of giving evidence. I know what happened.' He tried to walk away, but Marino grabbed him around the bicep and pulled him back.

'You went through some bad shit,' Marino explained. 'What you had to deal with was beyond what anyone should have

318

to see. A man killing his own family – damn near killing you. You don't just get over that.'

'I don't know what you're talking about,' King lied, images of the young girl in the white dress with the spreading crimson tide flooding his tired mind.

'So,' Marino tried to persuade him, 'you've done some *questionable* things, but it's not too late to turn things around. This thing with Swinton went way too far. The man could have died. If that had happened there wouldn't be anything anyone could do to help you.'

'We had a man running loose on the estate attacking young children,' he answered. 'CID failed to deal with it so I did.'

'Jesus, Jack,' Marino said, looking around the car park to ensure they were still alone. 'You probably didn't even get the right guy.'

'I didn't get anyone,' King rounded on him. 'You accusing me of something, Frank?'

'You said you dealt with it.'

'You misunderstood me.'

Marino said nothing for a while. 'Get your career and your life back on track, Jack. Quit the Unit first thing tomorrow and come see me in my office. We can sort you out an extended attachment to the CID where I can look out for you – get you cleaned up.'

King suddenly looked defeated – like a man without hope, set on a preordained road to self-destruction.

'It's too late for that,' he quietly told Marino.

'It's not too late,' Marino pleaded. 'We can still fix this.'

King prised Marino's fingers from around his arm. 'Ever considered I might not want to change?' he asked. 'Ever thought I might like things the way they are?'

'That's not you talking,' Marino argued. 'Not the real you. The job will support you – they have to. You didn't get the help you should have. Anything you've done can be laid back at their door. Trust me, they won't want the stink. Anything you've done can be sorted out – so long as you stop now.'

'And what?' King shook his head. 'Claim temporary insanity? That I lost it because of what happened?'

'You won't have to,' Marino tried to assure him. 'Everything will be smoothed out and forgotten before it comes to that. It'll be like nothing ever happened.'

King was silent for a while as he tried to comprehend returning to his previous sober world, being everything to everybody – trapped in a passionless marriage to Sara – the occasional dinner with friends and a bottle of wine as wild as it would ever be. How could he return to a life like that after tasting life around the extreme edges – the mind-blowing effects of crack compared to the slow drowsiness of alcohol? Predictable sex with safe women or being inside the wild, writhing Kelly. The drugs helped him forget – took him to a better place and so did Kelly. He could never leave that world now. It had trapped him.

'I'm not going anywhere,' he finally told Marino. 'Too much unfinished business to take care of. I'm not ready to go back to how things were. I'm not sure I ever will be.' He turned his back on Marino and walked towards his car, but Marino grabbed him by the shoulder and spun him back round. Before he could speak King knocked his arm away and pushed him hard in the chest with both hands, making him stumble and fall against another parked car. A look of shock spread across Marino's face.

'Don't fucking touch me,' King warned him. 'Don't ever fucking touch me.'

'I can't protect you much longer,' Marino recovered enough to plead with him. 'You're pissing off some heavy people, Jack. You go too far across the line and they won't care about the uniform you wear – they'll come looking for you. They'll do the same to you they would to anyone who moves in on their manor and starts shaking down people under their protection. You give them no choice.'

'I don't need or want your protection,' King insisted. 'Just stay away from me and stay out of my business, Frank. Someone wants to come after me, let them. I can take care of myself.'

'You don't know what these people are like,' Marino pleaded. 'You don't know what they're capable of.'

'And you don't know what I'm capable of,' King replied. 'Just stay out of my way, Frank. Just stay out of my way.'

King stood next to Sara as they waited for the front door to be opened, feeling agitated and paranoid, partly due to the decent hit of cocaine he'd taken before meeting Sara and heading to his parents' house, but more so due to the confrontation with Marino in the station car park. He and Sara had hardly spoken to each other during the long cross-town drive, although he'd managed to ask a few polite questions about how things had been at work for her, the cocaine stimulating his brain enough to actually speak, even if he could barely remember her answers. They never discussed their relationship and they never touched each other. Several times he'd had to shake the image of Kelly from his racing mind and resist the almost overwhelming compulsion to tell Sara all about her, but somehow he managed not to. Better to let his relationship with Sara fade to a natural conclusion – a drift more than a deliberate split. There was no need to torment Sara with how little she ultimately meant to him and how much Kelly, a young woman he hardly even knew, did. The door swung open and his mother stood in silence looking back and forth between them, concern etched into her face.

'Good Lord, Jack,' she said. 'You don't look too good. You OK?'

'I'm fine,' he told her. 'Just a little tired from work.'

321

'I see,' she replied, unconvinced. 'And you, Sara – how are you?'

'Good thank you, Emily,' Sara lied and managed a slight smile.

'Well don't just stand out here,' she encouraged them enthusiastically. 'Come in and join the others.' She stepped aside and allowed them to enter. 'It's been months since we saw either of you.'

King found himself momentarily frozen. The space beyond his mother suddenly appeared dark and foreboding, as if it was trying to lure him inside and trap him forever, his mother's accusation that they hadn't seen him in months when he *knew* it had only been weeks adding confusion to his fear.

'Jack,' Sara tried to bring him back. 'Jack.'

'What?' he asked as he came back to the world.

'You all right? You look like you've seen a ghost.'

'Yeah,' he insisted. 'I'm good.'

She stepped towards the entrance, but still he didn't move. 'You coming?' she asked, looking frustrated and annoyed.

'Yes,' he answered, forcing himself to move towards the door and the dark interior as Sara and his mother passed knowing looks of disapproval between them – his behaviour clearly a mystery to both of them. He followed them through the house to the kitchen where his father, brother and his fiancée sat around the table sipping from glasses of wine and talking cheerfully until he entered the room – his mood and distance from them trailing behind him like a poisonous vapour expanding and filling every inch of space.

'Sara,' his father acknowledged them. 'Jack.'

'Dad,' King barely answered, falling onto the chair next to his brother.

'Hello, Graham,' Sara answered a little stiffly.

Graham smiled as he stood to fetch extra wine glasses. 'Drink?'

'Yes thanks,' Sara answered quickly.

'Jack?'

King looked at the wine on the table as if it was toxic. The last thing he wanted was to drink alcohol and risk numbing the effects of the cocaine he hoped would see him through the evening. 'No thanks. I'm driving.'

'Ah,' his father nodded. 'Probably for the best. You look bloody knackered as it is. Too much time in the pub with the other coppers sharing tales of the latest arrests?'

'I don't think so,' King replied flatly. 'I've been working long hours. Doing what it takes to get the job done. Know what I mean?'

'You do look tired, Jack,' Scott interrupted. 'Everything all right?' He'd seen too many soldiers in Afghanistan take drugs to briefly escape the horror and fear that surrounded them not to immediately recognize it in his own brother.

'You're all right,' King snapped at them slightly. 'I'm tired. So what? No big deal.'

'It's not just that,' Sara told them. 'The man who . . . hurt Jack is appealing his sentence.'

'What?' his mother asked. 'How can he do that?'

'Don't worry about it,' his father smiled. 'Any appeal by that monster will be refused.'

'It's already been agreed there are grounds for the appeal,' Sara explained. 'Something about an unqualified psychiatrist.'

'Under-qualified,' King corrected her. 'Not unqualified.'

'What?' Graham pushed.

'One,' King said. 'One of the shrinks who declared him sane to stand trial may not have the level of expertise the prosecution thought. That's all.'

'You're not seriously talking about a re-trial, are you?' Graham asked.

'No,' King answered, 'but I might have to give evidence again.'

'That would not be good for you,' Sara told him.

'I'll be fine,' King lied.

'Of course you will,' Graham tried to reassure him. 'It's only a matter of standing in the box and telling the truth.'

'And what would you know about it?' King suddenly snapped – awkwardness suddenly sweeping through the room.

'Leave him alone,' his mother tried to rescue him, smiling as she made the final preparations for dinner. 'He's allowed to be tired if he wants.'

'It's not a choice I made,' he corrected her. 'I work hard – keeping the streets safe for people like you.'

'We're quite capable of looking after ourselves,' his father argued. 'Thirty years in the army taught me a thing or two about survival.'

A heavy silence hung in the room as father and son locked eyes. Sara tried to break the oppressive atmosphere. 'How've you been, Scott?' she asked.

'Good, thanks,' he replied politely. 'Got out of hospital a while back now. Everything seems to be on the mend nicely.'

'He'll be returning to his regiment soon,' Graham interrupted. 'Get back in the saddle – best thing to do.'

Scott smiled and nodded, but made no comment. 'And Hannah's been great,' he addressed Sara. 'Put up with all my . . . *moods*.'

'Not easy,' Sara sympathized, 'recovering from something like that.'

'No shit,' King found himself saying almost involuntarily, killing the improving atmosphere and reminding everyone Scott wasn't the only one who'd spent weeks in hospital recovering from terrible injuries.

'We found ourselves a right pair,' Hannah tried to salvage the good will. 'Didn't we, Sara?'

'Found?' King attacked again. 'What are we – stray dogs?'

'That's not what she meant,' Sara chastised him – weeks of frustration surfacing. She knew she was losing him, but wasn't even sure if she cared any more. Their relationship

324

felt more and more like a sick pet that needed to be put down.

'Anyway,' Graham tried to exert his authority, 'without these lovely young women I don't know what would become of you two careless so-and-sos. About time you made honest women of them.'

'Well,' Scott stumbled slightly, 'we've only been engaged a few weeks.'

'If you're engaged what are you waiting for?' Graham asked. 'When you know you know. No point waiting around. In the old days you'd be engaged for a couple of months – just long enough to sort out the logistics – and then you'd get married. That's what we did.'

'Jesus,' said King, resisting the temptation to pull out the paper fold of cocaine he had in his pocket and snort it in front of all of them. 'What century we in? Sara and I aren't even engaged. We're living in sin. We like living in sin. Don't we, Sara?'

'Living?' she asked, her eyes watery. 'Is that what we're doing, Jack? Just living?'

'Food's ready,' King's mother interrupted quickly.

'Good,' Graham welcomed the distraction and began to clear space on the table for the plates and dishes his wife carried. 'Everybody just help yourselves. It's just a kitchen supper, not a dinner party.'

The others politely began to place selected items onto their plates, but King just looked on, the mundane normality of the scene making him want to turn the table upside down and flee from the house. The only thing that stopped him was his affection and respect for Scott. But it was hard to sit there surrounded by faces he didn't even recognize any more – as if they were just old photographs of people from a previous life he no longer ever thought of.

'You need to eat something,' his mother told him. 'You don't look like you've been eating properly at work.'

325

'Nor at home,' Sara added, not looking at him.

'Fine,' he sighed, leaning forward and spearing a few small items that he spread out on his plate.

'All you're having?' Scott asked.

'I'm not very hungry,' he replied.

'You can tell you've never been in the army,' his father unhelpfully joined in. 'You never turn down the chance of a good feed when you're a soldier. Never know where your next meal's going to come from.'

'Well I'm not a soldier and this isn't the army,' King snarled and pushed his plate away. 'I do what I want when I want.'

'As do most of the police force by the look of things,' his father laughed mockingly. 'All I ever hear about is police incompetence. Too busy having public spats with politicians instead of doing the job required.'

'People should just stay out of our way,' King argued. 'Let us get on with what we have to do instead of sticking their noses into our business. What the hell do you care about how we do things? So long as we take out the bad guys and keep our boots on the throats of the little thugs who think they rule the streets – what do you care?'

'Sounds like you want a police state,' his father said disapprovingly.

'Better than one run by the military,' King baited him. 'At least we live in the real world.'

'It doesn't get any realer than a combat zone,' his father told him, puffing out his chest. 'Just ask Scott if you don't believe me.'

'So what do you want me to do?' King demanded, giving way to his rising temper and desire to divorce himself from their world. 'Join the army and get sent to Iraq or Syria? Drop bombs on women and children?'

'Don't go too far, Jack,' his father tried to warn him.

'You know,' King ignored him, 'all I ever hear is how useless the police are. How useless I am. That it was my fault some fucking madman stuck a knife in my back.'

'Jack,' Sara appealed to him, tears welling in her eyes.

'What the fuck do you want me to do?' he refused to relent. 'Go to some shithole in the Middle East and stand on an IED? Maybe this time you'll get really lucky and I'll get my arms and legs blown off and then you can prop my torso up in the corner of your sitting room and point to me every time one of your old friends comes round so they can see just how much you've fucking sacrificed – because Scott wasn't enough, was he? Now he's out of hospital you can hardly tell he was even wounded at all. He's still in one piece – except for his fucking mind of course.'

'Jesus Christ,' Sara said, turning away from him and looking at the floor before finding the courage to look at Scott. 'I'm so sorry, Scott. I'm really sorry.'

'Forget it,' he told her, even managing a slight smile. 'Jack's been through as much as I have. It's not easy adjusting to everything after something like that.'

'Don't make excuses for me,' King fuelled the fire. 'I'm glad it happened to me. It woke me up. I was sleep-walking towards a life like yours,' he addressed everyone in front of him. 'Life's for living – being on the edge for as long as you can until you fall off, but at least you are alive – even if just for a while. You think I want to be sitting round a table like this in thirty years' time with grown-up kids who can't stand me and a wife I haven't fucked in years? Do I fuck. That's your lives not mine.'

'That's enough,' his father shouted across the table. 'That's enough.' He breathed deeply, calming himself enough to speak with quiet authority. 'I think it's best if you just leave.'

Everyone sat in silence looking at the floor, except King and his father who stared into each other's eyes, their faces twitching with hate and rage.

'Fine,' King calmly replied, getting to his feet. 'You think I want to stay here anyway? You're doing me a favour. Let's go, Sara.'

'I'm not going anywhere,' she said, glancing at him briefly. 'Not with you.'

He shrugged his shoulders as if he'd lost nothing more than some small change. 'Whatever. Have it your own way.' He threw his chair out of the way and strolled out of the kitchen as if he didn't have a care in the world.

After a few seconds Scott jumped to his feet and headed after him. 'Let him go,' Graham told him. 'He's not worth it.'

'He's my brother,' Scott reminded him. 'I have to try.' By the time he caught up with King he was already climbing into his car. 'Jack, wait,' Scott implored. 'Just wait a minute.'

'What the fuck d'you want, Scott?' he asked almost sympathetically, shaking his head to warn him anything he tried would be useless.

'Come back inside,' Scott pleaded. 'Come back inside and apologize. They'll get over it. I'll tell them you've been under a lot of pressure at work lately and that you've been having a hard time dealing with what happened to you. They won't push it – trust me – I know.'

'Why you doing this, Scott?' he asked. 'You think you can save me from whatever it is you think I need saving from?'

'Only you can do that,' Scott insisted. 'But you're still my brother. You don't turn your back on your brother – whether it's your blood brother or the guy standing next to you in a dried-out river bed when the Taliban are closing from all sides. You don't abandon your brothers.'

'Jesus, Scott,' King answered, shaking his head. 'It's just the world's changed now – everything changed. I don't know why it happened – it just did. But I can't go back. I don't want to go back.'

'It's not too late to put this right,' Scott tried to persuade him. 'For Christ's sake, just come back inside.'

'No,' King finished it, climbing the rest of the way into his car. 'There's nothing back there for me.'

'Then at least call me,' Scott told him as King started the

car. 'If you need to speak to someone. If you ever need help. If you're ever in trouble.'

'I just need to sort a few things out,' King lied, pulling a pen and a piece of paper from the centre console and scribbling something on it before handing it to Scott. 'If for some reason you can't get me on my mobile, that's where I'll be.'

Scott looked at the address – some place called Millander Walk. 'What's this?' he asked.

'It's on the estate I told you about,' King explained. 'It's where I'm staying.'

'Not at your flat?' Scott questioned him. 'Not with Sara?'

'No,' King said bluntly. 'I can't think there. Not at the moment. I need a few days to work things out and then I'll go home.'

'Really?' Scott asked – not believing anything he was being told.

'Really,' King repeated, before shrugging his shoulders. 'I don't know. Maybe.'

'And Sara?'

'Take her home for me,' King answered. 'Tell her I just need a little time and space. If she doesn't want to give it to me I'll understand. She's a good-looking girl. It wouldn't take her long to meet someone else. She'll soon forget about me. I didn't want to hurt her, you know. I didn't want to hurt anyone. It was the last thing I wanted. Sara – she's such a good person, but fuck . . . shit just happened. I'm no good for her now. She's better off without me.'

'Sounds like you've already made your mind up about everything,' said Scott.

'I haven't made my mind up about anything,' King told him, 'other than I want to feel alive – really alive – for a while at least.'

'The world won't wait for you, Jack,' his brother warned him. 'By the time you've worked whatever this is out of your system it could already be too late to come back. I don't want to lose you, Jack. I've already almost lost you once – remember?'

'You're not going to *lose* me,' King tried to convince him. 'No one's going to lose me. I just need some time.' He put the car in gear and released the handbrake. 'Just make sure Sara gets home safely.' He pulled the door shut and drove away – leaving Scott clutching the paper with the address on Millander Walk in his hand and an almost overwhelming sense that the brother he once knew and loved was lost to him forever.

15

King knocked quietly on the door before stepping back and looking both ways along the walkway – wary of anyone or thing that could be lurking in the shadows of the night-time estate. To his relief the door was soon opened slightly as Kelly peered out, looking him up and down – the slight smile on her naturally pouted red lips instantly enough to seduce and excite him.

'It's late,' she told him, opening the door a little further so he could see slim athletic legs. Her torso was covered with nothing more than a cut-off t-shirt, her long wavy brown hair tumbling over her shoulders and throat.

'You alone?' he asked.

She inhaled deeply on the joint she'd been hiding behind the door – blowing the smoke high into the night sky before answering – enjoying making him wait for the simplest thing. 'Yeah. I'm alone.'

'Can I come in?' he asked, smiling despite his anxiety that she didn't want him any more.

'OK,' she shrugged, pulling the door wide open for him to enter and then closing it quietly behind him. He breathed her in as he passed her – his fingertips brushing across her naked stomach, making her take a short involuntary breath, her eyes for a split second blazing with desire for him. He noticed it and slipped an arm around her waist, feeling the warm velvet of her pristine skin, pulling her towards him, his other hand coming to the side of her face and guiding her lips towards his. Gently she stopped him – holding his head in her hands.

'Slow down,' she told him, looking into his red eyes and recognizing the signs of someone on crack or cocaine – something she'd witnessed in dozens of people throughout her young life. 'Coke's got you all wired up,' she warned him. 'Here,' she offered him her joint. 'This'll bring you back down softly.'

He took the joint and drew deep and hard, holding the smoke in his lungs until he could feel its first effects beginning in his brain and replacing the mad energetic rush of the cocaine he'd taken almost as soon as he'd left his parents' house with a gentle calming, his heart rate dropping and his racing mind slowing. He took another deep hit and handed the joint back to Kelly who increasingly felt like something to be cherished and savoured, instead of devoured in a rush of drug-enhanced passion.

'Feeling better?' she asked.

'Yeah,' he replied, already sounding relaxed and content.

'It'll help you get some sleep,' she told him.

'Sleep?' he smiled as he pulled her close. 'I don't want to sleep.'

'Oh,' she smiled back. 'You want some more of *that*, do you?' He kissed the side of her neck in reply. 'Well, I suppose it'll relax you,' she said. 'Help you rest.'

'I need to be with you,' he whispered into her ear before gently biting her lobe – feeling her quickly and efficiently unbuckling his belt and unzipping his trousers – her fingers diligently pulling him free and softly stroking him hard.

'Well, well,' she said, never looking up from his swelling. 'What we gonna do with this?' She turned so her back was pressed against him and stepped towards the kitchen table, dragging him with her. When they reached it she leaned forward over it and pulled her own shorts and knickers down enough so she could feel him behind her and began to search for him – her hand finding him and guiding him inside her. They both moaned in pleasure as he began to rhythmically move in and out of her until King suddenly stopped. He wanted more – more than this.

'What's wrong?' she asked him, looking over her shoulder. No man had ever done anything other than just take her once she'd offered herself. She was as confused as she was concerned.

'Not like this,' he explained. 'I need more.'

She turned to face him, sitting on the edge of the table with her legs wrapped around his waist, arms draped around his neck as they searched for and found each other's lips – kissing somewhere between uncontrolled passion and a tenderness Kelly had never felt before. She broke away and spoke softly in his ear. 'What do you want?' she asked. 'What more do you want?'

'All of you,' he whispered back. 'Body and soul.' He lifted her from the table and easily carried her across the room to the sofa – his powerful physique hardly straining despite her athletic body. He gently laid her down and slowly slid her shorts and knickers the rest of the way from her legs, letting them fall to the floor before pulling her tiny top upwards, Kelly assisting by straightening her arms over her head. Once she was completely naked he kneeled next to her, taking time to absorb all her unspoilt beauty – her natural perfection – skin, legs, breasts, shoulders, stomach, all perfect, as were the long wavy ringlets of her shiny mahogany hair and her irresistible red lips. But more than anything else it was her deep black eyes like a swirling nebula from which there could be no escape, only destruction.

Together they unbuttoned his shirt and threw it to one

side as he stood and let Kelly pull his trousers and boxer shorts down – dragging his socks off as he kicked everything away, leaving him standing in front of her naked – his skin pulled taut over young conditioned muscle as he showed himself fully to her, enjoying their shared vulnerability of nakedness – their eyes washing over each other in a mutual wanting and admiration.

She could feel his strength without even touching him. Not the wiry strength of the feral teenage boys from the estate, made lean and powerful by the constant struggle to survive and borderline malnutrition, but a deep-set power from thick muscle tissue stretching across his chest and abdomen. She could wait no longer, leaning forward and placing her palms on his lower stomach muscles before gently sliding them up his body until they rested on his heaving chest, her mouth slightly parted as she bit down on her own lip. He slid one arm under the base of her back and with one smooth, effortless movement sat on the sofa and lifted her so she was now sitting astride his lap. One hand softly caressed her breasts while the other supported her weight as she leaned back, her eyes closed in anticipation of the pleasure to come. But he hesitated, making the moment last before they joined together – taking his hand from her breast and wrapping it around the back of her neck, gently pulling her swollen lips towards his own until they touched, generating an almost static shock between them as they both parted only milli-metres from each other for a brief last moment before committing to the kiss completely until Kelly eased her mouth away from his and spoke softly into his ear.

'I'm ready,' she told him. 'I want you now.' He responded by kissing her neck and lifting her weight, allowing her to move her hips upwards and forwards as her hand searched between her own legs until she found him, lowering herself slowly and only slightly until the tip of his erection slid easily inside her. They both froze as if they knew they were at the beginning of something neither of them would ever forget and may never surpass – their eyes locked together, mouths slightly open as they panted gently in anticipation until Kelly could wait no longer and sank him as deeply inside her as she could, moaning loudly as she felt him beating and pulsing within her.

They moved slowly in effortless rhythm together, never breaking eye contact, allowing their souls to experience the same joining their bodies were sharing. While they were coupled, she owned him and he knew he owned her.

'You think you're in control, don't you?' she whispered into his ear. 'That you control me like you control everything on this estate.'

'No,' he quietly spoke his reply as she rose and fell on him, moving ever faster, their eyes still never moving from each other's. 'No. You control me,' he told her. 'You control me completely.'

'I know,' she smiled slightly and closed her eyes, moving in harmony with him for a few more seconds until she fell forward, pressing herself down on him as deeply as possible, their lips once more sealed together while their hips twitched with pleasure as he released his seed inside her, making her reach simultaneous climax. They held each other in place, taking short, stunted breaths as their singing bodies slowly returned to something like normal until finally she could speak again.

'Fuck,' she told him, still holding him tightly. 'It's never felt like that before. Never.'

'That's how it's supposed to feel,' he replied. 'It's supposed to make you feel alive – more than alive. It purges the bad – leaves only the good. Takes away the fear and the pain.'

'Fear?' she asked. 'I doubt you fear anything. It's you everyone's afraid of.'

'Really?' he asked, the effort of ecstasy leaving his muscles taut and twitching. 'I doubt that.'

'You shouldn't,' she assured him. 'I hear what people think.'

'Never mind them,' he smiled and lifted her forward, releasing himself from inside her. 'Fuck,' he laughed slightly. 'I need something to smoke,' he told her. 'Make us something to smoke.'

'Why not?' she agreed. Turning her back on him she walked across the room like a leopard moving silently through long grass. She stood casual and confident next to a small side table as she prepared the joint, twisting her head back towards him only slightly as she spoke, her long hair obscuring her face. 'So,' she asked him, 'what was that? What just happened?'

'What d'you mean?' he asked, despite knowing exactly what she meant.

'Between us,' she said. 'It's never felt like that before for me.'

'Nor me,' he admitted.

'Is that what it feels like to make love instead of fuck?'

'I think so,' he told her. 'I hope so.'

'Then,' she asked hesitantly, 'do you love me?'

'Bring that thing over here,' he ignored the question. She lit the joint, spinning round like a ballerina and floating back towards him, but as she went to sit next to him he took her in both hands and again made her sit astride his lap so he could feel her touching him. Her hips instinctively began to rock backwards and forwards until he stopped her. 'Just sit still,' he told her, resting his hands on her shoulders and allowing them to slide down her body before wandering wherever they pleased. 'I just want to look at you.' She swayed slightly from side to side at the feel of his touch, placing the joint between his lips and allowing him to take a deep draw before doing the same herself – watching his searching hands before looking into his face – his eyes telling her he'd gone to a different, enchanted world.

'What?' she asked him with a smile.

'You,' he answered.

'What about me?' she pressed.

'You're so fucking beautiful,' he laughed. She moved in his lap, making him wince with pleasure as she blew a long plume of smoke into his face that he willingly sucked in and held in his lungs. 'What you doing hiding on this estate? You should be conquering the world.'

'I'm only seventeen, remember,' she reminded him, smiling with sweet sexuality.

'Going on twenty-five,' he teased her.

'You grow up fast around here,' she told him.

'I noticed,' he said, letting his hands move to her breasts, feeling her large dark nipples pressing into his palms. She moved again and felt him begin to swell between her legs.

'You need some more of this,' she insisted, leaning forward and placing the joint between his lips, the end burning brightly as he drew hard. They were quiet for a while as they enjoyed the increasing effects of the cannabis and looking at each other's bodies.

'So why haven't you?' he finally spoke. 'Why haven't you got out of here – become a model or actress or something?'

'I don't know,' she shrugged. 'Mum needs helps with my brother and sister, I suppose.'

'She'll cope,' he told her. 'You need to look out for yourself.'

'It's not as easy as that,' she replied. 'I'd need money. Somewhere to live. Someone to look after me.' She leaned forward and kissed him on the lips.

'I'll look after you,' he said, suddenly looking deadly serious.

'And what about your pretty policewoman girlfriend I know you've got hidden away somewhere?'

'Over,' he told her coldly, but truthfully. 'Was probably over the first time I saw you.'

'Why so sure?'

'I don't know,' he admitted. 'I just knew.'

'Were you married?'

'No.'

'Engaged?'

'No,' he answered, 'although I think she thought we kind of were.'

'Have you told her?'

'As good as.'

'How was she about it?'

'Fine,' he shrugged. 'She knew it was over – that we were just going through the motions.'

'And you think *we* can be a normal boyfriend and girl-friend?'

'Who wants to be normal?'

'So you won't be introducing me to your parents any time soon?'

'Why the fuck would you want to meet them?' he asked, laughing spitefully. 'Sitting around a fucking dinner table feeling them watching us, making their disapproval as obvious as they can. Fuck them. Fuck everybody. With you by my side I can do anything.'

'You mean take over the estate?'

'To start with,' he admitted. 'Then I'll expand.'

'You could upset a lot of dangerous people,' she warned him.

'I'm a cop,' he reminded her as he stroked her thighs, feeling the strength of her youth. 'No one's going to fuck with me.'

'You won't be a cop for long if you carry on like you have been,' she told him, taking a drag on the joint before placing it between his lips for him to do the same.

'I don't have to be,' he explained. 'I'm planning on making a lot of money very quickly – then we disappear.'

'Where?' she asked excitedly, her shoulders dancing. 'Where shall we go?'

'I don't know,' he confessed. 'Haven't decided yet. India

maybe? South America? Somewhere where money talks and we can live like a king and queen for life on a few hundred thousand. So long as it's far from here I don't care.'

'You can earn that much that quickly?' she questioned, sounding unsure.

'Why not?' he asked. 'If you'd seen how much cash that fool Astill had in his flat you wouldn't doubt me. If a clown like that can earn that sort of money, imagine what I can do. That uniform's like my shield. Out here it makes me fucking Superman. I can do anything I want. Soon every dealer within three miles will be working for me or paying me off. That sort of money adds up quickly.'

'Which is why some very serious people will do anything to keep control of it,' she told him.

'Even fuck with a cop?'

'Maybe.'

'I don't think so,' he assured her.

'And what about your own kind? What about other cops? What if they come after you?'

'I'll be careful,' he smiled confidently. 'I know what to look out for. I'll see them coming before they can do anything. But I need to make it as fast as I can. The longer it goes on the greater the chance of something going wrong. That's why I need to keep a hold of the drug trade across the estate. It's the only way I can make enough money fast. We won't be millionaires, but we could have enough to make a start somewhere else. I don't like it. If there was another way maybe I could try it, but there isn't. Things have already gone too far. I need to move fast. At least there are no victims here – just people who want to get high.' Even as he spoke he knew he was being self-delusional – trying to in some way excuse his actions, but even his damaged mind couldn't be entirely fooled by his own lies.

'People don't smoke crack just to get high,' she told him. 'They do it to escape from life.'

'Their choice,' he answered coldly, 'and it's our best chance.'

'I hope you're right,' she said, leaning forward as if she was going to kiss him before veering away and resting her chin on his shoulder – one hand wrapped around his neck while the fingers of the other walked down his back until they found the first of the two thick scars that decorated his skin, 'because I won't spend my life visiting you in prison, or worse. I've seen too many women on the estate waste their lives doing that.'

'Losers who got tied up with other losers,' he told her. 'That won't happen to me . . . or you.'

'So,' she teased him, 'you're indestructible then?'

'Something like that.'

'Is that how you survived whatever it was that caused these?' She ran her finger over the scar so he would know what she meant.

'Oh,' he said casually; for the first time in a long time he'd forgotten the scars were even there. 'Those.'

'I noticed them before,' she admitted.

'Hard not to,' he smiled slightly.

'I was gonna ask about them, but didn't know whether you wanted to talk about it. Most of the blokes round here, if they had scars like this, would walk around with their shirts off all the time – to make sure everyone could see them. But you never said nothing about them, so I thought maybe you didn't want to talk about them.'

'You want to know how I got them?' She shrugged as if she suddenly wasn't really interested. 'You sure you want to know?'

'Only if you want to tell me,' she lied.

He sighed and took the last of the joint from her, inhaling and burning it down to the cardboard filter before stretching for the nearest ashtray and stubbing it partially out. 'I was on foot patrol on the other side of Canning Town when I got a call about a domestic kicking off not far from where I

340

was.' It was the first time he'd spoken about it to anyone other than a doctor or therapist since it happened. 'It was supposed to be the last thing I dealt with before heading off on my sergeants' course. Ironic. Unlucky. Call it what you will. Anyway, I made my way to the scene, expecting the usual shouting match and pathetic accusations. I already had it in my mind to nick the male and leave the woman – give them a little time apart to cool down before they declared their undying love and ran back into each other's arms – the usual domestic dispute shit.' He fell silent, images of the fateful day suddenly rushing quickly into his mind, strong and vivid.

'But?' Kelly brought him back.

'But when I got there the house was in complete silence – no shouting, no screaming – nothing. I knew something was seriously wrong. I just felt it – like an evil presence or something, I don't know.'

'What did you do?' she asked innocently.

'Nothing,' he shrugged, 'for a while. I just stared at the front of the house trying to work out what the fuck was going on.' He felt his throat swelling as the memories threatened to overwhelm him before he managed to continue. 'Turned out I didn't have long to wait.'

'Why?' Kelly encouraged, somehow sensing the importance of him being able to tell her. 'What happened?'

'A girl,' he stammered slightly, 'about ten maybe . . . She came walking out of the house – looking straight at me – making straight for me. She had on this white dress, only it was turning red. The blood was turning it red. I think I went towards her . . . I can't really remember, but she ended up falling into my arms. I'll never forget those eyes. Jesus, I'll never forget those eyes just staring up at me. Then *he* came from inside – like something from hell – knife in his hand and covered in blood. He came at us – not so much me, but the girl. He wanted the girl. I turned my back on him to

341

shield the girl and he gave me these.' He looked over his own shoulder at the scars he couldn't see.

'Who was he?' she asked, her mouth suddenly dry and her voice faint as she realized she was listening to something real and close – not something from a film or a news item about a distant land.

'Her father,' he told her without emotion.

'Why?'

'Because he thought his wife – the children's mother – was going to leave him and take the children with her.'

'Was she?'

'No. They all died for nothing,' he explained.

'They?' Kelly seized on it.

'I went inside the house,' he told her, as if he was a child telling a friend about something he'd done as a dare that no one would believe, watching her eyes dance with the possibilities of horrors he was about to describe. 'I beat the shit out the father and cuffed him – and then I went in the house.'

'Oh my God,' she swallowed hard. 'What did you find?'

'Downstairs was clear, so I went upstairs. The blood was pissing out my back – made it feel like I was climbing a mountain, but I eventually got to the top.'

'What was there?' she asked, stroking his scars.

'Nothing,' he answered. 'Except the bloody handprints and smears on the walls. I knew that whatever I was going to find wasn't going to be good, but I had to know – had to see it with my own eyes. If there were more children inside, I figured I might still be able to save them.'

'Was there?' she asked, afraid what the answer might be.

'Yes,' he said quickly and firmly, as if he was breaking bad news to someone. 'There were more.' He felt her body tense against his. 'You don't have to hear this,' he explained. 'I had to go into the house. You don't.'

'I want to,' she almost whispered into his ear. 'Tell me what you found upstairs.'

'In the first bedroom I found a girl,' he told her without emotion, as if he was reading from a report. 'I later found out she was twelve years old. He'd strangled her and laid her out on a bed face up – arms crossed across her chest. No blood. No knife wounds. He'd tried to kill her *clean* – as if that somehow made it all right.'

'Bastard,' Kelly swore quietly. 'He must have been insane.'

'That's what he tried to tell the court,' said King, 'but they didn't believe him and neither did I. He just couldn't handle the thought of losing them – of his wife and kids being with someone else. The only insanity he had was the insanity of jealousy, but that doesn't work in court.'

They both thought silently for a few seconds before she spoke again. 'His wife?' she asked. 'What happened to his wife?'

'I found her in the next bedroom,' he explained, 'on the double bed she probably shared with the man who killed her – tangled up in the white sheets, although they'd turned red by then. He gave the wife special attention. Went to work on her with the knife. More stab wounds than you could count. You could see the hate in what he'd done to her. He blamed her for everything – although she'd done nothing.'

'You should have killed the bastard,' Kelly said, harsh words spoken softly into his ear.

'If I could have made it back downstairs I probably would have,' he admitted, 'but I passed out. Blood loss caught up with me.'

'So he killed his wife and daughter,' Kelly summarized, 'and almost killed the little girl you saved.' She sensed his hesitation – the flickering of his muscles as he tensed and she knew there was more. 'Jesus,' she said. 'That's not all, is it?'

He tried to speak, but the words became trapped in his constricting throat – forcing him to swallow hard several times before he could talk without his voice trembling.

'No,' he managed to tell her. 'No. That's not all. In the room with the mother, sticking out from the side of the bed, I saw a foot.' He felt her hold her breath while he described what happened. 'It was the teenage boy. Turned out he was fifteen years old. He walked in on his dad stabbing his mum to death. How he didn't just freeze or run from the house, I'll never know. But instead he tried to save her – tried to drag his own father from her, and it cost him his life. Later we found out this was when the girl I saved walked in and saw what was happening. The father momentarily turned from the boy to stab her once in the abdomen, but the boy was still fighting to save his mother and sisters, so he had to turn his attentions back to the boy and that's how the girl escaped outside. He saved her.'

'And so did you,' she gently reminded him.

'Maybe,' he tried to agree, although he'd never felt like he had – always questioning the world he'd abandoned her to, with no family other than a murderous father and physical scars to always remind her where the cause of her emotional pain came from. Saved her from one hell only to deliver her to another. 'But the mother and the boy weren't the worst,' he said – talking to himself now more than Kelly. 'I went to the last bedroom and that's where I found her – like her sister, lying face up on the bed, arms crossed over her chest, eyes open, staring at the ceiling in her best white dress. Her tiny throat crushed. She was so small. Only six years old. Somehow she still looked alive, but she wasn't. That was the worst. For me that was the worst. It's the one room I can't get out of my dreams. She was so tiny.'

'I'm sorry,' Kelly whispered and kissed his shoulder, tracing the thick ridges of his scars with the tip of her finger as he pulled her even tighter to him – holding her in a silent embrace that seemed to last forever.

King sighed deeply. 'It only feels right when I'm here with you. Out there, nothing makes much sense any more. Here, with you, I can sense time passing, you understand? Out there one day turns into the next and days turn into weeks and weeks into months, but I can't feel them passing. I can't even remember how long I've been here for.'

'Quiet,' Kelly whispered and pulled him closer. 'I love being with you.'

'I love being with you,' he replied sleepily. 'Sure your mum won't be coming back?'

Kelly suddenly stiffened and pushed herself away from him as she remembered something she had to tell him that couldn't wait any longer. 'Fuck,' she began, excitement etched across her face, the horror of King's monologue swept away by her urgent need to tell him. 'My mum,' she said, shaking her head at the confusion she knew she was creating. 'I almost forgot to tell you – Swinton – it wasn't him.'

King felt the blood rushing from his brain as the dizziness of disbelief swarmed over him making the here and now feel like a distant dreamland; Kelly's words seemingly echoing and reverberating around the room until he was sucked back into the present and reality.

'What?' he asked. 'What did you say?'

'Swinton,' she repeated. 'It wasn't him that touched up that little Bickley girl or the others probably.'

'What are you saying?' he demanded, desperately gripping her by her shoulders as if getting ready to shake the truth from her. 'How d'you know?'

'The girl spoke,' she explained. 'She finally told her mum who it was and you won't believe who she said.'

'Who?' he asked impatiently. 'Who was it?'

'Only my mum's fucking boyfriend,' Kelly almost laughed. 'It was Chris. Chris O'Connell. I always knew there was something wrong about him.'

King was momentarily unable to speak as the images of the beating he'd given Swinton spun in his mind, making him feel dizzy and nauseous – any and all justification for

345

kidnapping and torturing him turned to dust by Kelly's revelation. All the others he'd fucked over were dealers, would-be rapists or thieves, but Swinton now appeared to be nothing more than the wrong man in the wrong place at the wrong time – something proper investigation, something the rule of law would almost certainly have established.

'Fuck,' he called out, almost throwing Kelly from his lap onto the sofa. 'Why didn't you tell me?' he demanded. 'As soon as you knew it was me at the door, why didn't you tell me?'

'I was going to,' she pleaded – her black eyes showing a trace of fear for the first time since he'd met her, 'but you looked so strung-out I knew that if I did you'd run off and try and find him. I wanted to straighten you out a bit first and then tell you, but you made me forget.'

'Damn it, Kelly,' he chastised her. 'You can't wait to tell me this sort of shit. I need to know straight away.'

'What difference does it make?' she asked. 'Chris doesn't live on the estate and Mum says he's done a runner anyway. Nobody round here's smart enough to find him . . . except *you*.'

'I couldn't give a fuck about O'Connell,' he admitted. 'Fucking witch-hunt's done enough damage already. Swinton's done nothing, but we almost put him in his grave. I must have been out of my mind to listen to that damn Bickley woman. She said the first name that popped into her head and I went for it. Jesus Christ, what have I done?' He struggled to his feet and staggered across the room to the downstairs toilet, making it there just in time before he retched yellow bile from his empty stomach. Once the convulsions stopped he rinsed his mouth with water from the tap and doused his face in the same before shakily walking back to the waiting Kelly.

'What's so bad?' she naïvely asked. 'Everybody knows Swinton is a paedophile anyway. He got what he deserved.'

'He was the wrong man,' King tried in vain to explain.

'Don't you understand that? The people on this estate with their rumours and suspicions. They know nothing, but think they know everything. Taking out the *right* people's what separates me from them. Now I'm no better than they are,' he told her and headed to the kitchen to find a drink.

'You mean no better than I am?' Kelly questioned as she gathered her discarded clothes from the floor and clutched them to her chest.

'No,' he told her as he poured himself a large vodka and took a long gulp. 'You know that's not what I meant. You're different. Different from anyone I've ever met. Fuck,' he suddenly swore, as if too late he'd remembered something important. 'Your mum must be coming back here. I need to go.'

'Relax,' she told him. 'Mum's gone to my gran's in Essex. She won't be back until everything dies down.'

'She needs to get your brother and sister checked out too,' he advised her, thinking like a cop again for a few seconds. 'If O'Connell likes children it could be what drew him to your mum in the first place.'

'That's fucking sick,' Kelly replied, shaking her head.

'Maybe,' he agreed. 'It also happens to be true.' He looked her up and down in silence for a few seconds trying to imagine how much younger she would have had to be before she looked like a girl and not a woman. 'What about you? Did he ever . . . *touch* you?'

'Mum's only been with him about a year,' she explained. 'It's been a lot longer than that since I was a child.'

He nodded his understanding and drained his glass before quickly refilling it. 'Do you know if the Bickley woman reported any of this to the police?' he asked. 'She hasn't come to me to sort it out.'

Kelly took a breath before answering. 'From what I heard she did. Chris don't live on the estate so she thought he was out of anyone's reach – except the real police.'

'The *real police*?' he asked.

'You know what I mean,' she said apologetically.

'Whatever,' he let it go. 'I need to get back to the station and see what I can do. If people start talking to CID this could all lead straight to my door. Fuck.'

Kelly looked at him – naked, strung-out and drinking neat vodka on top of cocaine and cannabis. 'You can't go anywhere,' she insisted.

'I don't have a choice,' he argued. 'I need to put this fire out before it takes hold.'

'What can you do,' she asked, 'if it's already been reported?'

'I don't know,' he thought out loud. 'Maybe I can find a way to delete the report or mark it "no crime" and bury it where no one will look. I don't know, but I have to do something.'

'Fine,' she agreed sympathetically, 'but not now and not looking like you do. Stay the night. Get some rest and get cleaned up then go in first thing. Is anyone gonna be turning up stones during the night investigating what happened to Rosie?'

'No,' King admitted. 'I guess not.'

'Then stay,' she told him, letting the clothes she was holding fall to the floor.

'Fine,' he agreed, drinking the vodka in one go and sliding the glass away from him over the work surface. 'I'll stay.'

16

King entered the small CID office in Canning Town Police Station first thing in the morning confident that only the cleaners and the early shift uniform team would have beaten him in. If there was any CID there at all it should only be the remnants of the night shift, unless something major like a murder or rape had occurred during the hours of darkness, and if that was the case the chances were that any detectives involved would have headed over to the main CID office at Newham Police Station – the Borough HQ.

His heart sank a little when he saw DC Paul Morris sitting at his desk, head down, typing away. But at least there was no one else around and, most importantly, there was no sign of Marino. He made his way across the office to the old-fashioned ringbinder that was still used as the 'Overnight CID Occurrence Book' or 'Night Duty CID OB', as it was known by all. He could have found a copy of the previous night's events by logging on to the borough's computerized Aware system, but that would leave an indestructible footprint that he'd been looking. This way no one could prove anything.

He searched through the record of the night's events and soon came across a brief mention of the indecent assault on Rosie Bickley by a named suspect – Chris O'Connell. He felt sick to his stomach as the blood seemed to rage in torrents around his head. What he'd thought he'd contained on the estate was now out in the open for any and all police eyes to see. Marino may have kept quiet out of some sort of twisted sense of loyalty before, but now the allegation had become official, it was impossible to tell what he'd do next. He unclipped the bindings and slipped the page containing details of the indecent assault from the OB then quietly folded it and pushed it into his pocket while he kept an eye on Morris to make sure he wasn't being watched. He knew it was probably a futile gesture as Marino was the sort of diligent detective who nearly always checked the OB on the Aware system, but he was prepared to try everything and anything to protect himself.

With the crime concealed in his pocket he approached Morris and stood over him while he typed – Morris seemingly oblivious to his presence as he hurried to finish the paperwork and get home before the morning rush-hour traffic built.

'You the Night Duty CID?' King asked to get his attention.

Morris glanced up but never stopped typing. 'For my sins.'

'I hear there was an indecent assault reported last night on my estate,' King said, trying to sound casual. 'Happened a few days ago, but only just got reported.'

Morris' brow wrinkled as he tried to recall one allegation from dozens. 'Oh yeah,' he eventually said without interest. 'Some young girl who was able to name her attacker.'

'Yeah,' King imitated his disinterest. 'Rosie Bickley. I know the family. Any allegations they make aren't to be taken too seriously. Said Chris O'Connell's the suspect?'

'That's the fella,' replied Morris.

'I've nicked him for domestic violence,' King told him. 'Didn't seem the type to be preying on kids.'

'You never can tell, eh?' Morris answered in a tone that made it clear he wanted to be left alone to finish the last of his dawn reports.

'I'll take this one,' King said casually, 'have a word with the mum and see if I can't get her to withdraw the allegation. Save the CID a bit of work. You can assign it to me on CRIS.'

'Too late,' Morris told him. 'Someone's already taken it.'

King had to clear his constricting throat before speaking. 'Who?'

'Frank,' Morris broke the news.

'DS Marino?' King asked, trying not to choke.

'Yeah,' Morris replied, sounding increasingly irritated at being disturbed. 'He was in really early today. Took the investigation as soon as he saw it.'

'Did he say why he was so keen to take it?'

'No,' Morris shrugged. 'Looks like a load of grief to me. If he wants it, he's welcome to it.' He turned from his computer and looked King up and down. 'You all right? Look like you've seen a ghost.'

'I'm fine,' King lied, his mind racing with possible scenarios, all of which led Professional Ethics and Standards straight to his door. 'Shouldn't this one have gone to Sapphire or even the Child Protection Team?'

'It should have,' Morris sighed, turning back to his screen. 'Told Marino that myself, but he seemed pretty determined to keep it for now. Maybe he's trying to protect an informant or something.'

'Yeah,' King replied without really listening any more.

'Anything else?' Morris asked, trying to prompt him to leave.

'Sorry?' King answered, staring into space.

'Anything else?' Morris repeated with increased irritation.

'No,' King told him without looking at him. 'Thanks,' he managed to say before heading across the office and the exit, leaving Morris at his desk shaking his head. He never heard him mumble 'Fucking lids,' under his breath as he burst into the corridor and headed for his own office, hoping to be able to spend a little time alone to think. But to his surprise and disappointment both Brown and Williams were already there. They looked as surprised to see him as he was them.

'What the fuck you two doing here?' he blurted out.

'The early bird gets the worm,' Brown managed to say unconvincingly.

'It's barely seven am,' King reminded them, eyeing them with suspicion. 'Our early shift doesn't start till ten.'

'Thought we'd take a look at what stirs on the estate first thing,' Williams added. 'We've never seen it at this time in the morning.'

'That's because fuck all happens there this time in the morning,' King told them. 'Half of them aren't out their beds till gone midday. Why don't you tell me what's really going on?'

Brown and Williams looked at each other before Brown answered. 'It's Knight,' he told King. 'I don't fucking trust him.'

'Same goes for me,' Williams backed him up.

'How do we know he's not here to spy on us?' Brown continued.

'You don't,' King answered with a slight smile, as if it was to be expected. 'So this is why you're both in so early – to avoid working with Knight?'

'He's down for the late shift,' Williams explained. 'We plan to be long gone by then.'

'I see,' King nodded, 'but if you want to avoid him why not just send him to the other side of the estate? If he keeps coming to work to find an empty office, everyone packed up and gone home, he'll get suspicious and then he might just start talking to someone. Someone like Inspector Johnston. Is that what you want?'

'No,' Brown agreed as King slumped into his chair.

'Anyway,' he told them. 'We've got bigger problems than Knight. Either of you two early birds read the Night Duty CID OB yet?'

'No,' Williams admitted. 'Why?'

'Because if you had,' he explained, 'you would have seen we took out the wrong man.'

'What the fuck you talking about?' Brown asked, his face twisted with concern.

'Swinton,' King told them, trying to sound casual despite his thundering heart – trying to deceive them into believing he was still in total control. 'He never touched the girl.'

'*What?*' Williams questioned.

'Oh, fucking Jesus,' Brown cursed, placing both hands behind his neck as if trying to catch his breath after exercise.

'Hold on a second,' Williams recovered enough to think straight. 'You said it was in the Night Duty OB. The mother left it for us to deal with, so why is it in the OB?'

'Looks like she lost faith in us,' said King, spreading his arms in a gesture of disappointment. 'Her daughter finally put a name to her attacker: Chris O'Connell. He doesn't live on the estate so apparently the mum decided he was out of our reach and reported it.'

'Fuck,' Brown cursed again.

'Relax,' King told them. 'So she's reported it. Big deal. Doesn't mean anyone's gonna make the connection to Swinton or Swinton to us.'

'But once Sapphire start digging around who knows what people are gonna start saying?' Williams argued.

'Sapphire aren't investigating this one,' King broke the news.

'Why,' Brown asked warily. 'Why aren't Sapphire investigating?'

King cleared his throat before speaking. 'Because Marino's taken it for himself.'

'Fuck,' Brown swore once more. 'Fucking Marino. He's out to do us, I swear he is.'

'Not necessarily,' King told him. 'For all we know he may be trying to bury it – to protect us all.'

'No. No,' Brown insisted. 'This is bad. This is really fucking bad.'

'You need to calm down,' King said almost threateningly. 'We need to stick together.'

'Calm down?' Brown mocked him. 'Stick together? It's too late for that.'

'Davey,' King warned him.

'Let me tell you something,' Brown told him, stepping forward and pointing an accusing finger at him, 'Knight's not the only reason we're in so early. He's not the only one we don't trust – not the only one we don't want to work with or even be seen with. This has all gone way too far and me and Danny want out. We're gonna put in requests to be transferred off the Unit today. We've had enough of your shit. We want out while we still can.'

'No one leaves until I say they can,' King insisted. 'You two fucking belong to me until I say different.'

'So that's how it's going to be?' Brown nodded.

'That's how it's going to be,' King confirmed.

'So be it,' Brown agreed, but his eyes said otherwise.

'And you?' King looked at Williams.

'Fine,' he sighed, 'but no more beatings. I've had a gutful of that shit. I won't do it again.'

'Agreed,' King lied, 'and don't worry about the Bickley girl's allegation or Marino. I'll think of something. I'll think of something and I'll take care of it. Just leave it with me. For now just get down to the estate. Show a presence. Let everyone see we're still in control.'

'In control,' Brown laughed ironically.

'What about you?' Williams asked. 'Where you going?'

'The estate,' King answered, standing and pulling on his body armour, 'but I need to get there quickly and I need a car. I'll take what I can find in the yard. When I've done what I have to do we'll meet up and remind a few people who's in charge.'

'Fair enough,' Williams surrendered.

'And you?' King asked Brown who after a second simply nodded. 'Good,' King told him coldly as he clipped his utility belt around his waist. 'Then I'll see you both later.' He spun on his heels and was gone.

King scoured the small yard at Canning Town looking for a patrol car that had been abandoned by its careless owner with the keys still in the ignition. Not an uncommon practice in a busy but secure police yard. He could have booked one out correctly from the station office, but he was in no mood to answer questions or waste time with paperwork. Better to *borrow* one and ignore the pleas over the radio from the owner for its return. When he finally brought it back he'd blame a faulty PR for not heeding the requests.

He jumped into the driver's seat – his body armour and utility belt making his movements awkward and uncomfortable as he started the engine and sped towards the automatic barrier, ignoring the flashing light and irritating *dinging* sound that warned him his seat belt wasn't on. As soon as the barrier lifted he pulled into the traffic, switching on the bar of lights attached to the roof to clear a path for his flight and driving recklessly fast towards the estate. The estate was his kingdom, his principality, his caliphate and he wasn't about to let Marino or Caroll Bickley bring it to an end. The power he felt when he patrolled its walkways and rat-runs was as seductive as Kelly's oil-black eyes, and he wasn't about to let any of it go. He saw her long brown curls twirling and falling around her neck and shoulders and could have sworn he could smell their dizzyingly beautiful scent. He needed to see her soon – to get his fix. But first there was business to take care of. People to see and straighten out. Kelly and all her delights would have to wait a while longer.

King hammered on the door of Carroll Bickley's flat and waited impatiently for it to be answered. He could hear the sounds of life inside, which only fuelled his anxiety and anger. Again he hammered on the door until he heard the protesting voice of a woman coming from inside.

'All right. All right,' she called out in her thick East London accent. 'Give us a fucking chance.'

He stood back, hands on hips as he tried to roll some of the pent-up tension from his neck muscles until finally the door was opened by a disinterested-looking Carroll Bickley.

'Oh,' she barely acknowledged him. 'It's you.'

'We need to talk,' King told her as he barged past and into the cool dimness of the flat. 'Shut the door,' he demanded and headed for the lounge area, followed by Bickley.

'What about?' she asked as if she didn't know.

'Don't play dumb with me now,' King warned her. 'You know what the fuck about – about Rosie and the fact you've been blabbing to the CID. I told you I'd take care of it and I did.'

'You took care of the wrong man,' she reminded him without mentioning her own part in Swinton's wrongful identification.

'Only because you pointed the finger at him,' he accused her.

'Never said it was him for sure,' she argued. 'Never said Rosie said it was him.'

'Shut the fuck up, you stupid bitch,' King's temper snapped – tired of the pointless conversation. 'You came to me wanting things done *your* way, remember? No courts. No . . . *police*. I took care of it like I take care of everything on this estate. Now you need to keep your fat, ugly mouth shut and do whatever I tell you to do.'

Bickley stood in silence for a few seconds with her mouth hanging open. Few people had ever dared speak to her like that before. Like most women on the estate she could hold her own in a fistfight against all but the hardest of men.

356

'Too late,' she finally recovered her ability to speak. 'I've already reported it to the CID.'

'I know that, you fucking idiot,' he snarled at her. 'Why d'you think I'm here? The question is what else have you told them?'

'Like what?' she asked – confused.

'About me,' he growled. 'What else have you told them about me?'

'Nothing,' she reassured him, shaking her head.

'You didn't tell anyone about our . . . *arrangement*?'

'No.'

'You sure?'

'I'm sure. I never said nothing to nobody about it,' she pleaded.

'But you did report Chris O'Connell?' he checked – paranoid thoughts of some sort of undercover set-up swirling in his mind. 'It was you who reported him to the police?'

'Yeah,' she answered. 'Of course it was me. Who else would?'

'Nobody,' he dismissed it, 'although it still doesn't explain why you went behind my back. You should have told me it was O'Connell. I would have taken care of it.'

'You already got the wrong man once,' she told him, enjoying some payback, 'and he don't live on the estate. How you gonna get to him if he don't live on the estate?'

'You should have left that to me,' he replied. 'It would have been my problem to solve – not yours.'

'Yeah, well,' she shrugged. 'Too late now.'

'I don't think so,' he said. 'You need to undo the damage you've done before other Old Bill come sneaking around the estate asking questions that could lead them back to me. People round here like the way I run things. No one wants that to change.'

'Maybe they used to,' she told him before immediately regretting it.

'What's that supposed to mean?' he seized on it.

'You've changed,' she tentatively explained. 'People liked it because you brought a bit of order without the need for people to have to give witness statements and waste their time going to court. It don't go well for you round here if you're seen to be cooperating with the Old Bill and the law. Just the way it's always been, I suppose. But we still needed someone to bring a bit of order and you did that – in your own way. But now you just bring fear and trouble. What you gonna bring next, eh, with what you been up to? What you gonna bring next?'

'What the fuck you talking about?'

'You'll see,' she told him, sounding like an old witch warning of the fulfilling of an ancient prophecy. 'Just keep going the way you're going and you'll see.'

'What?' he sneered. 'You think some half-arsed local wannabe gangster's got the balls to fuck with me? I don't think so. All you need to do is keep your mouth shut and say nothing. Fine – you've fucked up and reported the allegation. Now you need to tell the CID it was a mistake. Your attention-seeking daughter made it all up and you, being a dumb bitch, believed it. No need for anyone to ask any more questions that could lead back to the Unit.'

'It's too late,' she stabbed him in the chest with her words. 'They already suspect you've been up to something. Only asked me a few questions about my Rosie, then it was Sergeant King this and Sergeant King that. What did I tell you and what did you say you were gonna do? They know. They know.'

'Who asked?' King almost shouted as his blood began to freeze in his veins – numbing his brain and palpating his heart. 'Who was asking the questions?'

'The fella from the CID investigating it,' she told him, trying to remember his name. 'DS Marino, yeah – DS Marino.'

'Fuck,' King exploded, spinning away from her before turning back on her like a wolf about to pounce. 'Marino was here? Already?'

'First thing,' she confirmed. 'I was still fast asleep when he starts banging on my door. Him, then you – makes me wish I hadn't told any of you lot. Should have gone to the Campbells straight off.'

King grabbed hold of her by the collar of her t-shirt and pulled her close. 'What did you tell him?'

'Nothing,' she tried to convince him – panic rising in her eyes as she recognized the hate and anger in his. 'I swear I told him nothing, but . . .'

'What was he asking about?' he pushed her.

'I told you,' she pleaded. 'Questions about you.'

'What questions?' he demanded. 'Be specific.'

'Whether I'd told you about Rosie being assaulted,' she explained.

'And what did you say?'

'Nothing. I mean I told him you knew nothing about it. I told him Rosie had only just told me and he was the first Old Bill I'd talked to.'

'What else?'

'He was asking about Swinton. What I knew about Swinton getting a beating.'

'And?'

'And I said nothing. I knew nothing. That I'd heard it was local men who'd taken care of him like the police should have.'

'Did he buy it?'

She shrugged her shoulders and shook her head. 'I suppose he may have believed I didn't have anything to do with it,' she told him, pulling his hands from her t-shirt. 'But none of that matters to you, does it – because he knows, doesn't he? He knows you're up to something – otherwise why all the questions?'

King didn't answer as all his suspicions about what Marino did and didn't know became near certainties, although he still couldn't guess Marino's end game. *Was he out to gather evidence and fuck him properly or was he, for some reason, still trying to cover his back in the hope of bringing him back into the fold?*

'Maybe it's time you got off the estate,' she told him.

'What?' he asked, drifting back from his thoughts.

'I said maybe it's time you left the estate.'

'No,' he insisted. 'I can't do that. Not yet. Too much unfinished business.'

'Well,' she said, a trace of empathy creeping into her voice, 'don't say I didn't warn you if it all comes on top. If the Campbells get hold of you it'll be you who's finished business.'

'What the fuck have the Campbells got to do with anything?'

'There's rumours,' she told him conspiratorially. 'I hear things.'

'What things?'

'That they're not happy with what you're up to,' she explained. 'That you're costing them money and making them look bad.' She paused as if to emphasize the importance of what she was to say next. 'You know who they're connected to, don't you?'

'No doubt you're about to tell me.'

'They work for the Balcan family,' she almost whispered, 'and the Balcans own the East End. You make the Campbells look bad, you make the Balcans look bad, and they won't tolerate that. Why don't you get out while you still can? Go back to your own kind.'

'It's too late,' he told her – some regret and sadness seeping into his words before he steeled himself. 'Like I said, I have unfinished business here and if that means dealing with the Campbells as well, then so be it. They're all just cheap criminals. I'm not afraid of them or the Balcans.'

'You should be,' Bickley warned him – her voice quiet and foreboding. 'You should be.'

*   *   *

360

A few minutes later and King had escaped from the confines of the flat to patrol the walkways of the Grove Wood, trying to clear his mind and form some sort of plan that would ensure he maintained control of the estate and the Swinton situation. But his ever increasing use of crack, cocaine and cannabis dulled his mind, robbing him of the sharpness he'd once taken for granted. Ideas came to him only in sporadic, unformed, broken pieces. He would have to rely on other people's fear to keep things manageable until he could focus his thoughts properly. Thoughts that were continually inter-rupted by images of Kelly – semi-naked as she gracefully floated around the small council maisonette that had become the centre of his world.

As he was trying to shake her from his mind, at least until he'd worked out what to do about Marino, he suddenly saw Dougie O'Neil scuttling around the corner and into a stairwell, as if he was trying to avoid him – the side-effects of his drug use making him paranoid enough to believe that was exactly what O'Neil must be trying to do. He quickly doubled back and sprinted down a parallel stairwell that led to the back of the housing block and a rat-run alley he knew O'Neil wouldn't be able to resist taking. He listened intently to the sound of O'Neil's rapidly approaching footsteps and jumped out just as he was about to pass – making O'Neil rear up as his mouth dropped open with fright.

'Going somewhere, Dougie?' King asked.

'Jesus Christ,' O'Neil complained, trying to catch his breath. 'You scared the shit out of me.'

'You'll survive,' King ignored his distress. 'Question is – what you doing out the flat? Brown or Williams covering for you? And don't lie.'

'No,' O'Neil admitted sheepishly, 'but it's cool. The flat's all locked up safe and sound.'

'With no one in it?' King asked – his anger and frustration

growing by the second. He didn't have time to deal with O'Neil's mistakes, not now.

'Like I said,' O'Neil pleaded nervously, 'it's all good.'

'And my gear?' King said. 'My money?'

'In the flat,' O'Neil answered. 'Secure and safe.'

'And the key to the grid?' King snarled. 'Where exactly would that be?'

'Here,' O'Neil admitted, pulling a small set of keys from his trouser pocket.

'You fucking idiot,' King reprimanded him and slapped him across the face.

'Fucking hell,' O'Neil moaned. 'What was that for?'

King snatched the keys from him and dangled them in front of his face. 'What if someone's been watching you, you moron – waiting for the chance to rob you? Now you're walking round with the keys to our entire fucking security system in your damn pocket. All anyone's got to do is turn you over out here and they could help themselves to everything that's mine out the flat.' King looked deep into O'Neil's pale and shaking face. 'You're fucking stoned, aren't you? You're not thinking straight because you're fucking stoned.'

'I just had a little taste,' O'Neil pleaded his case. 'Just enough to keep me right.'

'I told you,' King reminded him, 'one rock a day and you do it inside the flat.'

'Sorry,' O'Neil apologized pathetically.

'You're a sad fucking loser, O'Neil,' King told him, shaking his head. 'Now answer my question – where you off to in such a hurry?'

'To see a friend,' O'Neil tried to convince him.

'Don't lie to me, Dougie,' King warned him. 'You don't have any friends. So I'll ask you again – where were you going?'

O'Neil sighed before answering. 'Just to do a bit of business.'

'Business?'

'A geezer,' O'Neil said, looking around to make sure they were still alone. 'Reckons he's got some proper top A-grade horse. Just thought I'd score a bit – see if it's as good as he reckons.'

'You left the flat empty to score some heroin?' King accused him. O'Neil just shrugged. 'With my money?'

'I'd only use my cut,' O'Neil assured him.

'Your cut?' King laughed. 'And what exactly is your cut, Dougie?'

'I don't know,' O'Neil admitted.

'No,' King mocked him. 'You don't know. Your cut is whatever fucking bone I choose to throw you and until I say differently that's a rock a day. You don't have my permission to spend my money.' The paranoia swirled in his mind. 'You sure you aren't trying to fuck with me, Dougie?'

'I don't understand,' O'Neil answered, looking and sounding confused.

'You sure you aren't using my money to start dealing smack behind my back – cutting me out of the profit? You fucking me over, Dougie?'

'No,' O'Neil shook his head desperately. 'I ain't fucking you over. I just wanted to chase a bit of brown.'

'Not with my money you ain't,' King told him. 'Thought you could skim off a little from the top and I'd never notice, eh? Let me pay for that shit you want to pump into yourself.'

'Looks like I ain't the only one who likes a little taste of something heavy,' O'Neil fought back before immediately regretting his fleeting bravery.

'What you talking about?' King asked, his paranoia growing by the second – his eyes seemingly vibrating in their sockets as he tried to guess what O'Neil had seen in him.

'Your lip,' O'Neil answered nervously. 'Looks like the first signs of crack-lip.' King's hand involuntarily shot to his mouth – his fingers quickly finding the sore, burnt area of his bottom lip where his homemade glass crack-pipe had overheated and left its mark. The homemade bong had worked well – cooling the smoke and the pipe used to draw it through the water and into his mouth, but it wasn't easy to conceal if he needed a hit on the move and it took precious seconds to prepare. Lately he'd abandoned it altogether in favour of a small glass tube fashioned from some meat-basting contraption someone with little money or imagination had bought him and Sara for Christmas. The crack went on one end and his lips around the other. He simply had to burn the crack and inhale the hot smoke through the short pipe – the pain of his burning lips instantly obliterated by the effects of the drug.

'You don't know what you're talking about, O'Neil,' he tried to dismiss him. 'It's just a cold sore – from the stress of having to deal with morons like you.'

'Really?' O'Neil risked asking, his fear of King fading as the realization that he was as flawed as anyone swept over him. 'Crack can bring anyone to their knees. Maybe even you?'

'Shut the fuck up,' King demanded. 'You think I could ever be a crack-head like you? I'm the fucking police. You remember that. Don't ever make the mistake of thinking I'm like you. Now empty your pockets.'

'What?' O'Neil asked, scared and confused.

'Empty your pockets. I want to see what you're really up to behind my back.'

'I ain't up to nothing,' O'Neil pleaded as King pushed him against the wall and started patting down his pockets.

'What we got here then?' King asked as he felt something square and padded in O'Neil's trouser pocket – pulling it out to reveal a small wad of notes folded in two. 'Just going to make a small score of smack, eh? Fuck you, Dougie. There's enough here to buy quarter of an ounce. Enough to start dealing for yourself.'

'I wasn't going to cut you out, honest,' O'Neil pleaded his case. 'I was gonna tell you about it once I'd shifted the gear.'

'What?' King barked in his face. 'You think I'm some sort of idiot. You lying little fuck. What else of mine have you got on you?' O'Neil said nothing as King continued to search him, but found no more – although he wasn't finished yet. 'Drop your trousers,' he ordered, 'and your underwear.'

'You fucking serious?' O'Neil asked. King slapped him hard enough across the face to momentarily stun him.

'What's the matter, Dougie? Don't I look serious?'

'Jesus,' O'Neil complained.

'Do it,' King demanded. 'Do it now.'

Slowly O'Neil began to undo the button and zip of his filthy jeans, constantly looking around, as much in hope of salvation as wishing to avoid an embarrassing interruption, but no one appeared. He stood meekly in front of King with his trousers around his knees, arms held out to his side to show his innocence.

'See,' he declared. 'Nothing.'

'And the boxer shorts,' King reminded him. Reluctantly O'Neil carefully slid the shorts down to his knees – standing in a crucifix position with his pathetic-looking genitalia hanging vulnerably – his humiliation almost complete. 'You know the drill,' King told him. 'Turn round and touch your toes.'

O'Neil's eyes closed for a second before he did as he was ordered. Even though he knew it would condemn him, he had no choice but to dig his own grave. As soon as he was fully bent a small package wrapped in clingfilm fell to the ground.

'You lying little bastard,' King accused him, stepping forward and kicking him hard in the crotch from behind – sending O'Neil to the floor in a crumpled heap. He stuffed the wad of cash into his pockets and pulled a latex glove and a small evidence bag from his utility belt as he bent to recover the package. A quick look confirmed what he already suspected – he could clearly make out the dozen or so rocks of crack wrapped inside.

'Oh, this is just beautiful,' he told O'Neil sarcastically as he dropped the package into the evidence bag, tossing the now soiled glove before slipping the bag into his pocket. He stepped forward and kicked the still prostrate O'Neil in the stomach, forcing an ugly whimpering sound from his victim who rolled over to try and protect himself. 'What were you going to do with these, eh? Trade them in for more smack for you to destroy yourself with?'

'No,' O'Neil begged – panting for breath. 'I . . . I just thought it was safer to keep some of the gear on me. Just in case.'

'You're not here to think,' King snarled at him, leaning over and grabbing him by the hair, twisting O'Neil's face towards him and again slapping him hard. 'You exist to do what I tell you to do and no more. You're too stupid to think and I'll warn you now – if you become a liability, you'll be replaced – understand? You are completely and utterly replaceable. Without me you are nothing.'

Suddenly O'Neil's expression changed from one of fear to one of surprise as he seemed to look past King – his eyes wide with warning. Slowly King looked over his shoulder to find PC Rana Knight standing at the foot of the stairwell staring at the scene of O'Neil on the floor with King standing over him like a bird of prey readying itself to tear its victim to shreds.

'Shit,' King muttered under his breath before straightening and turning fully to face Knight. 'How . . . how long have you been standing there for?'

'Long enough,' Knight answered straight, looking wary and alarmed.

'Then you heard me questioning this suspect?'

'I heard something,' Knight told him.

'Things get done a little differently round here,' King tried to explain. 'A little more force – a little less bureaucracy. It's how we keep the local wildlife in check.'

'And that's what you're doing, is it?' Knight asked.

'That's exactly what I'm doing,' King replied.

'I get it,' Knight reassured him.

'Good,' King nodded, 'because on the Unit we stick together – understand? We don't stab each other in the back. What happens on this estate stays on the estate. That way we all benefit.'

'I understand,' Knight lied.

'Then we have no problem,' King smiled like a hyena. 'Just make sure you don't mention what you saw or heard to anyone. Can I trust you to do that?'

'You can trust me,' Knight lied again. 'I'm just here for the arrests.'

'Then come over here and help me with this one,' King told him, but Knight didn't move, his eyes narrowing with suspicion of what King intended to do and what he was capable of. 'I said get over here,' King repeated.

'I don't think so,' Knight answered and began to back away – relieved to finally have the evidence Johnston needed. Now he could get the hell off this God-cursed estate.

'I said I need your assistance,' King hissed through gritted teeth, but Knight just continued backing away then dived into the stairwell and was gone. 'Fuck,' King shouted. 'Fuck.'

'Why did he run?' O'Neil asked in a panic.

'Shut up,' King told him, turning back to O'Neil. 'Question is, what am I going to do with you?'

'Please,' O'Neil pleaded. 'I wasn't trying to fuck you over. I promise.'

'Shut up, Dougie,' King told him, staring into the sky for answers. 'I'm thinking.' After a few seconds of silence he spoke again. 'Go back to the flat and lock yourself inside. I'll be along later to sort this shit out. Just wait for me inside. Now fuck off.'

O'Neil scrambled to his feet, pulling up his shorts and trousers. 'What about that other copper?' he asked, looking like a trapped rat. 'He might say something. He could get us both nicked. He looked like he knows something.'

'I'll speak to him,' King explained. 'Make sure he's not going to be a problem. I'll tell him you're just one of my regular informers who needs to be turned over now and then. Now . . . get out of my sight.' As O'Neil scurried back along the alleyway King whispered to himself. 'You shouldn't have tried to cross me, Dougie. That was a mistake. A very serious mistake.'

King knocked on the door that had become his gateway to a world of raw, intense pleasure. After only a few seconds it was flung open and Kelly pulled him inside without speaking and attached herself to his lips. His arm searched for the door, found it and flicked it shut as he stumbled forward, almost tripping over Kelly who threw her slender arms around his shoulders before jumping from the ground and wrapping her legs around his waist. They kissed long and hard before he finally eased her lips from his and sat her on the table – her arms and legs refusing to release him.

'What's the matter?' she asked, faking a frown. 'Don't you want me any more?'

'I want you,' he told her. 'You'll see in a minute how much I want you.'

'But what?'

'Just need a little hit of something first,' he explained and slid his hand under his body armour before it reappeared pinching a small fold of paper between his fingers.

'Never needed that with me before,' Kelly continued the charade of concern.

'Been a long morning,' he told her as he carefully unfolded the paper and tapped a thin line onto the back of his hand. Without ceremony he sniffed the white powder hard through

368

his nose, coating the inside of his lungs with the tiny white crystals where their effects would be hotwired through his body. He tapped another uneven line onto the back of his hand and offered it to Kelly who steadied his hand by cupping it in her own before inhaling deeply. They stood silently wrapped together as they waited for the cocaine to charge their bodies and minds. After a minute Kelly broke the silence.

'You seem jumpy,' she said.

'Just got a lot of shit I need to sort out, that's all,' he re-assured her.

'Well,' she told him, gently kissing his neck and the side of his face, 'don't burn yourself out. You're no good to me if you're worn out.' She dropped a hand to his belt, her fingers dexterously working at the buckle – whispering in his ear as she did so. 'D'you think we'll ever have a normal relationship?' she asked. 'Meet each other's parents, go out for a drink or something?'

'Christ, I hope not,' he answered. 'Who wants a *normal* relationship? I like the way we are – just the two of us in our own world where no one can fuck with us. Besides – I'm finished with my parents and all their shit. They were just baggage holding me back, keeping me trapped in their pointless world. I'm on my own now – the way I want it to be.'

'And your pretty policewoman girlfriend you never admitted having?'

'Gone too,' he assured her.

'So where you gonna stay?' she asked.

'I'll need to stay here for a while,' he told her. 'Until I can get something else sorted out. So long as your mum's not planning on coming back any time soon.'

'She won't be back until things have blown over,' she answered. 'She may not come back at all.'

'Good,' King nodded.

'I've never lived with a man before,' she laughed slightly.

'I should hope not,' he said, 'but I won't be around much for a while. I'll be in and out a lot till things calm down.'

'Why bother?' Kelly suddenly asked. 'Why don't we get out of this dump? We could, you know. There's nothing stopping us.'

'We will,' he agreed. 'But first I need to put a few grand together. Maybe even chuck this job in and go abroad somewhere.'

'Still thinking of running away to another country?' she asked. 'I've never been abroad. Where would you take me?'

'I don't know,' he told her as she slid her hand inside his trousers. 'Where would you like to go?' But before she could answer there was a loud knock on the front door. 'Shit,' he cursed. 'Who the fuck is that?' His eyes darted around as he thought fast for a second. 'You'd better see who it is then get rid of them,' he told Kelly. 'If it's anyone looking for me I'm not here. You don't know where I am.'

Kelly uncoiled her legs from his waist and glided towards the front door – her hips moving like the hypnotizing pendulum of an old clock. She put the chain on the door, opened it slightly and peeked through the gap to see two heavily muscled men standing outside – one of whom she recognized, the other she did not.

'Yeah?' she introduced herself. 'What you want?'

'I need to speak to the copper,' the younger, smarter one said.

'What copper?' Kelly lied expertly.

'Don't mess me around, little girl,' he warned her.

'I ain't messing anyone around,' she defiantly told him. 'I just don't know what you're talking about.'

'D'you know who I am?' he asked her – expecting the usual reply of 'Yes' he received on council estates across East London.

'No,' she shook her head as if he was nothing. 'Why don't you tell me?'

He cleared his throat of his rising anger before answering. 'I'm Josh Campbell and this here,' he pointed to the older thick-set man in his forties whose face bore the scars of many a fistfight, 'is George. George helps me with my . . . *negotiations.*' George said nothing, as did Kelly as she stood eyeing them with disdain. 'You're Debbie Royston's girl, ain't you?' Campbell tried to unnerve her. 'Kelly, isn't it?'

'So you know my name,' she told him. 'A lot of people around here do.'

'I bet they do,' Campbell smiled – his green eyes shining from his tanned face. 'Especially the men, right?'

'Anything else you want to say?' she asked, sounding bored.

'Look, little girl,' Campbell snapped at her. 'Ain't nothing goes on around here without me hearing about it and I hear the copper's been staying with you – so why don't you go get him?'

'Why don't you fuck off?' Kelly told them and grinned sarcastically.

Campbell took a step forward. 'Be a shame if I had to come in there and teach you some fucking respect.'

Before she could answer a strong hand fell on her shoulder and pulled her backwards as King stepped in front of her, removing the chain and opening the door wide, although his right hand remained hidden behind it as did the CS gas canister it held.

'No need to threaten the girl,' he told them – his voice cold and calm, but seething with menace. He was close to ten years younger than Campbell and nowhere nearly as muscled as either man, but his lack of fear made them wary. 'I'm who you're looking for.'

'Well, well,' Campbell smiled. 'Haven't you been a busy boy? Gonna invite us in then?'

'No,' King told him flatly. 'Say what you got to say and leave me in peace. I'm a busy man.'

'Indeed you have been,' Campbell replied, 'and that's the problem. You've been overstepping the mark, my man – stepping on my family's toes, taking what's ours.'

'I do what I want,' he said. 'You just stay out of my business and I'll stay out of yours.'

'What happens on this estate is our business,' Campbell explained.

'Not any more,' King told him, his brown eyes burning into Campbell's who took a deep breath to compose himself before speaking.

'I think we're all getting off on the wrong foot here,' he tried to calm things. 'My family have discussed this situation and we all agree there's no need to cut you out of things. Far from it. We feel there's no reason why we can't have a mutually beneficial relationship.'

'I'm listening,' King replied, scanning the men in front of him for danger. They had nothing in their hands, but the one doing all the talking wore a shirt that wasn't tucked and could be concealing a weapon in his waistband, whereas the silent one could have had just about anything hidden under his jacket.

'Better if we talk inside,' said Campbell.

'Better for who?' King asked shaking his head. 'We can speak here.'

The two men looked at each other then back to King.

'Fine,' Campbell agreed, trying to hide his anger at the knockback. 'You see, Jack, it's like this. You've been drawing attention to yourself – moving in on our business interests – but we're reasonable people. We understand you probably didn't even know the likes of Micky Astill ultimately worked for us. But the fact remains that the money and gear you took off him belongs to us. A percentage of everything he earned came back to us – as does a percentage of everything that's earned by anybody through . . . shall we say, not strictly legitimate business practices. We're not talking about petty

372

criminals here. I'm talking about the decent earners. Real money. And Astill was one of them – as is Susie Ubana.'

'She's got a big mouth,' King told them matter-of-factly.

'Maybe,' Campbell moved on, 'but this is about more than just a couple of dealers. This is about my family's entire business. Our reputation. We can't be seen to be allowing a couple of uniformed coppers to undermine our authority, now can we? Other people might start taking the piss too and then everything goes to shit. You see, people pay us to keep the peace – to resolve disputes over whose patch is whose and who can sell what where. We're the police and the courts for people who can't go to the police and courts – d'you understand?'

'So?' King shook his head. 'Why should I give a fuck about your problems? I look after this estate now. I keep order here and I don't need you to supply my gear. I have other sources.'

'Don't be naïve, Jack,' Campbell warned him. 'Any time we wanted to cut off your supply we could. All we have to do is say the word and there wouldn't be a supplier in the East End would touch you.'

'You're assuming I use someone in your territory,' King said. 'I'm not that stupid. I bring mine in from further afield. Better price. Better quality too.'

'Who gives a fuck?' Campbell lost patience. 'Point is, we could squash you like a fucking maggot on a dead man, but . . . we see a better way. You could be valuable to us. Information. Information, Jack. We have a couple of Old Bill who tip us the nod now and then. Tell us when maybe someone's moving against us or if there's a rogue outfit trying to muscle in on one of our dealers. But you, Jack – we don't have anyone like you. You could give us information about the Old Bill – if they're looking at us, planning on putting an undercover cop against us. Perhaps you could even find out who's informing against us. Fucking grasses are the bane of my life. Be worth a lot of money to us if you could come up with some names. We could even let you carry on doing what you've been doing around here, although of course you'd have to pay us a percentage – just like everyone else. And you'd have to stay in the Old Bill and not get nicked. You're no good to us if you get yourself nicked and chucked out. That happens, you're just another nobody. This is a good offer, Jack – a one-time only offer. Everybody wins and nobody needs to get hurt. It's good business.'

King pursed his lips and rolled his eyes as if he was considering it before answering.

'No thanks,' he told them dismissively and began to close the door, which brought both men rushing forward, reaching for the backs of their waistbands – just as he'd expected them to do. But instead of trying to slam the door shut King reversed his action and threw it wide open – swinging the CS canister towards the men as they drew their small leather coshes – remembering his arrest and restraint training as he aimed at the older man's stomach and pressed the trigger on top of the device, releasing a long thin stream of noxious liquid. Once he saw it splashing off the man's chest he immediately raised his aim and fired the burning poison into his face before arcing the spray the few feet to his left and into the face of the fast-approaching Campbell.

The effect was instant and devastating as both men collapsed to their knees clutching their faces and clawing at their eyes, trying to find an escape from the pain, but only making it worse. Blind and barely able to breathe, they were lambs for the slaughter as King walked slowly and victoriously from the flat – strutting and posing like a peacock amongst the stricken men, hoping everybody on the entire estate was watching his merciless, triumphant march.

He looked down on the grovelling Campbell, speaking as he drew his ASP – extending the weapon to its full, lethal length.

'I don't make deals with scum like you,' he shouted. 'I'm

the police and this is my territory now. Mine.' He raised the ASP above his head and brought it down as hard as he could into the side of Campbell's face – tearing skin and breaking bone – his own face contorted with violent intent as he pulled the ASP back and hammered it into the brow of Campbell's head – all rational thought gone from his mind – the fact he was close to committing murder doing nothing to calm his assault until the sound of Kelly shouting from the doorway froze him like a statue.

He turned his head slowly to look at her, the fog of cocaine and rage subsiding enough for a moment of clarity. Her eyes were wide with terror.

'Please, Jack,' she almost begged. 'Don't kill them, Jack. Please don't do it.'

He looked from her to the bleeding Campbell and then back to her, nodding slowly as if he understood before the recovering moans of Campbell's henchman attracted his attention. Calmly he covered the short distance, speaking as he walked.

'I won't kill them,' he reassured her, 'but it's time to send a message – a message to anyone who thinks they can walk in here and take what's mine.' He turned in a full circle looking up at the windows of Millander Walk that looked down on the spectacle as he addressed the audience that he knew was watching and listening. 'Everybody needs to know,' he called out at the top of his voice, 'this is what happens if you fuck with me. You come after me – this is what I do to you.'

He raised the ASP above the henchman and whipped it down with a sickening thud into his ribs, then his spine, then his knee, over and over, punctuating each blow with grunt from the effort. Distracted by movement from Campbell, he lowered his ASP and stood tall – a slight smile spreading over his lips which had been made thin and pale by the bloodletting.

'Don't worry, Campbell,' he tormented the prostrate figure. 'I'll be back with you just as soon as I've finished with this cunt.' The smile fell from his lips as once more he lifted the ASP and brought it down hard on the motionless henchman.

King hammered on the door with the base of his ASP – the rage and adrenalin from beating Campbell and his enforcer still coursing around his body as he grabbed the bars of the metal security grid and tried to pull it from the bricks where it was riveted with screws that ran deep.

'Ubana, you slag,' he screamed for everyone to hear. 'I know it was you. I know it was you who told them where they could find me. I know it was you who set me up. You'd better open this fucking door or it'll be a lot worse for you later.'

His demands were met with silence. Ubana held her fourteen-year-old daughter close as they cowered inside, wiping the girl's tears away and humming to her gently the way she had when Nakiya was a young child awaking from a nightmare.

'Open this fucking door,' King screamed again as he jammed his ASP through the gaps in the metal grids over the downstairs windows and began to systematically smash the panes of glass. The acoustic boom as they first imploded was followed immediately by the tinkling sound of thousands of pieces falling to the floor, making Ubana and her daughter flinch and whimper as they held each other closer against the threat of the madman outside. 'You can't hide from me forever, you fucking bitch. You live on this estate – you deal with me. You live on this estate – you pay me.'

Once all the windows were smashed he beat the front door relentlessly with his ASP until exhaustion finally slowed and then stopped him. He waited a few seconds until enough breath returned before shouting one last threat.

'You're a dead woman, Ubana. You're a fucking dead

woman.' He kicked the door once through the grid and stormed off back along the walkway to Kelly's maisonette where she stood waiting for him at the front door. She grabbed him by the arm and dragged him back inside, slamming and locking the door behind them.

'Fucking hell, Jack,' she warned him. 'That was Josh Campbell you just beat the shit out of – the oldest brother of the family. They ain't just gonna sit back and do nothing. They'll come after you now. They have to.'

'I know who it was,' he answered. 'Fuck the Campbells. You think I'm afraid of them?'

'And Susie's connected,' she ignored his question. 'Everyone knows she's connected. She ain't gonna just do nothing. She's gonna try and make things bad for you, Jack.'

'Then I need to be ready,' he said – lost in the belief of his indestructability. 'Give them something they won't be expecting. They think they're dangerous. I'll show them what dangerous really fucking means.'

'There's too many of them,' Kelly reminded him. 'They'll keep coming.'

'They're just cowards,' he told her, pulling out his mobile and speed-dialling a contact. 'Once they know how far I'm prepared to go they'll back down.'

'What are you talking about, Jack?' she asked, her voice cracking with concern. 'Listen to what you're saying – it's madness. You can't go to war with the Campbells. You wouldn't stand a chance.'

'We'll see.'

'You can't, Jack,' she insisted. 'Let's just run. Let's run now. Maybe if you move to a different police borough or even a different force they won't come after you. Maybe they won't find you.'

'No,' he barked at her. 'Not yet. I can't leave yet.'

'Why?' she pleaded. 'Because you're afraid to leave this shithole of an estate? There's nothing worth anything here.

Nothing worth dying for.' He held up his hand to silence her as his phone call was answered.

'To what do I owe the pleasure of this call?' Scott asked cheerfully.

'I need your help,' King told him without ceremony.

'You sound like shit,' Scott said – serious now. 'You all right?'

'I'm fine,' King lied. 'I just need you to do something for me.'

'Such as?'

'You still got that piece of paper with the address on it I gave you?'

'Yeah,' Scott assured him. 'I've still got it.'

'I need you to bring me a gun to that address.'

'You fucking what?' Scott asked – almost laughing at the madness of the request. 'You're joking, right?'

'No,' King told him. 'No I'm not. I need a firearm – a handgun – and I need it now.'

'Jesus Christ, Jack. What sort of trouble are you in?'

'Nothing I can't handle.'

'If you need a handgun to handle it then I'd say whatever shit you're in, you're in over your head. Where are you now?'

'On the estate I told you about. At the address you have.'

'Is that where you're in trouble?'

'Could be,' King answered.

'Then get the fuck out of there,' Scott demanded. 'If you can't go back to your flat, get round to my place. You'll be safe there until we can work something out.'

'I can't do that, Scott,' he insisted. 'I don't want you getting involved.'

'And how is getting you a gun not getting involved?' Scott asked.

'I just need you to do that one thing for me,' King pleaded. 'Just drop it to me and go. No one will ever know. I'll take care of everything else myself.'

'Jesus, Jack,' Scott told him. 'I can't get hold of a gun.'

'Don't give me that shit,' King said. 'You're in the fucking army – an officer in the army. Book one out of the nearest armoury and get it to me. I can do what I've got to do and get it back to you before anyone even knows it's missing. The police don't have a record of military weapons to compare ballistic records to. Even if it gets used no one will ever know. I need that gun, Scott.'

There was a long silence before Scott spoke again. 'OK,' he finally agreed, 'but I'm not even in London. Give me about two hours and I'll meet you at the address. Just stay safe till I get there.'

'Don't worry about me,' he reassured him.

'Jack,' Scott told him. 'I've been worried about you for a long time. I'm not about to stop now.' King pressed the *end call* button without replying.

Kelly was on him immediately. 'A gun, Jack? A bloody gun? What you going to do – shoot them all?'

'It won't come to that,' he promised. 'I'll give them a fright and they'll back off.'

'No they won't,' Kelly told him mournfully. 'And nor will you.'

'I need to go somewhere,' he explained. 'I'll be back in an hour or so.'

'Where?' she asked.

'Just somewhere,' he answered. 'I need to clear my head – work out what I'm going to do.'

'Can I come?'

'No,' he insisted. 'I have to do this alone.'

'What if the Campbells come back? What am I supposed to do?'

'They're not interested in you. It's me they want. If it makes you feel better, go stay with a friend till I get back. Or here,' he told her, pulling a rolled-up wad of cash from his pocket and handing it to her. 'Go shopping or something. Get yourself into the West End and treat yourself.'

'Shopping?' she asked in disbelief. 'You want me to go shopping? Now?'

'For fuck's sake, Kelly,' he snapped at her and made her jump – the black pools of her eyes threatening to well over. 'I don't care what you do. I just need to get my head straight. Just for a couple of hours. Damn it, Kelly, I'll see you later.' He closed his eyes and breathed for a moment. 'I just need a little time and keys. I need keys to get in if you're not here when I get back.'

'Take mine,' she told him, grabbing her set from the side table and handing them to him. 'I've got a spare set some-where.'

'Thanks,' he told her as he turned and headed for the door before her voice stopped him.

'Jack,' she called out. 'You will come back, won't you? You are coming back?'

'Of course,' he reassured her without knowing if he was telling the truth or not – the siren who'd led him to physical pleasures he'd never experienced before suddenly looking like the little girl lost she really was. 'Of course I'm coming back.'

'I love you,' she blurted out, taking a step towards him before freezing, afraid she would only chase him away.

King tried to find the words to answer her, but they all just swirled around in his head before becoming stuck in his throat. Eventually he said the only words he could push from his mouth before fleeing for the door and the world outside. 'I'll see you later, Kelly. I promise. I'll see you later.'

Susie Ubana surveyed the damage King had caused to the windows of her maisonette as her daughter began to sweep the thousands of glass shards from the floor. They moved silently and carefully, only talking in whispers for fear of his return and wrath. Ubana shook her head as she considered her next move – her business forgotten as all her thoughts turned to her daughter's safety.

The girl looked up from the floor at her mother and spoke. 'He's not coming back, is he, Mum?' she asked. 'He's not coming back to get us?'

'No,' Ubana reassured her – struggling to speak as a lump formed in her throat. 'I'll take care of it.' She left her daughter sweeping glass and headed for the front room, lighting a cigarette and inhaling deeply before calling a number on the phone she'd been gripping since King had first hammered on her front door. The phone was answered within two rings.

'Susie,' Marino greeted her informally – like someone who'd known her a long time. 'You got something for me?'

'It's King,' she told him. 'He's completely out of control, Frank. He's just smashed in all the windows at the front of my house – says I set him up with the Campbells.'

'And did you?' Marino asked, making Ubana pause before answering.

'Christ, Frank, I talked to them,' she admitted. 'I had to. He was muscling in on my business – which means he was muscling in on their business. I had to tell them. If I didn't they would have thought I was skimming from them.'

'Jesus,' he sighed, knowing she was right. 'I understand.'

'That's not all,' she told him.

'I'm listening,' he encouraged her.

'Josh Campbell and one of his heavies came looking for him.'

'And?'

'And they found him.'

'Where?'

'With Kelly Royston,' she explained. 'In her flat.'

'Kelly Royston?' Marino questioned. 'Bloody hell – please tell me he's not involved with Kelly Royston.'

'Been spending his nights there. You can take from that whatever you want.'

'This is getting worse by the second,' Marino complained.

'Listen, Frank,' she warned him, 'that's not the worst of it.

When Josh came looking for him King somehow got the drop on them – used gas or something. He beat the shit out of them. You don't do that to Josh Campbell and walk away. They'll find him, Frank. Your man's in serious fucking trouble. I warned you this was gonna happen. You should have just turned him in to Internal Affairs and let them deal with it. They could have saved him from himself.'

'I couldn't do that,' he admitted. 'He was a good man. A good copper. I had to try and bring him back. I had to.'

'Well he ain't no good any more,' she told him, sounding sad, 'and if you don't find him before the Campbells he won't be anything.'

'You think they'd hit a cop?'

'As far as they're concerned he's not a cop any more,' she warned him. 'He's fair game.'

'Shit,' Marino cursed. 'Where is he now? Still on the estate?'

'No,' she answered. 'I saw him taking off in a patrol car.'

'D'you know where to?'

'No,' she told him. 'Why don't you have your people look out for the car he's using? They'd find him soon enough.'

'No,' Marino disagreed. 'He's probably monitoring his radio, even if he's not answering it.'

'You've tried?'

'Yeah, I've tried,' he told her. 'I've been trying to catch up with him since I got into work this morning.'

'Why?' she asked. 'Something else already happen?'

'You could say that,' he admitted.

'You gonna tell me what?'

'No,' he answered. 'It's irrelevant now anyway. Most important thing is to find him.'

'And how you gonna do that?'

'I don't know,' he admitted. 'That's my problem.'

'You're not still trying to solve this on your own, are you, Frank?' she asked. 'Not still trying to give him a *chance*?'

'That's up to me,' he reminded her sharply. 'If he turns up back on the estate you just remember to call me straight away. Understand?'

'I understand,' she assured him before hearing the line go dead. She let the hand holding the phone fall into her lap – looking at it and speaking as if Marino could still hear. 'You're too late. You can't save him. Gone too far for that now.'

King opened the door and stepped into the cool interior of the flat. This place seemed to belong to another life now, one that had ended long ago, although he couldn't sense how long. A life that had had a long-term future – one that offered stability, a lasting relationship, a career, a family and something like love. But also one that could never make him feel the way he felt when he walked the estate like an emperor or how he felt when he was inside Kelly – watching her move, inhaling her scent. Yet surrounded by the trappings of his previous existence he suddenly felt melancholy and anxious – for the first time he realized he'd gambled everything on something that he could never really have. All the things he'd given up his life for, the crack, the cocaine, the cannabis and even the serenely beautiful Kelly, were things that merely offered short-term escapism from the reality of the moment, without offering any sort of future other than violent death at the hands of organized crime or a long, slow destruction by the ravages of hard drugs.

He began to wander around the small flat, picking up photographs of himself and Sara she hadn't yet cleared away or thrown in the bin. He looked happy in the photographs, relaxed and confident – content with his lot and what the future with Sara promised. As he looked away he caught a reflection of himself in a mirror that made him freeze. He looked much older than his twenty-four years – pale and tired – every line and contour of his face showing the signs of stress his new life had brought. The anxiety of living on the edge had etched itself into the very fabric of his face. It had felt so good – even beating the crap out of Campbell and his hired muscle only minutes ago had felt good – but now, standing in the middle of his old comfortable life, he just felt exhausted. He'd become a hamster on a wheel – forever running just to stand still. He'd burnt too brightly and now the darkness was coming to swallow him. He swept the framed photographs from the sideboard and sent them crashing to the floor where the glass frames broke apart like the pieces of his life – tearing and ripping at the pictures they used to protect. But somehow one remained undamaged. One of him with Sara shortly after he'd been discharged from hospital. He bent and picked it up from the floor, lifting it close to his face. Its difference from the others was striking and he realized that he'd already changed forever at that point. The *incident* had already changed him forever – long before the estate – long before Kelly and the drugs, Astill, Ubana and the Campbells. That day had robbed him of who he used to be and shattered any chance of living the ordinary life he'd thought was his right. The ghosts of that day were never going to stop haunting him – were always going to chase him into the dark world he now lived in. They would drag him towards the abyss and watch him throw himself over the edge. Only the memory of the girl he'd saved shone enough light in his nightmares to show him the way back from a self-inflicted eternity of darkness. Standing alone in his flat, suddenly aware it had all been made a lie since the *incident*, that it was a life he could never have had, he began to desperately want it – for things to be the way they had before, although in his soul he knew it was too late. Since the madman had slaughtered his own family, it had been too late for him. He was too numb and lost to feel his own tears running down his face until the sound of the front door being closed made him spin around.

'Sara,' he smiled, wiping tears away with the back of his hand.

'What do you want?' she asked coldly as she walked deeper into the flat – looking at the smashed pictures on the floor. 'Come to destroy the flat like you're destroying yourself?'

'I just wanted to see you,' he told her. 'I've made some terrible mistakes.'

'I don't think so,' she replied. 'Last time we saw each other you made it very clear how you felt about me. There's no way forward for us, Jack. It's over.'

'I didn't know what I was saying,' he pleaded. 'I was fucked up.'

'Jack,' she sighed. 'I think you should just leave. I want you to leave.'

'We're good together,' he ignored her. 'I just lost my way, but I can fix everything. I just need some time.'

'No you can't, Jack,' she said. 'You can't fix this. I waited long enough, but you just kept pushing me away. I've met somebody else. I'm sorry.'

'I don't care,' he pleaded. 'I can fix anything. I just need you to believe me.'

'No, Jack,' she raised her voice. 'Now you need to leave.'

Again he ignored her – slumping onto a kitchen chair to let her know he wasn't going anywhere. 'I've done bad things, Sara. I've really fucked up.'

She wanted to push him away – drag him from his chair and throw him out of the flat – but her feelings for him still ran deep. She didn't want him back, but she wasn't ready to completely exile him from her life either, not while he was wounded and hurting.

'You in some sort of trouble, Jack?' she asked softly.

'Trouble,' he laughed through his pain. 'I'm in more than trouble. I'm on the fucking edge here.'

'What's going on, Jack?' she pushed. 'What the hell's happened to you? Tell me what's wrong.'

'It wasn't supposed to happen like this,' he explained, his voice little more than a whisper. 'Going back to work. Going onto the Unit – it was supposed to make me feel like me again . . . but it didn't. I couldn't get those . . . thoughts out my head.'

'What did you do, Jack?'

'I started taking more painkillers than I should – with drink.'

'Christ, Jack,' she told him. 'You can't mess about with buprenorphine. It's practically a class A drug.'

'It worked for a while,' he continued, 'helped with the pain and the memories, but it stopped working – so I tried something else.'

'What do you mean you tried something else? What did you take?'

'At first just cannabis,' he admitted.

'*At first*?' she seized on it – her voice growing increasingly concerned and disbelieving.

'After that . . . crack, cocaine.'

'My God, Jack. What have you done? No wonder you look like you do. Haven't you seen what that stuff does to people? It destroys their lives.'

'I know,' he confessed, 'but I *needed* something and it made me feel good. It took away the pain and made me forget.'

'OK,' Sara said, trying to rationalize the situation and find a solution – thinking like a cop. 'If it's just the drugs we can get you cleaned up without anyone knowing. I'll call in and tell work you're sick with flu. That'll buy us a week to ten days to get whatever shit's in your system out of you.'

'It's not just the drugs,' he told her, hanging his head, unable to look her in the eye any more. 'I've done . . . *other* things.'

'What have you done, Jack?' she asked – afraid of the answer she was about to be given. 'What have you done?'

'I . . . I just wanted to shake things up,' he tried to explain.

'Put the fear back in the criminals and the thugs and the dealers. We roughed a few up – took their dope off them and . . . and planted it on others.'

'Oh my God.' Sara slumped into the chair next to him. 'What the hell were you thinking, Jack?' They sat in silence with each other for a while before Sara spoke again. 'Does anyone else know? Does anyone else know what you've been doing?'

'Davey Brown,' he told her. 'Danny Williams.'

'And Renita?'

'No,' he answered firmly. 'She knows nothing, but . . .'

'But what?'

'Maybe Frank Marino knows,' he said. 'He's been sniffing around my business for weeks. I think he has a grass on the estate.'

'Your business?' she questioned him. 'D'you know what you sound like?'

King ignored her as he purged himself through confession. 'There's more.'

'More?'

'Butler,' he said, as if the name alone should be enough.

'Butler?' Sara shook her head – confused. 'Ronnie Butler?' He said nothing as she began to work it out for herself. 'Jesus Christ, Jack. I heard rumours police were involved in what happened to him, but I thought it was just silly canteen whispers. When you said it was vigilantes I believed you. My God. Maybe I just wanted to believe you. Maybe I was fooling myself because I didn't want to believe you could do something like that – now you're telling me it was you?'

'He deserved what he got,' King retaliated – a fire flashing in his eyes.

'It wasn't for you to decide,' she told him. 'You should have left it to the CID – the courts. We don't get to decide the punishment, Jack. We just catch the bastards. What happens to them after that is out of our hands.'

387

'People were laughing at us,' King argued. 'I had to do something or they'd never have respected me.'

'You're wrong, Jack,' she disagreed. 'You're wrong.' Again they sat in silence, but Sara's mind was racing as she recalled everything she'd heard about reported incidents on the estate until another name surfaced from the darkness. 'Swinton,' she accused him. 'Alan Swinton. It was you, wasn't it? It was you who beat him nearly to death.'

He leaned back in his chair and looked at the ceiling. 'It was a mistake,' he answered.

'Oh my God, Jack,' she said, pinching her forehead between her thumb and fingers to ease the pain of what she was being told. 'That's what happens when we become judge, jury and executioner – we start making mistakes. But that's not why you're here, is it, Jack? You're not afraid of Butler or Swinton, but I see fear in your face. So what is it? Are Professional Ethics and Standards on your case?'

'No,' he sneered. 'They got nothing on me. As far as I know they don't even know I exist.'

'What then?'

'The Campbells,' he admitted. 'I turned one of them over.'

'*The* Campbells?' she asked – already shrinking from the answer. 'What the hell do you mean, you turned one of the Campbells over?'

'They came after me,' he explained, 'so I beat him and his crony like dogs so everyone could see I wasn't going to be pushed around by anyone.'

'Wait,' Sara told him. 'You're confusing me. Why would the Campbells be coming after you? What are you to them?'

'I . . .' he tried to tell her, but the words kept sticking in his throat. 'I . . .'

'You what, Jack?' she pushed him.

'I . . . I moved in on some of their . . . businesses,' he finally confessed.

'Businesses?' she queried. 'The only businesses the Campbells

388

are interested in are drugs, prostitution and gambling. How could you possibly . . .' She stopped mid-sentence as the realization of what he'd become dawned on her. 'Which is it, Jack?' she insisted. 'Prostitution? Gambling?'

'Drugs,' he spurted out before she could torture him any more with her questions.

'A fucking drug dealer,' she shook her head – her voice heavy with disgust. 'A fucking peddler of misery and death. Get out of here, Jack. Get the fuck out of my home.'

'I thought you were going to help me,' he pleaded. 'You said you'd help me. I lost my way. That's all. I wasn't ready to go back. Being on that estate these last few weeks – I just wasn't ready for it.'

'Jesus, Jack,' Sara told him, shaking her head in dismay. 'A few weeks? You've been in that damn place for almost six months.'

'*What?*' he asked, swaying with the shock of her words – the reality of how far he'd drifted from the real world cutting through the fading effects of the drugs and his own paranoia. 'What are you talking about?'

'You've been there almost six months, Jack,' Sara spelt it out for him. 'Now get out. I just want you to get out. You bring drugs and drug dealers and the Campbells to my front door and you want me to help you?' she asked. 'I want you to leave and take all your shit with you. I won't tell Professional Standards what you've done. That's all I'm offering.'

'Fine,' he growled as he stood. 'I might have known you'd turn your back on me.'

'It was you who turned your back on me, Jack,' she reminded him.

'You were happy to stand by me when things were good,' he pointed at her. 'When you thought you were on to a good thing with me on accelerated promotion – happy to play the part of a senior officer's wife. But now I'm in trouble you're showing your true colours.'

389

'Just leave, Jack,' she told him, looking away.

'At least it proves I was right about you,' he said. 'Nothing about you is real. It's all false – all just for show. You're barely alive – just a pathetic social climber. Even fucking you was like having sex with a robot – and you expected me to be *grateful* that you'd allowed me to fuck you.'

'I swear, Jack,' she warned him, 'if you don't leave I'll call 999.'

'At least I know what it feels like to be alive now,' he told her. 'I know what it feels like to make love. You'll never know what it feels like to have true power – to have thousands of people do anything you tell them to. To see the fear in their eyes when they look at you.'

'So,' Sara picked over his words, 'you left me for some little whore on the Grove Wood Estate. You probably deserve each other.'

'She's not the whore,' he accused her. 'She's not with me because she sees a ticket to a semi-detached in South Woodford. She's with me to be with me – the real me.'

'You've lost it, Jack,' she told him. 'Run back to your little Grove Wood Estate slut. I wish you both luck. You're going to need it.'

'Fuck you, you stuck-up bitch,' he cursed her and stormed towards the front door. 'And fuck your pointless life.'

'Do yourself a favour, Jack,' she called after him, 'and hand yourself in to the station. Tell them everything. Maybe they can save you from the Campbells and yourself.'

'Fuck you and fuck the Campbells,' he shouted before yanking the door open and slamming it shut behind him.

Sara slumped in her chair not knowing whether she wanted to cry or just enjoy the quiet relief of knowing now why he'd left her and that he'd never be coming back.

'Goodbye, Jack,' she whispered to herself, looking at the broken pictures on the floor. 'Goodbye.'

* * *

'Look at the state of you two soppy cunts,' Archie Campbell, the father and leader of the family, reprimanded his eldest son and his supposed minder George. Despite being in his mid-fifties, Archie had lost none of his menace as his piercing blue eyes glared with violent malevolence and intelligence, his short, stocky, muscled body tensing with rage. 'You let one fucking beat copper do this to you?' He waved his hands around to indicate the multitude of wounds that covered their bodies and heads as they looked sheepishly away. 'What was this cunt,' Archie continued in the only way he knew how, 'ten foot tall and built like a silverback gorilla? Some sort of fucking superman?'

'He got the drop on us,' Josh complained through split lips that still seeped blood.

'Got the drop on you?' Archie shook his head with disgust. 'Fuck me.'

'He had CS spray,' Josh tried to explain. 'We couldn't see a fucking thing. I could hardly breathe.'

'He's fucking Old Bill,' Archie screamed. 'They all have that shit. What did you expect?'

'We was just talking to him,' George tried to help. 'Next thing we get a face full of CS gas.'

'Did I ask for your opinion?' Archie asked calmly, but his voice was still full of foreboding menace that made the much larger man visibly shake. He knew all too well what Archie was capable of. 'Did I say you could fucking speak?'

'Sorry, boss,' George managed to splutter.

'Get the fuck out of my sight,' Archie ordered.

George knew Archie's words could be a death sentence. 'But, boss . . .' he tried to plead his case.

'I said get the fuck out of my sight,' Archie screamed, causing George to spring to his feet and head for the door, passing Josh's two younger yet even more vicious and violent brothers – Tyler and Callum. Their eyes were fixed on him like vultures just waiting for their father to give the word they could feast on his carcass. 'You're supposed to be his fucking minder. Some fucking minder you are. Get the fuck out of here. I'll deal with you later.' George left the comfortable study of Archie's council house that had doubled as the meeting room where the family business had been discussed in private for decades. 'And you,' Archie turned on Josh, 'you've embarrassed the whole family. I can only imagine what people are saying about us. I give you one simple job and you fuck it up. Pray word of this doesn't get back to the Balcans. They start thinking we're a Mickey Mouse firm what can't even handle one rogue copper – they'll cut us loose.'

'I'm sorry,' Josh apologized. 'I'll put it right – I promise.'

'No you won't,' Archie told him. 'You had your chance and anyway – look at the state of you. You ain't going anywhere till you've healed up a bit. The less people see you looking like that the better.' He turned to his other sons. 'Tyler, Callum – I want you two to find this slag copper and show him what happens to people who fuck with us. Understand?' Tyler and Callum nodded their stony faces. 'Beat the shit out of him if you have to, but don't kill him. He's still Old Bill at the end of the day. Don't want half the Met after us looking for payback.'

'Fine,' Callum, the youngest but most intelligent and violent of the brothers, agreed. 'I'll use a hammer on his knees. He won't be walking the beat any more.'

'Just make sure the message is sent loud and clear,' Archie told him. 'You don't fuck with the Campbells.'

'No,' the soft voice of a woman emitted from an oversized armchair in the corner of the room, making the men tense as they turned towards Iris Campbell – the wife and mother of the family. If Archie was the muscle and front man, then it was Iris who was the brains and tactician. 'You're right,' she said, cryptically. 'He's Old Bill.'

'Meaning?' Tyler asked.

'Meaning you can't just beat the crap out of him like he

392

was any little slag,' she explained. 'He may be bent Old Bill, but he's still Old Bill. You beat the shit out of him and let him live – what's to stop him going crying back to his old mates looking to make things . . . *difficult* for us? We got too much on the line with this thing with the Balcans to be having Old Bill breathing down our necks right now.'

'So what you saying?' Callum asked.

'I'm saying we have two options,' Iris told them calmly, as if discussing a simple business decision. 'Either we do nothing and leave this copper alone to continue his expansion into what is supposed to be our territory, which leaves us looking like a laughing stock and jeopardizes this thing with the Balcans, or . . .'

'Or what?' the middle son and largest of all asked.

'We find a *permanent* solution,' she said.

'You sure, Iris?' Archie asked. 'Never heard of anyone taking a copper out before – even a bent one.'

'Does he look like he's going to stop if we do nothing?' she questioned. 'Take a look at Josh's face,' she insisted, jutting her chin in his direction. 'If he wasn't scared of us before he's even less scared of us now, which means he's not afraid to go after more and more of our business interests. And a little bird tells me he's not alone. There could be as many as four of them working together. Four bent coppers is quite a force, but this Sergeant King is the leader all right. Cut off the head and kill the beast.'

'And have the Met come after us?' Tyler reminded them. 'How long we gonna last with half the Met looking to take us down?'

'Not necessarily,' Iris told them. 'We've got *contacts* in the police, right?'

'We have an arrangement with one or two,' Callum answered. 'Sensible ones we can deal with.'

'Which means we have a line of communication,' Iris pointed out.

393

'So?' Tyler asked.

'He's been a very bad boy, this Sergeant King,' Iris explained. 'Be very embarrassing for the Met if what he's been up to ever got out. After we've taken care of this little problem we talk to them through our contacts – tell them that should their investigation be unsuccessful as to who took him out, then our lips would be sealed, but if they come after us, we'll let every newspaper and journalist in London know what he's been up to.'

'Think they'll go for it?' Callum asked.

'Don't see how they've got any choice,' Iris said, pausing to sip tea from her fine china cup, the saucer balanced expertly on her thigh. 'They can't afford another scandal right now – they'll cut a deal.'

'You sure, Iris?' Archie checked.

'Have I ever been wrong before?' she asked.

'No,' he admitted. 'Not on the big stuff.'

'But killing a copper,' Tyler worried. 'That's a major fucking call.'

'Things have to be done,' Iris wagged a finger at him. 'Sometimes things have to be done – for the business. We may not like it and God knows I hope none of you ever start to enjoy it, but sometimes *necessary* things have to be done. You don't think me and your dad built this business without getting our hands dirty from time to time, do you? You don't think I don't see some of their faces in my dreams sometimes? Taking a life should always be a last resort – to protect the business. To protect the family. But this rotten apple's given us no choice. Another time maybe I would have walked away and let him have that shithole of an estate, but not today. Not with this thing with the Balcans coming up – not while we're trying to move up. He has to go.'

'I'll do it,' Callum volunteered quickly and without emotion. 'I know what to do.'

Iris and Archie looked at each other for a long time, as if

communicating telepathically before Archie spoke. 'I could get one of the crew to do it,' he said, 'or even bring someone in from outside.'

'No,' Iris dismissed it. 'This needs to be kept tight and quiet. Need-to-know only.' She turned to her youngest son, her feelings a mixture of maternal fear and pride in what he was willing to do for the family. 'It needs to be quick and clean,' she told him, 'which means using a shooter. Get him in the open, corner him and take him down. Take Tyler with you for back-up. You know who to see about the shooter?' she asked. Callum just nodded. 'Good. Once you've used it lose it in the deepest part of the Thames and make sure it's untraceable. If it gets dredged up thirty years from now I still don't want it leading back to anyone who can put us in the frame. Understand?'

'I'll take care of it,' he assured her.

'Then time waits for no man,' she told them, 'or woman. Do what you gotta do and get back here. I'll take care of your clothes while you two scrub yourselves clean in the shower.' The two brothers nodded that they understood. 'It's settled then,' Iris finished the meeting.

King knocked on the door of the maisonette in Millander Walk and it was quickly opened by Kelly. He barged past her into the cool of the interior while she bolted the locks behind him.

'What's going on?' she asked, panicked, as she watched him pull the plastic bag of cocaine from under his body armour and tip a small pile onto the kitchen table before pulling a credit card from his pocket and slicing and shaping it into a long, thin, white line. He bent over the table, covered one nostril and inhaled half the line before swapping nostrils and snorting the rest – the effects instant, making him stand bolt upright and wide-eyed.

'Fuck,' he declared with satisfaction.

'Where have you been?' Kelly asked – now standing at his side.

'I had to sort some shit out,' he replied, blinking as the drugs took hold. 'It's done now. I thought I told you to stay at a friend's or go shopping in the West End – out the way.'

'I couldn't,' she told him. 'I wasn't in the mood. I was worried, Jack.'

'About what?' he asked as if nothing had happened.

'You,' she shook her head. 'The Campbells. They're not gonna just forget what you did to Josh. He's not just one of their faces, he's an actual Campbell – one of the brothers.'

'Fuck the Campbells,' he dismissed it. 'They come back – they'll get more of the same.'

'Only next time there'll be more of them and they'll be ready.'

'The Campbells are finished,' he told her. 'I've decided to expand. Push them out for good.'

'How you gonna do that, Jack?' Kelly asked, sounding a little dismayed.

'One by one I'll take every estate and every street in Canning Town and then maybe even beyond that,' he explained – the cocaine rushing around his mind and making him irrational and unrealistic. 'I'll set myself up as an estates policing unit expert – persuade the senior management to let me set up and oversee units all over the borough – use the cops under me to take control of the streets. No one will get in my way.'

'I'm not sure, Jack,' she said, unconvinced by his drug-fuelled dream. 'Maybe we should just get the hell out of here. You've still got your job – we don't need this . . . this . . . *dead* place. Nothing good ever happens here, Jack.'

'I'm not running from the Campbells,' he told her through gritted teeth. 'I'm not running from anyone.'

'Why, Jack?' Kelly pushed. 'Nothing wrong with running – if it's the right thing to do. If it's for the best – for you and me.'

'No more running,' he told her. 'I'm tired of running.'

'I don't understand,' she admitted. 'You're not running from anything.'

'Really?' he asked, suddenly sounding tired and broken. 'I've been running ever since I walked into *that* house – one way or another. I've been running from the nightmares, but they always find me. It's time I stopped running.'

A gentle knock on the door made both of them jump. 'See who it is and get rid of them,' he demanded.

'What if it's the Campbells?' she whispered.

'When the Campbells come back they won't knock,' he told her and nodded his head towards the door. Kelly peeked through the spyhole to see a man in his mid-twenties who looked vaguely familiar, although she didn't know why. 'Who is it?' King asked quietly.

'I don't know,' she answered. 'I've never seen him before. Could be a cop?'

'The same one as last time?'

'No,' she told him. 'A different one.'

'Shit,' King cursed as he headed towards her and peeped through the fisheye lens. 'Thank fuck,' he declared, breaking into a smile, confusing Kelly even further before he unlocked the door and threw it wide open. 'Scott,' he welcomed his brother. 'I knew you'd come through for me. Get inside, quick.' Once Scott was in, King re-locked the doors and led his brother into the open-plan kitchen–diner.

'Who's this?' Scott asked, nodding towards Kelly, his eyes squinting with distaste.

'Kelly,' King answered dismissively. 'Kelly, this is my brother Scott.'

'The one you called earlier?' she asked.

'Yeah,' King confirmed hurriedly, eager to move on. 'Well? Did you bring it?'

'How old are you, Kelly?' Scott ignored him – his eyes fixed on Kelly – her beauty and her youth equally undeniable.

'Old enough,' King answered. 'For fuck's sake, Scott – did you bring it?'

'No,' Scott told him. 'Of course I didn't fucking bring it. I'm not going to bring you a firearm. You think I'm insane?'

'You lied to me,' King accused him as his world seemed to be collapsing in on him – lied to by the only person he really trusted in the entire world – left defenceless and exposed to the unstoppable tide of the Campbells that was surely sweeping towards him. 'You've fucked me.'

'I had to lie to you,' Scott insisted, grabbing hold of him as King stood motionless, still in shock. 'It was the only way I could be sure you'd meet me. You said you were in trouble?' Scott waited for an answer, but King could neither move nor speak.

'A local family,' Kelly eventually answered for him. 'A crime family called the Campbells. They're heavy people – capable of most anything. Jack's pissed them off.'

'Then tell the police,' Scott told them. 'If he's been going after a criminal family and they're threatening him because of it, have them arrested.'

'He's not been going after them like *that*,' Kelly explained. 'He's been moving in on their interests.' Still Scott looked confused. 'Taking over their business,' Kelly spelt it out.

'What?' Scott asked in disbelief. 'You've been what?'

'It wasn't supposed to happen like that,' King tried to explain. 'I was just trying to shake things up. It just went too far, that's all.'

'Then you need to hand yourself in,' Scott told him. 'Tell Internal Affairs everything.'

'What,' King shook his head, 'and go to prison for dealing – for abduction and assault? I don't think so. They'd lock me up for years. Do you know what happens to Old Bill inside? I'm not telling anyone anything.'

'I'll use all the influence I can to help you,' Scott tried to convince him, 'and so will Dad. He still has contacts. If we can establish you're suffering from PTSD we can claim you weren't responsible for your actions. Prison's not a certainty.'

'That's not a risk I'm willing to take,' King told him.

'You don't have a choice,' replied Scott.

'Yes I do,' King insisted. 'I take the Campbells on head to head. I wipe them out and take over this whole manor. I can get the manpower to do it – I just need you to bring me a gun.'

'Jack,' Scott tried to snap him back to reality. 'I'm not going to bring you a gun. It's not going to happen. Everything you say – it's the drugs talking. That mark on your lip, I've seen it before – on my own men when they came home after tours in Iraq and Afghanistan. Not all of them could handle it. It's crack, right? Jesus, Jack. I've seen that shit destroy good men faster than you'd believe. They'd have been better off with a bullet through the head. At least it would have been quick and painless. Instead they rotted away. Their minds went first, then their bodies – all sense of loyalty and morality lost. I saw men, who in Helmand would risk their lives for their fellow soldiers, come home happy to sell their own children if they could get more of that poison once they'd started using. You're not thinking straight, Jack. You can't with that crap in your system. Come home with me. Let's get you cleaned up – then we can work out what we're going to do.'

'No,' King insisted. 'I'm not going anywhere. I'm not one of your squaddies you can play that caring officer shit with. I just needed you to get off your high horse for once in your life and get me a fucking gun, but you couldn't even do that. You betrayed me, Scott. You let me down, just like everyone else did.'

'The drugs are making you paranoid,' Scott warned. 'You don't know what you're saying.'

'I know exactly what I'm saying,' King sneered. 'I don't belong with you people any more. This is where I belong. I don't want to go back to my old life. I couldn't even if I wanted to – I know that now. Don't you understand? I've come too far. There's only prison and some pointless pretence of a life there for me now. I don't want to live like you or Mum and Dad – each new day the same as the last. After a few years with that mannequin of a fiancée of yours you'll wish you died in Afghanistan instead of just being wounded.'

No one spoke for a few seconds. 'I'll pretend I didn't hear that,' Scott managed to swallow his anger. 'That's the crack talking, not you.'

'No,' King raised his voice. 'It's the truth.'

'Bullshit,' Scott argued. 'You were never the same after what happened to you. You needed help and you didn't get it. It's not your fault, Jack. It's not your fault.'

King sighed. 'Just go, Scott. Go back to your life and leave me to live mine.'

'If I go you'll have no life,' Scott told him.

'Just go,' King shouted at him.

'Not without you,' Scott answered, taking a step towards him. But King's hand firing to the CS canister on his utility belt stopped him in his tracks.

'I will,' King warned him. 'I swear I will, Scott. Just go and don't come back.'

'Don't do this,' Scott pleaded. 'You're my brother.'

'Not any more,' King said cruelly.

'Then you're lost,' Scott told him.

'Only to you,' he pushed the knife in further. 'Get out, Scott.'

Scott stood still and silent for a long time – his eyes moving from his brother's to the CS canister his hand still rested on. Finally he spoke. 'This isn't over. I won't give up on you.' Slowly he headed towards the front door hoping King would change his mind and accept his help, but he said nothing – watching him unblinkingly. Scott turned the locks and opened the door, calling back to King. 'I'll keep coming back,' he said, 'until you have no choice but to accept my help.'

'Don't come back,' King warned him. 'There's nothing here for you.' Scott nodded once and stepped through the door. 'Lock it,' he told Kelly who moved quickly to do as he'd said. Once the door was secure he allowed the tension in his body and mind to try and find a release. 'Fuck,' he cursed – the act of swearing giving him some sort of small relief, but not enough. He pulled the bag of cocaine from under his body armour and again tipped a small pile onto the kitchen table, although this time he hurriedly turned it into a straight line with his fingertips before inhaling entirely through one nostril – swearing as he bolted upright. 'Fuck.'

'Take it easy,' Kelly warned him. 'You're getting too wired. You won't be able to think straight.'

'I'm fine,' he assured her as he sniffed repeatedly and wiped the powder from the end of his nose onto the back of his hand before licking it clean – its bitterness making him wince. The sound of his mobile phone ringing saved him from any more discussion. The caller ID told him it was Davey Brown. 'Davey,' he answered it as he tried to clear the stinging saliva from the back of his throat.

'Where the fuck are you?' Brown demanded.

'On the estate,' King answered. 'Why? Is there a problem?'

'I've had the Duty Inspector banging on the door wanting to know if one of us took off with one of his team's motors from the yard. Wouldn't happen to be you by any chance?'

'What did you tell him?'

'I told him fuck all,' Brown said. 'Denied all knowledge.'

'Good,' King replied. 'Keep it that way.'

'Aye,' Brown moved on, 'but that's not the only problem. Marino's been going crazy trying to get hold of you. Says he needs to find you before *they* do. Who the fuck are *they*?'

'Don't worry about it,' King told him. 'I've already taken care of that. Marino's just trying to trip us up – get us to turn on each other or something. We just need to stay solid and we'll be fine – better than fine.'

'What you talking about?'

'Just do as I tell you and you'll see,' King assured him, 'and get hold of Danny and Knight too – make sure they keep their mouths shut. Understand?'

'Aye,' Brown agreed, sounding concerned. 'I understand.'

'Once you've found them,' King told him, 'I want you all to get down to the estate and meet me here – Millander Walk.'

'OK,' Brown played along. 'We'll be there.'

King hung up without replying and reached for the bag of cocaine still on the table before Kelly stopped him. 'You've had enough,' she warned him. 'Do any more and your brain'll explode.'

'I need something,' he complained.

'Fine,' she agreed. 'I'll make us a joint. It'll help bring you down. Sit,' she ordered pointing at the sofa. He did as he was told, unclipping his body armour and utility belt as he did so, letting them fall to the floor. Kelly dug out the box she kept her stash in from its hiding place and took it over to where he sat, kneeling on the floor next to him while she expertly prepared a large joint – lighting it without ceremony, taking one drag before passing it to King. 'Here,' she told him. 'This'll make you feel better.' She watched him inhale deeply – making the end of the joint glow bright red and crackle like a camp fire as he swallowed the smoke into the depths of his lungs, his pursed lips drawing her attention to the burn mark Scott had mentioned. Kelly had seen enough crack-heads in her own life to recognize the signs when she saw them, but she hadn't yet found the right moment to challenge him about it and still hoped he'd burnt himself smoking a joint down to the roach instead. She waited for King's body to slump as he relaxed before asking.

'Is he right?' she challenged him. 'Is the burn on your lip from a crack-pipe?'

Instinctively his hand came up to his mouth and touched

his lip. 'I've done it a couple of times,' he lied. 'Nothing I can't handle.'

'Nobody can handle crack,' she warned him. 'No one comes back from it. Get off that shit now, Jack – before it eats you alive.'

He looked into her eyes – as black as fresh drops of blood in the moonlight. She should have been experimenting with make-up and dreaming of teenage boys. Instead she was making joints for a corrupted cop and lecturing him on the all-consuming dangers of crack cocaine. 'OK,' he told her and meant it. 'If that's what you want.'

'Good,' she smiled, taking the joint back from him and inhaling more gently and calmly than he – blowing the smoke slowly from her red lips into a long, thin, white stream towards the ceiling before handing the joint back to King who took a long drag, holding the smoke in his lungs for as long as he could. His eyes become irresistibly heavy as Kelly stroked his skin and began to make soft sounds like gentle waves breaking on a sandy beach as if she was calming an infant.

'Sleep,' she told him. 'You need to sleep.'

He could deny her hypnotic demands no longer. Everything in his vision suddenly went blank and the soft sounds of Kelly's soothing faded to nothing as dreams quickly swept into his unconscious mind and dragged him deep into their world.

King woke abruptly from a dream involving suffocating and overheating to find Kelly lying across his chest fast asleep. He touched his own face and realized he was soaked in sweat – the rapid thumping of his heart telling him something was wrong, but he didn't know what. He rolled her off his chest and inadvertently woke her at the same time. He did up his trousers and leapt to his feet as Kelly yawned and stretched like a ballerina.

'You should sleep some more,' she told him, but he wasn't listening as he tried to focus on his wristwatch.

'Fuck,' he declared angrily. 'I've been asleep for almost two hours.'

'You needed it,' she reminded him.

'I can't afford to sleep,' he argued. 'Not right now. Fuck,' he cursed again. 'Anything could have happened in the last couple of hours. I need to get back to the station and find out what's going on. I'm going to get cleaned up and take a piss. Make me a sandwich or something, will you? I need to eat,' he told her and headed for the stairs, leaving his body armour and utility belt on the floor where he'd dropped it earlier.

'Cheese all right?' she asked. 'I ain't got a lot in.'

'Fine,' he answered over his shoulder and climbed the stairs slowly, feeling the effects of the fading drugs, stress and lack of sleep on his creaking body. He made it to the bathroom and urinated dark yellow water that stung as it escaped – warning him he was dehydrated. He zipped himself up, wincing slightly, and stepped over to the sink, turning the tap and filling it to the brim with cold water before burying his face in it. Water spilled over the edge and splashed on the floor as he submerged even deeper, the cold liquid covering and filling his ears, bringing a sense of peace and tranquility – escape – until a sound like the distant rumbling of thunder made him surface long before he needed to for air, the speed of his action throwing droplets high onto the walls and ceiling. He wiped the water from his face in an almost panic – as if it was a barrier between him and senses he needed to remove.

Satisfied he'd imagined it, he pushed his wet hair back with his hands and stared at the image of himself in the mirror. His appearance shocked him, as if each hour was ageing him by years, his skin pale and waxy, his eyes hollow and sunken and his lips colourless and cracked. 'Fuck,' he cursed himself a second before the rumbling noise returned. He hadn't imagined it – it was real – someone hammering on the front door. The sound had previously been distorted by the water he'd buried himself in, but was now as clear as the danger he sensed.

He flew from the bathroom, the warning he was ready to shout to Kelly already formed in his mouth, but as he burst into the upstairs hallway he realized it was too late. Kelly opened the door only slightly, believing the thin door chain would keep her safe, but the second she did so the door exploded inwards – knocking her backwards and to the floor as the two men strode into the maisonette – their handguns clearly visible.

'Shit,' King whispered to himself. He flattened himself against the wall and spied on the scene unfolding in front of him downstairs. Even from his position and with everything seeming to move on fast-forward, he recognized the two men from the many and varied mugshots and surveillance photographs he'd seen pinned to walls or circulated in intelligence bulletins. It was Callum, the youngest of the Campbell brothers, he saw lift Kelly from the floor before slapping her so hard with the back of his hand that held the gun that she spun through three hundred and sixty degrees before crashing back to the floor – her lips instantly split and bleeding, her face stricken with terror.

'Where's the fucking copper?' Callum was straight into her. King saw Kelly's mouth open, but no words came out. Instinctively he reached for the CS gas on his utility belt but felt only air.

'Fuck,' he cursed almost inaudibly as he remembered abandoning his belt and all its equipment downstairs. He looked to the heavens for solutions, but there weren't any. He was defenceless against men armed with guns.

Callum half lifted Kelly from the floor by her hair and started to drag her deeper into the maisonette. 'You got about three seconds to tell me where he is before I cut your fucking face off.'

'He's not here,' Kelly screamed through her fear and pain.

'Really?' Tyler asked as he lifted King's body armour and belt from the floor. 'Then what the fuck is this?'

'He left it here,' she pleaded. 'He's gone.'

'Lying fucking whore,' Callum snarled and punched her with a short jab on the nose that produced an instant and heavy nose bleed. 'Check upstairs,' he told Tyler. 'I'll finish with the whore.'

King didn't hesitate. He moved quickly and quietly into Kelly's bedroom and headed to the open window. He climbed agilely out onto the window ledge and used the drainpipe to climb to the flat rooftop of the long low building that was Millander Walk – heading off along the dwellings below until he felt he had at least some distance between himself and the Campbells – searching his own pockets and almost weeping with relief when he realized he'd kept his mobile phone in his trousers.

'Jesus Christ,' he rejoiced. 'Thank God.' He fumbled with the phone trying to find the number he needed, before the image of Kelly, terrified and bleeding, swept all other thoughts away. 'Fuck. Fuck, Kelly. Fuck.' Tears filled his eyes and his throat closed with fear for her and loathing for himself for having deserted her, while his belly tightened and his chest pounded with an overwhelming desire for revenge against her captors. 'They're dead men,' he promised her as if she could hear. 'I swear they're fucking dead men.' He wiped the tears from his eyes and composed himself as he searched for and found the number he needed. It was a long time before it was answered, every second feeling like hours, and somehow he was sure he could sense the reluctance of the person he was calling to answer, but eventually they did.

'Hello,' Brown answered, sounding weary and disinterested.

'Where the fuck are you?' King snarled into the phone – speaking through gritted teeth to prevent himself from shouting and betraying his whereabouts. 'I told you to come to Millander Walk.'

'Aye,' Brown replied. 'Sorry about that. We got side-tracked.'

'Fucking side-tracked?' King asked – incredulous at what he was being told. 'I'm on the estate,' the urgency of his situation moved him on. 'I'm in trouble. I got two of the Campbells down here after me and they're armed – with guns. They've already turned over the place where I was staying. I escaped through the window – onto the roof. It won't take them long to work out where I am.'

'Call for urgent assistance,' Brown told him, although there was no concern or urgency in his own voice.

'I can't,' King answered. 'My PR's still in the house. All my gear's back in the house. I've got fucking nothing.'

'Then use your phone,' Brown tormented him.

'Listen,' King tried to get through to him, 'I can't . . . can't get other people involved. Too many . . . too many questions. Get hold of Danny, but not Knight, I don't trust him, and get the fuck down here now. Use a car. Lights. Sirens. Be visible and noisy. I need you to scare these fuckers off.'

'I can't do that,' Brown told him coldly.

'What?' King demanded, his voice faltering slightly – beginning to understand Brown's true intentions.

'I said I can't do that,' he repeated.

'You back-stabbing bastard,' King accused him – his voice growing louder as he spoke. 'You won't get away with this. I'll come for you. I swear I'll fucking come for you.'

'I'm sorry, Jack,' Brown told him without sounding like he meant it, 'but it's just the way it has to be. You went too far, Jack. You just went too far.'

King heard the connection go dead and with it any chance of help. He was alone now. Completely alone.

'Fuck,' he cursed the world and everyone in it but Kelly – Kelly who he'd abandoned to the hands of violent thugs. 'Bastards,' he swore again before stuffing the phone in his pocket and looking out across the sprawling estate that stretched before him. The kingdom he'd taken control of with violence and threats that now seemed to turn on him in every way.

His loneliness and desperation made him as sober as he'd been in weeks – his bravado and ambitions swept away by a tidal wave of harsh reality. He felt like he was awakening from a dream – as if it hadn't really been him who had beaten Butler and Swinton or moved in on the Campbells' small empire. But he knew there could be no reasoning with them now. He couldn't blame his alter-ego for all his crimes and intrusions and hope to be spared. It was he who was going to have to pay – the real Jack King.

All he thought of now was escape. If he could escape and never return to this God-cursed place perhaps the Campbells would forget about him and leave him alone. Desperately he looked for a way to flee, all too aware it was only a matter of time before they realized where he must be. If they caught him on the flat roof he'd have nowhere to run to and nothing to hide behind. They'd shoot him down like a rat in a barrel.

He ran across the rooftops until he reached the end of Millander Walk and peered over the edge. It was only two stories high, but it looked higher from the top – his only way down another fragile-looking drainpipe. He had no choice and swung his body over the edge, gripping the pipe and trusting it could take his weight without even testing it. It creaked and moved a little as he shinned his way down to the walkway and sprinted into a stairwell that led to the rear of the block. He checked the coast was clear before moving into the open, but as soon as he did so he heard the angry cries of the Campbell brothers shouting warnings to each other that he was out in the open and trying to escape.

Without looking back he ran as fast as he ever had, through the rat-runs of the estate he'd grown to know so well – always listening with terror for the sound of a handgun exploding into action, fully aware that by the time he heard the sound the bullet would have either ripped through his fleeing body or whistled past him – leaving behind it a faint sonic boom as it distorted and warped the air around it. But no such dreadful sounds came – just the howling of the chasing brothers.

As his legs and chest began to burn with the effort of the sprint, he realized his best and possibly only chance of survival was to hide. He knew the estate so well and surely there were still people who would be prepared to offer him temporary sanctuary. The Campbells couldn't search every flat, every garage or shed on the estate. If he could lie low for a couple of hours surely they would tire of the hunt and crawl back from whence they came. He could even wait until darkness and slip away unseen by anyone.

Without even thinking about where he'd been running he came across a stairwell he knew well – one that could lead him to the place where he could wait until the circling hunters retreated to search for him another day. With the last strength in his legs he climbed the stairs two at a time until he reached the landing that led to his goal. He half ran, half stumbled along the walkway until he reached the door he'd pounded upon dozens of times before – cursing the fact he'd never kept a key that would unlock the metal grid over the door and windows. Even if the Campbells somehow found him here their guns and threats would be useless. All he'd have to do would be to keep his head down in one of the back rooms and they wouldn't be able to touch him. If they fired shots surely someone on the estate would panic and call the police – the noise and commotion of approaching sirens and engines would no doubt be enough to scare his pursuers away.

Suddenly an idea leapt into his head and he wondered why he hadn't thought of it before. All he had to do was make an anonymous call to the police himself and covertly summon the cavalry. One phone call to save himself. He pulled his mobile from his pocket and went to press 999 when he suddenly stopped – his mind clearing enough for him to remember why he hadn't already made the call: his mobile was legitimate and registered in his name. It would only be a matter of time before the call was traced back to him, giving rise to ever more awkward questions.

'Shit,' he whispered and banged on the door even harder – the memory that O'Neil's phone was untraceable spurring him on. Once safely inside he'd make the call on O'Neil's phone and that would take care of the Campbells. The closer he felt to salvation the faster his heart beat – the fear of despair giving way to the excitement of victory, but still the door wouldn't open. He leaned forward to thud the side of his fist on the wood once more just as the door finally opened slowly – the hollow face of O'Neil peering out at him from the shadows like a ghost.

'Open the fucking grid,' King demanded without any expla-nation, but O'Neil just stood, looking straight through him as if he wasn't there. 'Open the fucking door,' he repeated, his hands desperately gripping the bars of the grid and shaking them in a hopeless attempt to make them yield. 'What the fuck's wrong with you?' King screamed. 'Open the fucking door – now.'

'Why?' O'Neil blinked, as if he was coming round from unconsciousness.

'Because I fucking told you to,' King told him. 'Now do it.'

'I can't do that,' O'Neil said, sounding like a robot.

'What – are you fucking stoned?' King asked desperately. 'The Campbells are all over me. Open the fucking door.'

'I don't think so,' O'Neil told him without any emotion as he began to close the door.

'No,' King screamed, reaching through the bars. 'Dougie,' he pleaded. 'Don't do this to me. We can help each other. I can get you drugs. Money.' But still the door slowly closed. King tried to lean his weight into it, but the metal bars took the strain. Desperately he pushed at the door with his arms, but O'Neil was easily able to force the door shut just as King wrapped the fingers of both hands around the edge of the door in a pitiful attempt to keep it open – the fragile bones breaking and splintering as O'Neil first slammed it almost closed and then kicked it to force the prising fingers away. King pulled his hands free and screamed like a wounded forest animal – the sound of his pain and anguish reverberating around the estate – the king of the jungle's last cry of defiance.

'You're a dead man, O'Neil,' he shouted at the closed door as he staggered backwards cradling his broken fingers in his other hand – the pain taking his breath away as he looked for a new place to run.

He fell against the wall trying to clear his head and think – looking back and forth for any sign of impending danger. He was just about to launch himself into an exhausted stuttering run when a red brick close to his head seemed to explode into a cloud of dust – filling his mouth with powder and almost blinding him. A second later he heard the deafening crack of the gunshot that had caused the brick to shatter. Instinctively he threw himself behind the low wall – giving himself a moment to recover his bearings and work out that the shot had come from the stairwell of the tenement block opposite – no more than sixty feet away. At least one of the Campbells had his position pinned.

'He's over here,' he heard the gruff voice, thick with an East London accent, call out. 'First floor – behind the wall.'

'Fuck,' he damned them and began to run, crouched over to deny them a target as he made his way to the stairwell – adrenalin and fear making him forget his pain as he jumped down the stairs, never knowing if he was about to run into one of his hunters – the instinct to flee overpowering any strategy or plan of escape. He just had to run.

After running and running – constantly turning left and right, climbing stairwells and descending others, always fleeing from the calls of his hunters that seemed to surround him – somehow he found himself back in Millander Walk. *Kelly*, he told himself. *Just get to Kelly*. But as he staggered exhausted towards her he found himself passing Susie Ubana's front door. He fell backwards onto the wall behind him where he and Ubana had once stood looking out over the estate together. He looked at the woman on the other side of the metal grid who stood smoking a cigarette and staring back at him with tear-filled eyes. He nodded to her as if he understood what she was silently trying to say before continuing his journey back to Kelly, only to be stopped in his tracks as Tyler appeared from the stairwell, a slight smile of satisfaction on his lips as he slowly, confidently, started to move towards him – the handgun held casually at his side. King spun quickly and sprinted two steps before the sight of Callum appearing from the other stairwell froze him where he stood. He was trapped. Nowhere left to run or hide.

As the Campbell brothers closed in on him from both sides he turned to Ubana – his only hope. 'Please,' he whispered to her as tears of hopelessness slipped from his eyes and ran down his face mixing with his sweat. She gently shook her head and looked at the floor as his last chance of escape closed in front of him. He spun towards Callum who was no more than fifteen feet away now, moving slowly towards him, the light flickering across his gun and making it look like a living creature – a black scorpion or writhing snake. A hot wind as warm as the devil's breath blew along the walkway and seemed to sweep everything away with it, leaving him in a void where only the Campbells now existed. He considered jumping over the wall, but it was a long fall to the car park below – one that would surely break his ankles if not his legs – leaving him to the mercy of the two vultures. Instead he tried the only thing left for him to try. He stood as straight as he could, ignoring the pain of his broken fingers and looked hard into Callum's eyes.

'Don't go too far, Campbell,' King warned him. 'I'm the law round here. You don't shoot coppers.'

'You're not Old Bill any more,' Callum sneered, raising his gun and pointing it straight at him.

'Fuck you,' King shouted in defiance as Callum squeezed the trigger smoothly and professionally, sending a 9mm Parabellum bullet hurtling towards him at four hundred metres per second. It smashed into the right side of his chest knocking him backwards almost six feet, although he managed to stay standing – the last effects of the cocaine mixing with his own adrenalin, enabling him to do what should have been near impossible. The bullet had ricocheted off a rib before ripping a hole through his lung, causing it to immediately collapse as the projectile continued on its journey through his body and leaving an exit wound in his back the size of a cricket ball. Frothy pink blood bubbled from both wounds as King looked down at the ever-increasing spread of crimson across his white shirt and suddenly he wasn't there any more – he was back outside *the house* with the young girl lying in his arms. He forced one last breath into his surviving lung and looked up at Callum, who no longer meant anything to him, as if he didn't exist any more. He saw the flash from the end of the gun as if it was happening in slow motion – the sound of the explosion a warped, muffled boom.

The second bullet crashed into the left side of his chest, shattering a rib and narrowly missing his heart, although hundreds of shards of bone embedded themselves into it, sending it into fibrillation if not full cardiac arrest. It tore another huge hole through his surviving lung before bouncing off a rib and exiting out of his side. He staggered backwards and fell to

413

the ground – his head impacting hard. He lay motionless, staring at the blue sky above. The same powder-blue sky he'd seen on *that* day. And as he listened to his own deep wheezing as he tried to breathe through shattered lungs, he felt no pain any more – only peace. Until the sun was blocked out by the shadowy figures of two men he could barely see, although he could hear their voices coming from a far-off place.

'Finish him,' Tyler told his brother. 'Put one in the fucker's head.'

'No,' Callum said, but not through mercy or pity. 'Can't afford for it to look like an execution. Plans have already been made. Let him drown in his own blood.'

'Fair enough,' King heard the voice say, although he no longer understood what was happening in the real world, only that the shadows had gone and the blue sky had returned. He felt his heart and breathing slowing to almost nothing as he sensed another presence at his side and momentarily returned to the real and present world. He turned his head slowly to the side and saw small feet in training shoes. A child's feet. The boy knelt down next to him – his innocence making him unafraid.

'Do you remember me?' he asked quietly.

King used almost the last of his strength to manage a slight nod. It was Billy Easton – the boy from the basement who he'd taken cannabis from so many days ago – his first step to what he'd now become.

'You shouldn't have come here,' Billy told him, not unkindly. 'Nothing good ever happens here.' King nodded that he understood – the movement making him cough – blood spluttering from his mouth. 'Can I get you anything?' the boy asked as a last act of kindness.

'Stay with me,' King said, his voice barely a whisper now. Billy took hold of his hand and sat next to him – ignoring the spreading pool of blood forming under King's body as he watched his eyes at first flicker and then softly close.

17

Marino bounded up the stairs towards the first floor of Millander Walk where he'd been told he'd find King. In the distance he'd heard the two shots being fired as he'd approached the estate in his unmarked car and knew he was probably already too late. In the background he could hear the wail of approaching sirens. As he rounded the corner he stopped in his tracks when he saw the prostrate figure of a man in black trousers and a white shirt on the ground – a young boy he didn't know sitting next to him holding his hand. Susie Ubana stood outside her flat holding her teenage daughter close. They both flicked tears away from their eyes.

'Oh Jesus, no,' Marino implored quietly as he began to walk slowly towards the body.

'You're too late,' Ubana accused him as he passed her. 'You can't help him now.'

Marino ignored her and went to King's side – kneeling next to him and taking his other hand. 'Oh dear God, Jack,' he said, looking down on his motionless, lifeless body. 'What the hell happened to you?'

'Is he dead?' Billy asked.

Marino looked up into the sparkling blue eyes of the boy. 'Go home, son,' he told him as kindly as he could. Billy began to stand, wiping the blood from his hands on his jeans as if it was just dust. 'And thank you,' Marino added. 'You're a brave boy.'

Billy just shrugged. 'I thought he wouldn't want to be alone.'

Marino choked back the tears and grief that threatened to swamp him on hearing the boy's words of kindness. 'No,' he struggled to reply. 'He wouldn't have wanted to be alone. Now go. Go home.' The boy nodded once and wandered off along the walkway, occasionally looking over his shoulder in case something miraculously changed. Marino watched him all the way until he disappeared into a stairwell then his gaze returned to the stricken King. The holes in the chest of his shirt told him all he needed to know – that King couldn't have survived. But he knew he had to be sure – for the final report if nothing else. He held his middle and index fingers together and pushed them deep into King's throat, close to his trachea. He was desperately struggling to detect even the slightest trace of a pulse when King's body suddenly lurched as he sucked air into what remained of his lungs and his eyes sprang open as if from a nightmare – blood spitting from his mouth. Marino fell back with shock before recovering himself. Leaning over King, he tried to remember his first aid training – tried to remember how to seal holes in punctured lungs – but King chased all thoughts from his mind as he grabbed him by the collar of his jacket and pulled him close, his lips trying to form words. Marino twisted his head and held an ear as close as he could to King's mouth and waited for him to speak.

'I saved her, Frank,' he managed to say – his voice so quiet it was almost inaudible. But Marino knew what he meant. The young girl in the white dress with the spreading crimson – he'd saved her and lost himself.

'Yeah, Jack,' Marino told him, holding his hand tighter than he'd held anything before, as if that could somehow stop him from slipping away. 'You saved her. You saved her.'

416

King smiled as peace washed over him and took away all the pain and anguish of being alive – his bloody lips even forming a slight smile. His eyes fluttered like the beating wings of a tiny bird before closing for the last time as his chest stopped heaving against impossible injuries and his heart fell still.

Marino remained crouched and silent – still holding King's hand as he tried to comprehend the magnitude of having watched the life of a young man he'd known so well end right in front of him. His trance was broken by the sound of feet running towards him. He spun round to see Kelly closing in on them, her face a mess of blood and bruises, her pace slowing to a staggered walk as she realized what she was seeing. She was already crying, but now her tears intensified as she covered the last few steps and collapsed to her knees next to King's bloody body. Marino made no attempt to stop her, despite the fact he knew she was contaminating what was now a crime scene. None of that seemed important any more.

'Jack,' Kelly said, cradling his lifeless head in her hands. 'Jack,' she repeated louder and more desperately.

'He's gone,' Marino told her.

'No,' she sobbed. 'No. He can't be. I love him.'

'I'm sorry,' was all he could say.

'He said something to you,' Kelly almost accused him. 'I saw you leaning over him. He said something to you, didn't he? You got to tell me – you got to tell me what he said.'

Marino sighed deeply and looked into the deep pools of darkness that were her eyes – now so stricken with grief and fear he knew he had to tell her something – something she could anchor herself to and stop her being carried away by a tidal wave of sadness. 'He asked me to tell you that he loved you,' he lied. 'That was all he said: "Tell Kelly I love her."'

She raised her hand and covered her mouth as her

417

heart-wrenching sobbing intensified, but Marino also registered a faint bright flicker in her oil-black eyes – a flicker of happiness, as if although he was gone, she could never lose him now.

'Why did you come back, Jack?' she asked through her tears. 'Why did you have to come back?'

'I think he came back for you,' Marino told her what he thought she needed to hear.

Suddenly she stiffened slightly – drawing on a hardness that lived within her, nurtured by years of living on the estate. 'Nothing good survives here,' she told him. 'I'm leaving. I'm getting as far away from here as I can and I'm never coming back. Never. The people who live here are already dead, but I'm alive. He showed me that – told me I could be anything. Now I'm going to be all I can be and this place can't stop me any more.'

A few days later

Inspector Johnston stood in silence in Superintendent Gerrard's office at Newham Police Station, watching him as he silently read a thick report wrapped in a pink cardboard jacket that marked it as 'Confidential', only occasionally pausing to shake his head or make disapproving tutting sounds. Eventually he closed the report and pushed it away from him across his desk as if its mere presence offended him.

'This is an absolute fucking disaster,' he finally declared. 'Rogue, corrupt police officers on the streets of London. Worse – rogue, corrupt *uniform* police officers. Christ, you almost expect the odd detective to go bad, but a uniformed sergeant selected for accelerated promotion? This could rock the Met to its very foundations. And all this about King suffering from post traumatic stress disorder – a condition, and I quote . . .' He scrambled for the report, skimming the pages until he found what he was looking for . . . '"a condition his senior officers failed to recognize or act upon". Let me tell you, Joanne, this does not look good for you . . . or me.'

'Sir,' Johnston interrupted, clearing her throat before she began in earnest. 'I should remind you that at this stage the report is merely a preliminary and *confidential* report.'

'Meaning?' Gerrard snapped impatiently.

'Meaning,' Johnston explained, 'the Senior Investigating Officer into the matter has not yet submitted his findings to the CPS or anyone else for that matter. Turns out he's an old training school friend of mine – also on the accelerated promotion scheme.'

'So?' Gerrard asked – more interested now.

'So it's fair to say he understands the possible implications of an *open* and undiscriminating investigation,' Johnston told him. 'He's the sort of officer who is . . . aware enough to understand the damaging implications a fully disclosable investigation would have on the reputation of the Metropolitan Police and all the hard-working and *honest* officers who carry out their duty daily with self-sacrifice and no thought for their—'

'For God's sake,' Gerrard stopped her. 'Save the rambling job-speak for your Chief Inspectors' Board and tell me what we're suggesting here.'

Johnston smiled her pixie smile before speaking. 'Although there is no solid evidence yet, as such, there are *suggestions* that a local family engaged in organized crime called the Campbells could have been involved in King's death.'

'Yes, yes,' Gerrard hurried her along. 'I heard the rumours.'

'Well,' Johnston calmly explained, 'it appears they are not without their *connections*.'

'Connections?'

'People,' Johnston answered. 'Legal people.'

'And?'

'And these *people* have been in contact with my friend and

419

his investigating team,' Johnston explained, 'by way of sounding us out, so to speak.'

'Sounding us out?' Gerrard asked. 'About what?'

'It appears they have information in their possession – information about Sergeant King's *activities* that could be very damaging. Even more damaging than we first thought.'

'Christ,' Gerrard declared, stroking his short brown hair. 'Then we're all royally fucked.'

'Not necessarily,' Johnston told him.

'Really?' Gerrard asked suspiciously.

'The people acting on behalf of the Campbells have made a suggestion,' she explained. 'An offer, you could say.'

'An offer?' Gerrard encouraged her, his eyebrows arched high in his forehead.

'They are aware that eventually any investigation into King's death would lead to their clients' door,' Johnston went on.

'You mean the Campbells' front door?' Gerrard huffed. 'Good. About time we nailed that family for something.'

'And if that was to happen,' Johnston spoke quickly to dampen Gerrard's appetite for revenge, 'then they would not hesitate to release the information they hold to any media outlet that would want it – which of course means all of them.'

'This sounds more like blackmail than an offer to me,' Gerrard complained.

'However,' Johnston continued, 'if the investigation was to head in a different direction, one that led away from the Campbells—'

'You mean one that led nowhere,' Gerrard interrupted.

'One that was eventually to be *inconclusive*,' Johnston corrected him, 'then they see no reason why any such information relating to King's activities should be . . . made public.'

'Christ,' Gerrard shook his head, 'and you think this could actually fly?'

420

'I can assure you, sir,' Johnston told him, 'my friend leading the investigation has the ear of some *very* senior officers. As do I.'

'And he's already run this by them?'

'That is my understanding.'

'And they believe this is the best way to go?'

'They believe it would be best all round,' Johnston assured him. 'For the good of the Metropolitan Police.'

'My God,' Gerrard shook his head in disbelief. 'What's it all come to?'

'It's for the best, sir,' Johnston added.

'Maybe,' Gerrard played along, 'but we still have a murdered police officer on our hands – who has a family and friends who want answers.'

'And what do we tell them?' Johnston eased herself into a position of control. 'That their son was rotten to the core? That he was gunned down by a rival gang protecting their *turf* from his expanding criminal endeavours?'

Gerrard said nothing for a while, Johnston's words bouncing around inside his mind like jumping beans in a can. 'No,' he finally agreed. 'I suppose not. But we have to tell them something.'

'We . . .' Johnston began before stalling – remembering her place in the pecking order, 'the SIO and the people he's spoken to have suggested that perhaps Sergeant King was the victim of a gang who were apparently planning to commit an armed robbery at a betting shop on the edges of the Grove Wood Estate. It's *possible* he disturbed the gang as they left a flat in Millander Walk prior to committing the intended robbery. The estate is, after all, notorious for producing armed robbers. It is *believed* that Sergeant King challenged the gang and was mercilessly gunned down in the line of duty. No doubt his actions saved several members of the public and the staff at the betting shop a terrible and violent ordeal. My friend, the SIO, thought a Commissioner's

421

Commendation for bravery would be the very least he deserved.'

When Johnston was finished Gerrard just sat in stunned silence – as if he'd been shot in the head with an invisible bullet.

'Sir,' Johnston tried to bring him out of his trance.

Eventually Gerrard showed signs of life. 'Christ,' he said shaking his head. 'Is all this really . . . *doable*?'

'Oh yes, sir,' Johnston told him – trying to suppress a smile of satisfaction. 'I can assure you it's very *doable*.'

'Then so be it,' Gerrard sighed, looking down at the file on his desk – *the life and death of Jack King*. He shrugged his shoulders and gave a short unpleasant laugh.

'Sir?' Johnston asked, confused by Gerrard's unexpected reaction.

'Ironic really,' Gerrard replied – only serving to further confuse Johnston.

'Ironic?'

'The King is dead, Inspector,' Gerrard told her, as he closed the file. 'Long live the King.'

Acknowledgements

A big thank you to all the team at HarperCollins for supporting me in my latest venture and allowing me to do something quite different from the DI Corrigan series. It's still quite early in my writing career, so it's very brave and admirable of them to go for it. A special thanks to my editor – Sarah Hodgson – who worked very hard and showed a lot of patience and skill. Also the Publisher – Kate Elton – who has always backed me. And a big thanks to Hannah Gamon from marketing, Jaime Frost in publicity, all the guys on the wonderful Killer Reads team and everyone in sales.

More thanks to my talented agent – Simon Trewin at WME – who continues to look after me – and my wife and children who continue to stand by and encourage me, not to mention motivate me.

And lastly, I want to acknowledge all the cops I've ever worked with each of whom have shaped me into the person I am and given me the best, funniest and most valued years of my life. I miss you all and the job I loved. I see each and every one of you in the characters in my books.

LD